Always and Forever at Glendale Hall

Victoria Walters writes uplifting and inspiring stories. She's the author of the bestselling Glendale Hall series, which continues with its fourth book *Always and Forever at Glendale Hall*, as well as two other standalone novels – *Summer at the Kindness Café* and *The Second Love of my Life*. She has been chosen for WHSmith Fresh Talent and shortlisted for two RNA awards. Victoria was also picked as an Amazon Rising Star, and her books have won wide reader acclaim. Victoria is a full-time author who lives in Surrey with her cat, Harry.

Also by Victoria Walters

Glendale Hall series

Coming Home to Glendale Hall
New Beginnings at Glendale Hall
Hopeful Hearts at Glendale Hall
Always and Forever at Glendale Hall

Standalone novels

The Second Love of my Life
Summer at the Kindness Café

eBook short stories

Dancing in the Fire
The Summer I Met You

Coming September 2021

Murder at the House on the Hill

Always and Forever at Glendale Hall

Victoria Walters

hera

First published in the United Kingdom in 2021 by

Hera Books
28b Cricketfield Road
London, E5 8NS
United Kingdom

A CIP catalogue record for this book is available from the British Library.

Print ISBN 978 1 80032 506 7
Ebook ISBN 978 1 912973 61 3

Look for more great books at www.herabooks.com

Printed and bound in Great Britain by Clays Ltd, Elcograf S.p.A.

To everyone who loves reading about Glendale as much as I love writing about it… this is for you. Thank you.

Prologue

Twelve years ago

When I woke up, I had no idea where I was.

I could hear something beeping…

I could smell bleach…

I could feel softness beneath me…

I blinked, trying to get my eyes to adjust. And then I could see three familiar faces sitting around me. My parents. And my brother. I let out a breath, relaxing a little to see them with me.

'Thank you, God,' I heard Brodie say as my mother let out a sob and reached for my hand, squeezing it so hard it hurt a little.

'You've come back to us,' my dad said, his voice breaking. 'I'll get a doctor.' He jumped up and hurried out of the room.

I opened my mouth but it felt dry, and my throat felt like it had a long, deep scratch down it. I tried to move my legs but I couldn't. I turned to Brodie, my eyes widening in panic.

'It's okay, Anna,' he said. 'You were in an accident but you're okay. You will be okay.' I was shocked to see tears in his eyes as he spoke fiercely to me. I'd never seen my brother cry before. He looked across at my mother, looking for a moment like a little boy again. 'She will be okay now, won't she?'

'Of course she will,' Mum said, fiercely. She leaned over and brushed my hair back off my forehead.

And then it came flooding back. The flash of two head-lights coming straight for us. The force that sent me flying. The sound of broken glass. And someone screaming.

I realised that person had been me.

A doctor and two nurses appeared then, and the room became a whirl of activity as they checked me over and asked me questions. I was able to move my legs after a minute, to everyone's relief, but the pain was excruciating. The doctor told me that I'd been in a coma for two weeks after a driver had ploughed into my dad's car. I hadn't been wearing my seatbelt and had flown through the windscreen. The doctors did test after test. There was no lasting brain damage. Both of my legs were broken and I'd need a lot of physical therapy to build my muscles up again. My ribs were cracked and breathing was painful but they would heal. I had a deep gash in my cheek but they didn't think there would be too much of a scar. They said I was lucky.

I tried to ask my mum about the accident, about what had happened, but she kept crying, kept saying that I had survived, that was all that mattered, and my brother kept thanking God, and my dad… well, he said nothing. Soon, I learned that my family didn't want to talk about it. And I was too scared to keep asking because I feared what they would say.

Especially when I overheard my dad telling Brodie that the driver who had hit us had died.

Flashes kept returning to me of that evening. Flashes that would plague me long after my physical recovery.

2

Flashes that made me sure the accident had been my fault, and as such I shouldn't have survived it.

And that fear rooted itself inside my chest and refused to shift.

It wouldn't leave me. Not after Brodie told me he'd made a bargain with God to save me, or when I was allowed home and my parents helped me onto our sofa, the relief radiating out from them, or even when I could finally walk around the block without my legs feeling like they were going to collapse.

The fear followed me all through my recovery.

When the consultant signed me off from the hospital, I walked outside and sucked in the air.

I could breathe again.

I could walk again.

I was alive.

But I was terrified that I didn't deserve any of it.

And that fear...

It never left me.

Chapter One

'Come on, Anna, give us one more round!'

I leaned on the bar as Dave waved his empty beer glass at me, grinning hopefully. It was well past eleven now. I'd rung the last orders bell ages ago, but the table of Dave's rugby mates were still here. 'I need to lock up,' I said, shaking my head.

'So, lock the door… and then give us another round of beers. Come on, gorgeous, the boss is away, he'll never know, will he? He'll be glad of the money anyway. And you can have one with us.'

I smiled, wavering. I'd worked at The Thistle pub for three months and my boss was known to be a grumpy old sod so the idea of us getting one over on him while he was away at some landlord convention was appealing. Plus, I felt like celebrating. I had just booked a flight for the end of the summer to Ibiza so I didn't have to put up with working here for too much longer. 'Make mine a double and you've got yourself a deal,' I replied. The whole table cheered and Dave leaned over to plant a wet kiss on my cheek. I laughed along with them and slipped out from behind the bar to lock the doors. Outside, Glasgow was dark and quiet, the sky crystal clear and dotted with stars.

Once we were locked in, their table became even more boisterous, and I busied myself getting everyone a drink, and one for myself, before joining them, sitting on the edge of the table, the only space left. 'Here's to Hamish,' I said, raising my double vodka and coke up as I toasted my absent boss, tossing back my long, candy-floss pink hair.

'To Hamish!' The six big rugby lads roared back at me, their fists thumping on the table as we all took a long drink. I had been on my feet behind the bar all day, Hamish having abandoned me even though it was the day the rugby club met, making us busier than usual. So I felt like I deserved this. And, let's face it, breaking the rules was something I was always up for.

'We need some music,' Dave declared.

'I'm on it!' I downed the remainder of my drink, climbed off the table and went over to the CD player Hamish used with a lot of grumbling on a Saturday night, the only time he allowed music in his pub. The pub was small, situated in a quiet road on the edge of the city, frequented by locals only, some of whom had drunk here for fifty years or more. I had caused a stir turning up with my pink hair, and being well below the age of the average customer, but Hamish had been through five different bar staff in the past year alone by being infamously difficult to work for, and I'd worked in pubs and bars for years so he had begrudgingly given me the job. The reason I'd chosen to stay at The Thistle for the past three months was the job was easy, and came with board in a tiny bedsit upstairs, and was just a twenty-minute walk into the city centre, and I'd just wanted any work so I could save up to spend September in Ibiza. I longed for runs on the beach, bars that served cocktails and tourists up for a good time.

'Ooh, I love this song,' I cried as Queen started playing. Hamish didn't think music existed after the eighties but I didn't mind. I loved anything old school. I turned it up and jumped on an empty table to sing along.

Dave climbed up with me and wrapped his arms around my waist. 'You know we still haven't gone on that date you promised me,' he said into my ear, pulling me closer.

'She's too good for you, mate,' a burly man they called Badger, for some inexplicable reason, yelled as one of the others wolf-whistled at us.

'We could have another drink upstairs once these clowns leave,' Dave said then, turning me towards him. He reeked of alcohol but he did have a nice smile, and his muscly arms were strong and safe around me. I let him pull me closer, tipping my face up to meet his, aware of whooping from his mates but not really caring after the vodka I'd just had. When his lips met mine, they did the thing that I kept seeking – they drowned the world out for the moment and let me just stop and breathe.

Which was why I didn't notice the door opening behind us or that Dave's mates had stopped cheering. It wasn't until Queen suddenly stopped, and the room fell into silence, that Dave pulled away from me and we turned around to see Hamish standing under the table, hands on his hips, his face bright red. 'What are you doing here?' I gasped in horror.

'The convention finished early so I thought I'd come home rather than fork out money on a hotel...' He shook his head. 'More importantly, what the hell is going on here?'

'Um... they were just helping me clear up,' I said, stepping away from Dave and wiping stray berry lipstick from the side of my mouth.

'Do you think I'm stupid, Anna?' Hamish practically growled at me. 'I know a lock-in when I see one. You could have cost me my licence! For God's sake get down from there, and all of you lot clear out,' he said, jabbing his finger towards the door. 'As for you.' He looked back up at me. 'I want you out. Tonight.'

I stared at him in horror. I needed this job until my flight. I jumped down. 'Come on, Hamish, it was just once and...'

He shook his head. 'I went against my better judgement hiring you in the first place. I knew there must be a reason why you never stick at a job, why your CV is almost as long as my arm, why you were happy to live out here in the sticks. You need to sort your life out. But not under my roof. Pack your bags now.'

'It's midnight,' I said, my voice annoyingly small. His words had stung more than I cared to admit.

'Have a heart, Hamish,' Dave said, hanging back as his mates sheepishly began to file out of the pub. He had the grace to look thoroughly ashamed of himself at least. But I couldn't fully blame him; I had gone along with it after all.

'Fine,' he snapped. 'Out first thing. I mean it, Anna. And don't even think about getting a reference out of me.' And with that, he spun and walked out the back furiously.

'I'm sorry,' Dave said as he walked to the door. 'You could always come back to mine?' He looked hopeful again.

I almost laughed but this was not funny. 'I need to find somewhere to go. I've lost my job and home tonight.' I walked over and held the door open pointedly. He shrugged and left, not even giving me a backwards glance. Why had I let him kiss me? I slammed the door and locked it, sagging against it with a sigh. It had been me all over tonight. Grasping at fun, no thought for the consequences. Even though this was a dead-end job and a pretty crap place to live, I now had neither. What would I do next? Where would I go?

I was no stranger to moving, as Hamish had pointed out, but I'd never lost a job in the middle of the night like this with nowhere planned for me to work or live. I tried not to panic. There must be someone I'd worked for or met that would have something for me. Surely?

I hurried upstairs to my room and pulled out my phone. I scrolled through the contacts. Exes were out, of course. I hesitated over the name Donna. I'd burned that bridge by dating her grandson. I carried on and stopped at the name of a landlord I'd worked for in Edinburgh – it wasn't that far away. I tried not to think about how little I had in my bank account after booking my flight. Just enough for the train fare, I hoped.

'Blimey, I didn't think I'd ever hear from you again,' Graham said after he answered. 'I've got nothing, hired all my summer staff.' And then he hung up.

I tried a girl called Amy that I'd spent many nights out with after work in London. 'I can hardly hear you, I'm in a bar,' she shouted. 'Who is it? Who?' This time, I hung up.

I tried a few more pubs but no luck. I hated myself for doing it, but then I phoned a man I'd been seeing last year who ran a restaurant in Manchester. 'You told me that you didn't do relationships; well I don't do second chances.'

'This is going well,' I announced to the empty room. My phone rang then, making me jump. I was hopeful as I looked at the screen that someone had changed their mind but then I sighed, seeing my brother's name flash up. 'I can't talk, Brodie. Something's come up,' I said, making my way to the wardrobe and pulling my bag out.

'You sound stressed.'

'Yeah, well, it's been a rubbish night. Did you want something?'

'I haven't heard from you in a month, I wanted to make sure you were okay.'

I usually brushed off questions like that but tonight frustration burned in my throat, and my eyes stung as I felt tears well up in them. God, I could not cry to my brother. 'Not really. I need to leave my job… unexpectedly. And I need somewhere to stay. So that's why I can't talk. I need to sort something out.' I felt tired suddenly. Tired of scrambling to find someone to help me.

The fact that I knew deep down it was my choice that there was no one to call for help was really not making me feel better about the situation.

'But that's perfect. Remember the job I told you about? It's live-in…'

I did remember and I shook my head quickly. I'd shut him down about it more than once before. 'No, it's fine, I can find something…'

'Anna, for once, please listen to me,' he said, sounding pained. 'Glendale Hall needs a housekeeper and you need a job and a place to live, why would you not want it? The pay is really good and you met them all at the wedding. They're a lovely family.'

I barely remembered them, to be honest. I hadn't bothered to talk to many people at Brodie's wedding, the one and only time I'd been to Glendale before, and I'd left as fast as I could after it was over. 'Village life isn't for me,' I protested. It wasn't only the thought of spending the summer in the back of beyond that had put me off, though: it was the fact that Brodie would be living nearby. And I knew that my brother longed to heal my life, and me. 'And besides, I've booked a flight in September to Ibiza…'

'That's fine,' he said, quickly. 'Beth needs help this summer as she's a wedding planner. She would happily have you for any time you can give her. And it sounds like you need her as much as she needs you. I'll come and pick you up in the morning. There's no good reason for you to say no.'

Ugh. My brother was too convincing for his own good. I sighed heavily. 'I can't think of one, no.'

'Exactly. Text me the address.'

'Uh, my boss needs me to leave first thing…'

There was a short silence. 'Fine, I'll be there as early as I can,' he said, hanging up. I could feel the disappointment travelling down the phone line. I flung my phone on the bed. I couldn't quite believe what I had just agreed to.

I was going to Glendale. A small village in the Highlands. Where nothing ever happened, and everyone knew your business. And my brother lived there.

The brother who thought exactly the same way about me as Hamish did, and would no doubt give me a hard time all summer. After all, he was the perfect Minister of Glendale, and I was his black sheep of a little sister.

'It's only for three months,' I said aloud before I reluctantly started packing.

Chapter Two

It was the first Saturday in June, but in Glasgow the morning was still chilly. I could see my breath in the air as I paced back and forth outside the pub to try to keep warm while I waited for Brodie to pick me up.

I longed for a coffee and hoped Brodie would let us stop on the way to Glendale for one. I couldn't stay still, and not just because of the temperature. I felt jittery about going to Glendale. Now that my moment of crisis was over, I was nervous. I wasn't thrilled about being under my brother's watchful gaze and spending the summer in the countryside. I was a city girl through and through. What was I going to do in a village?!

A beep from a horn drew me from my thoughts and I watched as Brodie pulled into the road. Too late to back out now. Unless I made a dive from the moving car on the way. I decided not to rule that idea out just yet.

'Are you okay?' Brodie asked, after he'd parked and jumped out of the car. 'Is that all of your things?' He regarded my two bags sceptically.

'I'm fine. And, yes, I travel light, makes things easier especially if you're thrown out by a grumpy old man early in the morning.' Brodie raised both eyebrows as he picked up my bags, and I sighed. 'I'm cranky because I need coffee.'

'Well, if you look inside the car you might cheer up a little,' he replied, putting my bags into the boot. I went around to the passenger side and saw a takeaway coffee waiting for me.

'You're a legend,' I said, climbing in much more eagerly than I'd planned to. I took a sip. A black, sugary coffee, still piping hot – just how I liked it. I was pleased he had remembered that. Since I'd left home at eighteen, we hadn't lived together and with all my moving around I hadn't spent much more than the occasional Christmas visit or Sunday family lunch when I couldn't avoid it with him.

'It has been said,' he replied with a grin as he climbed in beside me. I was relieved he was wearing a warm jumper and jeans this morning and not the dog collar: it always made me feel on edge. Like I was being judged or something. Brodie was naturally fair like me and we had the same big, blue eyes but whereas Brodie was tall and muscly, I was tiny in height and had always longed for boobs to fill out a bra to no avail.

Brodie started the engine and we set off. I settled into the seat, sipping my coffee, glad of the car heating warming me up. 'So, are you going to tell me?' he asked after a moment, glancing across at me. 'Why your boss told you to leave?'

I braced myself for the inevitable lecture. 'I accidently had a lock-in, and he came home unexpectedly and wasn't at all happy about it.'

'How do you accidentally have a lock-in?'

'It was just one last drink for the road.' I shrugged. 'Hamish was supposed to be away for the night. Oh well, he was a complete bore to work for anyway.' I swivelled to look at him. 'I hope Beth will be a better boss.' I'd only met Beth Fraser once before, when Brodie married Emily – the reception had been at Glendale Hall, and organised by her. She owned that vast estate and it was hard to believe that I'd now be living and working there. I had barely spoken to her, or anyone else at the wedding, making the most of the open bar that night, so I didn't really remember much about her.

'Beth and her family are lovely but they all work hard so they'll expect you to do the same.' He gave me one of his looks, one that made me feel like a big disappointment to him. 'The Hall is going to be really busy this summer – Beth has started a wedding planning business, which was why she really needed a housekeeper so she wouldn't have the house to deal with as well. They used to have a full-time live-in one, Sally, but she's retired now.'

'Will I have to wear a uniform?' I laughed and Brodie tittered at me.

'I know it's a big estate but they are all very down-to-earth. I've already told Beth all about you.'

'I bet you sung my praises,' I said, dryly, draining my coffee cup dry. I felt slightly more myself after it at least.

'Actually, I did, I just said you were a bit… lost.'

'Here we go again,' I muttered, folding my arms across my chest.

'If there's anyone who can understand, it's Beth. She ran away from Glendale Hall when she was a teenager because she didn't want to do what her family wanted her to do. Her mother, though, might be less keen once she sees your hair. What happened to the blonde?'

'I fancied a change. It's fun,' I said, touching my pink locks. 'At least there's one rebel at the Hall, I suppose.'

'Takes one to know one,' he replied, and then reached for the radio. My brother's music tastes were a little conservative for me but I was happy to put up with his choice if it meant conversation could be stalled for a bit. Instead, I looked out of the window and watched the city slowly be replaced by countryside. As we drew closer to Brodie's village, I turned back to him. 'There'd better be something for me to do in Glendale besides work otherwise it'll be a very long summer.'

He smiled. 'Even you're going to struggle to get into trouble here.'

I grinned. 'That, dear brother, sounds like a challenge.'

He groaned in response.

–

Glendale was a small countryside village but it was busier this morning than I expected as we drove through the pretty High Street with its hanging baskets bursting with colourful flowers. Brodie pointed out his wife's bakery, which had a queue outside, and the shop that Beth and her family owned, and then we passed the church and vicarage where Brodie lived and worked. I'd seen it all briefly when I came here for his wedding but I'd refused to stay the night so I hadn't spent any time in the village. I felt a bit guilty about never having stayed with Brodie since he'd moved to Glendale, but he'd always come to where I was or met me at our parents' home in Inverness without complaint. Although that was Brodie all over – he was a giver.

'Emily is meeting us at the Hall. She wanted to be there with Beth to welcome you and introduce you to everyone. I mean, I know you met them all at the wedding but you didn't stay long.'

I tried to ignore that comment. Like most of the things Brodie said, it made me feel like the worst sister. 'How is

Emily doing?' I asked. Emily was pregnant with her and Brodie's first child although she had a little girl already from a previous relationship, who I knew that Brodie adored.

'She's really well. I can't believe she's due at the end of September, it seemed so far away but now it feels really close. She's tired though. I keep telling her to do less at the bakery but she loves it so much. She needs to let others help her more. Beth too. It's really good that you've come, Anna. I know that you're only here now because you didn't have another choice but...' He smiled across at me. 'I'm still pleased.'

I forced out a smile. I knew I should be grateful that I had a job and place to live, and that it was down to him. The problem was – I hated that my brother was disappointed in me, which was why I didn't look forward to spending time with him. I was always torn between wanting to please him and wanting to do the exact opposite of what he thought I should do. And behind it all was the guilt and fear I still carried with me from my accident, something I could never share with him or my parents, and it was part of the reason I kept a distance from them. 'I'm sure Emily can handle things; you worry too much. You always have.'

'I just want to look after her. That's not a crime, is it?'

I knew he wished I would let him do the same for me so I didn't answer that. Instead, I looked out of the window again as the village faded away and we drove along the road to Glendale Hall. I sat up in the seat to watch as we passed through the large iron gates, which were flung open to let us in. The gravel crunched under the tyres as Brodie drove up to the front of the house. It was a grand cream-stone building with ivy climbing over the large oak front door. I was used to staying in one-bedroom flats. This was something else entirely.

Once he had switched the engine off, and removed his seatbelt, Brodie paused with his hand on the door handle before turning to me. 'I just want you to know that I only want to see you happy, Anna. I know you're not excited to be here, but these people mean a lot to me, and I really think if you let us in a little bit, you might find we can help you find the happiness you seem to have always been searching for.' I opened my mouth to protest, my default position, but Brodie held up his hand and I stopped. 'I know you're about to tell me that I don't know what I'm talking about, that you are happy, but I won't believe a word. You're my sister. I know and love you.

'I still think about those days at your bedside in hospital praying and hoping and wishing that you'd wake up out of the coma, that'd you'd pull through. God granted you a second chance. And me too. I became a minister because of how He saved you. I know you don't have faith like me, like Mum and Dad, that you think it's all, well, rubbish.' He smiled slightly. I looked away. 'But I know that you've run through life like you don't have a second to breathe since then. Trying new things, moving to new places, changing relationships as often as you've changed jobs, never settling. I wish it was making you happy but I don't think it is. All I'm saying is why not use this time to think about what you really want from your life? Make the next thing you do, or the next place you go to, something that fulfils you in some way. You can't convince me the grotty pub I picked you up from today was where you really want to be.' I hated that he saw through the barrier I had put up around myself. 'Right, I've said my piece. Now I'll shut up. I won't mention it again but I'm always here if you ever do want to open up to me. Okay?' I nodded once. It was all I was capable of.

He opened the car door, letting in a blast of cold air, and I sucked in a deep breath before I climbed out as well.

Chapter Three

The front door of Glendale Hall swung open when we reached it and there stood Beth Fraser, my new boss, and Emily, Brodie's wife, whose hands rested on her bump, both beaming at us. I bit back a quip about being shocked that they didn't have a butler to welcome visitors. Brodie carried my bags, leaving me to walk alone up to them, trying to summon my usual bravado, but it felt a little wobbly after the past twenty-four hours and the fact I was moving into, and was expected to help run, an actual mansion.

'It's so lovely to have you here, Anna,' Beth said warmly as I approached. And then she leaned in to kiss my cheek. 'Welcome to Glendale Hall.'

'Thanks,' I said, a little taken aback by her familiar greeting. Beth was tall and slim with wavy, dark hair, and she wore skinny jeans, a t-shirt and ballet pumps, looking most unlike the owner of such a grand house.

'You look really well,' Emily said, reaching out to give me a big hug. Emily wore a long, floaty dress, her blonde hair up in a messy bun. I had always envied her curvy figure, and how she always radiated happiness. Now that she was pregnant, the effect was rather dazzling.

'You're the one who's glowing,' I replied, sure that I looked a right mess after having to be up so early. The coffee had helped a little but I'd missed my usual morning run and felt crumpled from the long car journey.

'Where shall I put these then?' Brodie asked as he appeared beside me. His face lit up when he saw his wife, which should have made me cringe but I had to admit it was sweet.

'I thought Anna could have the room you stayed in, Em,' Beth replied, stepping back to let us walk inside. I looked around. I hadn't seen inside the house at my brother's wedding – it had all taken place in the garden. The hallway was practically as big as the flat I'd lived in above the pub. It wasn't decorated as traditionally as I'd expected – the walls were light, and there were wild flowers in vases all around lending a lovely fragrance to the room. 'Are you okay showing her, Brodie? We thought you'd both be hungry after setting off early so we made some food. I'll call everyone in.'

My stomach rumbled on cue – I hadn't had the chance to have any breakfast. I started to follow Brodie up the wide staircase.

'Can you please talk to Heather about her wedding shoes?' Beth said to Emily, linking arms with her. 'That's the only problem with wedding planning: I can advise on flowers until the cows come home, but shoes are so not my area of expertise,' she added with a chuckle as they walked out of the hallway together.

'I don't know how she'll pick just one pair. She's too excited to get out of her wellies for the day, maybe she should get a pair for the ceremony, and another pair for the evening…' Emily's voice trailed off as they walked out. I knew from Brodie that they had been friends for years. I thought about the fact I'd had no one to call for help last night and felt a prick of envy at their friendship.

'Are you coming?' Brodie asked over his shoulder.

I hurried after him. 'I'll get lost here,' I commented as we walked along the corridor, passing bedrooms. Brodie opened what was to be mine and I hovered in the doorway as he placed my bags down by the large, four-poster bed. It was like something out of a book. The window displayed the garden, although whether you could call so many acres just a garden, I wasn't sure. It was a lovely room, light and cream, and there was an en-suite bathroom too. 'This is a step up from rooms above pubs,' I said, walking over to the window to look down. The manicured lawn stretched out below me.

'So, you like it?' Brodie's eyes twinkled as if he was daring me to disagree. Annoyingly, I didn't think anyone could argue that Glendale Hall was anything other than a beautiful house. 'Shall I see you down in the kitchen?'

'No, I'll come now,' I said, not wanting to have to walk in by myself. I glanced at the full-length mirror as I trailed after Brodie, and quickly smoothed down my wavy, pink hair, and straightened my Beatles t-shirt. We went back down into the hall and then through into the vast kitchen. It was huge with a large, long dining table, and French doors which had been flung open leading out onto a patio. The kitchen was full of people and there was a delicious smell of cooking in there. My nose twitched.

'Is your room okay?' Beth asked me as she placed a basket of bread down onto the table.

'It's lovely,' I said, looking at her daughter Izzy, who was reading a book with one hand, and with the other handing a toddler a quarter of a sandwich. The table was crowded and noisy as everyone reached for food. I couldn't help but stare.

Beth noticed and cleared her throat for attention. 'Right, guys, stop devouring food for a sec...' she said loudly. The table grew quiet and all eyes turned to me. I stared as defiantly as I could manage back at them. 'This is Anna, Brodie's sister, and she'll be moving in with us for the summer, helping out around the Hall. No one can replace dear Sally,' she said, turning to an older lady at the table. 'But I think we all agree we need help around here.'

There were some nods and titters at that.

'Anna, let me remind you who everyone is but don't worry if it goes in one ear and out the other, they are always here so you'll soon know everyone.' She pointed out everyone as she introduced them. 'My husband, Drew, Izzy our daughter, that's Drew's brother Rory and his fiancée Heather, and their little boy Harry. That's Sally, our dear former-housekeeper, my mother Caroline and her husband, John, and of course, you know Brodie and Emily, and little Iona too.'

She paused for breath as everyone waved hello and I nodded, unsure if they all lived at the Hall or not. Had I moved into a commune or something? Beth noticed me frown.

'Rory and Heather live on a farm not too far away, with her dad Don, who I'm sure you'll meet soon, and Angus who works on the farm. They've also recently bought another farm and the manager there, Cameron, pops in now and again too. Sally lives in a cottage in the grounds. So it's just you, me, Drew, Izzy, Mum and John in the house. Oh and that's Ginny,' she added, pointing to the cat walking out of the doors into the garden. 'Right, sit down and help yourself to whatever you like.'

She disappeared back into the kitchen and I sunk into a chair, thinking I'd never lived with so many people before.

I glanced at Brodie, who was talking to Drew about an upcoming garden party, and at Emily, who was bouncing Iona on her lap as she sipped some orange juice. She gave me a reassuring smile. I decided to just eat and listen to what they were all talking about. There was a tray of mixed sandwiches, crusty bread, different cheeses, pâté, hummus and vegetables sliced up, a bowl of salad, and sausage rolls. I worked out what I could eat and piled up a plate, and then poured myself another cup of coffee. I needed to be as alert as possible.

'Do you not eat meat, Anna?' Izzy, who sat opposite me, suddenly said. I was startled as it had appeared that she had been lost in her book. 'I like your hair. Was it easy to dye like that?' The conversations around us halted as everyone waited for my response.

'I'm a vegetarian,' I confirmed. 'And it's just a home dye. I have light hair naturally so it was easy, although it fades quickly. What are you reading?' I crunched on a carrot dipped in hummus as the others began talking around us again. It was shop-bought hummus, so not as good as the one I made, but I was too hungry to mind.

'It's about the suffragettes,' Izzy replied. 'Brodie said you went on a march once?'

'I've been on several animal rights and climate change marches. I really think we all need to do so much more to help the environment. Out here, it's maybe less obvious but I've mostly lived in cities and the pollution is out of control.'

'Well, we don't have many marches in Glendale, I'm afraid,' Caroline, Beth's mother, said from down the table. Her voice was posh and she was clearly full of disdain. 'We also have a cattle farmer at the table.'

'We are very interested in sustainable farming though,' Rory said, quickly. I smiled at that.

'You're not vegan though?' Izzy continued her grilling of me.

I took a sip of coffee. 'No. I haven't found a vegan cheese or chocolate that I can get on board with. Yet.' I looked at the lunch spread. 'Who's the cook here?' I asked, wondering if I could give them some tips. The sandwiches were pretty uninspiring.

'No cook, unfortunately,' Beth said. 'Sally used to do all our meals and I know I'm second-rate in comparison. She's always asking me to let her help but she deserves her retirement,' she said, smiling across at the older lady. 'Emily provided the baked goods for dessert so everyone will be happy about that. I don't know what I'll do when the weddings kick in; there will have to be a lot of takeaways.'

'Why? I'm here?' I asked, raising an eyebrow, confused.

'You can't cook,' Brodie said with a laugh.

'There's a lot you don't know about me, brother,' I replied, a little irritated. I'd spent my working life in pubs and restaurants and worked for some really talented chefs and cooks. I'd picked up more than a few tips, although I was yet to cook for anyone but myself. I was nervous but I wanted to prove to him that there was something I could do. 'Leave tonight's meal to me and I'll show you.'

'Will we still be able to eat meat?' Drew asked, glancing at his wife in panic.

'I may not eat it but I can cook it. Although wait until you've tried my veggie lasagne and you might change your mind.' I decided then to make two dishes and see if I could get them to enjoy a meat-free one as much as the meat one.

23

'Well,' Beth said with a smile. 'You might very well turn out to be more of a lifesaver than I first thought.'

I was so surprised I had no comeback. No one had ever said that about me before. Usually, I was told I was trouble. I glanced at Brodie, who gave me a nod. Of approval? Suddenly, it felt like this dinner was a bigger deal than I had planned for it to be.

But I was determined to do it well. It had been a long time since I had wanted to prove anything to anyone. Somehow though, I wanted to prove to these people that I could do this. That I wasn't just here as a favour to Brodie. I was the right woman for this job.

Chapter Four

Beth showed me around the Hall once lunch was over, and everyone scattered to various pursuits. 'Life is pretty busy here,' Beth said as we walked into the formal lounge. 'Which I love, but this means some things in the house have been slipping. If it's not a room we use much, like this one, it has likely been neglected.' I could see a line of dust on the mantelpiece and the heavy drapes needed cleaning. 'It's just so much work. I've had a local woman come in to do hoovering and dusting but not a proper spring clean, you know? I look after the grounds with John, and I keep an eye on our shop in the village with my mother although we have a manager there, and then we run a Christmas trail and an annual summer garden party for the village. This year, I've got two weddings that I'm planning at the Hall plus I'm helping Heather with her wedding to Rory. I think I may have bitten off more than I can chew so I can't tell you how relieved I was when Brodie said you'd decided to come and help after all.'

We walked into the smaller living room then, where the TV was. It was much cosier and more lived in. 'Well,' I said, hesitantly. 'I sort of had to leave the pub where I was,' I said. 'I thought Glendale would be a bit too quiet for me, but I'm grateful to have somewhere for the summer.'

'You're honest,' she said, tilting her head. 'I like that. And don't mind my mother. We butt heads sometimes but she cares a lot about this house and our family. Let's show you the garden now. Are you sure about the cooking by the way? I don't want to give you too much to do, I'm guilty of that sometimes.'

We stepped out into the sunny afternoon. Birdsong was the only sound to greet us. I'd never stayed anywhere so peaceful before. We walked across the lawn side by side. 'I'm happy to work hard,' I said, in case she thought I was a shirker or something. Even Hamish hadn't been able to say that I didn't work hard. 'Although I won't be any help with weddings, they are really not my thing.' I shrugged. If I was honest, I found weddings boring. I had never understood why people got so emotional about them. I could concede though that the Hall's grounds were a stunning backdrop for one.

'I didn't think they were mine either, but after I had mine to Drew here, people started to ask if they could have theirs here too. I ended up helping Em organise her and Brodie's wedding, and it's all just spiralled from there really. I'm not into dresses and flowers and all that, I just love organising things. And Glendale Hall has a magic to it sometimes,' she said, smiling at me as if I would soon see that for myself. 'So I'm happy to share it with others.' She took me to the stream and gazebo where the weddings would be held, and there was a woodland area where she pointed out the cottage behind the trees that Sally lived in. It was hard to believe that all of this land belonged to her. We walked for ages until we'd finally seen it all and then Beth stopped and looked back at the house behind us. I paused too. 'I hope you'll have a fun summer with us, Anna. Even if there will be some weddings around you. Now, I need to go into the village. Why don't you take today to just settle in? We can start tomorrow. You can leave the meal too if…'

'No, it's okay, I'll cook,' I said, firmly. 'Do I need to go into the village for anything?'

'I did a big shop yesterday so there should be plenty in, have a look and see. But if you need to go into the village for anything anytime then you can use my car, and here,' Beth produced a credit card. 'For any Hall supplies. Just keep the receipts, for the tax man.'

And to check I wasn't shopping for myself, I assumed, which was fair enough. I nodded and pocketed it. 'Thanks. I'll have a look, and then I'll have a quick run. I had to miss my usual one this morning, and it's a lovely day.'

Beth shook her head. 'I won't say I understand but I hope you enjoy the run. I'll see you later. And listen, make yourself at home.' She strode off with a wave. I watched her go, pleased to find her down-to-earth but I was still intimidated by her owning all of this, especially when she was only a few years older than me. I set off back to the house to change for my run, needing the reassurance of the ground pounding beneath my feet.

–

When I jogged out of the Hall gates, I turned away from the village, not wanting to bump into any people, and headed instead in the other direction into the winding Highland countryside. There were green fields either side of the road, and only a narrow path for walkers. There were no cars on the road though so I ran on that instead. The afternoon sun was warm through the fluffy clouds and I let some of my tension slip away as it always did as

I started to run, turning up my music, playing my rock chicks playlist, my favourite one to exercise to.

I started running when I was thirteen, after my accident. It was, at first, a way to build strength in my muscles on the advice of my doctor, but I found it was good to calm my mind and use up the excess energy I always seemed to have inside me. I tried to do one every day, unless it was bitter cold or pouring with rain. I also did yoga when I could. Anything I could really, to try to de-stress. Sometimes it worked, other times the only way I could release the restless feeling that itched under my skin was to pack up and move on and try to find a new life to sink my energy into.

Wanderlust. That's what they call it, I suppose. But it wasn't particularly a desire to travel that pushed me on to new places. Often I stayed in the UK, and didn't feel the need to run off to Thailand, although I had tried that in my early twenties with a man I met sky-diving. And I had my flight booked to Ibiza as I fancied seeing some sun again. No, it was more to do with the fact that I never seemed to be able to settle anywhere.

The problem was I felt a weariness that I never had felt before. The prospect of moving on didn't hold quite as much appeal as it once had. And I wasn't sure why.

I ran harder and faster, following the twisting path until it disappeared and I was forced to follow the verge on the side of the road. The hills rolled past me, endless land that was empty and lush, reaching all the way up to the sky. Soon I passed sheep and in the distance I could see cattle chewing on the grass at the top of a hill, but I hadn't seen one person, and only a couple of cars had passed by. I didn't think I'd felt this alone in months. Living in a cramped pub you rarely had moments to yourself, but I preferred that. It was too easy to think when I was alone. Self-analysis was something to be avoided at all costs, I had found.

Hearing a vague noise ahead, I turned from looking up to the cattle on the hill back to the road and saw a tractor had suddenly pulled out of the side road. I hadn't noticed and I was about to run headlong into it. Letting out a shocked gasp, I saw the man on the tractor waving his arms madly and I dived out of the way, landing on the grass in a tangled heap. My earbuds fell out as I hit the ground and then I heard the shouting I appeared to have missed by listening to my music at such a loud volume.

My heart raced as I slowly sat up and tried to catch my breath.

'What the hell were you doing?!'

I looked up to see an angry Scottish man standing over me, hands on his hips. He wore jeans with holes in, clumpy boots, a plaid shirt. The sun was behind him so I couldn't see his face but it didn't take a genius to work out that he was pretty pissed off. 'I didn't see you,' I said, brushing the dirt off my palms and trying to stand up. A hand reached out to help me but I ignored it and stood up. My ankle hurt a bit and my palms stung from the ground but I was okay thankfully.

'You need to be careful; you're running on a road. I could have hit you! I was shouting, why didn't you move sooner?' He spoke with a thick, gruff Scottish accent but now I was standing I was surprised to see he was younger than I had first thought, and had short dark hair, a line of trimmed stubble around his chin, and olive skin. A contrast to the men I'd met so far here that weren't my brother, who were very pale and very ginger. I saw him give me a look up and down as well but his expression didn't change. I was in leggings and a tight top, my hair in a ponytail, my skin glowing from my run, but I wasn't bothered – he was good-looking but too disapproving to be attractive. I didn't need another disapproving man in my life.

'Blame Joan Jett,' I said, lifting up an earbud. I glanced behind him. 'I didn't think those things moved fast enough to be a hazard, to be fair.'

'It's heavy enough to hurt even if it is slow,' he half-growled. 'Besides, it could have been a car. You need to watch the road. Everyone thinks it's so quiet out here but there are a lot of hazards in the country too, you know.'

I was fed up now. I hoped he wasn't a typical example of a Glendale man otherwise it really would be a cruel summer. 'Chill out, no one got hurt,' I snapped, popping my earbuds in and backing away. He had definitely ruined my run.

'Bloody tourists,' I heard him mutter as he walked back to his tractor.

'Actually,' I called to his retreating back as I started to jog. 'I just moved here, so I'm sure I'll be seeing you around!' I ran off feeling his eyes on my back, and I broke into a grin, pleased I had got the last word.

Chapter Five

The country-style kitchen at Glendale Hall was huge, with an Aga and a double fridge, and although I'd always worked in more modern places, and it wasn't the style I'd have if I ever had my own kitchen, it was pleasant to work in, especially with the view out from the French doors into the garden. The late afternoon sun streamed into the room as I cooked dinner and the family started to gather at the table. They mostly ate in here, Beth said, and only moved to the formal dining room for occasions when there were too many to fit at the table, usually at Christmas and other big celebrations. She had also warned me that people tended to drop by unannounced so I made sure I prepared extra just in case.

I'd showered after my run, put on skinny jeans and my Fleetwood Mac t-shirt, and let my hair down loose and wavy, humming along to the radio as I cooked. I could always feel at home in a new place once I got into the kitchen.

'How come Brodie didn't tell me that you love to cook?' Beth asked as she poured some wine, glancing at me as I mixed up a salad dressing.

'I guess we haven't lived together for years; it's not something you just announce, is it. People find out when you make them a meal. And I've never done that for him,' I mused as I drizzled balsamic vinegar. I didn't add that

I'd never cooked for anyone. My mum always cooked when I reluctantly came home, and I never mentioned that I could help. I didn't really tell them much about my life, I supposed, a habit that had grown since I left home feeling like they were disappointed in me. I wondered what Brodie would think of this meal. I couldn't help but hope he'd be proud that I had some life skills after all.

'Well, I'm excited to try it, it smells great.' Beth turned then as the door opened and in walked Heather and her family. 'Oh, Cameron, you came,' she said, going over to greet them. At the name I didn't know, I glanced over my shoulder and did a double-take. I muttered under my breath. Of course the man who almost hit me with his tractor earlier, and blamed me for it, had to be one of our dinner guests. Awesome sauce.

'Now, you're not going to poison us, are you?' Brodie appeared then, coming over to nudge me with his elbow, carrying a bottle of red wine which he added to the line-up at the side of me. It seemed they all felt they had to bring something to dinner.

'I've made a separate dish just for you actually,' I replied, throwing him a glare. I moved to the Aga to check the meal, and shooed him away with my hands. He grinned but did as I asked and joined the others. Beth checked to see if I needed any help but I told them to all sit down. I hadn't cooked for this many people ever, I only ever cooked for myself. Even when I'd had jobs in pubs and restaurants, I'd never been allowed to do more than prepping veg or making a sauce, I had just watched and absorbed any knowledge I could get and then practised by myself so I really hoped this would go down well.

The room was loud and merry as I carried everything over to the table. There was Beth, with her husband Drew and daughter Izzy, Brodie with Emily and Iona, and the farming lot – Heather and her husband Rory, their son Harry, and Heather's dad, Don, had come too. I was officially introduced to Cameron by Heather, who called him manager of Hilltop Farm. I couldn't have missed the farming vibe from him really, could I? I was pleased to see him also do a double-take when he recognised me, his neck flushing slightly. I hoped he was embarrassed by how he spoke to me out on the road. But he just gave me the briefest of nods before looking away. What was his problem?

I ignored him and focused on serving everyone. I had made baked vegetable pasta and a beef lasagne for the vegetable-adverse, alongside a salad with my homemade dressing, and a basket of home-made cheesy garlic bread. Seeing what they had had for lunch earlier and the vibe I got from Beth, I thought it was a good starter meal for them.

'This looks amazing, Anna,' Emily said, breathing in the garlicky smell with a big smile on her face.

'Much better than what Mum makes,' Izzy agreed, reaching for a big serving spoon.

'Thanks, Iz, keeping me grounded as ever,' Beth replied, dryly. 'Sit down, Anna, here's a glass of wine. Cameron, you can tell us if this is authentic or not.'

I glanced curiously at Cameron, who took the plate of pasta she had passed him across the table. 'I'm half-Italian,' he said. That explained the dark hair and olive skin then. Usually I was attracted to dark looks but it was hard to compute his attractive exterior with his complete lack of manners.

'You cook yourself, then?' I took a bite of the veggie pasta and was pleased that it tasted as good as usual. I noted that they seemed to have all had a taste of both dishes despite them all being meat eaters.

'Oh my god, this bread,' Heather said beside me. 'It's so good, Anna!'

'No,' Cameron had to admit. 'My father is Italian but he's not around anymore. My family all live there so I haven't had much contact with them.' He looked away after his terse speech and had a spoonful of lasagne. I watched as he ate and he looked across at me before looking away. I felt inwardly triumphant at the surprised expression on his face, which I took to mean the food was good but he didn't want to admit it.

'Okay, how have you kept this skill quiet from us?' Emily asked me then. 'Also, can I sell this garlic bread in my bakery please?'

I chuckled, pleased that they all were enjoying it. I'd kept the meal comforting and family-friendly, it was an easy-win kind of meal, not the meal that would win *MasterChef*. But, let's face it, that really wasn't what people wanted to eat at home. 'One of the first restaurants I worked in was Italian,' I remembered. 'The owner and chef was this really larger-than-life Italian woman called Donna – she lived for food. She was so strict, she would hit you with a spoon if you did something wrong,' I said with a fond smile. She was ballsy, that woman, you couldn't help but admire her. 'She'd learned from her grandmother back home in Italy and wanted everyone to eat good food. She taught me a lot.' My smile faded and I took a swig of wine. I had been really upset when they had told me to leave that place. All because I supposedly broke her grandson's heart. It still smarted years later. I had told him I didn't want anything more than casual. Why did men never listen when you told them that? 'I've just watched, really, in all the places I've worked, and picked things up. I've also watched a lot of cooking shows and YouTube videos,' I added with a self-deprecating laugh. I glanced at Emily. 'You can definitely have the recipe for a cut of the profits.'

'My sister, everyone,' Brodie said but his eyes twinkled. I felt for the first time he was getting a glimpse of me as my own person, and not just the wayward sister he worried about. It made a nice change.

'We like a businesswoman around here,' Emily said, raising her glass to me.

'I just had the best idea,' Heather said excitedly, putting her cutlery down with a clatter. 'Cameron, we were only saying the other day that we needed some help in the kitchen department at Hilltop, didn't we?'

Cameron's lip curled in distaste. 'I think Anna has her hands full here though.'

'What do you need?' Beth asked them.

'We have our first retreat guests this week and are testing out offering bed and breakfast. But Cameron can't even cook bacon without burning it, and I can't always be there in the mornings to do it.' She turned to me. 'I don't suppose you'd be willing to show him the breakfast ropes so to speak?'

'We can find someone else,' Cameron said quickly.

'But look how amazing Anna's food is,' Heather interrupted him. 'Could you spare her for a morning, Beth?'

I looked at Cameron, who was mildly furious and it got my back up. Why did he seem so freaked out by the idea of me showing him how to cook? Because I was a newcomer who didn't know to look out for tractors about to knock her over? I couldn't help it: when there was an opportunity to annoy someone who seemed to unreasonably dislike me, I had to take it, right? 'It would be easy,' I said. 'I can make brunch tomorrow and show you the ropes as I do it so it's not taking me away from my work here or anything.' I grinned as he looked at me full of disdain. 'And I'm an excellent teacher,' I added, giving a piece of garlic bread a good old bite. I was certain that I saw his lips twitch.

'But that's your day off,' Beth said. She had told me Sundays were my own. I had no idea what I would find to do out here on them though.

'It's okay, we still need to eat, right?' I glanced at Cameron. He was staring down at his plate, picking at his food, quite obviously annoyed. I'd never met anyone quite so grumpy under the age of fifty before.

'Well, if you're happy to then I won't turn down a good brunch.' Beth definitely seemed pretty easy-going. But I knew based on experience that that could change in an instant if she thought I was doing something wrong. 'We can have a big feast after church.'

I raised an eyebrow. I hadn't thought that I'd be around now to watch my brother work on a Sunday.

'Thank you so much!' Heather said to me then. 'Well done on bringing her here, Brodie.'

'I think we should be thanking Hamish,' he replied with a raised eyebrow.

Honestly, he never gave me a break.

'Can we have seconds yet?' Izzy asked then, reaching for the veggie pasta before anyone could stop her. I watched her happily, glad I'd made extra food. I couldn't help but warm to people who loved to eat, and who appreciated my cooking, and I'd got one over on Cameron too. He was still glowering.

And when I announced I'd made cheesecake for dessert, I even got a round of applause.

Chapter Six

I didn't sleep well my first night at the Hall. The whole house was so quiet, it was disconcerting. I hadn't slept somewhere so quiet since Christmas night at my parents' house. All of my jobs usually had me living above pubs and restaurants, or when I travelled I slept in youth hostels. I was used to noise and people coming and going in the night. Glendale Hall, though, was completely silent.

When I woke up after finally drifting off to sleep in the early hours, all I could hear was birdsong. I started Spotify up on my iPhone to break the silence and wake myself up. It was going to take some getting used to having all this peace and quiet. I sat up and looked around my room. It was so much more luxurious than I was used to, it felt rather unreal to be waking up here. I supposed because I wasn't sure I deserved to be here.

Shaking off that dark thought, I told myself to get going and that would stop me sinking into any over-thinking. It was something that plagued me too much, more than usual already, and I had a busy day ahead so there was no time to let myself dwell.

It turned out that most of Glendale Hall attended church on a Sunday morning. Some did it because they always had, and maybe believed in God I don't know, but the rest did it to support my brother, which was actually quite sweet, I thought. Although that meant I felt I had to go to church as well.

Growing up, we had gone every week but now I only attended when I had to, for things like my brother's wedding. But I couldn't be the only one at Glendale Hall who didn't attend.

So, after my morning run, I showered and got dressed and went downstairs. It was a sunny, warm morning so everyone who lived at the Hall walked together to the village – Sally, the former housekeeper; Beth's mother Caroline and her stepdad John; along with me, Beth, Drew and Izzy.

'Is it weird having a minister for a brother?' Izzy asked as we walked along, taking up most of the road, which was empty of traffic although I was keeping an eye out for tractors, just in case. I liked how inquisitive Izzy was, it reminded me of me growing up. I always had a lot of questions. A thirst for knowledge and experience, a desire to know everything. I still felt like that even now. Izzy seemed to get most of her information from books, whereas I wanted to get it from living, not reading.

'It's a lot to live up to,' I admitted. 'When I was younger, I was sure I often saw the words in my parent's eyes: "Why can't you be more like your brother?"'

I laughed but it sounded hollow to my ears. I felt like they still thought that way. I certainly knew that I didn't measure up to him.

'Thankfully, I'm an only child otherwise I'm sure that's what my mother would have said too,' Beth said from beside us. She looked at Drew, who chuckled, their hands entwined. 'So, you're not as religious as him then?'

I didn't think I'd ever been interrogated quite as much in a new job before. This family were pretty nosey but they did it in such a straightforward way, I couldn't get annoyed. 'No. I mean, our parents are so we both grew up going to church but Brodie kind of stopped for a while when he was a teenager, and then after my accident I couldn't go and I guess I just slipped out of the habit. When I was eighteen, I left home and I don't go when I'm away from my family but when I'm at home, they kind of expect it.' It was a source of contention between us all sometimes. My accident had led Brodie back to God, back to his faith in such a way he became a minister, but it had pushed me away, and kept me running from it ever since. I knew my parents and Brodie were upset by my lack of faith, and confused too. They believed that God had spared me. If that was true, I had never felt as if I deserved it. Instead, I felt like I had been given a burden that I wasn't strong enough to carry.

'Oh, well, you shouldn't feel you have to join us,' Drew said. 'We're in the habit but it's not a prerequisite of living at the Hall.'

'He's her brother,' Caroline said, glancing back, evidently having listened to our conversation. 'Surely she wants to support him? Same as if he were an actor, you'd go to his plays, wouldn't you?'

I honestly hadn't thought about it like that. I hadn't listened to a sermon of his for years. My last time in church was for Brodie and Emily's wedding and, obviously, he hadn't led that service. Had I been letting him down all these years? 'Of course,' I said quickly, a little embarrassed. I cleared my throat. 'So, when Heather was talking about Hilltop Farm, I didn't really understand what they do there?' I asked Beth and Drew, trying to take the heat off me. Thankfully, Caroline turned back ahead and began talking to John and Sally. I felt that I needed to be careful around her. She felt more like how I'd imagined the owner of the Hall to be than Beth was. I'd have to ask Brodie how come it wasn't her who ran the place.

'Well, my brother Rory and Heather recently bought the neighbouring farm to theirs,' Drew explained. 'They've opened it up as a retreat for the first time this week – a group from the Midlands are staying at the farmhouse. They are learning about farming and enjoying getting to live in the quiet countryside for a week. But they also plan to make it a working farm with sheep: they're training their new dog and looking into buying sheep but they wanted to get the farmhouse sorted first. Cameron is living on site and managing it.'

I nodded. 'Even though I love animals I don't think I've ever set foot on a farm in my life. I'm more of a beach holiday person.'

Beth smiled. 'They've actually had a lot of inquiries. I think lots of city people and workplaces love the idea of a rustic, peaceful getaway. Heather found this group through her Instagram; they're a mother and baby group. They are really enjoying it.'

'Her Instagram?'

'She's so popular on there,' Beth said. 'I'm trying to get the Glendale village accounts as popular but I can't compete. Do you do much on social media?'

I was surprised. I hadn't expected that. Maybe because Glendale was so in the middle of nowhere, the last place you expect to find any kind of influencer. I shook my head. 'Not really. I hate the idea of people you've met in the past being able to track you down and see what you're doing now.' I caught Beth share a glance with her husband, they clearly found that strange, and I suppose nowadays it was unusual, but let's just say I probably had more ghosts I preferred to lay to rest than most women my age.

Conversation paused as we reached the village and made our way to the church. I was taken aback to see how many people were walking inside. Brodie was in the doorway in his dog collar, greeting them all with a friendly smile. I thought church congregations were dwindling but Glendale's appeared to be thriving.

'Anna, I'm so pleased you're joining us,' Emily said, hurrying over as we walked past the vicarage. She wrapped her arm through mine. 'I definitely need your garlic bread recipe. I've been thinking about it since last night: I could do a week of bread specials from other countries. It would be really fun, don't you think?'

'Of course you can have it,' I said, thinking that Emily reminded me of sunshine. I felt like I was more of a cloudy day kind of girl. 'I can email it over.' Emily and Brodie had emailed their baby scan to all the family so I had her address. I hadn't spent any time alone with Emily since she met my brother, we'd only seen one another at Christmas or family gatherings, which I made sure were few and far between, and she was sweet but like everyone in my life, I had no intention of doing anything other than keep her at arm's length. Although I did love how enthusiastic she was about bread. 'I didn't expect to see so many people here,' I admitted as we walked towards the church door.

'It's all down to your brother,' Emily said as we approached him. He smiled at us. It was obvious how happy she made him. 'Just don't tell him or he'll get an even bigger head,' she added so only I could hear.

I laughed as he looked at us suspiciously. We walked on through into the church and I looked around. The church itself was small with light streaming in through the stained-glass window at the back above the altar. People were filling up the pews. Emily led me right up to the front where a pew was empty, clearly left for those at the Hall. I realised then what a big part this group played in this community. It took them ages to join us as they greeted the whole village on the way, it looked like. Finally, they all sat down and Brodie came to the front.

'Welcome, everyone. I'd like to say a special note of welcome to my sister, Anna, who has come to stay in Glendale with us for the summer. Anna was the reason that I became a minister in the first place so it's particularly special for me to look out and see her in the front pew.' He gestured to me and I felt all eyes turn towards me. I shrank down, embarrassed. Now everyone knew I was the minister's sister. Thanks, Brodie. It was like the headmistress of a school pointing out her daughter on the first-day assembly. Not what I wanted. I glanced around and caught a smirk across the aisle in the next pew. I recognised Cameron – he seemed to be enjoying my discomfort. Hmmm. I would have to get him back for that in our cooking lesson later.

'I hope you'll join me in welcoming Anna to the village.' Several people turned to smile at me. I squirmed in my seat, feeling the pressure of living up to my brother's expectations once again. 'Now, let's have a song…' Brodie turned to the band behind him, to my relief. No stuffy organ hymns in Brodie's church but a guitar band singing worship songs, which the congregation joined in with enthusiastically.

I tried to sing along to the words on the projector at the front but I couldn't stop thinking about Brodie's words. How I was the reason that he became a minister – he really believed that God had saved me and he'd wanted to repay that debt somehow. I, however, felt like an utter fraud – completely undeserving of being saved.

Brodie saw me almost dying as giving him his life's purpose whereas I felt like it had left me without one. It was part of the reason I wasn't as close to him, or my parents, anymore.

I tried to tell myself that I kept moving because my life had been saved so I needed to live a big life. I needed to travel and have new experiences. I needed to be fearless, and not settle, but I knew it wasn't what made me so restless, what kept me from getting close to anyone, what made me run from place to place, and never want to return home. Because having adventures was meant to make you happy. And I wasn't.

No, the real reason behind it all was my survivor's guilt. Well, that's what the therapist I had seen after the accident had called it. But she never knew the whole truth behind my guilt. No one knew. It was something I didn't talk about and tried not to think about. It followed me around, though, like a dark shadow. It was the reason I couldn't talk to my family about the accident. And why Brodie thinking that God had saved me horrified me.

Because I knew that I'd survived an accident that was all my fault in the first place.

Chapter Seven

Cameron walked into the kitchen at the Hall after church. I had asked everyone to stay out of the kitchen until brunch was ready because I didn't want them listening to me teaching Cameron. I wasn't looking forward to it and was prepared for him to be difficult so it was better for everyone if the others stayed out of the line of fire. It was a pleasant late morning so the others went readily into the garden, leaving us alone.

Cameron looked almost bored, and that was irritating. I mean, I was doing him a favour after all. What was even more irritating was how he rolled up the sleeves of his white shirt and I caught myself looking at his muscly arms. They were rather distracting. Why did someone so grumpy have to be so good-looking? Life was often unfair in that way though, I had found.

Turning away, I pulled my hair into a bun, put on an apron and handed him one. I had to look up at him to speak. That wasn't a rare event – I was always smaller than other people – but Cameron loomed large in the kitchen. But I had never once backed down from anyone, and I wasn't about to start. And, thankfully, he put on his apron and it dulled his intimidating effect a lot. In fact, I let out a laugh. It looked ridiculous on him.

'What?' he asked, not getting the joke.

'I just love a man in an apron.'

He didn't smile. 'Shall we get on?'

I stared back at him. 'Fine. I will teach you how to make an easy brunch if you answer a question first. Deal?'

Cameron's eyebrows shot up. I loved that I'd wrong-footed him. It was one of my favourite things to do – the last thing people expected. His mouth twitched. 'I can't let Heather and Rory down at Hilltop so I'll have to say yes.'

'My question, then, while we get all our ingredients,' I said, walking over to the fridge. I handed him things behind my back, passing them to him – eggs, bacon, sausages, tomatoes fresh from the garden, milk for pancakes, yogurt, berries. There was bread from Emily's Bakery already on the counter, smelling inviting. I thought he'd run a mile from the idea of baking muffins or anything so we'd keep it simple. 'So, we're going to make the kind of breakfast people staying at a rustic farm would expect. You have to play to your crowd. If I had served up a soufflé in my old pub, I would have been laughed out of there. But just because you're making a simple menu, it doesn't mean it shouldn't taste just as good as a fancy meal. In my humble opinion. Right, so my question…' I turned to see Cameron, surrounded by food behind him on the counter, looking quite bewildered. By the food or me, I wasn't sure. Could have been both actually. 'Why were you so against me showing you how to cook?' He was still looking at me strangely. Maybe he was attractive but dim, like Dave back in Glasgow. 'Go ahead. We can cook afterwards.'

He sighed. 'I wasn't against it, exactly. It's just I need to focus on this new job. I didn't think learning to cook was a high priority, to be honest.' He didn't quite meet my gaze, though, so I definitely didn't think I'd heard the whole truth. I still couldn't shake the feeling that it was me he hadn't wanted to teach him, not that he hadn't wanted to learn. But we'd only just met. Had I really offended him that much already?

'Why did you want to be a farmer?' I asked, determined to worm the correct answer out of him soon.

'I love being outside, I love animals, I love hard work, and it's all I've ever known. Like I said, my dad wasn't around much so my uncle, Angus, took me under his wing. I used to spend loads of time with him at Fraser Farm where he works. After uni, I came back to Glendale and Rory and Heather offered me a full-time job. It was a no-brainer.' He shrugged. 'So, what do you do first then?' he asked, steering us back to the matter in hand, clearly not wanting to elaborate further.

I'll be honest, I hadn't expected that he would have gone to university. But then he came back home. I felt like there was more to his story. Like anyone, I suppose. Who tells someone they just met the real truth anyway? I knew I never did. Or even people I had known for longer. But I at least knew that he wasn't afraid of hard work and it sounded like he was determined to do a good job at Hilltop, so hopefully we could make it through this lesson without anything getting burned. 'Let's make scrambled eggs. If you get that right then everyone will be happy.'

Cameron focused on the task straight away. He listened and followed my instructions, and actually produced a notebook to write down what I was saying. I couldn't remember a man listening to me so carefully before. We moved on to sausages and bacon then, and I bent down to put them under the grill and glanced over. He was chewing on his pen as he checked his notes, oblivious to my skinny-jeans-covered bum. 'So, you'll want to provide some non-cooked options because not everyone likes a cooked breakfast. So, make sure you have cereals, yogurt and fruit, granola, pastries, that kind of thing. And all bread options.'

'Options?'

'White, wholemeal, granary, rye, gluten-free... You know what, I'm sure Emily can deliver to Hilltop or something,' I said when he looked blank. 'Same for milk. Dairy-free options.'

He wrote that down. 'I really thought I'd just be doing cornflakes and toast. This is nuts. You'd better show me the pancakes,' he said, taking a deep breath.

I smiled. 'For someone happy on a huge tractor, the kitchen seems to scare you.'

'I've never been around anyone who cooks. My uncle can just about make beans on toast, and my mum only really makes pasta with a jar of sauce. We have a lot of takeaways or ready meals. I eat the best when they invite me here, to be honest.'

'No girlfriend to cook you a meal, then? Although in this day and age, you should be cooking for her, of course.' I couldn't resist the sly question. Not that I cared either way.

'No girlfriend for either of us to do it,' he said, looking away from me. I saw a flicker of something in his eyes. Pain maybe.

I wasn't surprised he was single with the attitude he'd shown me so far but it made it all the more interesting that he appeared to be so resistant to my charms. 'Hey, don't let that bacon burn!'

Cameron spun around to check it, muttering something about me being as bossy as Gordon Ramsay. Cheeky.

We managed to get through the rest of making brunch without incident or any conversation apart from cooking instructions. When it was all ready, I poked my head out of the French doors. 'Do you all want to eat out there? I think we're ready.' They all agreed to that suggestion so we served up the food in dishes and carried everything outside, along with a pot of coffee, teapot, and a jug of juice. 'You think you'll be able to get through a breakfast now?' I asked Cameron before we carried out the toast and pastries.

'Honestly, I'm not sure but I definitely know what I'm aiming for now. I didn't before.' He turned to me and for the first time in the hour we'd been in the kitchen, looked me straight in the eyes. It was a little disconcerting. 'Thanks then,' he half-grunted.

I supposed that was the best I was going to get. I gave a terse nod. 'Sure,' and then I pushed past him and went outside. I really couldn't make him out at all.

We sat down to brunch and everyone was complimentary. Cameron was quiet through the meal and at the end said he had to be off to the farm, legging it as quickly as he could get away with, I thought.

'He's not a big talker, is he?' I asked Heather once he had gone.

She was bouncing her toddler on her lap, passing him some toast, and turned to smile at me. 'Just like his uncle. They don't say much but when they do it seems to count more. I trust them like family. And that counts for a lot. Thank you for helping us today. I really don't have the time to get to Hilltop every day to make the guests breakfast.'

'I'm always happy to get into the kitchen.'

Chapter Eight

The vicarage was at the end of the High Street, next to the church, and it was small but cosy, the scent of lavender and baking greeting me when Brodie opened the door. I had only been inside once before – when I had come for their wedding. Emily had asked me and my mum to join her and her bridesmaids to get ready before the wedding, and I'd felt awkward the whole time. The vicarage reminded me of my parents' house in Inverness, so my feet felt almost itchy as soon as I crossed the threshold. It was a family home through and through. Something I had run from when I was eighteen, and was still running from now.

'Hey, sis,' Brodie said with a grin. Despite myself, I smiled back. When he called me that, I remembered happier times before my accident, times when he had just been my big brother. He'd changed out of the dog collar, thank goodness, and now wore a casual shirt and jeans. 'Come on in. We thought we'd go in the garden, it's such a lovely day.' Brodie led me through the kitchen and out the back door into their square garden, which backed on to the church cemetery, although you couldn't really see it as there were trees at the bottom of the garden. I could, however, see the church steeple rising up behind it. It was weird to live in the shadow of a church, surely? I felt like I'd always be anxious to be on my best behaviour or

51

something. And that would not be something I would enjoy.

'Lovely to see you again, Anna.' Emily greeted me with a warm smile. She was at their white patio table, Iona on her lap. A picture of summer happiness was before me. Emily with her blonde hair and floaty floral dress. Iona with a cute hat and sundress on, colourful flowers in full bloom all around them, the sun shining down. On the table stood a vase of wild flowers, a jug of homemade lemonade with ice in glasses that had lemons on them, and a pretty lemon cake under a dome with plates all ready.

'Is lemonade okay or would you like a coffee?' Brodie asked behind me as I stared, wondering if I was going to destroy this scene with my presence. I felt uncomfortable. Out of my depth. I wanted alcohol, to be honest, but I murmured that lemonade was fine and sat down, Brodie joining us.

'How are you settling in at the Hall?' Emily asked me as she poured us all a drink. Brodie lifted the dome and cut up thick slices of cake for us all. I was glad I went on a run this morning. From what I'd seen so far, Glendale appeared to be determined to feed everyone up.

'Fine, I think. I had to show Cameron how I make brunch so he can feed people who come to stay at Hilltop Farm. I'm not sure if he took it all in or not. He didn't say very much. So I haven't had much of a chance to look around. Beth took me on a tour when I arrived but that's it. I feel like I'm going to get lost.' I took a sip of the lemonade and it was refreshing, I had to admit.

'The hall is so lovely,' Emily said. 'I lived there for a while when I first came to Glendale – I'm sure you'll work out all the nooks and crannies quickly. It will soon feel like home like it did for me, I bet.'

'Well, as long as I don't have to give any more cooking lessons, I should be able to get on with my actual work tomorrow.'

'I still can't believe my little sister can cook,' Brodie said with a shake of his head. 'I'm not sure why you kept that quiet though.'

I shrugged. 'Usually when I come home I get a lot of lectures. There's not much time to show off my skills.' I said this lightly but it hurt to know that my family thought that my life was all wrong. It made me feel as if they wouldn't care to know about things that I was enjoying in it.

Brodie did look a little shamed by that. 'I'm sorry you felt that way. We really didn't mean to do that. I know Mum and Dad would love to know you had a passion. And it was kind of you to show Cameron the ropes. I'm sure he appreciated it. I know Rory and Heather will. They are keen to make a real success of Hilltop.'

'He's a bit hard to work out, to be honest.' Reticent and reserved, I thought, most unlike his gorgeous exterior. I shrugged. 'Hopefully that's my first and only lesson with him.' I couldn't be bothered with people who didn't make an effort. It was clear he had no interest in me so I would have no interest in him either.

'I always thought he was a little shy,' Emily commented, picking up her fork to have a bite of cake. 'Probably used to spending loads of time alone outside on the farm, only having to deal with animals and not people, you know? I mean, Rory and Angus are similar, aren't they? Heather brings them out of their shell, I've always thought.'

Brodie nodded. 'Not everyone is as outgoing as you,' he added to me.

That felt like more criticism. 'I'd say he was rude, not shy, actually.' I couldn't help but snap at my brother. Like I wasn't entitled to have an opinion of someone I'd spent time with trying to help, and who had treated it like he was the one doing me a favour just gracing me with his presence. 'Anyway, how are you feeling, Emily?' I swivelled to face her instead of Brodie. I saw a flicker of hurt in his expression but I ignored it.

'I'm okay, I just get tired, which is frustrating as there's always so much to do. But I know I need to let people help more.' She smiled across at Brodie as if this was something he was always telling her. 'Not something I'm naturally good at, I must be honest.'

I knew what she meant. I was fiercely independent and hated relying on anyone. Which was why it had been so hard to accept the job here. And why I was happy that I wouldn't need to stick around for long. 'I think you're doing just fine. Don't let people tell you that you can't do things if you want to do them.' I gave Brodie a pointed look.

'There's nothing wrong in letting people carry some of your load for you, Anna,' he replied, mildly. He rarely rose to my cross tone. He was too calm for that. It was frustrating. 'They're just trying to show that they care.'

I snorted.

Emily looked between us and bit her lip. 'Thank you for emailing me the garlic bread recipe,' she said, quickly. 'I can't wait to make it. Is cooking something you'd like to do more? You really are a great chef.'

Emily was definitely trying to be peace-maker but she was too nice for me to snap at.

'I don't like staying in one place long enough. I just take jobs that let me live. I've picked up bits from people

54

I've worked for along the way, that's all. I doubt I know enough to do it professionally.'

'Well, I would say you do based on that meal,' Emily replied. 'If it's something you love, you shouldn't let the idea of staying somewhere for a while put you off. Life is about finding what you're passionate about, I think. And if you've found it, that's what you should do. Have some cake, Anna. I'll put on double my baby weight if I eat any more of it.'

I took a bit to keep her happy. It was amazing. She was such a good baker. And was clearly passionate about it. I knew what she meant – I loved nothing more than creating something in the kitchen. I thought back to how sometimes I would sneak into the kitchen of a restaurant I worked in to make something at night when no one could stop me. But the idea of doing it as my job seemed just too unrealistic to even consider.

It was still sunny when I left the vicarage to walk to the pub in the village – the Glendale Arms. There was nothing I enjoyed more on a summer evening than having a drink in a beer garden. I maybe once would have been nervous rocking up somewhere new alone, but I'd worked in so many pubs and bars and had travelled abroad alone so it didn't bother me now. There was always someone to talk to if you were open to talking to them.

Pushing open the door, I walked up to the bar. I'd put on my ragged denim shorts, a faded t-shirt and sandals, my pink hair was loose over my shoulders and my arms jangled with bangles. 'Hi,' I greeted the man behind the bar. 'Can I have a Jack and Coke?'

'Sure. I haven't seen you here before,' he said, reaching behind him for the bottle. 'I'm Malcolm, the landlord.' He was in his fifties, slightly portly with fair hair but he had a friendly smile.

I leaned against the bar as he mixed my drink, and smiled. 'I am new. I'm Anna and I'm working at Glendale Hall for a bit.'

'I know the family well,' he said with a nod, passing me my drink. 'Tell you what, first one is on the house to welcome you to Glendale. Hey, Adam!' He called out to someone leaving the loos. 'This is Anna, introduce her around, hey? She's new.'

The tall, stocky guy who looked nearer my age than Malcolm stopped and grinned. 'Your wish is my command. Hey, Anna, come out in the beer garden with us.'

I didn't need asking twice.

Outside, the garden was small and sloping, the church again could be seen behind it. There were a few picnic-style benches and it was fairly busy with families but Adam led me right to the back to two tables that had been pushed together full of men, with empty beer glasses alongside ones they were drinking, looking as if they'd been out here most of the afternoon.

'We play football every Sunday and come here for drinks afterwards,' Adam explained. He whistled to get his mates' attention. 'Guys, this is Anna. She's new to Glendale and needs someone to have a drink with. What do you think?'

I laughed when feet stamping and cheers followed his question. Adam pointed to each of the seven-a-side who waved and said hi to me when he called out their names.

'So, this is Glen, Steve, Mark, Alastair, Mick and Cameron on the end.'

My heart sank as my eyes found Cameron. I hadn't noticed him there, and he looked equally startled to see me. He managed to lift one finger in a wave before turning back to his beer. I almost walked away but I wasn't going to let him scare me off. I planted myself down in the spare seat opposite him. 'Hi, boys,' I said. 'Looks like I have some catching up to do,' I said, gesturing to their drinks.

'Cheers to that,' Adam said, sitting beside me. 'What brings you to our tiny village then?'

'I'm working at the Hall for the summer. In fact, this morning I was teaching Cameron how to cook.' They all guffawed at that and I grinned.

'Wear an apron and everything, did you, mate?' Adam asked.

'It was very fetching,' I replied.

'I bet it was,' Adam said, laughing.

Cameron shrugged. 'Real men wear aprons.'

I was surprised by a glimpse of humour from him. And impressed too. He lifted his eyes finally, looked at me, and smiled. It displayed one dimple on his right cheek. I hadn't seen that before. I crossed my legs, and accidentally brushed my foot against his leg as I did so. I felt him flinch. What was it with this guy?

'So, is he going to be a domestic goddess?' Glen asked me from the end of the table.

'I'm an excellent teacher but no one is that good,' I called back to him. 'Besides, I'm the only goddess around here.' When I glanced back, Cameron was looking down at his glass again.

'You need another drink, Anna,' Adam said then, noticing my empty glass.

'My round!' Alastair jumped up to head to the bar.

'Not for me,' Cameron said, standing up. 'Got some things to do at the farm. I'll see you next week.' They tried to get him to stay but he laughed off their pleas and walked out of the side gates, striding out towards his truck parked nearby. I couldn't help but feel his hasty exit had more to do with me than any chores that needed doing.

But once I'd finished my second Jack and Coke, I really didn't care.

Chapter Nine

I had no idea what time it was. The sun had set and the stars were starting to sparkle in the clear sky. I looked up at it and decided I had never seen anything more beautiful in my whole life.

And then I walked straight into a wheelie bin.

I let out a surprised yelp and rubbed my shin as I stumbled backwards and wondered why the hell there was a bin in the road. I realised then I wasn't in a road but was by a gate, the bin positioned outside it.

There was a noise and then a stream of light appeared. 'Anna?'

I looked behind me, confused, to see Brodie in the doorway. 'What are you doing here?'

'You're outside my house!'

'Why do you have a wheelie bin here?'

'Because the dustbins are collected in the morning.' He called something out over his shoulder, then stepped into the path, closing the door behind him. 'Have you been at the pub?'

I giggled. 'Yep. Just heading home.' I wobbled and tried to grab the wheelie bin but it appeared to have moved so I stumbled again.

'In the wrong direction,' he said, coming over and taking my arm, steadying me. 'Do you want to stay here?'

I clamped a hand across my mouth. 'It's my first day of work tomorrow.'

'I know,' he snapped then sighed. 'I'll drive you back to Hall. Hopefully, no one will be up to see you like this. Not exactly a great first impression, Anna.'

'I made some new friends,' I said as he pulled me towards his car.

'Great friends leaving you like this.'

'Well, I wanted to walk and then I forgot the way. Then I remembered you live here!'

'At least you had the sense to come here. I was just heading to bed. Right, get in.' He helped me into the car and we set off towards the Hall. I leaned back in the seat. The whole evening was a haze but I felt giddy from the drink and the fun company. I had been the centre of attention all evening, and there was nothing I enjoyed better. Well, apart from free drinks, which I had also had all evening too. I felt on top of the world until I looked at Brodie as he drove, his face set in a grim line.

'So serious,' I quipped, kicking off my shoes to get comfy.

'It's not great to be drunk your first night in your new job, is it? Are you going to be able to get up and do your work tomorrow?'

'Of course! I have had plenty of practice.' I thought that was funny but my brother didn't. 'Give me a break, Brodie. I just wanted to meet some new people. Get to know the village.'

'But you always take it too far.'

'I had a few drinks, it's not the crime of the century!'

We pulled into Glendale Hall. The house was dark and quiet and Brodie stopped the car just inside the gates. 'The gravel will wake everyone up if I drive on it. Shall I walk you to the door?'

'I'm perfectly capable of walking,' I declared but I wasn't a hundred percent sure. I picked up my shoes and bag. 'Thanks for the lift then.'

'Please don't take this for granted,' he said. 'They don't have to give you a job and a place to live. You may be planning to move on as soon as you can, but I live here. This is my home, and these are my friends. Please consider that.'

I hated being lectured by him. Even more when he was right. 'Chill out, Brodie,' I replied, rolling my eyes.

'And be quiet when you go in. Believe me, you do not want to wake Caroline up.'

'Like this is my first time sneaking in.' I thought back to all the times I had climbed into my bedroom without my parents noticing. Brodie always had though. 'That Caroline does seem scary. How come Beth owns the house?' I asked, opening the door.

'Her grandmother left it to her. To make up for things that had happened in the past. To ask for forgiveness. The house is important to the family, to the community. I hope you will treat it with more respect than you show yourself sometimes.'

I climbed out, fed up with him now, and slammed the door a little childishly. I felt his eyes on my back as I made it to the door. My alcohol buzz had dimmed slightly thanks to my big brother, so I slipped inside and made it upstairs without anyone appearing. I had got away with it. Although I knew Brodie wouldn't let me forget this.

Shutting my door, I went to my new bed and flopped on it. Why did I have to let Brodie see me tonight? A tiny voice inside my head told me that maybe I had wanted him to. That maybe despite all my protests, I hoped my brother would help me while I was here. That maybe I needed saving from myself.

But would he really want to help me after everything that had happened?

So many times, I'd almost asked him if he still blamed me for the accident, if the reason he and our parents disapproved of my life was because they thought I didn't deserve one at all, but I couldn't bring myself to say the words aloud for fear of what his answer would be. It was better to keep quiet, to stay away from my family, to keep my distance, to keep on moving, to keep fixed the barrier between me and other people... wasn't it?

I lost my train of thought then, and passed out still fully clothed.

—

Monday morning. My first full day of work as the new housekeeper at Glendale Hall.

And I was hungover.

Sun streamed in through my window when my alarm went off. Beth had told me the family tended to all start getting up at seven a.m. for breakfast on a weekday. I took that to mean I should be ready for them then so I'd set my alarm for six. I groaned when I opened my eyes and sat up, my head pounding instantly.

I was still wearing the clothes I'd had on yesterday, and I felt, frankly, disgusting. And then I remembered that Brodie had found me and brought me back here. Great. As if I wasn't feeling bad enough already.

Crawling out of bed, I shuffled into the bathroom, wincing at the sight of myself in the mirror. I looked rough, there was no denying it. I slipped into the shower and turned it on to the hottest setting, letting the water and steam wake me up. I stayed for as long as I could stand and then got out, brushed my teeth and hair, and pulled it into a ponytail, unable to face the hair dryer noise. I put on jeans and a t-shirt, and my Converse, and some make-up to make me look less pale and puffy, and then I made my way downstairs.

The Hall was quiet but the sun was up and prom-ised another warm day. The kitchen was empty for now so I made myself a strong, black coffee and took two painkillers for my head before starting breakfast. Beth had bought a notebook to list things that needed doing and clipped it to the utility room door. I checked it again. I'd looked yesterday and she hadn't added anything else to it.

> *Breakfast please!*
>
> *Clean and air drawing room as dusty and gross*
>
> *Change beds*
>
> *BBQ tonight so no need to cook* :)

She certainly wasn't like any of my previous bosses. I was relieved there was nothing too taxing on the agenda for my first day, after all the alcohol I had consumed. I started on breakfast and slowly felt better as I busied myself cooking.

'Good morning!' Beth wandered in, still in her pyjamas. 'I need coffee before I can get dressed,' she explained her attire with a wry smile. 'Look at you, you busy bee, what a treat. We haven't had breakfast made for us since Sally retired.'

'How come she still lives here?' I asked. Sally lived in a cottage in the grounds, which was weird for an ex-employee surely.

'Sally worked for us since she was really young, before I was born, so for like fifty years. She's family. And John used to live in the cottage so once he married Mum, it was sitting empty. We didn't want her to go. So it all worked out perfectly.' Beth fed Izzy's cat who had come in to the kitchen and wrapped herself around her ankles then sat down at the table to pour herself a coffee from the pot.

I nodded, unsure what to say to that. I couldn't imagine working somewhere for fifty years and then wanting to stay living there afterwards. I started bringing over breakfast, assuming that the others in the house would soon follow her down. 'I hope I've put everything out you might like.'

'Honestly, we've just been having cereal or toast really. This is amazing. I'm so grateful that you can cook. I really didn't think we'd find someone willing to do everything again. The people I interviewed for the job had such strict limits, like they would hoover and dust but not tidy. It's very strange to me. I'm used to just mucking in with whatever, we all are.' She smiled. 'Join me and have some breakfast.'

'Oh okay.' I sat down and poured another coffee, and grabbed some fruit and yogurt and sprinkled granola over it. It was all I could face this morning, and usually I didn't eat much for breakfast. I had put out eggs, bacon, pancakes and muffins for the others along with cereal and toast to cover all bases. 'I suppose housekeepers are a dying breed. I guess there aren't many houses big enough to need live-in help.'

Beth smiled. 'Exactly. We're really lucky that we've been able to keep the house in the family. But it does take a lot of work and money. We've had to come up with lots of ideas, like these weddings I'm starting up this summer.'

The back door behind us opened, making me jump. Beth seemed used to it though and looked up over her coffee cup and waved. 'Come on in, Heather.'

Heather walked in, holding the hand of her little boy, who was beside her. 'I'm on my way to drop off things at our shop and I need your help,' she said but she seemed to be saying it to me, and not to Beth.

'Join us for breakfast and tell us what's going on,' Beth said, cheerfully, gesturing them over. I didn't think I'd been anywhere with an open-door policy like this. Once again, I was glad I had made a lot of food.

Heather was pretty with curly light brown hair and she wore old jeans, a baggy shirt, and trainers. She smiled broadly as Beth passed her a coffee. 'Glad you're a black coffee drinker too,' Heather commented to me. 'We're addicted, makes us feel better we're not the only ones.' She put Harry on her lap – he was the spitting image of his father, and immediately reached for a muffin to eat. 'So, good news in a way but also scary news… A woman called Chloe contacted me through my Instagram account to ask if she could come and stay for a retreat, she's a travel influencer and wants to post about the farm and give it a review on her blog,' Heather said, giving Harry a bit of the muffin and eating some herself. 'She wants to stay for the whole weekend. The only space we had was this weekend and she's free so she's coming on Friday night.'

'That'll be such great publicity!' Beth cried. 'Who knew how much you'd get out of your Instagram. I really think I should have asked for commission when I gave you the idea.' But she was grinning at her friend. 'But why is it scary? You're ready to go, aren't you? And you have your guests this week to try everything out on, right?'

'Well, Chloe messaged me to check she'd get all her meals but I explained it's just breakfast that we're offering at the moment and it's self-catering the rest of the time but she doesn't drive so can't get to any local restaurants. So it was basically feed her or she won't come. I've said yes and now I'm panicking. I don't have time to hire a cook and I can't be there all the time so...' She turned and looked pleadingly at me. 'I wondered if we could hijack Anna for the weekend, to make her meals. Cameron will be on hand to help too, of course.'

I felt a little nonplussed by her rapid-fire conversation. I looked at Beth for help.

'I suppose, if you think about it, a retreat is about getting away from your life. I think I'd prefer to not have to worry about food all the time too,' Beth said. 'But Cameron is definitely not up to it?'

'Even if he could cook well enough to please her, there's not enough time if he has to manage everything else, you know? I mean, he has to look after the grounds and the farmhouse already. We're all helping but we have Fraser Farm too.'

Beth nodded. 'And she's coming so quickly. I think you're right, get help for that weekend and bag yourself a great review. You can decide later if you want to do food.' She turned to me. 'Anna, would you be willing to help? It would mean working on a Sunday but you could have a day off in the week instead?'

'I'd pay you double,' Heather added desperately. 'Could you manage without her though, Beth?'

I opened my mouth to protest but they both spoke quickly and excitedly. I couldn't get a word in before Beth answered her. 'Of course. Anything to help. You know how proud I am of you starting this business. It's not a wedding weekend either so we'll all pitch in and it'll be fine.' They finally stopped talking to look at me.

'What do you think, Anna? Will you please help me out?' Heather asked, hopefully. Beth gave me a reassuring nod.

I stared at them. A weekend at this farm? I mean, I'd be cooking, which I would love, but Cameron would be there. Although I was sure if I told him to let me get on in the kitchen, he would disappear again. I wondered if he knew about Heather's plan. He was surely going to be pissed, based on his reaction to me so far. Kind of reason to do it. And double my pay... It meant more money for Ibiza. 'Can I cook whatever I like?'

They both smiled. 'Definitely,' Heather said. 'Are you really sure it's okay? I feel so bad hijacking you from your job here!'

'It's fine. I love to cook. I've never been to a farm though...'

'Cameron will look after you.'

My face fell as they both tucked in to their breakfasts, all smiles. I didn't dare say that I was sure he wouldn't. It seemed everyone was oblivious to the fact he didn't want to be near me. I would just think of the money to get through it. It was only one weekend after all.

'Oh, we need to arrange that final meeting with the florist,' Beth said to Heather. 'Did Em help on the shoe front?'

'I've ordered a pair. I really hope they fit. The only problem with living in the sticks is I have to order everything online,' Heather replied with a grimace. 'I still can't believe I'm getting married this summer.'

'It'll be perfect,' Beth promised.

I could never understand the amount people spent on weddings, and all the stress, so as they pulled out their diaries to check when they could meet the florist, I slipped away from the table to clear up in the kitchen.

Whatever Beth had said about their old housekeeper, I was most definitely not part of life here at the Hall.

Chapter Ten

The drawing room at the Hall was grand. There was no other word for it. It had a high ceiling with ornate coving bordering it. Long and narrow, it had a polished wooden floor, and the furniture was in tasteful shades of neutral with elegant chairs, heavy gold drapes framing the windows, and paintings hanging on the wall that I assumed were worth a lot of money. There was also a grand piano in the corner with family photographs standing on it in silver frames. They would be a bitch to clean. There was a huge vase of fresh flowers in the large fireplace, as it was summer and didn't need to be lit. On the mahogany coffee table there was a large scented candle, and a clock, which ticked loudly in the silence, took up most of the mantelpiece.

I felt very much like staff as I walked in with my cleaning supplies, my hair pinned up in a messy bun, rubber gloves on, and my earbuds playing The Smiths. This was my main task for the day and I could see that it would take me most of it, particularly as I was still feeling the effects of last night's drinks. Thankfully, I was used to working with a hangover and with my music and the air from the window I opened widely, I felt up to hard graft, which had seemed impossible when I had woken up.

Going to the piano, I lifted the photographs off so I could clean it. There was one of Beth and Drew on their wedding day with their daughter. Izzy had been there when they got married, I knew, because Drew hadn't known Beth had had their child as a teenager. I felt relieved that I wasn't the only one around here with a complicated past. I sometimes wondered what the future held for me when it came to relationships. I had always moved on from places so quickly that I'd only had casual ones, flings that really hadn't meant anything even if sometimes the men I had them with had felt differently. And although I did have fun, I couldn't deny a certain lurch in my stomach when I saw love captured like in this photo. Would I ever want something like that? Perhaps you never really knew until you found that someone to have it with. The problem was, would I ever stick around long enough to realise if someone was that person? What if I'd already met them and hadn't realised?

Shaking my head, I carried on pulling the photos off. I didn't want to get stuck in that kind of mindset. Sometimes I looked back at my old photos on Instagram and wondered what would have happened if I stayed anywhere longer than six months. But how could I when I had to hide the truth about my past from everyone?

I polished the piano until I could see my face in it and then set about cleaning the framed pictures and setting them back on it. I saw the whole history of Beth's family in those pictures. It was strange how sometimes a life came down to a photograph. I knew nothing about these people and their lives but they smiled back at me as if we were friends. There was one of Caroline as a younger woman holding a baby, who I presumed was Beth, with a woman who was clearly Caroline's mother, at the Hall. It was so much more formal than the one of Beth and Izzy in the garden one snowy day. I could tell through the camera lens how different their relationship was by how happy and relaxed they looked with one another.

I wondered what people would think about my life when they looked back on photos of me in the future. I think in all of them I'm alone. There was always someone to take a photo if I asked, but not really anyone I ever wanted to be beside me in one.

I lost a bit of time just staring at those photos once I placed them back. I was relieved when my phone vibrated in my pocket with a message to draw me away from thinking about my life. I knew I spent far too much time looking back. I had to look forward. I had to keep on moving.

I hope your head is as sore as mine today!

The name flashed up as Adam, so we had obviously swapped numbers last night even if I didn't really remember doing it. I knew it was bad when I drank so much the night became a blur. I tried not to do that but once I started knocking the drinks back, I lost track of keeping an eye out for the one that would push me over the edge, and just kept on going until I had forgotten what the edge was even like.

Pretty brutal and I've got to work all day :(
Fancy drinks again on Wednesday? It's pub quiz night, and we'll all be there

I paused, concerned by the 'all'. Did that mean Cameron? What would he do if I joined their quiz team? I decided not to promise anything. I'd find out from Beth what this quiz night was like first.

I'll let you know if I'm free!

Putting my phone away, I turned my attention to the mantelpiece. I didn't really mind cleaning. It was repetitive and actually more physical than I realised when I was younger. But I was used to scrubbing pubs now, and this was a whole lot cleaner despite Beth saying it needed a good spring clean. I sang along softly to my music and the tasks passed quickly. Lunch came and went. Beth told me firmly not to bother with making lunch for anyone other than myself unless there was a special occasion otherwise I'd just be feeding everyone all day. I didn't feel hungry so I just kept on going, heading into the kitchen once it was done to grab a cup of coffee and one of Emily's muffins. It was empty, which I was pleased about. I didn't think I had any energy left over to chat.

I took a quick break to eat and drink and then I went upstairs, feeling like the sooner I finished, the better. A run and a shower would be needed before this family barbeque. At least my headache had eased. All that was left was a slight taste of shame at the back of my throat, but I knew from experience that too would pass soon. I just hoped Brodie wouldn't mention it. I was dreading seeing him later. I already knew that he was planning to come for dinner with Emily and Iona. At least the farm lot were busy, Beth had said at breakfast, so there was no chance of having to deal with any grumpy farmers on top of my grumpy brother.

I stripped the beds and took it all to the laundry room. There were several sets for each bed so the washing could wait, and then I re-made all the beds.

Being a housekeeper in a house like this meant there was a lot to look at while I was bed-making. Each room had its own style and obviously had different belongings in. I hadn't known the household long but I thought it was pretty easy to tell who occupied each room, even if I hadn't been told on the house tour. Beth and Drew's bedroom faced the front and had once been her grand-mother's room, she had said. It was pretty messy as they had both been up and about early. Caroline and John's was the most elegantly furnished, in rich cream and gold with a large dressing table filled with expensive products that it was hard to resist trying – but I thought she was bound to notice so I didn't. And then Izzy's room faced the back and was filled with books – they lined the entirety of one wall and there were several piles of them stacked on the floor too. After I made her bed, her cat appeared, jumping up and curling up for a nap. I reached down to stroke her, smiling as she purred.

I then moved on to my room and changed my bed too. The room still didn't feel like me but then I kept most of the places I lived in pretty impersonal. There didn't seem much point in bothering to do things like put up pictures or buy ornaments to just pack it all away again when I left. But I had to admit, Glendale Hall felt so lived in it did give me a pause to leave the rooms full of character to come to mine with just furniture in and my small bags of belongings, most of which were still in my case. I really should at least hang my clothes up.

I looked at the room and tried to picture it the way I would have it if I wasn't moving on after the summer.

But the image wouldn't come. That helped. If I couldn't picture a place that I wanted to stay, then it surely meant I should keep on moving. If I ever felt like I had found a place to make my own, then that would be the time to stop. I couldn't help but hope I might find it soon. It had been so long since I left my family home when I was eighteen, and that had been the last place I had actually called home. Everywhere else was just a place to stay. And Glendale Hall would be the same.

Shaking my head, I changed into my running gear. I'd finished Beth's tasks and I had an hour before I needed to get ready for dinner so I wanted to go for a run to clear my head and the remnants of last night away.

As I walked towards the landing, Beth suddenly came up the stairs. She was beaming. 'Anna! The drawing room looks amazing! I don't even think my mother will find any fault with it.'

I relaxed at her praise. I couldn't help but want her to be pleased with my work. Brodie's words came back from last night. Despite what I said to his face, I didn't want to embarrass him, or myself either. Yes, I'd be moving on quickly but I was willing to earn my wage fairly while I was here. 'I'm pleased. I've done all the beds too so thought I'd go for a quick run before dinner. If that's okay?'

'Of course. Once you finish the list, your time is your own. You'll still join us for the barbeque, right? Drew makes a mean spare rib and Emily is making homemade burgers.'

'I'm happy to help too,' I insisted.

She waved a hand as she started to walk past me. 'We had it all planned before you came. You can just relax, although I might get you to help with the potato salad.

Apparently I don't use enough mayo in mine, so my daughter tells me.' She rolled her eyes as she headed off to her bedroom. I chuckled and carried on downstairs. Beth had a good sense of humour, which I appreciated. A boss you could laugh with was worth a lot, I had found.

I opened the door and smiled to see the warm late-afternoon sunshine greet me. I needed this after a day of cleaning. I headed out of the gate and hesitated. I was about to turn into the countryside but then changed my mind and turned towards the village. I really didn't want to bump into any farmers with tractors today – they would definitely spoil my good mood.

Chapter Eleven

'How are you feeling, or should I not ask?' Brodie asked when he found me in the kitchen later. He and Emily had arrived at the Hall with Iona, who was asleep in her pushchair. Drew already had the barbeque in full swing and Izzy, Beth, Caroline and John were outside getting the picnic table ready for our meal. Sally had walked through the garden from her cottage and was pouring out drinks for everyone. I was mixing up a potato salad, the only thing they'd let me help with.

I turned around, ready to snap, but his eyes were twinkling and he smiled, so he seemed to have decided to give me a pass on last night. 'I've just been for a run. You should come with me one day, make sure you don't get a beer belly like Dad,' I replied, picking up the bowl.

'You can grate cheese on this stomach,' he said, patting his white shirt.

'Only cottage cheese,' I said, following him outside.

'Em, please tell my darling sister that I don't need to go running, she seems to think I have a beer belly coming on.'

Emily laughed as she parked Iona in a shady spot. 'I don't think you have a beer belly. A cake belly on the other hand…'

I giggled as Brodie protested loudly. 'Here's the potato salad,' I said, adding it to the array of dishes on the table.

I did wonder how they weren't all suffering with beer bellies when I saw all the food laid out though. Sally passed me a fruity-looking drink, but when I tasted it it was pretty strong on the alcohol front. Maybe I needn't have worried about being caught drinking, after all. We all sat down as Drew served up the cooked meats. He had barbequed some veggie burgers for me, which was pretty thoughtful, actually.

'So, was Beth a slave driver today then?' Emily asked me, giving her friend a grin to let her know it was just a joke. She was having elderflower cordial again, along with Izzy, the rest of us drinking the cocktail Sally had made. It was refreshing on such a beautiful evening.

'Her list was fine,' I replied. 'I even got in a run before dinner.'

'It's all about the lists with Beth,' Emily said, fondly. 'Speaking of, how are the three weddings coming along? Not far off the first one now.'

Helping myself to salad and French bread, I listened as Beth chatted about the weddings. Not only was she planning Heather's wedding to Rory, which was at a castle somewhere, but another two, which would be taking place here at the Hall. The ceremonies would use the gazebo down by the stream and then there would be marquees in the garden for the receptions.

I looked out at the grounds beyond the table. Despite not ever fantasising about a wedding myself, I could see the attraction in having one here. The garden was really pretty, especially in the sunshine. I had to concede that the countryside did have some plus points over the city.

'But before the weddings, Heather is going to kidnap Anna on Friday,' Beth said, putting a big dollop of potato salad on her plate.

'I didn't know Heather was a kidnapper on the side,' Brodie joked.

'She has an influencer coming to stay to review the farm as a retreat, so they need Anna's cooking skills,' Beth explained.

'I am apparently in high demand,' I added, dryly. 'I'm meeting Heather tomorrow to agree the menu so she can buy everything I'll need.' I had started drafting it after looking at the Instagram reviewer's feed to see what kind of food she seemed to like. I was excited to cook for someone who appreciated good food and for the money, much less so about spending the weekend on an isolated farm where the only person I knew was Cameron. But I was sure that I could avoid him and just focus on cooking.

'Well, I'm sure Heather will appreciate the help,' Brodie said, smiling approvingly at me.

'And is paying me double,' I said, unable to resist. He rolled his eyes. 'I was going to ask… Do any of you go to the pub quiz at the Glendale Arms?' I said, remembering Adam's invitation. They all looked at one another. 'Am I missing something?' I couldn't help feel annoyed by in-jokes sometimes. I knew it was because I had never stayed rooted anywhere to have in-jokes with people, but it was still annoying, and always made me feel like the outsider I would forever be.

'We go every month,' Beth explained. 'It gets pretty competitive. Especially between us and the Fraser Farm team. We had to spilt into two groups last year as there were too many of us, and now it can get really heated. You want to join us? It's on this Wednesday.'

I smiled. 'I might just do that. And if there's a music round, I'm on it.'

'It changes each month, so could well be. Last month, Fraser Farm beat us, so we need to sharpen up.' She gave the others a hard stare.

'What do you win?'

'Pride,' Beth said at the same time that Emily replied with, 'A free meal.' I couldn't help but laugh. It definitely seemed like Beth took this very seriously. I had to go just to witness her there. I pulled my phone out to tell Adam I'd be there and even had a team to join.

'Someone back in Glasgow you miss?' Emily asked me with a smile.

I shook my head. 'Actually, someone I met in Glendale. He'll be at the pub quiz too. Plays on the local football team.'

Brodie nodded. 'Their team gets very rowdy at the quiz. They never win.'

I had a thought. 'What about Cameron then? Does he play on their team or for Fraser Farm?'

'Fraser Farm. Heather persuaded him to join when she realised their team severely lacked sports knowledge. I wouldn't put it past her to have made it a requirement when he took the job,' Beth said. I couldn't tell if she was joking or not. 'John has us covered for that, luckily. I have a feeling this is going to be our month now.'

Drew lifted up his glass of beer. 'Cheers to that.'

I smiled, agreeing silently that it would be enjoyable to beat Cameron.

—

I drove Beth's car to Fraser Farm the following day after I had given the kitchen a really good clean post-breakfast. Beth had walked into the village to work at the Glendale

Hall shop, which sold things grown on the estate, knick-knacks and souvenirs she said, so was happy for me to have the car for the morning. I put on the satnav and drove the twenty minutes down winding country lanes to reach the farm, set back behind large gates which were open for me. I drove up the gravel drive, more like a track, passed a paddock with two horses in then pulled up to the low red-brick building, which was surrounded by hills rising up in the distance. I could see cows grazing up there, almost touching the sky, it seemed, as they chewed on lush green grass. Heather rounded the farmhouse as I parked, with her little boy hurrying behind her, both in wellies, a black-and-white dog at her heels. 'Welcome to the madhouse,' Heather greeted me, cheerfully, as I climbed out of the car. Like everyone around here, it seemed, Beth had a jeep-style car and it wasn't easy for someone as short as me to get in and out of. I made a little jump and closed the door, turning to face her.

'Got to be honest, this is my first time on a farm,' I said, looking around. Behind them there were a couple of barns and I could make out some chickens wandering around, pigs in an enclosure to the side, and in the distance some goats.

'First of many, I'm sure, now that you're in Glendale. And you'll be spending all weekend at Hilltop. Right, come on, Harry, let's take Anna inside and get meal-planning.' She took her little boy's hand and led the way into the kitchen, which we came into through the back door. It was very much country-style, with an Aga like at the Hall. It was smaller though and had a lived-in, cosy feel to it. 'Please say you need a coffee because I'm dying for one?'

'Definitely. So, how long have you lived here?'

'Over two years now,' she said, lifting her son into a highchair and fixing us all drinks. 'I moved in once I became pregnant with this one, and it's been a challenge I don't mind admitting. But, I don't know, at Christmas it all just fell into place and I realised how much I love it here. That's when we bought the farm next door, Hilltop, and we've been renovating it and getting things ready for the first retreat this week. It seems to be going really well but I am nervous about this reviewer coming at the weekend. I want her to think it's worthwhile promoting, you know?'

I nodded. 'Of course. I'm happy to help on the food front. I once helped one of the restaurants I worked in serve a food critic for a newspaper. We weren't supposed to know... but someone recognised him. To say there was panic behind the scenes is an understatement but we got a great review.' I smiled as she came over with two coffees for us and a juice for Harry. She sat down with us with a contented sigh, as if she'd been on her feet all morning, which I realised she likely had. 'I think if we can make her feel like she's at her second home then she'll love it.'

'That is definitely the idea. That's really what I wanted to do when I decided to start the retreats – give people who don't have time for themselves a chance to recharge, you know? Let them breathe in some good old Scottish air, turn their phones off and be with nature, things they probably don't ever do.'

I nodded. 'Sounds like something people would enjoy.' I would be nervous of all that peace and quiet and time to think though. I hoped there would be too much to do at Hilltop while I was there for that to be the case for me. 'I suggest, then, we go for simple food, almost rustic. Just great flavours, local dishes and fresh, organic ingredients. Was that what you had in mind?'

'That would be great. We already offer that for break-fast – the food is either from our farm or our shop, all local, and all seasonal and the bread from Emily's, of course. So, yes, keep along those lines.'

I pulled out my notebook with my ideas written inside. 'I looked at her Instagram account and she likes pretty places and pretty dishes. Her aesthetic is very pink and girly so I need to try to make the food as good as possible so she will want to take photos of it. I liked the idea of this dessert as I can sprinkle flowers on it...' I showed her my ideas on my phone. 'And that will go really well with the lamb for main and this starter for her first meal on the Friday night. Then, as you say, the usual breakfast and the Saturday night...' I ran through my plans for that. 'And then we offer an extra special Sunday brunch with pancakes, piled high with toppings. I think she'd enjoy that?'

Heather was beaming now. 'Anna, this all looks so incredible. Are you sure you can manage? It's a lot of work just making it for her, I know. Though Cameron will be on hand to help.'

I ignored that comment. 'It'll be fine. I've made it all before, so we don't need to worry about anything not working. Better to be safe than sorry, I think. I'll enjoy it.'

'Well, I'm really grateful. I'll go to the shops later and get everything you need. I'm going to put you in the farmhouse with Chloe. Cameron's cottage isn't far if you need anything. Does that sound okay? And I'm planning to come on Saturday night so I can help and we can all eat together if she's happy with that?' I passed her a shopping list. 'I can't believe how lucky we are to have you here.'

I was surprised. I didn't think anyone had ever said that before. 'I really didn't think I'd be cooking this summer, just cleaning the Hall so I'm pleased.' Even if I was going to be on a farm with Cameron. Maybe he'd warm up in his own surroundings. And hopefully this Chloe would be fun. She did post a lot of cocktail photos on Instagram, I had noted.

'It's all worked out perfectly then.' She clapped her hands together. 'I love it when a plan comes together. Right, I need to pop over to Hilltop and then hit the shops. Beth is coming over tonight for some wedding planning. I knew my best friend was bossy but I thought it was the brides that were meant to be demanding, not the planners.'

I laughed, standing up. 'I'll let you get on. I don't envy you planning a wedding, I think I'd end up eloping if I ever wanted to get married.' I wrinkled my face, I couldn't help it. I really didn't get the whole marriage and babies thing. I looked at Harry and I thought he was cute but I felt no maternal stirrings of my own.

She smiled. 'We are getting married in the place my mum always wanted to. She's no longer here so it felt right. I think you just have to go with what works for you as a couple. Hopefully your future groom will feel the same.'

'Believe me, I'm not looking for one,' I said as she showed me out. 'I much prefer to be footloose and fancy free.'

'Brodie said you loved to travel around. Never found anywhere you want to plant roots yet?'

I shrugged. 'Maybe I never will.'

She glanced back at Harry, who was playing with a toy truck at his highchair. 'Depends if you find people that you don't want to leave behind, I suppose. I always think of Harry and Rory and my dad as my home, you know?

Right, see you Friday, and thank you so much again – you really are a lifesaver.'

I left her waving from the doorstep as I walked back to Beth's car. I envied how settled she was here as much as I felt like I'd never want a life like this. I wasn't sure which feeling was the strongest though.

Chapter Twelve

I had slept at the Hall for four nights when we all walked to the Glendale Arms on Wednesday evening. I was sleeping a little better now, slowly getting used to how quiet it was in the house at night, and waking up to only the sound of birdsong. The evening was cloudy but not too chilly so I'd put on jeans and a black shirt, letting my pink hair down loose over my shoulders, and wearing ankle boots on my feet. Beth, Drew, Caroline and John were with me. The quiz was over-eighteens only, so Izzy was back at the Hall with Sally, who had walked over from her cottage to spend the evening with her and look after baby Iona too. Brodie and Emily had come to the Hall to drop Iona off so were walking to the pub with us.

Although Beth's tasks were always achievable, the Hall was huge, which meant after my morning runs, I worked most of the day and then had to make dinner. So I was tired and keen to escape the house for the evening. I hadn't been out since Sunday, which was pretty tame by my standards so I was in need of some fun.

'So, you're our music expert, I hear?' Drew asked me as we reached the village.

'I do like my music trivia. I love going to gigs and I especially love seventies music and rock bands. My dad used to take me along to shows when I was little, he played guitar for a local band.' I used to love going with him and listening to the music, perched by the side of the stage, thinking my dad was a rock star. After my accident, though, all that had stopped. And he'd given up being in the band. I wondered if he missed it. We never really talked about it. We rarely talked about life before my accident. It had changed so much in our family. I had learned a bit of guitar myself – taught by a guy staying in a hotel where I worked. I would have liked to get one, but they weren't that portable for moving around.

'Why did the music gene bypass you then?' Beth joked to Brodie, who had listened with interest to my reply. I felt a little embarrassed about admitting that was why I loved music, I wasn't sure why. Perhaps because I didn't spend much time with my family now. Back then, I had loved being with them. Brodie and Emily strolled behind us, hand in hand, looking so at peace with one another that I almost couldn't bear to watch them.

'He was too busy with his mates to come along,' I replied for my brother. Four years older than me, Brodie had hung around with a slightly dodgy crowd when he was a teenager. My parents had been worried about him. He'd even started to question his faith, which was pretty hard to believe seeing him now. That was, until my brush with death, when he'd returned to God and I'd turned away from Him, and my family, and the life we had before instead.

'Yep, you cramped my style,' he joked, but I saw him frown as he thought back. I knew he regretted that time. He'd more than made up for it though; I doubted my brother ever put a foot wrong now. 'I can't remember that last time Dad picked up a guitar,' Brodie said.

'I tried learning for a bit,' I said. I suddenly wanted to play again.

'He probably still has his guitar.'

I shrugged. I'd never ask him for it. We just didn't have a close relationship anymore. Brodie looked like he was going to say something else but decided against it.

We reached the pub, which was full of people, and a lively atmosphere that made me smile. I had missed the buzz of a pub. The Glendale Hall team had a fixed table and made their way there. I hung back a bit, looking around, and waved when I spotted Adam standing at the bar.

'You came!' he said when I walked over. 'And just in time for my round. JD and Coke again?'

'Perfect. I'm joining the Glendale Hall team.'

'We're at the next table and on the other side are the Fraser Farm lot. I hope you've brought your game: it can get pretty competitive in here.' He laughed as he passed me my drink from the tray the barman handed him.

I grinned. 'I think I can handle it.' Now I not only wanted to beat the farm team but the football lot as well.

He clinked my glass with his beer. 'Bring it on.'

I walked off, feeling his eyes on me. I smiled to myself. He was fun to flirt with. I wasn't exactly interested but he was the only (non-grumpy) man I knew around my age here, and that was attractive in itself. I sat down with my team and looked behind at the table where Heather and Rory were. She waved at us. Beth told me that the other man with them was her father, Don. Then there was an older lady called Hattie who worked in their farm shop, and Cameron, who was nursing what looked like just an orange juice and who glanced at me as I sat down, averting his eyes when I smiled, like he couldn't even let himself smile at me.

I shrugged and took a sip of my drink. I had been looking forward to it all day. The guys at the football table greeted me enthusiastically, everyone who'd been in the beer garden on my first visit on Sunday was there apart from Cameron, and judging by the drinks lined up they wouldn't be too much competition for the quiz.

'Welcome to quiz night!' a voice boomed over the microphone. The room hushed immediately as the landlord, Malcolm, stood at the front of the room holding a clipboard. 'We have five rounds tonight and I want a good clean quiz, folks. No using your phones like last time.' He turned to the football table, who jeered back at him. 'I mean it, lads. Once more, and you'll be barred. Right then, the first round is general knowledge. Write the answers down on your sheets then pass them up to me at the end of each round. Are we ready?' Everyone cheered enthusiastically. I smiled at their spirit. 'First question then – in what century did the Scottish Reformation take place?'

Heads bent furiously around the room to confer.

'That's not right,' Caroline hissed furiously at her husband when he suggested a year, making me bite my lip to stop myself laughing. They weren't lying when they said they took this seriously. Beth, of course, was the one who wrote down our answers, undoubtedly the leader of the group, and she went with John's suggestion, her mother's lips pursing as she was forced to agree.

'Right, next question then,' Malcolm said over the noise. 'The Gaelic for whisky is *Uisge Beatha*. What is its literal meaning?'

'That's so easy,' Caroline declared with a roll of her eyes. Emily leaned in to whisper to me that the family had made whisky, so now I knew where their fortune came from.

'Give us a clue,' Adam called over to me.

I just raised my glass at him, and then drained it dry.

—

The room had become tense. It was the final round now. I was on my third drink and when Malcolm announced he was doing a music round, I banged my glass excitedly on the table. Beth beamed at me. I felt all eyes turn to me as Malcolm read out the questions. We were pretty much neck and neck with Fraser Farm, who were, as predicted, our main competition. The football lot seemed to have given up in favour of a shot competition, and were calling out insults to Cameron, who just ignored them.

The first four questions were easy for me, and Beth wrote down everything I said. It felt good to contribute to the team, and I knew I had got them all right. 'Okay, final question for the night then!' Malcolm called out. Everyone fell quiet. 'In 1975, "Bohemian Rhapsody" was number one for nine weeks. It was finally knocked off the top slot by a song with a name that appears in the lyrics of "Bohemian Rhapsody". Name the song and the band that ended Queen's number one success.'

I looked over at the Fraser Farm table. They were all staring at one another blankly. Everyone at my table looked at me.

'Any ideas, Anna?' Beth asked me, hopefully.

I knew that song like the back of my hand but what other song was in the lyrics, that would have got to number one then? I frowned, trying to think, beginning to regret the drinks I'd had. And then it came to me. 'Oh my god,' I whispered. I leaned in so I was almost touching Beth, desperate for no one else to hear. '"Mamma Mia" by ABBA.'

'Are you sure?' she checked.

'Hell, yes.' I looked at Brodie. 'Sorry.'

'If you're right, I really don't care.'

I stared at my brother, surprised again by his good humour, as Beth jumped up to hand Malcolm our final round answers. Cameron stared at her, then at me, before leaning back, crossing his arms over his chest, annoyed. Heather was hanging her head. Don told her to just write down what they thought and she took it up, glaring at Beth as they passed one another.

Malcolm made a big show of reading both sets of answers, and then everyone else's, even though we all knew it was between our two teams for the win. 'Well well well… last month's victors have—' He paused, dramatically. 'NOT done it again! Tonight's winners are Glendale Hall!'

The whole table erupted. I was pulled into Beth's arms and Emily clapped me on the back as we all cheered. I had never felt part of a team before. It was kind of nice.

'Another drink for Anna!' Drew declared.

'She drinks for free forever!' Beth added, throwing her arms up in the air.

I grinned. I liked the sound of that.

The evening soon took on a blurry feeling. Everyone seemed to want to buy me a drink. Slowly, our table faded away though. First, Brodie and Emily left to go and get little Iona. Emily kissed me on the cheek and Brodie gave me a cheerful wave while telling me not to stay out too late. I rolled my eyes in response but I couldn't help but return their smiles, it had been an enjoyable evening with them. Then Caroline and John left for home. Heather, Don and Rory left to go back to their son, who was being looked after by Angus, who lived and worked on the farm too. And then Drew and Beth began to yawn.

'We'd better head back,' Drew said. 'I'm on nights from tomorrow so I need as much sleep as I can get. You coming, Anna?'

'I'll walk back in a bit,' I replied. Adam and his mates were still there drinking and I really didn't fancy going back to the silence of my bedroom just yet. It was only ten o'clock; there was a good hour left of drinking time.

'Are you sure you'll be okay?' Beth checked. I reassured them so they left together and I went over to Adam's table. Cameron had joined them once the rest of his table had gone, but still seemed to be drinking orange juice. He was deep in conversation with Glen and didn't look up.

'Come to rub it in?' Alastair joked when I sat down next to Adam.

'I can't help knowing more that you, can I?'

'I'm sure there are things I could still teach you,' he replied with a wink.

I rolled my eyes. 'Does that line ever work?'

Adam chuckled. 'No, it really doesn't.'

'Yeah, because you're such a ladies' man,' Alastair said.

'At least I can get a lady...'

I smiled as they teased one another and finished my drink. This kind of conversation I was quite happy to just enjoy. Just fun. Exactly how I liked it. Glen got us all one more drink when the last-order bell rang, and by then I was definitely drunk, still riding high on my victory and enjoying the attention of the all-male table. Well, apart from one, but I didn't care.

'Right, you lot, time to go.' Malcolm's voice broke through our laughter. 'I've got to lock up. No arguments,' he added when they started to protest.

Adam leaned in to me. 'Let me drive you home. I want to talk to you.' I knew what that really meant. And I was happy to go with him. I didn't want to be alone. He took my hand as we stood up. Everyone was saying their goodbyes so we slipped out unnoticed.

Outside, the night was cool now and I shivered, so Adam slung an arm around my shoulders as we walked to his car. I stumbled a little and he held me closer, and tighter. 'You're gorgeous, Anna,' he said, his mouth close to my ear. 'And so fun. I've been waiting years to meet a girl like you.'

'I'm not a girl, I'm a woman,' I trilled back with a giggle. He opened up the passenger door for me. 'But definitely not a lady.'

Adam moved his hand down to the small of my back. 'I was hoping that,' he replied, leaning in towards me.

Chapter Thirteen

'What do you think you're doing?' A voice barked at us.

Adam drew back quickly as I turned, confused, grabbing the car door for support once Adam's arm left me.

Cameron was marching over. His big frame was intimidating in the semi-darkness of the car park. His face was thunderous. I blinked, wondering what the hell was wrong with him. Was he pissed off that Adam had been about to kiss me? That made no sense though: he barely wanted to speak to me. 'You can't drive, Adam,' he said when he reached us. 'You've been drinking all night. What the hell are you thinking?'

My alcohol-fuddled brain woke up a little then. 'Why did you say you'd drive me home?' I asked Adam. I hadn't even thought. Of course he'd been drinking along with me all night. It felt like a cold bucket of water had just been poured all over me.

'I wanted to be with you,' he said. 'I haven't had that many. Come on...'

'I'll drive you both home. No arguments. You can get your car tomorrow. Come on,' Cameron said, gruffly. He shut the car door and I stepped away from it. Adam looked at me sheepishly. I felt so annoyed at myself. I knew never to get in the car with anyone who had been drinking.

What was wrong with me? I shivered. The thought of another car accident...

Cameron slipped off his jacket and wrapped it around my shoulders before I could stop him. 'Let's go,' he said, not looking at me. I'd never seen anyone look so disappointed in me before, apart from my family. I suppose he was just worried about his friend. He clearly thought both of us should have known better. And I had to admit, he was right.

We trailed after him as we walked towards his 4x4. Adam tried to hold my hand again but I folded my arms across my chest. Cameron's jacket was huge on me but it was warm and smelled musky like he did.

We climbed into his car in silence – Adam in the front next to Cameron, and me in the back. He drove through the village to a block of flats on the edge, where he stopped and Adam got out. 'Cheers, mate,' he said. He looked at me. 'I'll call you?' It was a question. I didn't reply. He shut the car door and disappeared into the night.

Now we were alone. Cameron started to drive again, towards the Hall, leaving me in the back like this was a taxi. It was weird, but I didn't know what to say. I could feel the anger rolling off him still. And I felt sick. Not just from the drink but because of how stupid I had almost been. I tried so hard to forget the accident I was in when I was thirteen, but tonight it felt like it had happened only yesterday. The weight of the past felt suffocating.

Finally, we pulled into the gates of the Hall and Cameron drove right up to the door, turning off the engine, leaving us in complete silence for a moment.

I undid my seatbelt and slipped off his coat, passing it to him. He took it without comment, but his eyes met mine in the rear-view mirror. 'Thank you,' I said, finally, my voice croaky. I jumped out of the car, needing to get away. There was too much tension in that car. I always ran from tension.

I hurried up to the door and let myself in. I looked back once and Cameron was still sitting there in the car, waiting for me to go inside, but it was too dark to see his face and I decided that was a good thing. I closed the door behind me, sinking against it with a sigh, and letting out the tears I'd been holding back for the whole drive home.

–

I decided I needed to do as much work as possible the next day. It felt both like a punishment to myself and the best way not to think about last night. Even if my throat felt fuzzy and my head was banging to remind me. So I tore through Beth's list of jobs for the day then decided to brush the stairs on my hands and knees and then mop all the wooden floors. I also did two loads of washing and drying, and made a meat and a vegetable curry, leaving them to cook slowly in the Aga before heading out for a run. It was the only way to make it through the day without crumpling into a heap on the floor.

I fancied a coffee that wasn't one I made for myself, so I took off towards the village. It was a cool, cloudy day, no sign of any summer sun, but it was nice weather to run in and I pounded along the pavement, trying to burn my negative thoughts away. I knew it wasn't particularly healthy when I got like this but I couldn't sit and dwell, I had to keep on moving and then maybe the past wouldn't catch up to me.

Sweaty and exhausted by the time I reached Emily's Bakery, I was relieved to be the only customer inside.

She was behind the counter putting out fresh cakes, and looked up with a pleased smile as I went in. 'This is a nice surprise,' she said.

'I've just been for a run, needed a coffee,' I said as I got my breath back.

'Well, take a seat. I'll take a break with you. Go on, it's on the house.' She waved me off so I couldn't refuse and I did feel pretty shattered after my productive day.

I sank into a chair and Emily brought over a latte and a tea for her, and two brownies. 'I can't keep eating cake,' I protested, taking a sip of the coffee.

She smiled as she sat down. 'Please, there's not an inch of fat on you and you look like you need some sugar.' She looked at me. 'Are you okay, Anna?'

I wondered if I looked as tired as I felt. I took a bite of the brownie. God, it was good. 'It's just been a busy day on top of a late night, that's all.' I hadn't slept until the early hours after what had happened. 'But I got lots done at the Hall, dinner is cooking, and I've had a good run.'

'Well, make sure you relax this evening and get an early night. You have to look after yourself. I know, I sound just like your brother, but he's right sometimes.'

'He thinks he's right all the time.'

'Brodie just likes to protect the people he cares about. It's admirable really. I had never met a more caring man before. And he was right about me – I did put other people first sometimes and forgot to look after myself. I'm still learning on that score but he's helped me to realise it. Half the battle, right?' She took a big bite of her brownie. 'Are you settling in okay at the Hall?' she asked, perhaps sensing I didn't want to agree with her on my brother being right.

'I'm getting there. It's so different to anywhere I've lived and worked before, you know. I'm enjoying all the cooking though. It's been a while since I got to do that.'

'It's exciting about your Hilltop job. Heather was so worried about it but she popped in earlier and seems to be a lot calmer about it now that you're helping out.'

'Oh no, the pressure!' But I smiled. I felt pretty confident about the food I was planning to cook. And based on what I'd seen of Heather, I was sure she'd put a hundred percent into the farm retreat so hopefully Chloe, the reviewer, would be happy.

'Not at all,' Emily said, quickly. 'It's such early days for Hilltop, Heather knows that and she's so grateful you agreed to do it. Brodie is really proud too. He was telling your mum last night all about your cooking.'

'He was?' My eyebrows shot up in surprise.

She looked taken aback at my surprise. 'Of course. He couldn't believe you'd never talked about it before or cooked for them.'

'It never really came up,' I mumbled, uncomfortable. I didn't know how much Emily was aware of our family dynamic really. I took a long gulp of the coffee and another bite of brownie. She had been right that I needed a sugar fix. 'I suppose we don't talk as much as we used to,' I admitted.

'That's a shame. I always find Brodie to be a really good listener, you know. And your mum seems lovely. Your dad, I don't know that well yet but I see his smile whenever they talk about you. They were all so pleased that you decided to come to Glendale, you know.'

'So, they could try to save me?' I snapped. Her face fell and I felt like a real bitch. 'I'm sorry,' I said. 'I can't help but always try to do what they don't want me to, I think. Maybe it's a habit.'

'They only want you to be happy. And me too. I'm always here if you want to talk about anything. I'm not your real sister, I know, but I hope you'll think of me as a friend at the very least.'

It was impossible to not see that Emily was being genuine. But would she feel the same way if she knew the truth about my accident? I doubted that. I was ashamed at getting angry with her though. The stuff with my family wasn't her fault after all. 'Thank you. And for these, I did need them. I do sometimes overdo it. Like when I'm trying not to think about things, I guess. I push myself physically instead.' Ever since I started running to build up my muscles after my accident, it became a mental release. I had some therapy around that time and the doctor said I needed to sometimes just sit and be comfortable with my thoughts. She even suggested that I try meditation to help. But I found it too hard to this day. I needed to be constantly moving.

'I get that, and I do it too,' she said with a nod. 'Sometimes, though, if it's important, you do need to think about it and maybe if you talked it through the solution to whatever the problem is might be simpler than you think, you know?'

I couldn't think of a time when I'd told anyone my problems. Not since that therapist when I was a teenager. I wondered what she'd say if I told her that last night I'd almost got in a car with someone who was drunk and that I'd sat up most of the night panicking about it, remembering the moment that the car plunged into us when I was thirteen, the searing pain and the blackness that followed. How I felt guilty to this day that someone else died that day, and not me? How I felt like the accident was all my fault? That it felt like there had been a mistake in me surviving it. How could I say those words aloud to her, to anyone? Who could ever understand? 'I'll keep that in mind,' I fake-promised, standing up. 'I'd better run back now. Dinner will be ready soon. Thanks Emily for this.' I gestured to the table but I meant more, and she knew it.

Emily smiled warmly. 'You're very welcome. Good luck for the weekend. I'm sure I'll see you soon to hear all about it.'

I thanked her and left the bakery but instead of running back, I walked, and took in a few deep breaths, wishing it was as easy to exhale out the past as it was oxygen.

Chapter Fourteen

A summer storm greeted me when I woke up the next day. Rain thrashed against my window, and lightning dazzled the sky. I sat on the window seat watching it for a while. I had slept better as I had been so exhausted and I felt that familiar come-down after a day where I'd pushed myself. My legs were a bit achy and I didn't want to hurry downstairs to start the day. I'd enjoyed watching the rain too. There was something calming, something safe almost, about watching the rain pouring down outside while you were dry and warm inside. Thunder rumbled gently in the distance. I wouldn't be running today, it looked like.

Turning on a calming Spotify playlist on my phone, I decided to do some yoga before breakfast. This was again something that had been recommended to me to build strength and to help me relax too. I had nightmares after the accident and struggled to sleep, something that plagued me on and off still, so I had kept yoga up and it did help. Emily had been right. After pushing away all my thoughts and problems yesterday, I felt weary. I sat cross-legged on the floor and closed my eyes. The music mingled with the rain allowed me to just breathe for a few minutes, stretching out my limbs gently, and trying to summon some peace into my body and mind. And soul too, I supposed. It wasn't easy for me.

I knew I needed to let go of my anger with myself for not thinking clearly back at the pub. But it was so hard. What if Adam had crashed? I'd already lived through one horrific accident. I'd already seen how much hurt and pain it could cause. And loss of life too. I tried not to think about the driver of the other car but how could I not? I had lived but he hadn't. And I didn't think I'd ever let go of my guilt about that.

But I hadn't got into the car. No one had been hurt this time. And I felt so relieved about it. And grateful to Cameron for stopping us. I also felt so ashamed of how close a call it had been. I knew that I'd let myself drink too much. I didn't like it when I lost track of myself and my judgement went out of the window. It was too easy sometimes to use drink as a way to drown out my restlessness but I had gone too far. That happened too much for me to like to admit. Especially lately.

Whatever I did, I couldn't shake the feeling that I wasn't doing what I was supposed to be doing. I had been moving for so long that standing still felt impossible but, increasingly, I knew that moving wasn't working like it once had. I couldn't quieten my mind as well. I couldn't push away the past as much as I had once been able to.

I felt more lost than I ever had.

What should I do? I had no idea but I knew I had to do something, and soon. Otherwise it seemed like I could lose myself for good.

I thought about when I had first felt the restlessness inside me. Deep down, like an itch that I could never quite scratch. It was after I had recovered physically from my accident. I couldn't understand why I didn't feel whole again. I started to not enjoy things as I once had. Like school. Hanging out with my friends. I felt like I didn't know how to live as I had before. Nothing seemed to bring me happiness like it once had. And the guilt of carrying on with my life as I had before had been too much to bear.

When my parents started talking about university, I hated the idea but I saw it as a way to escape. I thought that would be the answer. That I needed to go somewhere new. Where no one knew about the accident, and then maybe I could forget it. Well, move past it at least. But it hadn't really worked. So I'd ended up leaving after a year to go travelling, thinking that it was just studying that wasn't for me.

But the restless itch, the guilt, and the fear all just followed me wherever I went.

'Why can't you settle anywhere?' Brodie had asked me not long after he had become a minister. He was filled with purpose. Whereas I still felt as if I had none.

'Why should I settle? I'm young, free, and single,' I had answered him flippantly but his words had worried me. Was there something wrong with me? Why did I always need to keep moving, why did nowhere make me feel like I wanted to stay? Why did I feel as if I didn't belong anywhere?

I turned off my music as I finished my final stretch. I needed to start the day, as much as I really didn't feel like it. I was scared that the accident had changed me forever. That I'd never settle, never find a place to call home, but the thought that scared me most was that I'd never be happy.

Because I couldn't shake the feeling that I really didn't deserve to be.

I couldn't tell my family. I couldn't tell anyone. So, I carried on running from myself.

But I was tired of running. Just once, I wanted to be still. To have what everyone else seemed to find so easy.

The problem was, I had no idea where to even start.

–

Beth asked me to help Izzy after breakfast – she had given her a small room on the ground floor, which was currently used for storage, because she had always wanted a library. It wasn't anywhere near big enough to be a library but she wanted to turn it into a reading room and it gave her a summer project. I knew Beth would have preferred her to be out in the garden but I quite liked that Izzy knew what she wanted to do. And, actually, I think Beth did too.

'Luke is coming to help us in a bit,' she said when I found her in the room, which was opposite her mother's office. 'My friend, he lives in the village and helps out at Fraser Farm,' she explained when I looked blankly at her.

'Friend or boyfriend?' I asked with a smile.

'A friend! I'm never going to date, there's too many other things to do. We just both really like books so we have a lot in common.' I had to hide a laugh. She was funny, sometimes such a grown up and then other times a kid again. 'He's two years older than me but doesn't act like it.'

'I don't think that ever changes,' I commented. I stood in the doorway and surveyed the room. 'Where are we going to put all this?' The room was piled with junk, basically.

'Mum said anything we need to keep can go in the attic, anything else we either give to the charity shop or she can hire a skip and get rid of it. She said to pile it up and she'll check it, and then I can decorate the room.' She knelt down in front of a pile of boxes. 'I definitely need a wall of bookcases, a comfy armchair and lots of fairy lights.'

I joined her on the floor and started to look at a different pile. The room was small and dusty but we'd flung the window open wide. I could see how it could become a cosy reading room for her. 'Sounds good. Where did you get the idea from?'

'The common room in Harry Potter,' she said, matter-of-factly. She turned to me. 'Your hair is so cool. I hate mine sometimes.' She fingered her long, thick auburn hair.

'It's a gorgeous colour. But when you're older, you can try different things if you want. I like changing my look up, it's fun.' I supposed that was part of my restlessness too. I liked to try out new things even if it was just a new hair style.

She sighed. 'I hate the expression "when you're older".'

I laughed. 'I used to hate it too. And did a lot of things before I should have because of it.'

'Like what?' she asked, coughing as she shook out a dusty rolled-up rug.

I was saved from having to answer her by the appearance of Luke – he was a skinny, lanky teenager, all awkward limbs, but he had a nice smile and his eyes lit up when he saw Izzy. 'This room is perfect,' he declared, taking it in.

'Isn't it? Here, take these outside ready for Mum to check. I don't think we want to keep any of it,' Izzy said, handing him a big box. She had definitely inherited bossiness from Beth. 'Mum said you're only staying for the summer,' she said once he'd staggered off with the box. 'How come? We really need someone here full time. Look at this.' She showed me the line of thick dust on the windowsill.

'I've got a flight booked to get some sun, I don't like staying in one place too long,' I said as I flicked through an old photo album. I recognised Caroline when she was younger with Beth as a baby. Definitely something to keep, so I added it to that pile.

'Why not?' She smiled as her cat Ginny walked in to see what we were up to, reaching down to stroke her.

I glanced at her as she looked at me curiously. She liked to ask questions, this kid. 'I get bored, I suppose. I want to try all different things and see different places.'

'But what if you find somewhere you really love?'

'Hasn't happened yet,' I replied. I held up a vintage lamp. 'This could work in here.'

'Ooh, I love it!'

Luke returned then and we made good progress sorting until Beth found us and told us all to wash up for lunch. 'You're staying too, Luke?' Beth asked him.

'If that's okay?'

'Of course. Drew can drive you home later. This room is actually looking clearer already,' she said with a smile. 'What you're willing to do for books, eh, Iz?' She threw me a grin before she left us.

'I'm so jealous that you're going to have a reading room,' Luke said to Izzy as I stood up, brushing the dust off my knees.

'You can come and read here whenever you like,' she replied. He broke into a huge grin.

'You two are so cute,' I found myself saying like I was their grandmother or something. Luke's cheeks turned bright pink as Izzy rolled her eyes. I took that as my cue to leave, chuckling under my breath.

I thought about Izzy asking me what I'd done when I was younger. I remembered the first boy I'd liked. He was older and could drive, something that had impressed me so much I'd lost my virginity to him just before my sixteenth birthday. He had been eighteen and had seemed so cool to me, but afterwards he'd acted like he didn't even know who I was. I cried myself to sleep then told myself I'd never let a boy do that to me again. I'd always be the one who left them, and not the other way around. Keep it casual and you wouldn't get hurt.

But something about Izzy and Luke made me feel a little pang for my teenage self who had never had a sweet boy to take that first step with.

Chapter Fifteen

Despite feeling like I'd only just arrived at Glendale Hall, I was already leaving it. Beth drove me to Hilltop Farm late that afternoon as she would need her car for the weekend. I wasn't sure I liked the idea of being stuck on an isolated farm with no means of escape but I tried to just think of the money Heather was going to give me for doing this. Money that I could use in Ibiza, which felt very far away just now.

It was a cloudy day, which I hoped wouldn't stop the Instagram reviewer from enjoying the weekend. It was meant to brighten up tomorrow at least and Heather had promised to join us for dinner, which I was relieved about. It would be the first time I'd been alone with Cameron since he stopped me getting into Adam's car, and I was nervous about it.

'I need to finalise the plans for the first Glendale wedding this year,' Beth chatted as she drove. 'I hope I haven't forgotten anything. I enjoy wedding planning but it's a responsibility having someone's most special day in your hands.' She glanced at me. 'I might get you to check over their menu for me. I hope everything goes well this weekend. I think Heather's very nervous about it.'

'It'll be fine, I'm sure. I mean, I know I'm only doing the food but from what I've seen of Heather, she likes to make things perfect.'

'She's such a worrier, bless her. But Hilltop is a lovely setting. And Cameron runs the farm like a tight ship so it will all be fine. Right, here we are.' She turned off the winding country lane down a bumpy gravel track that I would have just driven straight past. We could see the farmhouse then. It was set low in the valley, hills rising up around it, woods behind it – a white stone building that looked really old to me. We drove past a big green and gold welcome sign and Beth parked outside the farmhouse. Heather hurried out to greet us with a wave. She looked smarter than I'd seen her before, in navy city shorts and a blouse and neutral sandals. I had put on dark jeans, a white shirt, which was pretty smart for me, so I was glad I'd made the effort. I climbed out of the car, grabbing the bag of my things out of the back.

'You look great,' Beth told Heather as she jumped out of her car.

'Thank you, she'll be here soon – I thought I should be here to welcome her. Shall we get you settled in, Anna? Oh good, Cameron's coming over.' She gestured to where Cameron had appeared through the trees. He too looked as if he'd made more effort than usual, wearing trousers and a shirt, not the jeans and plaid shirt I'd seen him wear so far. He gave the three of us a curt nod. I smiled but he didn't look in my direction.

'I'll let you all get on then. And it'll be fabulous guys, I know it!' Beth gave Heather a warm hug then rubbed my arm before getting back in her car with a cheerful wave.

'Right, let's show you where you're staying. Hey, Cameron, can you take Anna up to her room? I'd better stay here in case Chloe is a bit early.'

'Right.' Cameron walked quickly inside. I hurried after him into the farmhouse. The ceiling was low and beamed, and the floor was stone. Heather had made it feel cosy and homely with the original fireplaces restored, wild flowers in vases dotted around, and faux fur rugs on the wooden floors.

Cameron led me upstairs in silence, showing me to a room that faced the front, standing back to let me go inside as if he was scared to be in there with me. It was a sweet room with a four-poster bed and en-suite bathroom, decorated in cream and plum with another vase of flowers on the bedside table and an ornate free-standing mirror in the corner. 'This is pretty,' I said, putting my bag down on the floor. It was even quieter out here than at the Hall, if that was possible. I couldn't hear anything but the sound of us breathing. It felt so awkward but I took a deep breath: I had to clear the air. We would be together the whole weekend. 'Listen, Cameron, I just wanted to say thank you again for the other night, I wasn't thinking clearly and—'

'It's fine,' he cut across me. 'I'll show you where Chloe will be.' He strode briskly across the landing. I frowned, following him. This guy really didn't ever give me a break.

Her room was the main suite, bigger and grander than mine but it still had a comfortable, homely feel, fitting in with the old farmhouse. Heather had done a good job, I thought. 'She'll love it.'

He nodded. 'I live in the cottage through the trees,' Cameron said, pointing outside. 'If you both need anything over the weekend.' He looked at me once then away. I was reminded of the disappointment in those eyes when he'd stopped me getting in the car with Adam and I decided I was happy for him not to look directly at me again. I asked him to take me to the kitchen, which he did, leaving me alone in there quickly to see if Chloe had arrived or not. I sighed when he left. I'd tried to clear the air but he hadn't wanted to so I'd have to leave it there and hope we could avoid one another as much as possible while I was here.

Turning around, my frustration melted as I took in the room. Unlike the rest of the farmhouse, the kitchen was brand new.

'What do you think?' Heather said, walking in. 'I wanted to keep everything else original, in line with when the farmhouse was built back in the seventeenth century, but the kitchen was in such a state, it needed completely gutting. I thought it was better to focus on making it a place to create great food. I want to offer cookery classes in the future so it would work for that and if I do decide to hire a chef for retreats in the future, it has everything they'll need. Right?'

I smiled as I ran my hand across the shiny counter. 'It's perfect.' There was an island, which I would want if I ever designed my own kitchen, a double sink, a huge double cooker, an American-style fridge, and everything was white and stainless steel. The floor was black-and-white tiles, and there was a shelf above the counter lined with different oils and spices in fancy jars. 'I can't wait to cook in here!'

She clapped her hands in delight. 'I'm so pleased. I've put all the ingredients you wanted away so it's all here and—'

'Here's Don!' Cameron called out from the hallway, interrupting her.

Heather's mouth dropped open. 'Eeek! Well, here we go then.' She looked mildly panicked so I gave her a reassuring smile and followed her outside, where Heather's dad pulled up in his car and out stepped Chloe. She was exactly like her Instagram pictures – pretty and blonde with long legs in denim shorts, a golden tan, and perfect glossy lips. I couldn't help but glance at Cameron to see his reaction, but his expression was unreadable as usual. Don lifted out a huge silver suitcase from the boot as Chloe walked over to us, lifting her sunglasses to the top of her head as she smiled brightly.

'Welcome to Hilltop,' Heather said, throwing out her hand for Chloe to shake. 'I'm Heather, thank you so much for coming. This is Cameron, the live-in manager here, and this is Anna, our chef,' she said, gesturing to us.

'It's so lovely to meet you all. This place really is rustic. You're right about it being a real getaway from the city,' she said, looking around, her London accent contrasting with our Scottish ones. 'I'm just hoping I can use my phone!'

'We put in Wi-Fi in the end but it can easily be turned off for those who really want to get away from it all. I knew you'd want to post online though. Right, shall I give you a tour? Cameron, take her bag up please. Would you like a drink? Thanks, Dad, I'll see you back at home,' Heather directed everyone.

'I could make a welcome cocktail,' I suggested as we all filed inside. Chloe beamed at that suggestion so I headed for the kitchen. I was making more of a relaxed meal tonight but I needed to start chopping vegetables so I mixed up a cocktail for Chloe and placed it on a tray with a bowl of nibbles and pulled my hair back and went to the fridge to get out the food Heather had stocked it up with. I felt a burst of excitement. I was going to be a chef for the weekend! Not just cooking for the family back at the Hall but for a customer, although she was staying for free in return for a review but still. I stopped and snapped a photo of the kitchen on my phone. I wanted to document this.

Heather came in a short moment later to collect the drinks. 'Cameron is taking Chloe out for a walk around after this and then she wants a nice relaxing bath. I told her dinner will be at seven and then the living room is all set up for a movie night. I'll be over after breakfast in the morning to take her to Fraser Farm to show her a working farm and give her a riding lesson. I really hope she enjoys it!'

'She will,' I assured her as I chopped vegetables. 'Although hopefully Cameron will be friendly to her,' I added, wondering how he'd get on alone with her on a tour.

Heather looked surprised as she picked up the cocktail tray. 'He's great with the guests.'

Huh, I thought as she left me alone to prep the dinner. Obviously he was just unfriendly towards me then.

I chopped the next carrot with more vigour than was required.

Chapter Sixteen

For dinner, I had made vegetable tartlets to start, wild Scottish salmon with new potatoes to follow, and then a cheesecake with fresh fruit on top to finish as a light, summery Friday evening meal. I had served Chloe in the dining room, with the doors thrown open as the evening had turned sunny and warm. She had been happy for me and Cameron to eat with her, which was a relief as I was worried I'd have to eat alone with him.

'Anna, this salmon is divine,' Chloe said taking a bite once she had snapped a photo of it. She had a fancy camera and had stood on the chair to take it. 'Honestly, I think this is better than some of the fancy restaurants I've eaten in.'

'Well, that's lovely to hear,' I said with a smile. 'Thank you. Is this your first time in Scotland?' I glanced across the table at Cameron who was tucking in and seemed to be enjoying it although he hadn't made any comment on my food.

'I've stayed in Edinburgh before but not in the countryside. It's stunning here. I think Heather is on to a good thing. I feel more relaxed than I have all week.'

I knew what she meant. There was something relaxing about the air in Glendale and life seemed to move at a slower pace than I was used to from the towns and cities I'd lived in before. 'So, you review things full-time then?'

'I do. I basically blog and post about my travels on Instagram, I've been so lucky to make this into a job, I know that. Although my boyfriend wishes I was at home more. He can't always come with me, so that's hard sometimes, you know?' I nodded although I didn't really have any experience of that. 'How about you? Have you been a chef here for long?'

I shook my head. 'It's very recent.' I glanced at Cameron, who appeared to be studying his plate rather hard. 'I've never run my own kitchen before.'

'Well, if this is anything to go by then you're brilliant at it!'

After dessert, I made coffee and then Chloe's boyfriend phoned her so she took it into the living room, leaving us to clear the table. 'I can do it,' I said to Cameron. 'If you need to get back to your cottage.' He didn't reply, just followed me with the plates. Outside, the sun was setting in all different colours, casting a golden light in the kitchen as I piled up the fancy dishwasher, hoping I knew how to make it work. 'I think that went well,' I pressed as he brought in our empty glasses. Was he really going to stay silent all weekend?

'It did. The meal was really good,' he said, putting everything down and reaching for his coffee cup to take a sip. 'I actually do need to head back and sort a few things... Will you be okay alone with her? My number is on the hall table or just holler if you need me.' He was already heading out.

'Sure,' I said, although he wasn't waiting for me to agree. 'Goodnight, Cameron.'

He paused in the doorway to glance back at me. 'Goodnight, Anna,' he said softly before disappearing. I watched him go and shook my head. He really was an enigma, that man. But at least he had complimented the meal.

After I finished clearing up, I went to check in on Chloe. She was curled up on the sofa with her coffee still chatting to her boyfriend and said she didn't need anything when I asked so I slipped out of the French doors, deciding to have a walk while it was still light outside. I felt pumped up after the meal had gone so well and knew I wouldn't be able to sleep yet.

Walking out the side of the farmhouse, I spotted a trail which weaved around the edge of the woodland towards the fields that rose up on a hill. I knew that behind the hill stood Heather's farm and their cattle grazing. I followed the path. The sun had dipped to the horizon now and the sky was a dreamy pink-and-orange haze, casting a golden glow over everything. There was complete peace here. I thought I'd find it unnerving but I didn't. Instead, I breathed in the clean air and felt some of my tension in my shoulders lift, something that usually only happened on a fast run.

I heard a noise then. Breaking the silence around me, catching my attention. A grunt followed by a splintering sound. Curious, I ducked under a low hanging tree branch and walked through a gap between two trees. I emerged into a clearing. At the back was a cottage and beside it, Cameron was chopping wood on a tree stump.

With an axe.

Shirtless.

Feeling my mouth form an 'o', I couldn't help but stop and stare for a moment. I was only human, after all. Cameron heaved the axe back and then sliced a piece of wood into two in one fluid movement. His back was bare and tanned contrasting with the green woods around him. I moved my foot and a twig underneath snapped. He stopped and looked up to see me.

My cheeks heated up instantly at being caught watching him. 'That looks like hard work,' I called over as casually as I could manage.

Cameron straightened and shrugged. 'You get used to it. I've got a pile for the farmhouse in case Chloe wants to light the fire, it's going to get cold later.'

'I'll take it back with me,' I said, walking over, trying to ignore his bare chest facing me directly. He didn't seem at all embarrassed so I was determined not to show that his skin was affecting me in the slightest.

'They're pretty heavy,' he warned, holding out a basket filled with pieces of wood.

'I'm pretty strong,' I replied, taking it from him. It was true. I'd worked hard to build up my muscles when I was a teenager and yoga and exercise had kept them strong. I was determined to never be weak again. 'Do you like living out here?' I asked as I turned to go. I was curious. The cottage was small, made of grey stone with a thatched roof, and was tucked away in the trees. The only sound came from the light breeze rustling the leaves stretching above us like a canopy, light trickling through the gaps.

'I like the peace and quiet,' he said, picking up his axe, turning to go the opposite way to me.

'I don't think I could survive being so far away from a coffee shop.'

'And I like being alone,' he added, turning to go into the cottage.

'No kidding,' I said with a chuckle. His whole presence screamed 'stay back', in my opinion. He faced me again and raised an inquiring eyebrow. 'You're not exactly what

I'd call… friendly,' I said. Surely he knew how stand-offish he could be?

Cameron glowered at me. It was annoying that it didn't affect how good-looking he was. 'Maybe I just keep my friendliness for people who deserve it.' And with that, he spun around and marched towards the cottage.

Hell no. I wasn't about to let him talk to me like that. I dropped the basket of wood and stalked after him. 'What is your problem? Ever since we first met you've been so hostile to me. Why?' I demanded to his retreating back.

He stopped just in front of his open front door and with a sigh, turned around to face me. 'I'm just not a fan of people who have no regard for their own safety. First, you almost ran into my tractor, and then you were going to get into a car with someone who was clearly drunk. If you don't care about looking after yourself, you can't expect other people to care either.' His voice was low and sounded calm but I heard it crack at the end. 'And—' he began, but stopped abruptly.

'And what?' I said but he just shook his head, turned and walked inside, slamming the door shut behind him.

I stared at the door in shock. Okay, so I almost walked in front of his tractor but I didn't see or hear him and I was new to the area. How would I have known he was about to pull out of that hidden road on that bloody machine? And okay, the drunk-drive thing… It was a bad judgement call. But I had apologised for that. I had no idea why it had made him so angry with me he couldn't even bear to be civil. I didn't understand what his problem was at all.

But I decided he was right about one thing – if he didn't care about me then I sure wasn't about to care what he thought of me. I left the basket of logs on the floor, I wasn't going to do him any favours, and I walked as fast as I could back to the farmhouse, raging inwardly the whole way.

Chapter Seventeen

Awake before sunrise, I was already finishing off breakfast when Chloe appeared the following morning dressed in silky pyjamas, her hair piled on her head. 'Please say there's coffee,' she greeted me, sleepily. She perched on one of the stools behind the island and I carried over a mug of coffee for her. I was already on my second of the day after not sleeping through sheer pissed-off-ness, if that was even a word, over what Cameron had said to me last night.

'Didn't sleep well?' I asked as I drizzled pancakes in lemon and blueberries.

'I'm just not used to waking up this early. Heather wants me to come to her farm so I set my alarm. I'm not a morning person, I guess.'

'This should help.' I passed her a plate of pancakes. 'Would you like anything else?'

'These look amazing. What a treat. Come and join me,' she added, tucking in.

I sat down with her with my coffee and pancakes, stifling a yawn. 'Are you looking forward to your riding lesson?'

'A bit nervous. I've never even been on a horse. Anna, these are so good.' She glanced at me. 'How come you're stuck out here on a farm when you can cook like this?'

I decided it was better to come clean. 'Well, actually, I'm just helping Heather out as a favour.'

'Oh, so you work in a restaurant? I thought it was weird…'

The door behind us opened and in came Heather so I didn't have to admit I was actually housekeeper of Glendale Hall. I fixed Heather a coffee and a plate of pancakes, thinking over what Chloe said. It made me feel good. She was used to eating at London restaurants and thought that I was good enough to work in one. I wondered whether my next step should be not to another pub job, but to try to get into a kitchen. I knew though that it was competitive and hard work and I had no formal training. Would they just laugh me out of there?

'Okay, let's go to Fraser Farm,' Heather said to Chloe once breakfast was finished. 'I'll have her back in time for dinner at seven. Cameron is going to make a bonfire tonight, it's meant to be a lovely clear sky,' she said. 'So, that will be fun. And we can toast marshmallows.'

'I'd love that,' Chloe said excitedly.

Heather turned to me. 'We're all coming by for the bonfire but it'll just be us three for your meal don't worry, and Cameron, of course.'

I tried not to flinch at that thought. I pasted on a smile and waved them off. I heard Cameron come into the farmhouse and head upstairs to sort out Chloe's room, avoiding the kitchen, and me. Thankfully. I cleared up breakfast and as there was plenty of time before I had to start on the evening meal, I went out for a run.

This time, I avoided the path that led to the woods and Cameron's cottage but instead went through the gate into the field that rose up into a hill. I locked the gate behind me and took off, enjoying the burn in the back of my legs as I ran up the incline. It was a sunny morning but there was a breeze that cooled the back of my neck.

When I reached the top of the hill, I stopped, breathless. Ahead was the top field of Fraser Farm and I could see the Highland cows up there grazing. I stood admiring the view in both directions. Up here it felt like nothing could touch me.

I watched as Cameron left the farmhouse and walked towards the cottage. I saw him pause and look up at me. It was too far for me to see the expression on his face. I was flummoxed by him. There seemed to be this tension between us and I didn't understand it. I'd never had anyone take against me before they even knew me.

Clearly, I'd annoyed my bosses before. Hamish at the pub I'd just had to leave for one, and there were past boyfriends who hadn't been amused when I'd left in a hurry, and there was Donna, who had been outraged when I hadn't wanted to marry her grandson. But generally I thought people enjoyed my company, and I tried to be friendly to people. Yes, I made sure I never got too close to anyone. I always moved on before that happened. But people still tried. And then there was everyone at Glendale Hall, and Heather too. They'd all been welcoming. Why, then, was Cameron determined to dislike me?

More importantly, though, why was I letting him get to me? Perhaps because I usually was able to charm people or because I quite liked being the one to walk away, not the other way around. Or, frustratingly, because I found him attractive and felt rejected?

Groaning out loud, I walked across the top of the hill, and pushed Cameron to the back of my mind. Chloe's words earlier came back to me. She loved my cooking, so much so she thought I should do it as a job.

But that would mean changing my habits of a lifetime.

I looked out over this Scottish farm and thought about my next planned stop – a beach, bar work watching the sunset over a deep blue sea, tourists just looking for fun... No one would want anything permanent with me on that island; they didn't want it for themselves. The only difference would be the fact it would be a holiday for them; but I would never be looking for more. That thought suddenly made me feel a little sad.

What was Glendale doing to me?

It was making me think about my future, and usually I tried really hard not to think far ahead. I had planned to go on living as I was, but was my brother right? Was it stopping me from being happy?

I closed my eyes and willed the universe to give me some answers because I certainly didn't have any right now.

—

I spent the afternoon alone in the kitchen in the farmhouse preparing dinner. I put on my favourite playlist to cook to, tied my hair up, put my apron on, and let all my worries slide away as I focused on making the best meal I could. I wanted to wow Chloe. And Heather and Cameron too. And prove to myself that I could do something special.

The sun had begun to dip in the sky when Chloe and Heather returned from Fraser Farm, Chloe heading up for a bath as Heather joined me in the kitchen. 'I'm exhausted,' Heather admitted as she sat on a stool. 'It smells really good in here.'

I smiled. 'The lamb is cooking so it'll be ready in half an hour. I'd better set the table. Was the day okay though? Is she enjoying herself?'

'I think so. She really liked riding and looking around the farm, and she was great with Harry. She took loads of photos so I'm hoping we're going to get good promotion on her Instagram and blog. She's sweet, I really like her so fingers crossed she likes us too. I'll go over and get Cameron, he's probably building the bonfire. Was he a good assistant today?' She hopped off the bar stool. I was starting to understand that she rarely stood still.

'I haven't seen him,' I replied truthfully as I headed into the dining room. I saw her look surprised at that but I had been determined not to ask him for any help, and he had clearly been happy to avoid me all day. I went into the dining room and laid four places, lit a scented candle and opened up the French doors as it was so warm. Heather came in with wine and glasses and soon we were joined by Cameron and Chloe. Chloe was wearing leggings and a long t-shirt, her wet hair in a bun, but she still looked effortlessly pretty. Cameron smiled at her and asked her all about her day. I tried not to show my irritation that he was able to be nice to her and not me. I really didn't want it to bother me but it did.

I concentrated on serving dinner and ignoring their friendly conversation, although it wasn't easy. After the starter, I served the lamb shanks. The meat fell off the bone, I could see as I ate my nut roast, wishing for once I could try the meat main for myself. I had to content myself with the appreciative noises from the others. Even Cameron. And then for dessert I had made a berry tart with homemade ice cream – all the ingredients were local and fresh and organic, and I was really pleased with it. Cameron made us coffees afterwards and I put out a plate of cheese and biscuits but everyone was too full to eat much.

'You're wasted here,' Chloe said in a low voice when I took her plate. I just laughed but I saw Cameron watch our exchange with interest. He headed out to light the bonfire and Chloe went up to dry her hair while Heather and I cleared everything up.

'I can't thank you enough for tonight,' Heather said when we were alone. 'You totally saved us.'

'Oh, well…' I mumbled, a little embarrassed by her praise. I hadn't really experienced that before. But I decided I liked it.

'Thank God Brodie brought you here,' she said, squeezing my shoulder as she passed me to stack the dishwasher. 'Oh, I can hear them all arriving. I think we've done enough for tonight. Let's go and relax. You definitely deserve it.'

I slipped upstairs to put on a hoodie as I knew it would be chilly outside now. When I walked downstairs, I saw Cameron by the front door on the phone. I paused, not knowing whether to go down or not.

'No, Adam, I can't,' he was saying with a sigh. 'I'm working… I'm sure you can manage without me. Yes, she's still here.' Cameron sighed again. 'No, I won't ask her because I already said no… You know I don't like Lorna like that. Yes, I'm well aware you think I'm crazy.' Cameron was becoming irritated. 'I have to go… Adam, you know why,' he finally snapped. 'I'll see you later,' he added before hanging up. He strode out of the door. Hmmm. That was interesting. I carried on walking downstairs, wondering why Adam had annoyed him so much, and wondered if they had been talking about me. And someone called Lorna, whoever she was. It was clear though that Cameron wasn't interested in dating anyone. Maybe we did have something in common after all.

I followed Cameron to the bottom of the hill, where everyone had gathered around the large bonfire. The sky was only just turning dark behind the dancing flames. Everyone was sitting on folding chairs holding drinks and snacks when I approached. Rory, Heather's dad Don and little Harry had joined Heather, along with an older man who Heather introduced as Angus. Cameron went to sit next to him and on his other side was Chloe. I sat down in the empty seat beside her.

'Here,' she said, passing me a skewer with a marshmallow on. 'How fun is this? I haven't done this since I was at Brownies.'

'Me neither,' I agreed. I'd missed out on things like that after my accident and when you were an adult campfires and toasting marshmallows weren't usually on the agenda unless you had a family. 'Although I did camp out on a beach in Thailand once. Slightly different to this.'

She smiled. 'I loved Thailand. Where else have you been?'

'Australia and New Zealand, all round Europe and I also spent a few months working in an American camp for kids.'

'Oh wow, that sounds like fun. I've never stayed anywhere longer than just a couple weeks' holiday.'

'I like moving around,' I said, holding out my marshmallow to toast. I caught Cameron watching us again.

'I feel so unworldly listening to you two,' Heather said. 'I've never left the UK. I just never had the travel bug I suppose.'

'You must go to Italy a lot,' Chloe said to Cameron.

'Not since I was a kid,' he replied, staring into the flames.

'I loved Venice, and Rome,' Chloe said, oblivious to his blunt tone. 'The food in Italy…'

I nodded. 'So good. The best place I ever worked was an Italian restaurant. Although the owner, Donna, used to shout at me if I got anything wrong. She was very particular about her herbs and spices.'

'Why did you leave?'

'Her grandson,' I replied to Chloe. 'He told her I broke his heart when he found out I was seeing his friend, even though we'd barely gone out. Blood is thicker though, right? Now I make sure I don't date anyone I work with,' I added with a rueful laugh. Cameron lifted his head and met my eyes through the flickering light of the fire. I wondered what he was thinking.

'Sensible,' Chloe said. 'Although you two work together,' she said to Rory and Heather. 'And are such a cute couple.' Heather and Rory exchanged an amused look. I didn't think they'd ever been called cute before.

'We've had our ups and downs but it works for our family, we love it,' Heather said. 'It's a real family business, with my dad, plus the fact that Angus is Cameron's uncle,' she explained to Chloe.

'For my sins,' Angus grunted, making them all laugh, even Cameron.

'And Anna is the brother of the minister of Glendale, so she's connected to the village too.'

'A minister?' Chloe looked surprised.

'We couldn't be more different,' I confirmed, smiling.

'He's thrilled you're here,' Heather said. 'I bet he's a protective older brother, am I right?'

'Ever since my accident,' I agreed, and then realised what I'd said. I was annoyed. Now I'd get lots of questions that I didn't want to answer.

'Accident?' Chloe asked.

'When I was thirteen. My dad and I were in a car accident,' I said in a rush to get my explanation over with. 'My dad hit his head but I had just taken off my seatbelt so I flew through the windscreen. I ended up in a coma and almost died. It took a long time to recover…' I trailed off, not wanting to admit that I still hadn't recovered. Or that the driver who had hit us had died. Or why his car had hit ours in the first place. I looked away from the fire and into Cameron's shocked gaze. In fact, it looked as if the blood had completely drained from his face.

Like he'd seen a ghost.

Chapter Eighteen

I knew I hadn't imagined it because Angus shot his nephew a concerned look as Chloe let out a shocked noise. 'Oh, I'm so sorry, Anna. How awful.'

'It's okay,' I assured her. 'All's well that ends well,' I said lightly but, inside, my heart raced as it always did when I thought back to that time. 'So, how was your first time on a horse?' I asked, changing the subject. I swear I saw Cameron's chest sag with relief when Chloe started talking about horse riding. Clearly, I wasn't the only one who would rather not be reminded of the past.

After that, the evening passed peacefully. Cameron was quiet, but his uncle was too so perhaps it was normal for them. After we toasted the marshmallows, we had a few drinks and the sun slipped away while the fire burned merrily.

When Harry fell asleep on his mother's lap, Heather said they'd better go home. 'I hope you've enjoyed the day, Chloe,' she said as she said goodbye to us. 'And thank you again for dinner, Anna.'

'I feel so relaxed,' Chloe said. 'This place is really beautiful, a real sanctuary. I think you've got a winner on your hands. I know so many people who would love to get away from it all here.'

Heather hugged her then and we waved them off, leaving Chloe, Cameron and myself and the dying fire.

'I'm exhausted. I'll see you both for breakfast. My last morning here, it's gone so quickly!' Chloe headed off into the farmhouse with a cheerful wave.

I drained the last of my glass of wine as Cameron pulled on his jumper. The air was growing cooler by the minute. It was so quiet now it was just the two of us. I should have jumped straight up and followed Chloe back into the farmhouse but I knew that I wouldn't be able to sleep. 'One more drink?' I said, picking up the last bottle. Cameron looked like he was going to refuse but then he nodded and held out his glass. Maybe he also wasn't looking forward to going to sleep. I wondered again what had shaken him so much when I mentioned my accident. As I poured his drink, our eyes met and it felt like he was thinking about it too.

We both took a sip as we watched the last of the flames flicker. It was dark now and the stars were out; silence wrapped around us like a blanket.

'I'm sorry,' he said, finally, continuing to stare at the fire embers and not at me. I pulled my legs up and wrapped my arms around them as I watched him trying to find the right words. 'I was really hard on you, and I don't even know you. Hearing what you said about your… accident. When I saw you with Adam I thought, well, I thought that you were reckless and it annoyed me, I suppose. But…' He was stuttering a little. He looked over at me. 'It's really me that I was annoyed with, not you.'

'It's not you, it's me. That's a cliché,' I said. There was this heavy atmosphere around us now. Something stirred in the pit of my stomach when he looked at me like that. I shivered and I wasn't fully convinced it was because of the dip in temperature. He looked away and I let out a breath. 'Sometimes I act like I don't care, I know that. It's a self-preservation thing. I want to be fearless. But I'm so far from it. I was stupid the night I almost let Adam drive me. I'm glad you were there. You were right to be angry. I was angry with myself. My accident, it… haunts me,' I said in a half-whisper. Perhaps it was the alcohol, the fire, the fact we were alone with just the woods to hear us but I felt myself be more honest with Cameron than I had been with anyone in a very long time.

'I know what it's like to feel haunted,' Cameron said, matching my soft tone. He faced me in his chair. 'I feel like I'm trapped in the past sometimes. And, I don't know, you sent me back there. But I was so rude to you, I know. I'm sorry. I'm not like that. It's, what did you say? Maybe it was a self-preservation thing too.'

'You don't need to be scared of me,' I said with a laugh. 'I won't be here long. It's what I do – I move on.'

'I just don't let people in easily, I suppose. And when I say self-preservation, I really mean for you and not me. I…' He trailed off, unsure what to say for a moment. 'I keep my distance for other people's sake, not my own. I'm not someone you want to get close to.'

'A guy told me once that I was toxic.' I let out a bitter laugh. 'So, I could probably say the same thing back to you.' It was strange to think that I had things in common with Cameron. He'd been so distant with me but I recognised what was behind it now. Maybe he'd even been more distant with me than other people because he'd felt the same attraction I had.

'You're not toxic, Anna. Just because you don't feel the same way about someone, it isn't your fault. Like when you lost your job… They shouldn't have done that.'

I was surprised he was on my side. What had happened back then still smarted. 'You're right but I never even let myself find out if I do feel the same way. I leave before it gets to that stage. Yeah, it was unfair of them but I didn't realise. I didn't even see that he was in love with me. Because I have never felt that way about anyone. Doesn't that sound like there's something wrong with me?' I gripped my wine glass hard. I hated that I didn't feel like everyone else seemed to about relationships.

He shook his head. 'Just because you haven't loved anyone doesn't mean you can't. You just haven't met that person yet. And, believe me, when you do it's not all it's cracked up to be.' He sighed heavily. Heartbreak? Was that what haunted him? I couldn't relate to that. 'It must have been so hard what happened to you.'

I usually shrugged when someone said that but I was tired of doing that. 'It was,' I said simply and finished off my drink. 'You could tell me,' I said then. 'What's on your mind. I'm the last person to judge anyone, you know.'

Cameron was silent for a moment. He looked across at me and I could swear that electricity crackled across the air between us. 'Sometimes I feel like the wall I've built around myself might never come down.'

'Me too,' I whispered. How was it possible that he was saying the exact thing that I worried about? That we had the same fears?

'I should go,' he said, standing up abruptly. 'I am sorry for being so hard on you. For being so unfriendly. But you really should stay away from me.' And with that, he turned and practically marched towards the trees, as if he had to put distance between us. I watched him walking away and was gripped by a sudden unexpected need to follow him.

I didn't think, I just followed my instinct. Jumping up, I went after him towards the woods. Following him all the way to his cottage.

At his front door, he turned and looked at me. 'What do you want, Anna?' he asked warily.

'I don't want to be alone tonight,' I replied, honestly. I knew I'd go back to the farmhouse and that I would toss and turn all night and if I managed to fall asleep, nightmares of the accident would wake me up. I could feel it. I knew when nights like that were coming. And I wanted to hide from it. I knew that in Cameron's arms, I could forget. Even if it was only for one night. That's all I was ever looking for. A way to escape my thoughts. My past. Myself, really, if I was being honest.

'I told you…' he began.

'Just one night, Cameron. Believe me, that's all I want. You and me – we're the same.'

He shook his head. 'You don't know anything about me. I haven't told you everything.'

I stepped closer. 'I know. Nor have I. But I don't care. I don't want to be alone tonight, do you?'

Cameron hesitated. 'This isn't a good idea,' he warned, but when I stepped closer again, he didn't move.

'I don't want to be alone tonight, do you?' I repeated, softer this time, tilting my face to look up at him, just inches between us now. He was so much taller than me. He looked down at me and I saw the indecision in his eyes. It looked like I would need to be the one to decide. I stood on my tiptoes and brushed my lips against his. I heard him hitch his breath and we looked at one another. There was only a beat before he pressed his lips against mine and wrapped his arms around my waist. I drew mine up around his neck and pulled him closer.

Cameron lifted me up then and I wrapped my legs around his waist as he moved his mouth to my cheek and then down my neck and along my collarbone. I gasped and he looked at me one more time, perhaps giving me a moment to be sure. I just smiled and he shook his head, and carried me inside, shutting the door behind us.

–

I wasn't surprised when I woke up alone. I was surprised, though, that I'd slept so well. Cameron had held me during the night, I remembered feeling his body wrapped around mine. And I'd slept through the night. With no nightmares.

Sun streamed in through Cameron's bedroom window as I sat up and looked around the room I'd barely registered last night. It was small with basically a bed, a lamp, a chest of drawers and a bookshelf. White walls, white bedding, and a wooden floor. Cameron obviously didn't care about décor or injecting any personality into his room. Once again, I couldn't ignore the similarities between us. I was always keeping my room impersonal. Cameron clearly did the same even though he lived here permanently. Or maybe he had one eye on the door, like me.

I wondered what haunted Cameron but then I shook my head. I had enough to deal with without delving into his past. Two broken people couldn't make a whole person, I knew that with certainty. It was better if we kept apart from now on. I got out of bed and pulled my clothes back on, eager to escape. The walls felt like they were closing in. I tried so hard to outrun my own past, and I recognised the same thing in Cameron. He had been right last night – this was a mistake.

Hurrying downstairs as quietly as I could, I glanced around but Cameron was nowhere to be seen. I walked out and through the woods towards the farmhouse. It was really early, I realised, so Chloe wouldn't have noticed that I hadn't slept there. As I walked, I saw a figure moving in the distance. I paused. It was Cameron. Out for an early run. He turned when he heard me and changed direction to jog towards me. I tried to make it to the farmhouse door before he could reach me but I missed it by just a couple of feet.

'You're up,' he said when he'd stopped, a little breathless.

'I need to get sorted before Chloe gets up, and then Heather is coming,' I gabbled, not looking at him. 'And then I'll be back at the Hall...'

'Anna, I'm sorry about last night.'

'Nothing to be sorry about.' I glanced at him, trying to ignore his bare legs beneath his shorts and the tight t-shirt he was wearing. 'We both got what we wanted, didn't we?'

Cameron raised an eyebrow. 'But...'

'I'll see you around, Cameron.' I walked inside before he could say anything else.

I leaned against the closed door and sighed. I tried not to remember the feel of Cameron's strong arms around me, the warmth of his touch or how he had looked at me like he'd never seen anything more beautiful. For one night, I had felt closer to someone than I ever had. As if maybe for one night the walls we had both built around us, had been shaken just slightly. But I knew it had just been a mirage. Those walls could never come down.

We were both runners.

And like the best runners, we ran alone.

Chapter Nineteen

When I returned to Glendale Hall, chaos awaited me.

Heather dropped me home and didn't appear to notice that I was quiet as she raved about how well the weekend seemed to have gone and how happy Chloe had been when she left Hilltop, promising that her content would be uploaded to her social media and blog soon. Cameron had stayed away from breakfast, only appearing to help Chloe with her bags and drive her to the train station and we didn't look at one another.

As I left the farm, I thought that apart from a few visits to the Hall I was unlikely to have to spend much time with him for the rest of the summer, and that was the safest thing for both of us.

Heather had to go to her farm shop so she waved me off from her car and I let myself back into the Hall with my bag and stopped short in the hallway as Beth hurried down the stairs, her hair flying out behind her. Her face flooded with relief when she saw me standing there. 'Anna, thank God! The bride for my first wedding next week has turned up and wants to call the whole thing off! Can you come with me?' She grabbed me by the arm to pull me with her. I tried to protest but I was quickly learning that Beth wasn't someone you argued with. I dumped my bag by the door and followed her into the kitchen where there appeared to be some kind of crisis meeting happening around the table.

'Meera, why not tell us what happened?' Caroline was asking a woman I hadn't seen before from across the table. She was clearly the distressed bride – her cheeks were stained with tears but I could see she was beautiful with dark hair that reached her waist and dark eyes. Caroline and Sally were there and they looked at us worriedly; it was obviously not going well.

'I'll make tea and snacks,' I suggested. I mean, it had to help a bit, right? Beth shot me a grateful look as she joined the table and asked Meera to tell them what was going on. I listened as I made tea and arranged an array of biscuits on a large plate. Thankfully, the Hall always had a lot of snacks in stock.

'Tarak has just found out he's going to be transferred with work. It means we have to move to Yorkshire for at least a year. I really don't want to move away from my family! I won't know anyone there. What if I need their support or advice? What if…' Her eyes grew wide. '…I get pregnant and I'll be on my own?' She started crying anew as I handed around teas and put the tray of biscuits down.

'Moving away really isn't anything to worry about,' I said, sitting down, as I could tell Beth wasn't about to let me escape from this. 'I move all the time. I haven't lived near my family since I was eighteen. You'll be with your husband, won't you? And there's so many ways to keep in touch…'

Beth nodded. 'Definitely. I left home for ten years and had no family with me. But you know what? I made a family with my daughter and our friends and I grew up so much during that time. And you won't even be alone

– Tarak will be with you, and don't forget he'll be new to the area too. So you'll try new places and things together and meet new people together. And it's not that far, you'll have loads of visits from your family and you can come home whenever you feel lonely.'

'Marriage is about being a team,' Caroline added. 'If you think Tarak is your partner in life no matter what it throws at you then everything will be okay because you'll face it together. That's what a good marriage is all about.' She gave Beth a quick glance. I wondered if she was hinting about Beth's father, her first husband. Perhaps that's why they hadn't worked out.

Meera looked at us each in turn, her tears easing a little. 'You really think so? I've never been away from my family. It was such a shock when he told me.'

'Of course it was.' Beth slid the biscuits towards her. 'But you told me the first time I met you that he is your best friend, so you'll make it work together. It won't be easy, of course not, but you have a whole lifetime together and plenty of time to come back home and be with your family. Try to enjoy this time just the two of you. Think of it like a very extended honeymoon.' She squeezed her hand.

Meera took a biscuit. 'That's a nice way to look at it. You really lived in London alone with your daughter?' Beth nodded. 'It must have been so hard.'

'It was but it made me the woman I am today.' I saw Caroline nod then. She looked proud of her daughter. 'You can do this. I know you can.'

'Do you miss your family?' Meera suddenly asked me as she chewed on the biscuit.

I missed the girl I used to be more, but I nodded. 'Sure, but I wanted to do things, see new places and meet new people, you know?' I reached for a biscuit myself then. Suddenly, I felt like the one who needed comforting.

'How did you and Tarak meet?' Sally asked and I was relieved to be out of the hot seat.

'Through my brother. He's so lovely. Isn't he, Beth?'

She smiled, and sat back in her chair, pleased that the crisis appeared to have been averted. 'He really is. I have no doubt you'll be really happy together.'

After the tea, Meera left to go and tell her mum what was happening and I carried my bags up to my room. Beth trailed after me. 'Thank you for helping. I really thought my first wedding here was going to be cancelled.' She smiled. 'So, how was Hilltop?' She perched on the bed as I put my bags down and went to sit on the window seat.

'I mean, I think it went well. Everyone seemed to like my food and Chloe had a great time. I think Heather will get a really good review, and I bet she will get loads more bookings too.'

'I'm pleased, although I hope she doesn't try to steal you from me again this summer.'

I shook my head. 'It was a one-off. I love cooking but it's not like I'm an actual chef. Besides, it's a bit in the middle-of-nowhere for me,' I muttered, casually. There was no way I could work again with Cameron. 'Are you ready for your first wedding?'

'I think so. It's really helped not worrying about the house so much with you here although I'm sorry we've let it get a bit messy with you gone. We lived on takeaways too. Are you sure you're okay? You look a little… tired.'

'I guess it was a bit stressful,' I lied. 'Can I ask you something?' She nodded, and waited. 'I was just thinking about what you said about having left Glendale for ten years. You've been back a while now but do you ever think about leaving again? Do you ever want to just run away again, I suppose I'm wondering.' I was interested to see how someone who had run like I had, and then returned, had settled back home and seemed content to stay put. I still couldn't picture myself ever doing that.

'Do you know what? I thought about it when things got tough after I came home that first Christmas. Drew didn't know I'd had Izzy – I'm not sure if you know. I got pregnant at sixteen and he was about to fly to America to study to be a doctor and I just couldn't tell him. I couldn't bear the thought of him giving up on that dream so I didn't tell him. My grandmother found out I was pregnant and she made me feel like my family wouldn't support me so that's why I ran away to London. And why I stayed away for ten years. When she got sick, though, I came home,' Beth explained. 'And it was so hard. There was so much to talk about the past. So many things that I thought my family felt, but it turned out they didn't, there were so many misunderstandings, and then Drew came home for Christmas and I told him about Izzy. I didn't expect him to forgive me but he did and we fell in love all over again. Well, I don't think I'd ever stopped loving him. But I wasn't sure if he felt the same way, if he wanted to stay, if I wanted to stay and I thought about just leaving again. It would have been the easy option. But what had made sense when I was teenager, didn't then. I wanted to be with people I loved. I wanted Izzy to be with them as well.' She smiled.

'And then my grandmother left me this house,' Beth continued, gesturing to the room. 'I think she wanted to make up for the past, you know? And that made my decision, really. I had too much here to walk away from again, I suppose. So, long story short – no. There is too much here that I would lose if I left. Too many people I love. And I never want to lose them again.'

'Wow,' I said. 'That's quite a story.'

'Why do you move around so much? Honestly, your brother hasn't said much but I get the feeling he wishes you were around more.'

'Really?' I was surprised. I had always thought my family, like me, found it easier when I wasn't around all that often. 'I get so restless. I want to do things, see the world. Maybe after my accident I felt like I needed to live life to the full because I had almost lost it,' I explained haltingly. It was so hard to share that feeling with anyone else but I had started with Cameron and it felt somewhat easier getting it off my chest. And it felt that, like Cameron, Beth did understand a little bit. She had run away when she was only a bit younger than I had been. 'And now I think it's become a habit, I suppose.' It was only half of my story though; the other half was so much guilt, it was easier to hide away from it but I couldn't bring myself to share that with anyone.

She nodded. 'I can see why the accident made you feel like that when you were younger. Like you needed to prove that there was a reason why you pulled through. But, honestly, I think the best way to repay that second chance is to live a life that makes you happy. Some people are happy travelling the world or making millions at work or getting up on stage and singing to a stadium of people. Some people are happy living in their childhood home and raising a family. Some people have never left the town they were born in. Others would never want to go back to that town. But really what makes one life better than another?' She used air quotes around 'better'. 'If you're happy living your life and aren't hurting anyone else, of course, then it doesn't matter what people think.' She stood up. 'And you can change your mind. Look at me. What makes you happy when you're younger might be completely different now. Heather too. She used to be a librarian and now she loves living on a farm and is about to marry a farmer. Sometimes people know exactly what they want out of life but for most of us, it takes time. You have to figure out who you are and what you're really looking for. And then comes the hard bit. Knowing when you've found it and grabbing it with both hands.' She checked the time then and stood up. 'Time for church, are you coming?'

My head was swimming with her words. I wasn't even sure how to process them, but somehow I felt a little bit better. Just a little bit. I nodded and got up. I felt like while I was here, I should attend for Brodie's sake. I thought about what she'd said about him being pleased that I was here, it felt good to hear that. I just wished that I could really believe it.

Chapter Twenty

The following week in Glendale was spent sorting the house out as much as I could while Beth made all the last-minute plans for the first Hall wedding at the weekend while wailing at the rain, which seemed to be coming down all day every day. Izzy and Luke were in the Hall every day working on her reading room, pleased they weren't being told to get out and enjoy the sunshine, as there wasn't any to be found.

I cooked each night, sometimes others dropped in, sometimes it was just the family but I always made extra just in case. The only person who had yet to come along again was Cameron. I knew he was staying away but I didn't blame him. After all, it was what I would have done if our roles had been reversed. And I was avoiding going back to the Glendale Arms. I wanted a drink and a night out but I didn't want to run into him there. Adam had messaged me a couple of times asking when I was going to come for a drink but I kept making excuses. It appeared Cameron hadn't told him about our night together, and I was relieved that no one but the two of us knew.

On my second Friday at the Hall, however, there was a change to my routine when Emily phoned and invited me for dinner at the vicarage, saying she had a surprise for me. Beth had already decided to order a takeaway for everyone the Hall to relax ahead of the wedding the next day so I didn't need to prepare any food, so I had no excuse and I did really love surprises. Unless, you know, it was a declaration of love or a proposal, obviously. I went along, walking there as the evening was dry and warm, curious and a little bit excited to see what surprise Brodie and Emily could possibly have for me.

I felt surprisingly relaxed as I strolled to the vicarage. The sun sparkled through gaps in the trees which leaned over the road as I walked from the Hall to the village in my cut-off shorts and white shirt, which I'd pushed up to show off my tanned arms. Perhaps I was getting used to Glendale's quietness and slower pace and I always felt better in summer. There was something about the longer days and the extra warmth that made you feel more positive. Plus, I liked my job more than I thought I would, maybe because the people at the Hall were pretty chilled, Beth especially. She was even someone I thought I could be friends with. I tried not to think about the fact I didn't really have friends and once I moved on, I'd likely never see her again. It was better to just live in the moment. And this moment was going pretty well.

'You look lovely, Anna,' Emily greeted me enthusiastically when she opened the door. Iona was on her hip and waved her tiny hand at me. 'Come on in.' I followed them through into the living room, the smell of something tasty cooking from the kitchen filled the house as well as the usual baking and lavender scents that seemed to permanently exist here.

I stopped short when I saw that Brodie was not alone in the room but my parents were with him. The three of them turned to smile at me. For a second I wasn't sure whether to turn back around and leave or walk on through. I took a breath and followed Emily and Iona, trying to smile even though I was confused to see them. Was this the surprise? I would have to tell Emily that her idea of a surprise maybe needed reviewing.

'Anna, darling,' my mum said, jumping up to give me a kiss. My dad gave me one of his quick bear-hugs too. 'We were visiting friends and thought we'd stop by before we head home after Brodie told us you were here.' My mum smelled of her usual floral perfume. She was small like me with fair hair like her children, but my dad was tall like Brodie, stocky and strong with short, sandy hair, and despite having been retired for about ten years, he still wore grey suits as he had done when he still worked at the bank.

'And you wanted to see how I was getting on in Glendale,' I guessed as I sat down on one of the sofas.

'We wanted to check you were okay,' my dad amended gently.

'Want a glass of wine, Anna?' Emily handed Iona to Brodie and hurried out, perhaps feeling guilty I hadn't been as happy about the surprise as she'd hoped.

When I was with my parents, I felt like I could easily revert back to a sulky teenager and almost told them to mind their own business, but I saw Brodie watching me nervously so I tried to shake off the compulsion. 'I'm enjoying life at the Hall and I spent last weekend over at a farm helping out by cooking for a reviewer, which was fun.'

'I'm so pleased you enjoy cooking,' Mum said, but then bit her lip as if she wanted to say more but had thought better of it. My parents were as careful with their words around me as I was with them.

'We actually did have another reason to pop by,' my dad said, getting up as Emily came in with my drink. I took a long sip of it and looked up as my dad returned with a guitar case. 'When we spoke to Brodie, he mentioned that you had learned to play and wished you had a guitar. This has been sitting up in the loft so...' His cheeks brightened and he looked a little embarrassed as he awkwardly passed it to me. 'I thought you might like it?' He cleared his throat and hastily sat back down on the opposite sofa.

I stared at the guitar on my lap – the one he had played with when I was younger and went with him to his gigs. I felt them all watching me as if I was grenade that could explode at any moment. I was surprised and embarrassed to feel a little lump in my throat. 'Are you sure?' I checked. I had never thought that he'd be happy for me to have this. I was touched and, as usual, wondered if I deserved it.

'Of course, I'd love you to have it,' Dad said back, his voice catching a little as if he too was a little emotional. Perhaps he was thinking back to that time in our family when we were all at ease, when we were all happy.

'Thank you,' I said, meaning it more than he could ever know. I undid the case and pulled it out and straight away I was back sitting at the side of the stage watching my dad play, thinking he was an actual rock star. Back when my childhood had been carefree and without pain or worry.

'Play us something,' Emily urged me then, breaking the silence in the room. I felt like I didn't dare lift my eyes to look at any of my family, I had no idea what they were thinking, or feeling. I wondered if they had been transported back as I had. The accident had changed our family forever. I couldn't be the only one who desperately wished it had never happened.

I was also worried I might start crying but I had never done that in front of them. When they made it clear they didn't want to discuss the accident, I had started to keep my feelings hidden from them. I waited until I was alone to let the tears out, and I still only ever cried alone. Taking a deep breath, I focused on the guitar and played how I was feeling instead.

I played 'Let it Be' by The Beatles, one of the handful of songs I had learned to play all the way through. It had been one of my dad's all-time favourite songs and I had grown up listening to it so much it was imprinted on me too. It felt right for this moment. I concentrated on getting the chords right, not looking at anyone as I played, and the room was silent save for the strumming of the strings. I had enjoyed learning to play and had been sad to stop when I'd moved on from Brian, who had taught me. But I had been unable to lug a guitar around with me after that. Playing the guitar was like when I ran or did yoga, I was taken outside of myself, swept away from my thoughts and was able to exist just in that moment for once, not wondering what was going to come next.

When I finished the song, I finally looked up. My mum was crying, my dad was beaming, Brodie just looked stunned, and Emily was cuddling a sleeping Iona, smiling over her head at me. 'I haven't played in a long time,' I said, still holding the guitar tightly.

'It was beautiful,' my mum said. 'I wish we had known you wanted to play, and your cooking too...' She had to stop as a sob escaped her throat. She stood up hurriedly. 'Excuse me,' she said, and almost ran from the room.

'I'll check on her,' my dad said, following her.

I looked at my brother. 'What's that all about?' I asked, wondering what I'd done now to upset them. Sometimes it felt like I did it without even trying, but I really was at a loss this time.

'I'll put Iona to bed and check on dinner,' Emily said, leaving us alone.

'You keep a lot from us, Anna,' Brodie said gently. 'I'm not saying that you don't have reasons for that but we know very little about your life. Having you here is the most I've seen you in years and them finding out that you love to cook, and how good you are at it, and that you learned the guitar and missed Dad playing it... I think it just hit them how much they didn't know and how much they wish they were a bigger part of your life.' He said the words carefully, again like he was worried about my reaction to them.

I looked down at the guitar. What he was saying was at odds with how I thought they felt about me. 'I always thought you all thought my life wasn't worth knowing about because I wasn't living the way you wanted me to,' I explained, being more honest with him than I had in a long time. 'Every time I saw you, you made me feel like I was doing something wrong so it made me want to keep things from you, I suppose.'

'We're your family, we know you and love you, and we could see you weren't happy. We were worried about you, that's all. And keeping things from us only made us more worried.' He smiled a little. 'It sounds like we need to up our communication game in this family.'

I wished that would be enough. 'But I know how you all feel about the accident...' I began, knowing that the real wedge between us couldn't be erased by just telling them more about my life. Brodie waited for me to continue my sentence but then Mum appeared in the doorway and we both looked up at her.

'I'm sorry,' Mum said. She and dad were watching us. I wasn't sure if they had heard everything we had said. 'I

147

didn't expect to get so emotional watching you play, Anna. And that song… it brought back so many memories, I suppose.'

'You played it beautifully,' Dad added, the pride loud and clear in his voice.

I wasn't sure what to say to any of them. This was all very new for us.

Brodie stood up then. 'Come on, let's go and eat. I'm starving.' He threw me a reassuring smile as he scooted them out. I put the guitar away carefully and followed them, my head swimming.

I had almost brought up the accident. I had been disconnected from my family probably since I was eighteen and there now seemed to be a fine thread reappearing between us. I wanted to grab hold of it tightly, but how could I when I knew that they could never forgive me for what happened? And I didn't blame them. I'd never been able to forgive myself.

But then I looked down at the guitar. Perhaps they did want to try to go back to how things used to be between us. I didn't know if that was even possible, but I smiled as I looked at the guitar and hope sprang up inside me.

I realised then that I wanted to be close to my family again. I just wasn't sure how.

But perhaps today was a beginning.

Chapter Twenty-One

The first Glendale Hall wedding of the season was upon us. Beth had been fretting about the weather forecast but she was in luck – although it wasn't exactly hot, it was dry and there were glimpses of sun poking through light, fluffy clouds, as we all got ready on Saturday morning. One stipulation from Caroline had been that no wedding guests should come into the house itself. It was her way of making sure the Hall remained primarily a family home. It was the same when they had the Christmas trail and summer garden party, Beth told me. So, the wedding ceremony was being held in the gazebo by the stream and then the reception in a large marquee on the lawn, refreshments and toilets all on site. There were also caterers and serving staff working the event as well as a florist, photographer, and styling team on hand.

This meant, therefore, that I didn't have an official wedding role but Beth had pretty much given everyone a task as she was so determined to make the day perfect for Meera and Tarak. She asked me if I wouldn't mind making sure the gazebo still looked perfect before the florist draped flowers around it while she supervised the staff putting out the chairs for the ceremony. Meera and Tarak were having a traditional English wedding here and then were going to have a second wedding in India next month. Their families were spilt across the two countries so it had made sense to have two weddings and keep everyone happy. I couldn't imagine having to go through all the stress twice although I did like the idea of having two parties. Beth said Meera was going to wear a stunning sari in India but had chosen a white dress for her Hall wedding.

I walked over to the stream to look at the wooden gazebo. It was painted white with steps leading up to it, an archway stretching over the top with the stream sparkling behind. The couple would be standing up on the steps under the archway for the ceremony. Even I could see it was a beautiful place to say your vows. I just couldn't ever imagine doing that myself. I had brought a bucket of cleaning supplies but it looked clean to me. Still, I wiped it over and swept the steps to make sure they were completely clear.

The florist arrived with the flowers to drape across the arches, matching the wedding colour scheme of pink and white. Beth directed the chairs to be placed on the grass, a temporary aisle between them. She was in her element telling everyone what to do. I'd never known someone who enjoyed organising as much as she did. I was surprised she didn't have a headset and a walkie-talkie with her.

'Where do you want me then, Beth?' a deep voice called out. I turned from watching the flowers being put up to see Cameron arrive, carrying a big wooden sign over his shoulder.

'Oh, brilliant. So, we need the sign Heather's made put up on the main road as I'm worried people will miss the Hall turn off. Anna, can you please go with Cameron to find the best spot? I don't want anyone driving past us. Oh, Ruby...' Beth hurried off before either of us could protest at her instructions.

Cameron glanced at me before averting his eyes. Great. 'Okay, then,' I said, setting off quickly – the sooner we got this sorted, the better. I tried not to feel Cameron walking next to me or notice the way his muscles moved as he carried the sign. He made sure to keep a few feet of space between us as we walked up the lawn and passed through the house into the driveway.

I hated silence, especially if it felt uncomfortable like this one did. 'Beth is starting to lose it a bit, but she's so organised I think it'll run like clockwork. I'm kind of glad that after this, I can just slink away into the house though. She can be scary.'

Cameron stopped and put the sign down. He seemed relieved that I was happy to just make small talk. 'She rang Heather last night in a panic about this. I think the turn off is fine – it's not like Hilltop or even Fraser, which people always drive past.' He shrugged. 'Heather's always happy to help out, though. We all help each other out, I guess.'

'That's nice,' I said sincerely. I'd never really experienced such a community before. 'I think we need it here, just before the turning,' I suggested, looking up the road.

'Looks good to me,' he agreed.

I watched as he pushed it into the ground. 'So, has Heather heard anything from Chloe yet?'

'Yeah. The review is up. It's really good.'

'Oh.' I pulled out my phone, annoyed that he hadn't volunteered this information. I went to her blog and Instagram and broke into a smile. 'She really loved it! Especially the food. Ooh the lamb looks really good in the photo. Aww she's tagged me,' I said, realising she'd found me on there. I was excited. Her account was really popular and I was getting some more followers thanks to her. I sent her a message thanking her and saying how happy I was that she had enjoyed herself. 'Despite everything, we pulled it off.' I looked up to see Cameron watching me, a strange look on his face.

'Despite everything?' he asked, averting his eyes again. He straightened the sign even though it didn't need straightening.

'Don't make me spell it out,' I replied, arching an eyebrow. I turned to go, our task accomplished.

'Anna,' he said, his voice sounding agonised. I paused. 'I feel bad for not... calling, I suppose.'

'Why? It was a one-night thing.' I shrugged. 'I'm used to it, Cameron. No need to worry about me.'

'I'm not used to it. I don't do that,' he replied. 'Usually. I mean, ever. I just wanted you to know that I meant what I said – I'm not good for you.'

'I don't do relationships, okay? I don't want anything from you,' I said with a shrug. I didn't appreciate the assumption that I had been upset that he hadn't called. 'I'd better get back in case Beth needs me.' I walked off but I could feel him watching me. I didn't think I'd felt so confused by a man before. Why wasn't he good for me? I wondered if I'd ever find out. But then I'd have to tell him why I wasn't good for him. It was pointless.

I glanced back when I reached the house and he was looking towards the horizon, a pained look on his face. I thought *I* had demons. Cameron looked like he needed help. Not that I needed to worry about that. I wasn't going to be here much longer. And I couldn't be the one to help him.

Yet, as I walked back into the garden, I felt a strange desire to do it anyway. Which was crazy. I shook my head. I blamed this wedding. It was messing with my head.

Once I'd fed anyone at the Hall who wasn't working at the wedding, I set off for the Glendale Arms. I drove Beth's car to make sure I didn't drink more than one glass of wine. The wedding was in full swing by then, the marquee alive with music, laughter and the clinking of glasses. It was strange having it in the garden. Drew, Izzy, Caroline and John had retreated into the snug living room to watch a film, and Sally was staying inside her cottage for the evening. Beth had said we weren't banned but it felt too strange to wander into someone else's wedding party, it was best to leave Beth to it, everyone had seemed to agree on that.

I took the opportunity to head to the pub as no one needed me at the Hall. I was tired of avoiding the place because of Cameron – I needed a drink and to chat to people otherwise I knew I was going to end up wallowing.

After parking Beth's car, I walked inside. The evening was dry but there was a cool breeze, not that that stopped the drinkers in the beer garden. I carried the glass of wine I got from Malcolm outside and spotted Adam, who was with his friend Glen and another woman. I hesitated, unsure if they would want me to join them but he waved me over.

'Anna, this is my sister Lorna,' Adam said as I sat down beside him, opposite Glen and Lorna. I could see the resemblance as she smiled at me. She was slightly younger and slimmer than her brother, but they had the same eyes and dimple in their cheeks. I wondered why the name was familiar to me, and then I remembered the conversation I'd overheard at Hilltop – Cameron on the phone to Adam talking about her. Adam had been trying to get him to ask her out maybe.

'I've heard a lot about you,' Lorna said. 'These boys get very excited when a pretty woman shows up,' she added, rolling her eyes as they protested that. I smiled at her compliment. 'Mind you, so do I after living here forever. It's nice to meet someone new. You're working at the Hall, I hear?'

'That's right. Doing housekeeper work really and cooking for the family. It's a summer job, my brother found it for me.'

'I still can't believe you're Brodie's sister,' Adam said with a grin.

'Brodie is far too good-looking to be a minister,' Lorna replied. 'Oh, sorry. I guess you don't want to hear about your brother's looks.'

'It runs in the family though,' Adam said, looking across at me.

'And I don't want to see my brother flirting!' Lorna cried, making me laugh. I liked her. I wondered why Cameron had been so against taking her out. Perhaps it was the not-being-good-for-her thing, like he had claimed with me. I wondered if anyone at the table knew what was up with him but I didn't want him to find out I'd been asking.

'Is that flirting? I wasn't sure,' I joked. He nudged my elbow with his. 'There's a wedding at the Hall tonight so I needed to escape.'

'Why, you don't like weddings?' Lorna asked.

'They're okay if you're a guest and can take advantage of the free bar.'

'Yes!' Glen cried. 'I don't get weddings apart from that.'

'You don't get two people falling in love and wanting to spend their lives together?' Lorna demanded. Both Adam and Glen agreed that they didn't. 'No wonder I'm single here: look at the Glendale men, Anna.'

'I feel like I let womankind down by not enjoying weddings either. I'm sorry. I understand getting married if that's what you want but not people who love to go to weddings and watch or even cry when they're not the bride or groom. It's weird. I think I'd just elope if I ever got the urge. Not that I will.'

'Unless you meet The One,' Lorna said. She looked behind me. 'Which feels less and less likely for me each day,' she added in a quiet tone. I followed her gaze to see Cameron walking over. His eyes found mine straight away and I thought I saw him slow his pace for a second but he carried on and sat down opposite me with his beer in hand. Everyone greeted him, I offered a small smile but I couldn't read his expression on finding me here. 'So, are we all hitting up the garden party next weekend?'

'We usually go every year. It's a fun day out if the weather holds,' Lorna said to me.

'I'll be helping out but hopefully I'll have some free time too,' I said. Knowing Beth as I felt I was starting to, she would want everyone to enjoy the day as much as possible once everything that needed doing had been done. I glanced at Cameron, who was watching me. I wish I knew what he was thinking. Not that I should care.

'We should all hang out there then,' Adam suggested.

'Sure,' I said. 'What exactly happens at a garden party, though?' They laughed, and even Cameron raised a smile.

'We have ourselves a garden party virgin,' Adam said, his eyes twinkling. 'Can't wait to fix that.' He winked.

Then it was my turn to roll my eyes. 'Somehow, I'm not sure anyone would want you to fix their virginity, of any kind.' That time, Cameron properly joined in with the laughter. His laugh was deep and loud and a surprise. I realised I hadn't actually heard him laugh before.

'Don't raise her expectations too high,' Lorna warned them. 'Anna is a city girl and this is a Glendale party after all.'

'From what I've learned, it doesn't matter where the party is, only the mood you bring to it,' I replied. I had once had a brilliant time at bingo with a girl I had worked with. I wondered where she was now. Maybe I should have kept in touch with her.

'Anna, you're trouble, aren't you? I knew it the first time we met,' Adam said, draping an arm around my shoulders.

'I don't know what you mean,' I said with false innocence. My gaze drifted back to Cameron, who was watching us. Again, I couldn't decipher his expression, which was annoying.

'Well, I for one am going to make a toast to causing some trouble in Glendale,' Lorna declared, raising her glass. 'This village could do with shaking up a bit.' Glen and Adam clinked her glass with theirs enthusiastically. I followed suit but Cameron just lifted his glass before taking a long gulp.

'I can't wait,' I said, smiling at Adam who still had his arm around me.

If there was one thing I was good at, it was causing trouble, right?

Chapter Twenty-Two

My pleasure! It was a well-deserved fabulous review. I came home feeling so relaxed and refreshed. And again, your food was so delicious! I'm so jealous you get to live in Glendale. I will definitely come back. I think my boyfriend would love it. Have you thought any more about working with food? I really think you should. Chloe xxx

'Everything okay?' Beth asked as I looked up from my phone. I put it down after staring at Chloe's message. It was early morning on Sunday so only Beth and I were in the kitchen at the Hall, both drinking strong black coffee. I'd come back from my run and then Beth had joined me in her pyjamas.

'Fine. I just heard from the woman who reviewed Hilltop. She really loved it.'

'I'm so pleased for Heather. She's already getting lots more bookings. She's decided to stick to bed and breakfast for this summer season and then see if she wants to hire a chef for the second year. I think she might ask you if you want to do it.' She looked over her cup of coffee at me. 'I mean, if you wanted to do it this year, I would find someone else. I wouldn't want to hold you back from doing something you really love.'

I shook my head quickly. 'Oh no, I wouldn't be ready for something like that.' My mind started thinking about next year, but that was crazy. I wouldn't be anywhere near Glendale then anyway. 'I like this for my summer job.'

'Well, it's something to think about. I see you smiling when you cook. It seems to make you happy.'

I hadn't realised that I did that. I shrugged. 'I enjoy it but I'm not a professional. Anyway, I already have a ticket to Ibiza.'

'That sounds fun,' she replied but I could tell she wasn't really telling the truth. 'Speaking of Heather, I need to book something for her hen do. She is happy to leave it up to me, but I'm feeling the pressure, I don't mind telling you.'

'You've known her a long time, huh?'

'We were at school together although we did lose touch when I lived in London. When I came back though, it was as if no time had passed. I guess that's what true friendship is like, right? So, yes, I need to make it special.'

I just nodded. I had no experience of that kind of friendship. Izzy came in then, followed by her grandmother.

'Oh look, a murder mystery weekend in a castle. It's Agatha Christie themed,' Izzy said, looking at something on her phone.

Beth stared at her daughter. 'Tell me everything.'

'Why do you have that look on your face?' Izzy asked her, suspiciously.

'Because you might have just saved my life, daughter of mine.'

'Well, it's not the first time, is it?'

I smiled as I poured out more coffee. Beth and Izzy were so sweet together, you could just tell how close they were. It made me think of my mum. I wished we were as close. We had been once. Same for my dad and Brodie too.

Maybe we could be again.

I thought of the guitar my family had given me. I had played it in my room last night, trying to learn a new song, and it was already bringing me joy. I was grateful for that. I pulled out my phone again and messaged Brodie. Maybe while I was here, I should see if there was any chance of us repairing our fractured relationship.

—

'This is one of my favourite spots,' Brodie said as we got out of the car. I had messaged him to ask if he wanted to hang out after he'd finished his service as it was my day off. Emily was helping Heather and Beth with some wedding planning at the Hall so he was on his own. He suggested we went for a picnic like we had loved as kids so he drove us out of the village to a park, which had a hill that we walked to the top of and spread out the picnic blanket there.

'Great view,' I agreed, looking out at the fields and trees stretching out below us. I settled down on the blanket and watched as he opened the basket he had brought and pulled out food and drink. 'Remember where we used to go when we were younger – where we could see the castle? We used to always wonder what they were doing inside it, not realising no one actually lived there.'

'Mum and Dad never shattered the illusion, did they?' he said, fondly. 'Here, I got you the vegetarian sausage rolls you like.' He handed them to me and poured lemonade into plastic cups. 'Is there anything better than bread and brie?'

I shook my head as I piled up my plate, touched he had brought along my favourite foods. I thought back to telling my parents I wanted to go vegetarian, when I was sixteen, and they had exchanged a look that said 'here we go again' and that had spurred me on to never go back to eating meat. 'So, does Emily spend a lot of time with Heather and Beth?' I asked him as I bit into a roll. I had never had best friends, and I couldn't help but be curious about their friendship.

'They try to but it's not always possible with how busy they all are. The three of them are really close though. I suppose we've all been through a lot together these past couple of years. So many life changes. Getting married, having children, changing jobs, starting businesses... I know you think that Glendale is quiet but there always seems so much going on to me.'

I thought about how they had all been through these big changes in life and suddenly I felt like I was trailing behind. I had done none of them. And I still wasn't even sure that I wanted to. 'There's more going on than I realised. Like the garden party next weekend. And then there's Beth and her weddings.'

'I still remember the first garden party I attended with Emily. She hadn't been here long and talking to her there was when I first realised that I had met someone important. Of course, I didn't know how important she would be but I felt it pretty much as soon as we met.'

'I really don't believe in love at first sight.'

'It wasn't love at first sight but we had a... connection, you know?'

I was annoyed to find an image of Cameron popping into my mind. 'I guess I understand what you mean. And it's all worked out for you two, hasn't it?'

'It'll happen for you too. I mean if you want it to, that is.' He smiled. 'How are you getting on with the guitar?'

'Still learning but it's fun, I've been watching YouTube videos and trying to learn some new songs. I was thinking maybe I could have lessons, if I was staying somewhere for a while.' I shrugged. It was hard to plan things like that when you knew you were going to move on again soon. 'Thank you for asking Dad about it. It was a really lovely surprise.' I knew now that was the surprise Emily had meant, and it made me happy that they had done that for me.

'I think Dad was touched that you had such fond memories of going to the gigs with him. He has them too, you know. And he'd love to teach you more songs. If you stayed closer to home that is.'

I took a bite of bread, avoiding his gaze. It was so hard to imagine staying in one area or being nearer home again, I'd been avoiding both for so long. 'So, how are you feeling? About being a dad soon?' Time to move the conversation off of me, I decided.

Brodie's face lit up like a light had been switched on inside. 'I really can't wait. I mean, I already feel like one with Iona. Obviously, Greg is her dad and he sees her every couple of weeks and she stays with him. But mostly, day-to-day, she lives with us, so she feels like mine. But to have a baby with Emily is the icing on the cake. I'm so excited and so is she. Em thinks it's a boy but we don't mind either way. I just can't wait to be a family of four. And wherever you are, you will come back, won't you? To meet him or her?'

Brodie looked so hopeful that I had to nod. 'Of course.'

'Because we would love you to be their godmother. I already talked to Emily about it,' he continued.

I stared at my brother. 'Really?'

'Why do you look so shocked?' He laughed. 'There is no one we want more.' He reached over and gave my hand a quick squeeze. 'You will, won't you?'

I was still so taken aback but I couldn't deny the burst of joy inside my chest. I nodded and looked away, trying to hide my pleased smile. Maybe we really could move on from the past. That thought was too incredible for me to really believe but I wanted to.

'I'm so glad you're here, Anna,' he replied, picking up another veggie sausage roll. 'These are surprisingly good, aren't they?'

I smiled, feeling for once the same way as my brother – pleased that I was here in this moment with him. I pulled my phone out and told him to lean in for a selfie. It felt like a moment I wanted to capture.

And when I looked at it, I realised I looked happier in the photo than I had for a long time.

Chapter Twenty-Three

By Friday, the day before garden party, the weather had cheered up and we were greeted with blue skies and sunshine each morning. The Hall grounds were being spruced up ready for the party. Beth was on a high after the success of her first wedding and was in her element directing everyone. She told me they held it each year to raise money for the village, charging an entry fee, and local businesses helped out as well with food and activities and a local band played during the day. Everyone was given a job to do to make sure it could be a success – even Izzy was shooed out of her reading room to join in.

'Thanks so much for helping me,' Heather said as we put up a folding table, which was going to be for her to sell their farm produce. Emily had set up a table to sell cakes and Sally would be running the Hall table, which was selling home-grown produce and cute bits from their shop, like watering cans with plants in, succulents in pots with faces on, and honey from the bee hives. 'Rory and Cameron are at an auction with our cows so Dad is looking after Harry at home. Chloe said you two had been in touch. I still can't believe how enthusiastic she was about her stay with us.'

'Lift on three,' I said as we stood the table up on the grass. 'I think everyone likes an escape from their life sometimes and where better than on a farm in the High-lands? It's so different from her London life. She loved toasting marshmallows around the fire.'

'That was so fun,' Heather agreed. She put her hands on her hips to survey the table. 'It looks good. Chloe really rated your cooking. She was right too: you should think about doing it for a job. I know you'll be gone soon but if you ever want to come back to Glendale, I think Hilltop could use you.'

I smiled. 'That's so kind of you. I will remember that. So, what exactly happens at a cow auction anyway?' I started pulling out the chutneys and jams from the box she had carried over from her car.

'We take the cows and basically show them off to other farmers looking to breed cattle. Our Highland cows have a good reputation so we usually are able to sell what we need to sell. And it's a good opportunity to meet with other farmers and talk about things going on – Rory loves it. He took Cameron along as we're looking to buy some sheep for Hilltop and there might be some there that will work.'

'Has Cameron always worked with you?' I asked, hoping that I sounded casual.

'He has helped out on Fraser Farm for years with his uncle. First, in school holidays and then he went to university so we didn't see him as much but when he came back we got the opportunity to buy Hilltop and he was looking for a job so it worked out perfectly. I thought he'd run off from Glendale actually but, thankfully for us, he stayed. I suppose I did the same coming back home after university. We're such a strong community. And some-times things happen, don't they? To throw off your best laid plans.' I saw her expression and I was intrigued. What had happened to make her and Cameron come back? She noticed my raised eyebrow. 'My mother died so I came back to be with my dad. I suppose we all have a story as to why we're here. Why we stayed, why we came back, but it doesn't matter in the end. I would never want to leave now.'

'Anna, can you hold this ladder for me, please?' Beth called over then, so I left Heather, thinking how it was interesting that everyone here had pasts but that it didn't seem to matter to them, they cared about each other and supported each other no matter what. Maybe I shouldn't be so scared of my own past. Maybe people here would understand more than I thought they could. But I had never really opened up before and I wasn't sure I would even know where to begin.

I felt, though, that maybe if I could find the words then there were people here who would listen. And I'd never felt that way before.

—

Saturday arrived and it was a gorgeous day. It was the last weekend in June and summer was in full swing. The sky was cloudless blue and the sun was bright and warm. It put the whole household in a good mood. I even caught Caroline humming to herself.

The garden party started just after lunch so we all headed into the grounds to check everything was ready, and people started filing in who were running stalls or games and the band did a sound check on the makeshift stage at the end of the lawn. There were even pedal boats on the stream for people to take out.

Beth pulled me away from house duties to help in the garden again, which was fine by me in such lovely weather. I put on my denim shorts and Converse with a shirt I tied up to leave a strip of bare skin above my belly button. I joined Emily, who had arrived with the baked goods, and helped her set up her table. Jules, the manager of her bakery, would be running the stall but Emily wanted to make sure it looked perfect. She was wearing another floral dress with sandals, her blonde hair tied up and looked as glowing as ever, her bump getting bigger by the day, it seemed. 'Brodie really enjoyed your picnic last week,' she said as she adjusted the blue gingham tablecloth, making sure it was straight. 'He hasn't stopped going on about the veggie sausage rolls either.'

I laughed, pleased. 'They were very good. I suppose we haven't done much just the two of us in a long time.'

'I think it's great you are now. It's never too late. And family is so important, right? I think this looks okay, what do you think?'

The table recreated Emily's bakery, with the blue and lemon colours and the delicious cakes. 'It's perfect. And I really like your dress, it suits you.'

'Thank you. Do you know, I was thinking the same thing about your outfit. I get very jealous of your figure. I'm really starting to balloon up.' She smiled. 'Right, I'd better go and get Brodie and Iona. We should all catch up later, yes? It'll be lovely for Iona to get to know her auntie better.' And then she gave me a quick kiss on the cheek before strolling off. I liked the sound of being an auntie, I admitted to myself.

'Anna, Mum says can you show the ice cream truck where to go?' Izzy called out as she walked past carrying a jug of what looked like Pimm's and lemonade. 'She wants it by the stage, I think.'

'No worries,' I called back, heading to the driveway to tell the driver where to go. People were bustling around everywhere getting things ready and I enjoyed the energy in the air. It was nice feeling like part of a team here, all pitching in together to make something special, and I was looking forward to the afternoon and getting some time to relax and enjoy everything we had set up this morning. Adam and Lorna and their friends would be here soon and we would have fun, even if Cameron came with them. I wasn't going to let anything shake off my good mood today, I decided.

After I had directed the ice cream truck, I had to help the band lug their gear to the stage and then Sally needed help setting up her summer punch stand, and the day flashed by until suddenly it was time to open and people began pouring into the grounds. Everyone walked from the village and the grass was soon covered with people. It seemed as if the whole of Glendale had showed up, which they probably had, as entertainment was few and far between, and I even recognised most of them already.

'Anna!' Heather waved to me as she and Rory walked over, their son holding each of their hands, and Heather's dad was just behind them chatting to John. I couldn't help but crane my neck to see if Cameron was also there but there was no sign of him or his uncle, Angus. Perhaps they were staying on the farms. I wasn't sure whether to be relieved or disappointed. 'What a great turnout already,' she added when they reached me.

'Ice cream!' Harry cried out in delight when he saw the van.

'He will never sleep tonight,' she said, shaking her head as she let him pull her and Rory towards it. I laughed as they went, and then I saw Cameron walking up the lawn with Adam followed by Lorna and Glen. Cameron was wearing long shorts and a shirt and I tried not to look at his legs but failed. Adam was also in shorts and Lorna had on a denim dress and looked really pretty. I wondered if Cameron had noticed or not.

'Go and hang out with your friends,' Beth said as she passed me. 'You've been a massive help this morning, enjoy yourself,' she called as she went to greet Heather. I smiled at her then took a breath before walking over, telling myself to treat Cameron as just that – a friend.

'There you are,' Adam said, breaking into a grin and leaning in to kiss me on the cheek. His arm rested on the small of my back as he kissed me and I couldn't help but flick my eyes towards Cameron, who had turned away. I felt a dip in my stomach and I knew that it wasn't from Adam's kiss. I hated the way my body was betraying me.

I threw on a smile. 'Right then, where are the drinks?'

'That's my girl,' Adam said.

'This way,' Lorna replied, setting off. I went after them and then couldn't help but glance back. Cameron waited a beat before following us.

Chapter Twenty-Four

I didn't think I would enjoy a garden party as much as I was enjoying this one. After several glasses of Sally's punch, everything felt fun. We played the games stalls, danced to the band and piled our plates at the buffet table before finding a quiet spot on the grass under the shade of a tree to eat as the afternoon faded into early evening. The sun had been out all day and my arms felt brown and warm and I was in a pleasant punch haze. Adam sat next to me as we ate and drank; Cameron, Lorna and Glen were opposite us, and some of their other friends were nearby. I could see Izzy and Luke playing with Harry, Izzy's cat sleeping in a patch of sun nearby, Heather and Beth eating with their families, and everyone looked happy and chilled as things began to wind down ever so slightly.

I spotted Brodie, Emily and Iona so I got up to go over and see them. 'Are you having fun?' I asked. They were sitting in a little circle near to their friends. Emily had a huge plate of food and Brodie was holding Iona to feed her. I had a funny feeling in my stomach again when I looked down at them. They just looked so comfortable and happy together. I felt for a moment as if I'd intruded on something.

'It's been a lovely day. We've hardly seen you though,' Emily said. 'Have you enjoyed it?'

'It's been fun.' I looked at Brodie. 'Do you remember when we went to that summer fair when we were on holiday in Cornwall? This reminds me of that.'

He smiled. 'I do. And Dad got out his guitar and we all had a sing-song as the sun set on the beach.'

'We should do that!' Emily cried excitedly. 'Now most of the crowd has gone home.' She looked up at me. 'You should bring out your guitar.'

'I'm really not good enough…' I began.

'It would be lovely,' Brodie agreed, cutting off my protest. 'I bet everyone would love it. Go on, Anna.'

'Please,' Emily added.

It was hard to say no to them when they were looking at me so hopefully, and I couldn't help but agree it would be a fun end to the day. 'Oh, okay, but don't blame me if I'm rubbish.'

I set off towards the house and was only aware of someone following me when I started to climb the stairs. I turned to see Adam behind me. 'What are you doing?'

'I've never seen inside. Where are you going? Can I see your room?' he asked, grinning as he climbed up after me.

I rolled my eyes. 'Come on then. My brother wanted me to get my guitar.'

He whistled as we walked upstairs. 'It's really huge, I reckon my entire flat would fit onto this landing. I can't believe you get to live here.'

'Just for the summer,' I said but I realised as I walked to my room it was feeling more like home than anywhere I'd worked before. I reasoned it was because the house was so old and had housed generations, so it was a special place. And the family were welcoming and warm too which helped. 'This is me.' I led Adam inside and went over to get my guitar as he slowly looked around.

'You sleep in a four-poster bed? I think I need to step up my game, you'll be getting used to the finer life here,' he said, grinning and stepped closer to me.

'That's right, I'm just waiting for my Prince Charming now,' I joked as I picked up my guitar. I looked at Adam objectively. He was nice looking and was clearly attracted to me. I knew that before I had come to Glendale, he was someone I would have had a fun summer fling with. But I thought about how it had felt when Cameron kissed me, and everything became a little bit cloudy in my mind. It was as if my world had always been black and white but Cameron was making it grey. And I didn't like it.

'I can be a prince,' Adam said. I felt like my guitar was a barrier between us and I was glad of it. 'If you'd let me. Why don't we spend some time together alone, and I'll prove it to you.' He reached out to stroke my bare arm. 'We're having fun today, aren't we?'

'Definitely,' I said. 'But I won't be here long, I'm not looking for anything...'

He shrugged. 'Works for me. I like you, Anna. Sometimes it's as simple as that.'

Again, Cameron flashed in my mind. It should have been that simple, I knew. It had always been that simple for me. Why was it not simple now?

'Come on, I need to take this outside,' I said.

'Let me carry it,' he said, taking it from me. 'See, I can be princely, right?'

I chuckled. He was funny. 'It's a good first step.' I led the way back downstairs, Adam close behind me, and he took my hand in his as we walked down the stairs. I didn't have the heart to pull it away but when I reached the bottom, I stopped short, and Adam walked into me.

Cameron had just come in through the front door and was looking up at us, and our entwined hands.

'Anna is planning a singalong,' Adam told him, not bothered in the slightest. It felt to me as if the room had grown smaller though. 'Come and join us.' He nudged my back so I carried on walking, aware Cameron was watching me closely, and my cheeks had turned pink. I didn't know why. I hadn't done anything wrong.

'Beth asked me to find you. She wants to make a speech,' Cameron said, finally, clearing his throat. He looked away from us. 'So, uh, yeah.' He shoved his hands in his pockets and walked back out the door.

Adam shook his head. 'Cameron is being even weirder than usual, I swear,' he said as we followed him outside.

'He's always weird then?' I asked, curiously.

'Not weird. Just quiet. He's had a lot to deal with, I know, but I keep telling him that he shouldn't hide out in those woods on Hilltop all alone. He'll end up turning into a caveman.' He chuckled but I saw genuine concern for his friend flash in his eyes. 'I'll get us some more drinks. Meet you over there,' he said, nodding to the group of people sitting on the lawn. I longed to ask him what Cameron had had to deal with but Adam took off. It was now mostly just family and friends left in the garden. Beth was standing up, ready to speak, so I hurried over with my guitar, joining Emily and Brodie again, watching as Cameron went to sit with Rory and not where we had been before. I thought about what Adam said. Cameron hadn't always been like this, it was clear, just as I hadn't always been the way I was. Did that explain the strange connection I felt with him? What had happened to Cameron to make him close himself off from the world, even from his school friends like Adam?

And why did I want to know so badly?

'I hope you've all had a lovely day,' Beth was saying. 'I love having this annual tradition so we can all get together and enjoy a summer's day out, and raise lots of money for the village too. Thanks everyone who has worked so hard to make it a really great day. Feel free to stay as late as you like, there is still plenty of food and drink left and I think there will be an incredible sunset to enjoy later too!' Beth gestured to the sky which was still bright. Everyone clapped and cheered as she raised her glass of punch.

'And Anna is going to provide some entertainment,' Adam declared loudly as he joined me with two drinks.

'I'm so excited,' Emily said as she placed her sleeping daughter in her pushchair. As there were only about thirty people left, everyone gathered closer and I took a long gulp of the drink Adam gave me for some Dutch courage.

Sitting cross-legged on the grass, I held the guitar on my lap, and called out for requests, warning everyone I was still learning and didn't know that many songs yet. Brodie beside me asked for another Beatles song we used to sing with Dad when we were younger, and one he knew that I knew how to play. I gave him a grateful smile and started playing. I sang along, hoping everyone would join in. Pretty much everyone knew the words to all The Beatles songs, didn't they? You just grew up with them.

It took a minute for people to join in but I didn't mind. I had an okay voice and one that suited an acoustic guitar, a little bit folksy I suppose I would describe it as – slightly husky, like my speaking voice. Soon Brodie joined in and then Rory, who surprised me with his strong, deep voice. Heather too sang beautifully. They had been keeping their talents quiet, I thought. I smiled as the chorus soared with Scottish lilts and I felt myself get lost in the music again.

I loved how I felt so present in this moment. I wasn't thinking or worrying about anything but keeping up with the chords.

I looked around me as we did another round of the chorus. Everyone was enjoying themselves, I was pleased to see. I couldn't help but search out Cameron. He wasn't singing along but was watching me with one of his intense looks. When our eyes met, he smiled, and it felt like we were back around the fire at Hilltop, the same electricity crackled across the space between us and I wondered if his mind was also replaying how it felt to be in his bed together.

'You're so talented, Anna. What with this and your cooking,' Emily said when everyone was clapping after the song had ended. 'I think maybe your sister got all the good genes,' she joked with her husband.

'Way to bruise my ego, Em,' he replied, looking wounded.

She leaned over to kiss him and I heard her say in a low voice, 'But you have many other talents, don't worry.'

'I love you,' he said back, and I felt the same dip in my stomach. I looked across at Cameron, who also seemed to be watching them. I longed to know what he was thinking.

'Do you know "Your Song?"' Lorna asked me then. 'That's such a great singalong song.'

'One of my all-time favourites,' I replied, glad that was one I had learned too. I started playing, and everyone quietened down again, joining in faster this time. When I looked at Cameron again, he was singing along softly, and my lips curved into a smile to see that.

–

I walked down the stairs humming to myself. It was late now. The sun had set and the garden was lit up with lanterns and solar lights that were hidden in flower pots. Most people had gone now, just leaving the Glendale Hall family, Heather and Rory, my brother and Emily, and Adam and his friends. Plus the ladies who worked at the shops in the village. And it was a merry party – we'd all had too much punch. I slipped inside to put my guitar away and grab a hoodie as there was a chill in the air now the sun had gone. I had loved the singalong and was glad Brodie and Emily had persuaded me to do it. It had really been a lovely day. Beth and Sally were making hot chocolates and bringing out cookies for everyone before we all called it a night and the kitchen smelled delicious as I walked through.

'I didn't know you could sing and play like that,' a quiet voice said as I went back out into the garden. Cameron was sitting alone on one of the stone steps just by the house, holding his phone. 'Just checking Angus was okay,' he said, gesturing to it. We were away from the others and I felt the same flutter of nerves being alone with him as I always seemed to.

I sat down next to him, listening to Beth and Sally laughing as they made drinks through the open kitchen door. 'I haven't for a long time. I used to love it growing up and then I learned to play a couple of years ago – my dad just gave me his guitar so I'm learning again. I think I forgot that it brings me joy, and that I should hold on to things that bring me joy.'

Cameron looked across at me. 'I think I forget that too sometimes.'

'After my accident, everything changed. I was only thirteen and yet I had faced death. I kept thinking "why was I saved?", and I thought I had to live this huge life for it to make sense, do you know what I mean?' I was vaguely aware that I was close to drunken rambling but I wanted him to understand me. Maybe so then I could understand him. 'I try to travel, to do everything I want, to try new things, to be fearless, to keep moving, never settling. Some days I think I'm living life to the full, other times I feel like all I'm doing is running away.'

Cameron was silent for a moment, still watching me. I had never met anyone who looked at me like he did. I wasn't sure if I liked it. I felt uncomfortable, like he was pulling back layers from me that I would much rather keep covered. 'You should never feel guilty that you survived, Anna. You are more special than you realise. Just being you is enough.' He reached out to push back a strand of my hair and then quickly put his hand down again as if he realised he shouldn't be touching me. I wanted to tell him to touch me more but then he spoke again. 'I feel like I'm the opposite of you. I hide, I don't run. I stay safely at Hilltop in my cabin and I don't let the world come near me.'

'You let me near,' I half-whispered, staring back at him. We were just inches apart and everyone in the garden felt very far away.

Cameron shook his head. 'That was a mistake. Something that I haven't let happen since...' He trailed off. 'Why can't I stay away from you?' he whispered.

'I don't understand why you think you need to.' I leaned in, unable to help myself, and Cameron moved too, our lips touching gently, so softly that I might have imagined it if not for how it sent a shiver down my spine.

Cameron pulled back and looked at me again. 'Anna, I...'

'What is it?' I asked, wishing he would pull me to him again.

'I can't.' He stood up so abruptly my mouth fell open. He turned and walked towards the driveway, walking away from me furiously, shaking his head.

I wasn't going to let him just leave like that. I jumped up and tore after him. 'Cameron, you can't just walk away!' I caught up with him before he reached his truck and grabbed his arm. 'What is so wrong with kissing me?'

He looked at me, his face full of anguish. 'Because I'm not good for you. I'm not good for anyone!' He shook my hand off his arm. 'We need to stay away from each other.'

I stared at him. I felt this need to stay away from people too but why didn't I feel it with him? It was so confusing. 'Cameron, I'm so scared. Of the past, the future, of saying my fears out loud but I don't know, when I'm with you, I feel like maybe I don't need to be as scared anymore.' I let it out in a rush. It was the most honest I'd been with anyone since my accident.

Cameron shook his head. 'You shouldn't feel like that with me. I can't let there be anything between us.' He opened his car door and made to climb in.

'Don't I deserve to know why?' I cried, angrily. 'I just opened up to you and you're not telling me anything. You know what? This is why I keep away from people. You're right, I'm better off on my own.' I was furious that I'd let my guard down for a moment. I turned to go.

Cameron took my arm this time, making me face him again. 'I'm sorry, Anna. I meant what I said before. This is not about you. You're… amazing.'

His touch burned my skin. 'Do you even hear how confusing you are?' I said, shaking him off me, fury raging through my veins. This man was making me feel things

I'd never felt before, and I was not a fan. My earlier envy of Brodie and Emily felt foolish.

'I lost someone, Anna,' he said, quietly. 'Someone I loved. When I was at university. She… she died.' He looked away from me. 'And it was all my fault. So, I can't be with you. I can't be with anyone. I don't deserve it. It was all my fault. And I can never forget that. Do you understand now?'

His words punctured me. They sounded so much like how I felt, I suddenly couldn't breathe.

Cameron looked at me then, as if willing me to say something, but I couldn't. It would mean telling him what I had done. And I'd never said those words to anyone. My head swam. I stepped backwards.

I saw his face crumble in front of my eyes. He nodded once and then climbed into his car, slamming the door. I watched as he hung his head and gripped the steering wheel for a moment. I opened my mouth to say his name but no words would come out. Instead, I watched as he started up his engine and drove away, not once looking back at me.

Standing alone in the driveway, what he said echoed around me as if it was on a loop, branding itself on my brain.

She died.

It was all my fault.

I thought about what I should have said but couldn't.

He died.

And it was all my fault.

Chapter Twenty-Five

A grey cloudy sky greeted me as I went on my morning run, which fitted my mood after the events of last night. I wasn't sure how long I had stood there after Cameron drove away but, finally, I started shivering. So I'd pulled the sleeves of my hoodie down and gone back into the garden, where I'd made my apologies, pleading tiredness, and left without any hot chocolate. Adam had tried to get my attention but I had pretended not to see, which I felt bad about this morning, but I had been desperate to be alone in my room.

Cameron's words hadn't stop repeating in my mind since he had left me.

Surely he couldn't have actually been responsible for his girlfriend's death? And yet he had looked so anguished when he had told me. He seemed to believe it, whatever the truth was. Maybe that explained our connection. Because I too was haunted by a death. One that I believed was my fault.

In my mind I replayed the accident that had injured me when I was thirteen.

Dad and I had been driving back from the supermarket. It was winter and it was dark, although not late, and the road was wet from an earlier rainfall. I was telling him about a party that a girl from school was having at a local nightclub, one that I really wanted to go to. 'It's not fair,' I said. 'It's a special under-eighteens' night.'

'You're thirteen, Anna. You're too young to go to a nightclub.'

'You played a gig at one last night.'

'You came with me, an adult. This would be with just your friends. You know your mum won't want you to go.'

'Everyone thinks I'm so sad at school. The fact I go to church every Sunday, and gigs with you on a Friday night. I never go to parties or sleepovers. But Brodie gets to do whatever he likes,' I complained loudly.

He sighed. This was an all-too-familiar argument. 'You know that your brother isn't supposed to stay out past ten p.m.'

'Well, he does and it's not fair.'

'I'll be speaking to him about that, don't you worry. Anna…' Dad turned to me. 'Be reasonable, love.'

'I'll be the only one not there.' I felt tears welling up in my eyes as I looked at him, pleading with him to understand. I slipped out of my seatbelt to swivel in my seat and look at my dad with pleading eyes.

'Anna, your seatbelt,' Dad said, reaching across to grab it.

'What about if I just went for one hour,' I said as he spoke. 'And— DAD!' I screamed the last part as two headlights were suddenly in front of us. All I remember then is my dad gasping and grabbing the steering wheel, a loud crunching sound, and then I was flying through the air and everything went dark.

I stopped running, bending over breathlessly. I squeezed my eyes shut to try to block it out but I couldn't. After Cameron said what he had said, it had been running over and over in my mind like a film on repeat.

A car had slid across the road and hit us head-on but I knew when I woke up that if my dad hadn't been looking at me and reaching for my seatbelt, he would have been able to swerve and miss it. Instead, I flew through the windscreen and ended up in a coma. My dad thankfully only suffered bruising from his airbag. But the other driver had died at the scene.

Everyone had called it an accident. But I knew that if I hadn't been arguing then Dad could have stopped it. It was my fault. And I had to live with that for the rest of my life.

And now I'd met someone carrying the exact same guilt as me.

I looked up at the road ahead. If I turned right, I would find myself back at the Hall. But I hesitated. I'd run for a long time but I still didn't feel ready to go back in and pretend I was fine, when I very much wasn't. It was Sunday so I didn't have to work. I turned left and looked ahead towards the village. There was one person who might help me to make sense of everything. The only person who would know what to do.

But it would mean speaking about something I'd kept inside for twelve years. I'd kept my guilt from my family for so long but I knew I couldn't move on until I spoke about it. And Brodie was a minister. He had to listen. It was his job. He had to tell me what God thought. What I should do. He couldn't turn me away.

Could he?

A bird flew overhead, making a high-pitched noise, snapping me out of my indecision. I decided to take it as a sign and I set off towards the vicarage, my body shaking with nerves.

Emily opened the door after I knocked, still in her pyjamas. 'Oh, sorry to come so early,' I said, faltering, having not really thought about the time.

But she smiled and gestured me inside. 'Not at all. We're just having breakfast. Would you like a coffee?'

'Okay,' I said, following her through into the kitchen. Iona was in her highchair and Brodie was eating toast and reading the newspaper. It reminded me so much of breakfast growing up that I paused in the doorway, overtaken by the memories.

'This is a nice surprise,' Brodie said, looking up to see me. 'Joining us for food?'

'Actually, I was wondering if you have a sec, please? To, uh, talk,' I said as Emily sat down at the table to pour me a coffee.

Brodie's eyebrow raised and he quickly glanced at his wife. 'Of course. Let's go into the living room.' As he stood up, I realised he was wearing his dog collar in preparation for the Sunday service but, for once, I was pleased. It lent an official atmosphere to our chat, making it easier to talk to my brother about something this important. I followed him into the living room with the coffee Emily had given me, Brodie carrying his tea mug. We sat on opposite sofas and he looked at me expectantly.

I was suddenly unsure where even to begin. 'I didn't think about what time it was, I was out for a run and...' I trailed off.

'It's fine, Anna. We have a couple of hours until I have to be in church and we like a leisurely breakfast on a Sunday before work. Is everything okay?'

I shook my head, taking a sip of the coffee to try to find the words. 'To be honest, no.'

'What's wrong?' he asked, immediately concerned.

I thought I should start with the easier part. 'Do you know anything about Cameron?'

He looked surprised again. 'I know him a little bit, why?'

'We sort of... got slightly close,' I said, not wanting to tell my brother I'd slept with him. 'But then he said he couldn't be with me because something had happened at uni. Something he blamed himself for.' I took a deep breath. 'It's really unsettled me. Because I'm not sure what he means but also because I blame myself for the past too. I've kept it to myself for so long. But I felt this connection with him and I can see he's pushing people away and I know I do the same thing, and I want to be able to stop but how can I after what I did?' The words all came out in a shaky rush. I had to stop to gasp in a breath.

'Slow down, Anna,' Brodie said, gently. 'What are you trying to tell me?'

I shook my head. Now I was here, I wasn't sure I could tell him anything. 'Okay, let's talk about Cameron then.' I nodded, relieved. 'Cameron came to talk to me not long after he returned from university, before he took the job at Hilltop. He was haunted by what had happened to his girlfriend.' Brodie sighed. 'I don't want to betray his confidence, Anna, but this has obviously distressed you. She died in a car accident and he feels a lot of misplaced guilt about it. I think you should talk to him. I couldn't make him see that it wasn't his fault. Maybe you can. But I don't want you to get hurt. I don't think he's ready to move on just yet.'

I nodded, taking that all in. 'A car accident?' We really do have so much in common. I wished, though, we didn't have *that* in common.

'Yes. Has it made you think about yours?' he asked, gently.

'Why do we never talk about it?' I blurted out.

'We thought it would upset you, I suppose.' He looked so confused. 'We can talk about it, though. I'm always here for you, I hope you know that.'

'Only because you feel you have to be, as my brother, as a minister...'

'Because I want to be.'

He said it so firmly, so sincerely, I looked up and met his eyes. 'Why, when you know what I did?'

'What do you mean?'

'The accident,' I whispered. I tried to swallow away the lump in my throat but it wouldn't budge. My eyes filled with tears that burned. 'I still feel so guilty.'

'What have you got to feel guilty about?' Brodie asked me, gently.

'When Cameron said it was all his fault, I was shocked but I understood because I know that my accident was all my fault too.'

Chapter Twenty-Six

'What are you talking about?' Brodie cried as he reached out to touch my arm. 'Why on earth would you think that?'

'Because I was distracting Dad when it happened. I was arguing with him. I took off my seatbelt and he turned to help me, to talk to me, to make me see sense, and then suddenly the other car was on our side of the road. He had no time to swerve or get out of the way. It was my fault that he couldn't stop it. That the car hit us.' I let out a sob deep from the back of my throat. 'It's all my fault that we got hurt, and that other driver… He died.' For the first time in years, I let the tears flow in front of my brother.

'No,' Brodie said so sharply that I looked up in surprise. He took my hand in his and squeezed it tightly. 'I can't believe you think that. That driver was drunk, Anna. His car skidded in the rain on the road and he couldn't control it. He was going too fast. He ended up on the wrong side of the road. He was driving so fast that there was no way Dad could have reacted in time. It was his fault, Anna. Not yours. My god. Have you really believed that it was? For all these years? Why didn't you say something?'

'Because I thought you all hated me,' I said, shocked. 'He was drunk? You never told me that.'

'But the police, they talked to all of us,' Brodie said, confused. 'They didn't tell you?'

'I got upset and the doctor told them to leave. My therapist kept telling me I had no need to feel guilty but I didn't believe her, and I couldn't bear to tell her what I'd done. And none of you wanted to talk about it. I thought... And then Dad stopped me going to the inquest.'

'He wanted to spare you the pain. He wanted to protect you, not to upset you. We all did. I can't believe you didn't know the truth. Anna, is this why you stay away from us, from your home?'

I buried my head in my hands.

Brodie wrapped his arms around me and I stiffened but after I moment, I opened my arms and hugged him back. We held each other tightly as I tried to get my tears under control. All the years I'd felt so guilty and ashamed. I thought my family didn't want me in their life. 'It really wasn't my fault?' I said, finally, looking up, wiping my tears away.

'I swear on God, on my family, on my unborn child... Anna, it wasn't your fault. And we want you here. We love you. We always have. We want to have you in our lives, to know you, to be there for you. We want to take care of you.'

'Why didn't I know?' I said, shaking my head. I'd had to write a statement for the inquest but I'd just written that I didn't remember anything clearly. I'd lied to the police out of fear and shame. And so much guilt. If only I'd spoken my fears aloud to someone, I could have saved myself years of running, of hiding, of being haunted by the past.

'Dad felt so guilty too. He used to talk to me about it. He thought he should have been able to do something.

Both of you felt guilty but you shouldn't have. Neither of you could have done anything. I promise you that.'

'I always felt angry with you,' I admitted then. 'That you thought my accident had given you a second chance, and a purpose, in life, when I felt the opposite.'

'God saved you that day, Anna. I believe that and I know He did it for a reason, even if you were unable to see it. I hope maybe you can start to see it now. You are special. You always have been.'

'I felt so restless afterwards. Like I had to do something to deserve being saved. Like I needed to run. I still do, but I'm tired. I look at what you have and I think that maybe I want that too. But I don't deserve it, I know that.'

'You do deserve it,' he said fiercely. 'You deserve to have everything you want. You went through something so traumatic, something that you should never have to go through so young, but you were given a second chance, Anna. And you shouldn't be scared of it, you should be happy about it. You should use it to live the life you want – not the one you think you should have or deserve, but the one you really want. One that will make you happy. One that will make all that pain you went through worth it.' Brodie took my hand in his. 'You are an incredible woman, Anna. You shine so brightly. I wish you could see that. You don't need to run. You don't need to feel guilty or scared. We all love you. God included. And, yes, I know you don't want to hear it but it's true. You deserve all your dreams to come true. I promise you that.'

For the first time in twelve years, I wondered if my brother was right. I felt relief. I felt lighter than I had in so long. I hadn't realised quite how heavy the burden was that I'd been carrying ever since that accident.

'You need to talk to Mum and Dad,' Brodie said then. 'We need to sort this out once and for all. We need to start being a close and supportive family again.'

'I don't know where to begin... Can I have some time?' I was so used to keeping things from my parents, the thought of being vulnerable and sharing everything I felt was scary. 'Please, Brodie. I will talk to them, I promise, but I need to think things through, make some decisions... first.'

Brodie thought for a moment and then nodded. 'I understand. And they will too. I promise. I won't say anything to them about what we talked about. I'll leave it to you.'

'Thank you. But what do I do about Cameron?' I asked then.

'I think you should talk to him,' Brodie replied. 'He needs to find a way to heal. And I think you can help him, and he can help you. You understand each other, and it isn't easy to find people you can connect with like that. Maybe if you talked to him, told him how misplaced your guilt has been, he might see that so is his. Even if the past has been hard, it doesn't mean the future can't be brighter. Maybe you can both let the past go and move on.'

'Thank you,' I said. I knew then why Brodie was such a popular minister. It wasn't easy to listen, to not judge people, to offer unbiased advice. I didn't think I could do it but Brodie thought I could. He believed in me. He always had. I'd always pushed back against that belief but now I wanted to grab hold of it.

I could be free. I could be free of guilt, of shame, of thinking that I didn't deserve my second chance. And if I could be, maybe Cameron could be too.

I had no idea what would happen but I realised that I wanted to find out. Brodie smiled at me, and I smiled back tentatively believing for the first time in a long time that maybe things would be okay.

–

I stayed for breakfast with Brodie and Emily and then I went back to the Hall.

Alone in my room, I allowed myself to do something that I had never let myself do before, out of fear. I picked up my phone and Googled my accident, searching the local press, and I found an article about it. Everything Brodie had said was true – the driver who hit us had been drunk and speeding, spinning out of control onto our side of the road, killing himself in the crash. They mentioned me struggling for my life in hospital, and there was a family picture before the accident. It wasn't as hard to look at us now. And there was a later report that I'd come home from hospital, and finally a report of the inquest, confirming again everything my brother had just told me.

I looked up after reading all I could find. I wished that I'd looked before but I also knew that I hadn't been ready until now. I was relieved and grateful that I knew the truth. My second chance hadn't been a mistake after all – I just needed to do something with it. I needed to try somehow to put it all behind me.

And maybe Brodie was right that I could help Cameron too. I wanted to try, otherwise I would regret it, I knew. And I didn't want to regret anything from now on. So, I got into Beth's car and drove to Hilltop Farm.

My stomach fluttered with nerves at the thought of being alone with Cameron again but I couldn't stand the thought of him feeling as guilty as I had. Even if he didn't want to see me again, I had to try to talk to him. He couldn't deny there was a connection between us. It terrified me and it obviously scared him too but I couldn't help remembering how his arms around me had made me feel. It was as if I had felt still and safe for once, and surely someone who had made me feel that way couldn't be the monster he seemed to think he was?

What if Cameron had been carrying a burden just like I had, a burden that he didn't need to carry? What if, like for me, just sharing the load made it feel lighter?

I still couldn't believe that I'd kept my guilt to myself for so long. I had no clue what to do now. Maybe I didn't need to run anymore. But what would my life look like if I didn't? It was a habit that would be hard to break I knew. I felt so much better though. I felt like I could have what I wanted now. That I did deserve it. I just needed to figure out what *it* was.

The farm was empty today and the breeze whipped my hair around my face as I left Beth's car and walked towards the wood. It was strange to be back at Hilltop. I walked past the farmhouse and through the trees towards the small cabin where Cameron lived. I walked as purposefully as I could up to the door and knocked quickly before I changed my mind and turned back the way I had come.

The door opened slowly and Cameron peered out. When he saw me, he sighed. 'Anna.' He didn't seem surprised, just resigned. He swung the door fully open and stepped back to let me in. I walked into the open-plan living area. The room was as clean and tidy as I remembered, with the bare minimum of furnishings. I sat down in one of the armchairs but Cameron remained standing, hovering by the TV, the only thing breaking up the white, bare walls. He folded his arms across his chest. 'Why did you come?' he asked, his voice sounding a little hoarse, as if he hadn't spoken for a few days. Perhaps he hadn't. Unless Heather or Rory or his uncle came to see him, without any guests, he was completely alone out here. Which was clearly what he preferred.

'We have to talk – you can't just say what you did to me yesterday and then never mention it again,' I said, leaning forward in the chair to try to reduce some of the distance he had put between us.

'Can't you just leave it alone? I told you why we—'

'I'm not here because I want to be with you,' I interrupted. I wasn't sure if I was fully telling the truth because when he met my eyes I felt a jolt in the pit of my stomach but that was something I was nowhere near ready for myself anyway. 'I want to help. I went to see my brother earlier. I told him that, after I spoke to you, I had to talk to him about my accident. When you said you felt guilty about your girlfriend, I understood that feeling. I've carried so much guilt around since my accident.'

'Why?' Cameron asked, surprised.

'I thought it was my fault. I was arguing with my dad and I distracted him. I thought if I hadn't then he could have swerved out of the way. Brodie told me that wasn't the case. That we were hit by a drunk driver on the wrong side of the road. He was speeding. The road was wet. There would have been no chance of my dad getting out of the way. And before I came here, I looked it up online. I have always been too scared to. But I found the inquest report. Everything Brodie said was true. It really wasn't my fault.'

Cameron sighed. 'I'm sorry that you thought it was. But you don't know anything about what happened to me.'

I decided to ignore that comment. 'Everything changed that day for my family and I always thought they blamed me in some way for that. But my brother, he was so shocked that I felt guilty about it. I don't know, maybe I've been punishing myself for a long time. Like I always wondered if I didn't actually deserve to survive that day,' I admitted in a rush, looking down at my hands, rubbing them together.

There was a short silence. 'That's crazy,' he said then. I looked up. 'That accident wasn't your fault and of course you deserved to survive. I've never met anyone so full of life before. You're so alive. You draw people to you—' he said before stopping abruptly.

'Tell me what happened, Cameron,' I said, my breath catching in my throat at what he said. He told me to stay away and then he said things like that. What was I meant to feel about this man? I'd never been more confused by someone before. 'Please. At least give me that.'

He hesitated but then he nodded. 'I met Kirsty at university. We lived in the same halls and on my first night there I spent hours talking with her. She was beautiful inside and out.' He shook his head. 'We fell in love so quickly. We spent all our time together and we talked about our future. She wanted to see the world, and I wanted to see it with her. In our final year though, things changed. She was spending more time with this guy who was on her course. I kept asking her about him but she swore they were just friends. And I tried to believe her. But I felt like she was slipping away. One night, she phoned to say she was having a drink with him and I went to the student union. I saw them together. They were definitely not just friends.'

'What happened?' I asked again as he fell quiet. I could see the pain it caused him to speak about it. It hurt me to see him upset. I wished I could go over to him but I knew it wasn't what he wanted.

He looked down then. 'I marched over and yelled at her. I felt like my heart had broken in that moment. She told me she was sorry but she loved him, not me. I walked away and I went home. It wasn't until the morning that I turned my phone on. I had lots of messages. I thought they were from her but no… I went straight to the hospital but she was already gone. She had got into a car with him. He'd been drinking too. They'd crashed. She died from her head injury. If only I'd been there…' he trailed off. 'I should have fought for her. I shouldn't have just walked away and left her with him.'

'No. You couldn't have known what was going to happen. She chose him, Cameron. That wasn't your fault.'

'But I always made sure she got home safely. I knew they were drinking. I should have checked.'

'You'll drive yourself crazy thinking like that though. "What if"s are impossible. Look at me. For twelve years, I've tortured myself with "what if"s about the accident. What if I hadn't been talking to my dad? Why did I take off my seatbelt? Why did we leave the supermarket when we did? Why didn't we wait just one more minute? And it's haunted me. Don't let this do the same to you. We can't change what happened. We can grieve. But we can't change it. What happened to Kirsty was awful. A tragic accident. But I promise you that it wasn't because of what you did or said — it wasn't your fault.'

'I still feel that guilt though. I loved her so much.'

'If you blame yourself forever, you'll ruin your life. She wouldn't want that, would she?'

'I don't know anymore. I thought I knew her but I didn't. I think that's why I keep away from people now.' He finally looked at me. 'When I first met you, I got so angry that you almost hit my tractor and then when you almost got in the car with Adam… But what made me angrier than thinking you were being reckless with your life was that I thought you were the most beautiful woman I'd ever met.'

'I'm sorry I put you through that. I felt so ashamed that I almost got in the car that night. I always think of myself as this fearless person but I'm not. I'm more scared than anyone. That's why I keep on running. I don't want to run anymore, but I don't know how to stop.'

'I don't want to feel guilty anymore, but I don't know how to stop.'

We stared at one another. How did two broken people begin to help one another? Maybe it was just impossible.

'Do you want me to go?' I asked him then.

'Yes and no. Do you want to go?'

I smiled thinly. 'Yes and no.'

Chapter Twenty-Seven

Cameron offered me a cup of tea. It felt kind of mundane after what we'd talked about but I agreed and when he asked me if I was hungry, I realised I was so he made us crumpets with butter and jam. It was a warm afternoon so we took it all outside behind his cabin where there was a wooden table and two chairs, the sun shining through the gaps in the trees. All I could hear was birdsong again. It really was completely isolated out here but it was peaceful and we sat in silence for a while as we ate and drank and just breathed it in. I could see why he liked living out here. It was calming for the soul.

'When did you start moving from place to place?' Cameron asked, breaking the silence.

'It started with uni. The only reason I went really was so I could leave home. I felt trapped there, I think. I couldn't talk to my family about how I felt. Brodie said they didn't want to upset me by mentioning the accident but I thought it was because they blamed me for it. I had to get away from all that guilt and silence, you know? I needed freedom. So, I went to uni but I felt trapped there too so I left after just a year. Then I went travelling and I just kept on moving. I always feel so restless. I can't settle. I'm always thinking about where to go or what to do next.'

'And there's never been anything or anyone that's made you want to stay somewhere?'

I took a sip of tea. 'No, not yet. Although I look at Brodie and Emily and I do feel envious. They seem so contented. I want that but I don't know how to feel that way. I worry sometimes that it's just not in me to be, well, happy, I suppose, like it is for other people.'

Cameron shook his head. 'Of course it is. What about when you cook or when you play the guitar? I've seen the smile on your face that they bring. You look full of joy.'

I smiled. 'That's a lovely way to put it.' This quiet man had a way with words. 'I suppose you're right. They do.'

'Then you should do them more.'

'What about you? What brings you joy?'

'At first, when I took the job here, it was because I wanted to be away from people and the world as much as possible. I couldn't face travelling without Kirsty so I came back to Glendale and when Heather and Rory offered me this job, it was perfect. But I found I do genuinely love it here. The peace and quiet. The hard work. Even the people coming to stay. I want people to know how wonderful it is out here. I like being with nature. But I also feel guilty. Like maybe I should be doing more. For Kirsty. Maybe I should do what she wanted to do with her life because she can't, does that makes sense?'

I smiled. 'You wish you did more, and I wish I did less. But I don't think there's a right way to live. You're right, though, about finding things that make you happy. And I think we both need to learn that it's okay for us to be happy.'

'Not easy, is it?'

I shook my head. 'Not easy at all.'

'It's like my Uncle Angus. He loved this girl once. Was going to leave Glendale and marry her but she passed away and then he got stuck. Stuck on Fraser Farm, alone. I

196

always told myself I'd be nothing like him. And now look at me.'

'He doesn't seem alone to me. He has Heather and Rory and Harry and Don and you… A family.'

'Yeah, I guess you're right.'

'You're not alone either. I feel like you all look out for each other here. It's nice. I was always kind of disdainful about Glendale. I thought it was this backward place, really. That I'd die of boredom here but I can see now why my brother loves it. There's a lot to be said for having supportive people around you. I always thought I was a loner. That I didn't need anyone. But maybe I don't need to push people away quite so much.' I smiled ruefully. 'Maybe it would be nice to get to know people better.'

'Maybe you should stay longer in Glendale then.' He reached over and brushed his fingertips over mine. I wasn't surprised now to feel a jolt of warmth from him but it still freaked me out. I wondered if he could feel it too. I decided not to mention my ticket to Ibiza. The count-down to the end of my time in Glendale. It felt both far away and far too soon. 'I've kept things to myself for so long. Just talking to you today has helped.'

'Same for me.' We looked at one another and my pulse sped up a little bit. I wondered if he was going to kiss me and I was sure he was wondering the same thing. But then he let go of my hand and I let out a breath.

'I wish I could give you more…' he said.

I shook my head. 'I'm not looking for anything.'

Cameron nodded. 'Friends then?'

'That's pretty new for me but yes. Friends.' I was sure I could get over my attraction to him. Neither of us were in a relationship place. I mean, I'd never had one and look at how Cameron's last one had ended. No, this was better. It would be enough for us. It had to be.

Cameron glanced at his watch. 'I have to go to Fraser Farm, I'm afraid. Angus and Rory asked me to help move some logs.' He looked at me. 'Don't suppose you fancy coming along?'

'Okay, why not,' I replied. I had no plans until later. Beth had asked me to have dinner with everyone tonight; they were having a Sunday roast even though it was summer, and my brother and Emily were coming along with Heather and Rory too. It still felt strange to be included in these gatherings like I was part of the family, but I was learning it was Beth's way. And although it was something I hadn't looked for before, I found that I didn't mind it half as much as I thought I would.

We drove separately to Fraser Farm and I thought over what had happened at Hilltop. Cameron was still carrying so much guilt about losing his girlfriend and I didn't think it would ever completely leave him, even if the accident clearly wasn't something he could have prevented. But I hoped I had helped a little bit. I knew what it was like to carry guilt over something that had been impossible to stop from happening. I knew how messed up I still was after my own accident. But after talking to my brother, it felt like there was a flicker of change on the horizon, like maybe things were shifting for me just a little bit. My summer in Glendale was helping me little brick by little brick. I hoped that it might end up being the case for Cameron too.

Fraser Farm greeted me then. I could see everyone was in the yard, turning to look at our two cars driving up the track towards the farmhouse. I wondered if they would think it was strange that I was with Cameron. Probably not, as they were all in each other's lives so much. Heather broke into a smile and waved when she saw me and headed over to greet me as I climbed out of the car. My eyes flicked to Cameron as he got out and he smiled over at me.

'This is a nice surprise,' Heather said. 'Don't tell me Rory has roped you into helping move our logs too?'

I laughed. 'I didn't have any plans so just tagging along really, but I'm game.'

'Well, when it comes to jobs like this it's definitely the more the merrier!' She slipped her arm through mine as we started walking after Rory, Angus and Cameron, who sloped off towards the barn. 'Basically, Angus built us a shed to keep logs in. We have a lot of log fires in autumn and winter so we go through a lot and thought we needed somewhere to store them. We need to shift the ones we bought from the yard into the shed. I'm sure we can keep up with the boys just fine, right?'

'Of course,' I replied, firmly. I looked at the pen of goats as we passed it. They were munching on the grass in the sunshine. I laughed as their sheepdog Darcy ran up to the fence to bark once at them before running off to catch up with Rory, weaving between his legs happily. 'I have always wanted a pet. I mean, I'm veggie, as you know, and I love animals but as I've moved around so much, I've never had one of my own. Except a hamster when I was really young.'

'Honestly, I was never a fan of animals and when I came here I thought they were all against me! I've had pigs in the kitchen, goats chewing through the fence, horses dropping apples on me and cows escaping. Darcy even chewed through my favourite slippers but now this place is home, and really they are part of the family.' She looked across at me. 'Maybe it's a sign you need to put down some roots and get yourself a pet.' She looked ahead. 'Someone to come home to. Or maybe a man instead.'

I couldn't help but smile. Heather's eyes twinkled. I knew she meant Cameron but I certainly wasn't going to comment on that. 'I think a dog sounds like less work.' She laughed along with me as we joined the men in the barn and Darcy came to sit beside me. I patted him as Rory showed us the pile of logs that needed moving to the shed, which was around the other side of the farmhouse, and suggested we make a line to pass them along to make it quicker and easier.

I didn't think I'd enjoy moving logs on a farm but it was quite fun tossing them back and forth to one another. Heather was in front of me and we chatted as we moved them. Behind me was Angus, who was even more quiet than his nephew, although Heather addressed several comments to him and received dry replies. His fondness for her shone through the twinkle in his eyes though.

'It must get really cold out here in winter,' I said as a summer breeze blew through my hair. Even though it was a warm day, the hairs on my arms stood up with it. The farm sat in a valley surrounded by high hills and I could only imagine how tough winters could be here even though it was an idyllic spot.

'It really does and when it snows we often have power cuts, which has taken a lot of getting used to for a townie like me,' Heather agreed as she passed me another log. 'This is why we need lots of logs! Getting up in the dark and cold was a huge shock to my system when I first came here.'

'You still complain now,' Angus reminded her as I passed him the log.

'Complaining builds up body heat. That's a fact,' she replied, airily, dropping me a wink. 'I thought I was a hardy Scottish girl before I moved here but nope. I was not.'

'I couldn't do it.'

'Probably not – you don't eat meat. You need a lot of beef stew to get through the winter, I can tell you,' she joked.

I smiled. 'I bet I could make you a veggie one that was just as good.'

'I actually bet you could. Angus, this girl is such a good cook. I keep hinting she should be the chef at Hilltop but she pretends not to hear me.'

'We all do that,' Angus said in a low voice. 'Cameron told me how great your food is. You don't want to be a chef though?' he asked me.

I was flattered Cameron had talked about me to his uncle and that Heather kept talking about me working at Hilltop. I shrugged. 'I don't know. I hadn't even really considered it before.' I couldn't pretend that the idea didn't excite me but there was no way I could work at Hilltop with Cameron, was there? Besides, that would mean living in the countryside, settling here in Glendale. I just couldn't picture myself doing that.

'Well, we have the whole summer to persuade you. I warn you – Glendale is very hard to walk away from.'

'Been here my whole life,' Angus called out cheerfully. 'We all have.'

'Emily was hooked after she came for Beth's wedding,' Heather said. 'You might not be able to leave even if you want to.'

'Are you going to kidnap me?' I said, shaking my head. 'Are you a cult in disguise?'

'If a cult eats way too much cake, drinks too much coffee and attends too many weddings then yes we are,' Heather said.

I was laughing too much to take the next log from her.

'What's the hold-up?' Rory called from the back.

'Anna can't stop laughing,' Heather called back. 'Angus is telling too many jokes again.'

That made everyone laugh and even Angus let out a snort at the likelihood of that happening.

—

When I got back to Glendale Hall, Beth pulled me excitedly into the utility room before the others from the farm followed me inside. 'Okay, so I was just going to tell you but you know what my mother is like so here,' she said, thrusting a cream and gold card at me. 'You know I said I was organising Heather's hen do?' she asked excitedly as I looked down at the invitation. 'Well, Drew and I got talking and we thought why not do a combined stag and hen do? We actually had one before our wedding at Loch Ness and Heather and Rory both said what a good idea it was. Brodie didn't want a stag do but the boys made him have a pint at the pub and we took Emily out for afternoon tea. I think we could all do with a little fun trip together. So, what do you think?' She babbled before demanding a response as I took in the words on the card.

'A joint hen and stag do murder mystery weekend? At a castle in Edinburgh?' I repeated, trying to catch up.

Beth nodded. 'Heather adores Agatha Christie, and we've never done a murder mystery before. I think Rory will love it there too. We can all have such a good night together. So, what do you think? Will you come?'

'You're inviting me?' I checked with surprise.

Then Beth looked surprised. 'Well, of course I am! You're part of the family now. We're all going.'

'All?' I enquired.

'Well, we'll never get Angus there, and someone needs to look after the farm, and Don has agreed to watch Harry for us, and my mum and John and Sally have bowed out gracefully to let us young ones enjoy ourselves, and Sally is up for watching Iona too,' she said with a laugh. 'But I checked and Heather has no retreats booked for next weekend so the rest of us can go – you, me, Drew, Heather, Rory, Emily, Brodie, Cameron, Izzy and Luke. So, what do you think? I think it will be really fun!'

I actually felt quite chuffed to have been included. I smiled at Beth who was staring at me impatiently. 'I'd love to come,' I said sincerely. It did actually sound really fun. I wasn't exactly an Agatha Christie fan but a night away at a castle was no hardship. The only other hen do I'd been invited on was Emily's but I'd pleaded work as an excuse, sure I wouldn't have any fun in Glendale. I could admit now I should have gone. I wouldn't make that mistake this time around. 'Thanks so much for inviting me.'

She beamed. 'Well, of course. I can't wait!'

'Me neither,' I replied, sincerely. I pocketed the invitation and followed Beth out into the kitchen to greet the others and prepare for dinner. I glanced at Cameron and wondered if he'd accepted his invite yet or not. Now we were friends, I thought it could be fun to have him there. I just wouldn't let myself think about the fact we'd be staying the night there together. I really wouldn't.

Chapter Twenty-Eight

Adam phoned me mid-week and asked me out for a drink just the two of us. I couldn't help but hesitate. Both because of my connection with Cameron and the feeling that Adam was just a friend to me. But I was in need of a night out. I had been helping Izzy and Luke finish off her library as well as the general house cleaning and the week was flying by. I was both excited and nervous for our upcoming weekend away so a few drinks at the pub sounded like a very good idea to me. I agreed to meet Adam at the Glendale Arms, hoping he wouldn't see it as a date but knowing deep down that he probably did.

I kept my outfit casual, and Beth offered to drop me off at the pub as she was going round to Emily's for dinner.

'So, you and Adam…' Beth glanced across at me as we drove to the village.

'He's just a mate.' I caught her smile. 'Well, okay, I guess he has said that he wishes we were more but I'm not sure. I've always been up for something fun, you know. I don't know why I'm overthinking it,' I said, half to myself as I looked out of the window.

'You don't have to do things just because you used to enjoy them. You can change… Sometimes what we want now is different from what we used to want, doesn't mean it's better or worse, just different.' She smiled. 'Maybe Glendale is working its romantic magic on you.'

'I think I'm immune to romance,' I replied.

'That's only the case if you've had any in the first place. Have you?'

I looked at her, startled. Perhaps she was right. After my failed first time, I had actively only sought out casual relationships. I couldn't describe any of my exes as romantic but then I certainly hadn't encouraged any romance in my life.

'I had flings during my time in London but no one I really cared about. Certainly no one I ever brought home to meet Izzy. Reuniting with Drew showed me that real love can't be stopped. It finds you when you least expect it, when you don't even want it sometimes. I didn't think I would get engaged in a Christmas trail or chase the man I loved through an airport but... that's what love does.'

'You chased him through an airport?'

She grinned. 'I did.' She pulled up outside the Glendale Arms. 'It was always Drew for me, even though I tried to pretend otherwise. Even though I didn't even see him for ten years. But it was worth waiting for.' She followed my gaze to where Adam stood waiting. He lifted his hand in greeting. 'You have to follow your heart at the end of the day.'

'I don't think I can trust mine,' I said, climbing out.

'Of course you can. You're just too scared to. Believe me, I know exactly what that's like. But one day you'll realise it's the only way you'll ever be happy. Have a good night, Anna.'

I watched her drive away, a little taken aback. I had never received as much life and love advice as I had since I came to Glendale. I felt like I should be annoyed that everyone kept trying to tell me how to live my life but I couldn't because I knew it was me asking them for advice, and all of them were on my side. Even though they hardly knew me. They all seemed to want to help me to be happy. But what if they were fighting a losing battle? Maybe I was missing the happiness gene.

Walking up to Adam, I smiled as he kissed me on the cheek and led me into the pub. 'You look great by the way. Do you want to get a table outside? I'll bring us out some drinks,' he suggested. I agreed and walked on into the beer garden, relieved that no one else we knew was out there.

I was replaying Beth's words when Adam reappeared. His eyes lit up when he saw me. I felt really bad that he liked me so much more than I liked him. It was weird. Usually, I would have enjoyed the attention and I would have just gone with the little bit of attraction I felt towards him. I would have been up for a fun fling with him. But now, I held back. Why did it feel different this time?

'I needed this. My boss was such a dick today,' Adam said after he'd taken a long gulp of has beer.

I sipped my wine eagerly, hoping it would put me in a better frame of mind. 'I don't actually know where you work?'

'I'm an estate agent,' he said. 'Yeah, I don't usually volunteer that information,' he joked. 'That's why I wanted to see inside the Hall finally. We always wonder if the family will ever sell the place.'

'Highly unlikely,' I replied. 'They love it. It's a special house so I can see why. Beth has so many money-making ideas on the go, I think they will be just fine.' I wondered how Izzy would feel once the house was passed down to her. Maybe she'd create an even bigger library then. That idea made me smile into my wine glass. 'Why was your boss such a dick then?'

Adam launched into the full story – basically, his boss came down hard on them for missing the weekly sales target and ranted at them for half an hour. 'What annoys me is he made no sales this week but I did.' He shrugged. 'But what is life without a manager to moan about, right?'

I nodded along. That had always been the case for me too, but I liked Beth too much to feel that way about her. I told him all about Hamish in Glasgow. 'Which is why I ended up in Glendale.'

'Well I'm glad you escaped him,' he said. 'And found your way here.' He smiled at me. He really was sweet. I felt bad for my lack of enthusiasm towards him being anything other than a friend. He went to the bar to refill our glasses and, after he left, the gate to the garden opened and in walked Lorna, Alastair, Glen and Cameron. As ever, my heart sped up at the sight of him, and when our eyes locked he smiled and made me wonder if his had done exactly the same. Adam returned then and sat down before seeing them. They all stared. It was obvious we were having a drink alone and no one knew quite what to do. I felt my cheeks turn pink as Cameron clocked Adam, and I wasn't sure why I felt so uncomfortable. I wasn't doing anything wrong, but it somehow felt like I was.

'I thought we'd be safe,' Adam said in a low voice as they made their way over to us. 'We never come here on a Wednesday if it's not quiz night. I'm sorry.'

'It's fine,' I reassured him before they reached us.

'Hey you two,' Glen said brightly. 'Mind if we join you?'

'Glen, they might want to be alone,' Lorna said quickly, flashing her brother an apologetic smile.

'We wouldn't want to intrude,' Cameron said, hanging back. I couldn't read his expression or his tone. We had agreed to just be friends so I was confused by the animosity I sensed. But I was also a little bit pleased by it, annoyingly.

'No worries, come and join us,' Adam said with his usual good humour. Under the table his foot brushed my leg. I moved away under the pretence of shifting to make room for Lorna.

'I'll get the drinks,' Cameron said.

'I need the loo,' I said watching as he walked away. I hurried after him. 'Adam just wanted to come for a drink. It's not a date…' I said when I had caught up to him, before trailing off because I knew Adam felt differently.

'You don't need to explain,' he said, softening a little as we walked inside the pub. 'We're friends. It's totally fine for you to have a drink with Adam,' he said, leaning on the bar. He glanced at me. 'I just wish you didn't look so good while doing it.'

I laughed. I liked Cameron when he was being like this – relaxed and slightly flirty. It made me think that maybe he could let go of the past one day. And that was good. For him, of course. I shouldn't think about what it could mean for me. Or us. 'Adam is just a mate to me. I feel bad though.'

'He's a good guy. Let him down gently, won't you?'

'Sure.' I leaned next to him. 'Do I need to prepare myself for seeing you here with Lorna?'

'Lorna? No. I told you, I only see her as a friend. And I still can't… Well, you know.' He shook his head.

'But if you could, who would you choose to have a drink here with?' I found myself asking, and hoping he might say me. Malcolm, the landlord, took Cameron's order then but I waited. I wanted an answer.

When we were alone, Cameron turned to me. 'You know it would be you.'

God. Why were his eyes so piercing? When he looked at me, I felt almost naked. He'd given me the answer I had been looking for but, somehow, I didn't feel good hearing it. What were we doing? 'I need to get back,' I blurted out, escaping quickly before things got even more intense between us.

Back at the table, Adam was telling his friends the same story he had told me so I sat quietly and finished my wine, not looking up when Cameron returned for fear that everything I was thinking and feeling would be written all over my face once I looked at him.

—

'I'm sorry we were gatecrashed,' Adam said as he walked me back to Glendale Hall.

'It's fine, I enjoyed it,' I assured him. We'd stayed for a few drinks and it had been enjoyable, even if I had tried to avoid Cameron's gaze all evening. Lorna had driven the others home, the designated driver, but Adam had suggested we walk back to the Hall and then he'd get a taxi. I knew we had to talk so we'd said goodbye to the others and strolled from the village together. It was a warm evening and the road was empty, sunset was only just approaching, another long Scottish summer day. Glendale was so peaceful in moments like this.

'I think you were relieved,' he said then, looking across at me with a sheepish grin, tucking his hands into his pockets.

I had to be honest. 'I'm sorry, I really am. I just think of you as a mate.' I nudged him with my elbow. 'You don't hate me, do you?'

'As if I could. I'm disappointed but I knew it really. Can't blame a guy for trying though, right?' He grinned and I relaxed. He wasn't heart broken or anything and hopefully we could just carry on as friends. I really did like him. 'You seem like you have a lot on your mind?'

'Do I? I mean yeah, I guess I do. It's a cliché but do you ever feel like you're at a crossroads and need to choose which way to go next?' I asked him as we made our way down the road towards the Hall. I could see it rising up in the distance and I was pleased to see it, looking forward to climbing into my bed. And I wasn't worried that I'd be alone or that it would be quiet there. I had got used to it. I even liked it more than I thought I would after being so used to noise and company and distractions.

'Sometimes. I was offered a transfer at work a few months ago, to London, but to be honest I chickened out.' He shrugged. 'I've lived in Glendale all my life but sometimes I think maybe I should do something like that, make a change.'

'I feel the opposite way. That all I do is make changes.'

'I guess I should go back to online dating too,' he said with a chuckle.

'I am sorry, Adam.' We reached the gates so I paused and turned to him. And he stopped too. 'I honestly don't know what I want.'

'It's all good, Anna. You don't need to worry. You'll figure it out. We both will. We're still young. No one has their life sorted, even if you think they do, right?'

'That's true,' I agreed. I had often felt like the only one who was lost but I knew now that wasn't true. And maybe I wasn't actually lost either. Just taking the scenic route through life instead. The long way round. 'Life would be boring if we all lived it the same way.'

'I think I can safely say you're not boring.' He leaned in and kissed me on the cheek. 'You've shaken up things around here without even realising it.'

'In a good way?' I asked tentatively.

'Might need to get back to you on that.' He grinned and I shook my head. 'Goodnight Anna.'

'Goodnight, Adam.' I waved and walked through the gates, pleased that things were good between us. I thought about the prospect of leaving here for Ibiza in September. My summer in Glendale was turning out to be much more enjoyable than I'd feared. I didn't like the thought of walking away from it as much as I had done.

For once, I quite liked the idea of being right where I already was.

Chapter Twenty-Nine

Friday arrived quickly and I packed a small bag for our overnight stay at the castle near Edinburgh. The whole house was in cheerful spirits and everyone assembled in the hall to wait for the minibus to take us to Edinburgh for the murder mystery weekend.

Izzy came out of her reading room holding her cat. 'I can't wait to see the bookshelves when we get back,' she said to me. John was putting up the shelves while we were away and then all it would need was the finishing touches and it would be complete. It felt almost like my project too and I was excited to see the end result. 'And I can get lots of inspiration on how to organise it because this castle has the most amazing library according to the internet.'

'We're supposed to be having fun this weekend,' her mother reminded her as she pulled on her camel-coloured wool coat.

'Books are fun, Mum,' Izzy said with an eye-roll. She kissed Ginny and put the cat down on the floor. 'And besides, the whole weekend is book themed so what did you expect?'

'Hmm. I didn't think this through, did I?'

'It's here!' Luke cried from the doorstep. He looked really excited. I got the impression that his family were a very different breed to Izzy's and it was lovely of Beth to include him, and me for that matter.

'Right, let's get this show on the road,' Drew said, picking up two bags.

'Have a lovely time!' Caroline called out to us. I followed Drew outside. We were making two stops, at Fraser Farm and the vicarage, to collect everyone else, before heading to Edinburgh. I couldn't remember the last time I'd gone away with other people – not since before my accident. I was excited. Like this was a school trip or something.

'Right, I've got music, I've got snacks, I've got games, let's hit the road!' Beth said as she climbed onto the minibus. Izzy cheered and even I clapped. Their enthusiasm was, as always, infectious. I sat by the window towards the back and we drove away from the Hall to collect Brodie and Emily and then we headed to Fraser Farm to pick up Heather, Rory and Cameron to complete our group of ten.

Cameron came to sit by me, the only empty seat left once he'd climbed aboard. He wore jeans like me although I was in a hoodie as it was chilly but he just wore a t-shirt. I breathed in the musky smell of his aftershave and returned his smile. As the minibus pulled away, I looked around me, suddenly suspicious. Everyone was in a couple – although obviously Izzy and Luke weren't a couple as such – but we were all paired up in twos, which put me and Cameron together. I looked at Beth, who was passing around a tin of sweets. I wouldn't have put matchmaking past her. She seemed to like to fix everyone's lives. But surely she hadn't noticed anything between me and Cameron. Or did she suspect something? Heather had made a couple of hints and they talked about everything, it seemed.

'I've never been to Edinburgh,' Cameron said as we set off towards the motorway.

'I went to uni there, for my one and only year. It's a lovely city.'

'I went to Loughborough uni. My love of football led me there. I studied sport science and education. I thought I might teach one day.' Cameron shrugged but I caught that haunted look again. His course had been changed by his girlfriend's accident. Like mine had been changed by my accident. It made me wonder where we both would be if they hadn't happened. We certainly wouldn't have ended up next to one another on this minibus, that was for sure.

'You still could. If you get tired of the farming life.'

'What would my uncle say?' he said with a smile but I knew he was still thinking about university.

'I studied English Lit, but I hated it. Staying in and reading? Nope I wanted to go out and have fun,' I said ruefully. 'If only I'd realised how much I enjoyed cooking, I could have studied that and would have stuck that out. I mean, maybe, I don't know.' I knew there was no point in "what if"s, but it wasn't always easy to stop yourself from thinking of them.

'It's never too late. You could study it now. You are really good at it.' He smiled across at me.

'Maybe.' I settled back in my seat. Yet another path that I could choose. But I didn't want to think this weekend. I wanted to just enjoy this trip. 'We really need to change the music,' I called out then. 'We need a singalong!' My suggestion was met with both cheers and groans. Cameron chuckled as we debated what to put on, and our conversation was left for now.

We arrived at the castle hotel in excellent spirits. We had sung until the driver had complained of a headache, eaten far too many snacks, and had a lively debate about the best sweets in a tub of Celebrations before quietening down as the castle came in view. It was outside of the city, set in lush green grounds, perched up on a hill, keeping watch over the city beneath it. It was made of light brown stone with two towers and narrow windows. The minibus drove up to the open door as a man in a green uniform stepped out to welcome us. We were ushered with our bags into the lobby and were transported into another world. The castle was decorated in dark wood and tartan, had beams across the ceiling and despite it now being July, a crackling log fire in the corner.

'Right, pre-dinner drinks and the mystery starts at four p.m.,' Beth said as she handed out the room cards. 'Meet in this room then,' she added, pointing off the lobby to the lounge. 'Until then, the day is yours.'

I took my room card but before I went upstairs Brodie waved me over to the corner with him. Emily was heading to their room already. Brodie touched my arm. 'I just wanted to check you were okay. You were sitting with Cameron. How did your talk with him go?'

'It was fine. Good, I think,' I said, realising belatedly that I should have told my brother what had happened. I was still not used to filling him in on my life like that though. 'He told me all about his girlfriend at university,' I added in a low voice.

Brodie nodded. 'It wasn't my place to tell that story but you can see why I thought you could help him. He has a lot of misplaced guilt. Like you do.'

'I'm working on it.' I smiled. 'I'll make sure he does too. I'm glad he talked to you. I'm glad I did too.'

He looked surprised and pleased. 'Anytime. For both of you. You know that.'

I nodded gratefully. I did now. We parted ways then and I made my way up the winding staircase to my room, which was in one of the towers, letting myself in and breaking into a smile as I stepped inside. The room was high up and looked out over the grounds – a wide window at one end offering a beautiful view, and in the middle of the room was a four-poster bed. Off the room was a lovely en-suite bathroom complete with white fluffy robe hanging on the door. My bag was next to the wardrobe, which was open. Taking a look, I saw a dress hanging in there with a note attached to it.

> *Dear Anna, this is for you to wear tonight. I bought us outfits for the era! Beth xxx*

I lifted the note off and looked at the dress – a long plunging silver gown. 'Wow,' I said aloud. Next to it was a fake fur stole, a pair of silver heels and a clutch bag. Beth had gone all out. I shouldn't have been surprised. No one had ever bought me a whole outfit like this before. I was touched to have been included in this and excited to dress up and solve a murder mystery. No wonder everyone at Glendale Hall was happy – they could afford to do things like this. I felt a little like Cinderella if I was being honest. This wasn't included in the housekeeper job description, that was for sure.

There were a couple of hours until we were due to meet downstairs so I ran myself a bubble bath in the en-suite, closing my eyes and letting myself relax into the hot water. I turned on my relaxation playlist on my phone and let the world slip away.

Afterwards, I pulled on the fluffy robe and took my time to dry my hair and put on make-up. I Googled the 1930s and pulled my hair into a wavy style, one side pinned back with a pearl clip I had brought with me. Obviously, my pink hair didn't really fit with the era but I did the best I could.

Pulling on the dress, I let out a little sigh. It fitted me perfectly. Beth really did have great taste. I stepped in front of the full-length mirror and appraised myself. The dress looked stunning and showed off my figure, the heels made me look so much taller, and I looked elegant, which I didn't think I ever had in my life before. Never having been someone who longed to dress up, I was surprised at how good I felt. I thought that maybe I could get used to this after all.

'Anna, you shall go to the ball,' I whispered to myself before sliding out of the room.

Chapter Thirty

Walking through the door into the hotel lounge felt like stepping back in time. The room itself was art deco inspired with a glossy marble bar, velvet shell chairs, a huge gold mirror taking up one whole wall, arty pictures on the other wall, and a black and white tiled floor. A white piano stood off to one side and someone was playing background music. The room was full of people dressed in 1930s style, with servers dressed in black and white handing out drinks and canapés.

I spotted Beth, who waved me over, so I walked through cocktail dresses and suits, taking a glass of champagne from a passing waiter. 'You look gorgeous,' I said, taking in Beth's sparkling dress. 'You too, Heather,' I added as I saw her smart suit. Drew and Rory were in dark suits and hats, looking a little uncomfortable in them. 'They've really gone all out.'

'You look so stunning,' Heather told me.

'Gorgeous,' Beth agreed. 'I can't wait for the murder. With how good we are at pub quizzes, we will definitely win,' she added, her eyes twinkling with her competitive spirit. 'Oh great, here are the others.'

I turned to see Brodie and Emily enter hand in hand, followed by Izzy and Luke, who both looked nervous and so sweet, and then following them was Cameron. I took in his grey suit and hat and drank a long gulp of my champagne. He looked way too handsome for me to handle. I saw him find me in the room and I was pleased to see that he did a double take. They joined us, all finding drinks, Beth checking that both Izzy and Luke had the mocktails and nothing alcoholic. Izzy looked much older than fourteen in her sequin dress and Luke looked so awkward in his suit but he kept glancing at Izzy, somewhat dazzled. I caught Cameron looking at me in a similar way. I thought that I was probably doing the same when I snuck another glance at him.

'I've got a notebook and pen,' Izzy said, showing us her handbag. 'So, we can take notes.' Beth beamed at her. The apple didn't fall at all far from the tree with that one.

The piano fell silent then and two people stepped into the centre of the room, the man clinking his glass for quiet. We all turned to them expectantly. 'Welcome to our home. For those who don't know I'm Lord Devilton and this is my good lady wife,' the grey-haired man in the black tuxedo greeted us, gesturing to the attractive blonde next to him who was wearing a floor length gown and a fur jacket, her lips the brightest red I had ever seen. She looked half his age. 'We haven't been married long and as we eloped we thought we needed to invite all of our dearest family and friends to our home for an evening of celebration,' he said grandly, smiling at all of us. 'I'd like to particularly welcome Reverend Snide, my son Charles and his wife Prudence, and my wife's dearest godmother Miss M to this evening!' There was an excited murmur among the guests at that introduction because she really looked like Miss Marple. We looked at the people he had introduced, obviously our actors for the evening, and I thought they all really looked the part. Izzy was bouncing on her feet beside me. 'We will shortly be making our way into the dining room for dinner but I think, Charles, you wanted to say a few words?'

Charles was at the other end of the room so we all turned to see him step forward. His wife was looking fed up next to him, sipping her drink, and looking at someone else in the room. A handsome man. She dropped him a wink when Charles couldn't see. 'Thank you, Father. Obviously it was rather a shock for Father to return from his trip to Paris married,' he said with a nervous laugh. We tittered. 'And to someone we had never met. But you know my father, he's always been a man determined to have exactly what he wants in life. I have always admired that,' he added, raising his glass towards his father. 'So, I propose a toast – to going after what will make you happy in life, and be dammed what anyone else thinks!' Everyone laughed as he raised his glass.

And then came a piercing scream.

I jumped along with everyone else, spinning around, my heart beating faster despite knowing this was all just a game.

We turned around to see Prudence holding her hands over her face in horror, having evidently been the one who screamed, clinging to her new husband. Just by them on the floor was the Reverend, his dog collar askew, his eyes closed, his face deathly white as he lay on the floor, a knife sticking out of his chest.

A man strode into the room wearing a dark brown suit. 'I heard a scream, what the devil is going on?'

'Inspector Keen-eye,' Lord Devilton cried. 'Thank God you're here! There's been a murder!'

The Inspector crouched down to look at the body as we all watched in silence, transfixed. 'Who on earth would want to kill the Reverend?' He looked at us all. 'I just came into the house. There was no one else around. It must have been someone in this room. None of you are to leave until I get to the bottom of this and find the killer. I will need to interview everyone who knew this man.'

'Let us all go into the dining room. We need to sit down from the shock,' Lord Devilton suggested. 'Everyone follow us!'

There was an exodus into the dining room, everyone chatting eagerly about what had happened, staring at the body as we passed, the Inspector eyeing us all suspiciously.

'Why did they have to kill the vicar?' Brodie hissed to us as we walked, making us chuckle.

'Miss M,' Prudence said loudly to her godmother. 'We need your help. There is no way any of us could have done such a dreadful thing,' she said. 'You need to find out who really did this!'

'Rest assured, my dear, I will get to the bottom of it.'

I followed the others into the dining room, conscious of Cameron beside me. As we walked through the door, he rested a hand on the small of my back and I shivered involuntarily.

'You're not scared are you?' he asked in a low voice.

I swallowed the urge to say I was, but not of the murder. I was nervous of the way his touch was making me feel. I wondered if he could tell or not. 'Just determined to find out the killer.'

'I'm disappointed there is no butler. It's always the butler.'

I took in the grand dining room as we walked inside, chandeliers sparkling down on the crystal glasses and crisp white tablecloths. 'I could get used to this. It's a shame it's all make-believe.'

'Like something out of a film,' he agreed with a smile. He had removed his hand and my back felt so much colder without it. We found our table – our group were spilt between two tables mixed in with other guests – but we were next to one another. I was now definitely convinced that Beth had put us down as a couple. As Cameron pulled out my chair for me and poured us both a glass of wine from the bottle on the table, I realised that even though I shouldn't be, I was perfectly fine with that.

Chapter Thirty-One

We were also sitting with Beth, Drew and Izzy and they threw themselves enthusiastically into trying to solve the crime. I was having more fun than I thought I would. As the starters were served, the Inspector told us that he had narrowed down the suspects to Lord and Lady Devilton, Charles and his wife. And then Miss M mentioned that there was another suspect – the butler who had answered the door to everyone – Harold.

Cameron leaned in to me. 'It's so the butler!'

'Too obvious,' I replied. 'I think it's the new wife – she's hiding something. She's way too young for him.'

'I didn't think you'd be judgey about that sort of thing,' he said with a laugh. He had poured us both another glass of wine and I'd never seen him so relaxed before. I liked it.

'Definitely a gold–digger. And I'm not judging, just stating the facts. I mean I'd be very willing to be wooed by an older man with lots of money...' I grinned as he pretended to look shocked. 'Beth, help me out here,' I said to her. 'Lady Devilton is so not who she's pretending to be.'

'You know, I wasn't too keen on Prudence when we talked to her. She's definitely having an affair behind Charles' back,' Beth said, checking Izzy's notebook. Each of the suspects were coming around to the tables so we could interview them and the Inspector and Miss M would occasionally let us in on a clue or a musing of theirs as they wandered around the room too.

'We still don't have a motive,' Izzy reminded us. 'I think the Reverend knew something that the killer wanted kept secret.'

'An affair,' Beth said.

'Or a shady past,' I suggested.

'Or the butler did it,' Cameron added.

I nudged him. 'You need a motive and you don't have one.' He scowled as I laughed. A second scream interrupted us, and I jumped yet again. This time, Cameron put his hand on mine as we all craned our necks to see where it had come from. I felt myself threading my fingers through his. He turned to me and we locked eyes as we held hands. Why was this friend plan suddenly feeling so hard to stick to?

'Look!' Prudence cried after she had screamed. She pointed in horror to a second body on the floor.

'Oh my god,' I said, bursting out laughing. 'You're the worst at this,' I told Cameron as he registered the fact that it was the butler who had now been murdered.

He shook his head. 'It's usually the butler,' he muttered but he squeezed my hand, smiling, his eyes looking brighter than I'd ever seen them.

'He definitely saw the murderer. They had to silence him,' Izzy cried out.

'You know, the person who was closest to the door when the Reverend was killed was actually Lord Devilton,' I said, remembering. 'Maybe his new wife was so interested in his money she missed the fact he was a killer.'

'Oh my god,' Beth said. 'What if he doesn't have any money after all?'

'I've got it this time,' Cameron said after thinking for a minute. 'He's still married to Charles' mother.'

'Bigamy!' I cried, thinking that I was pretty tipsy by this point. 'Charles!' I called as he walked by. 'We need to ask you something.' He came over. 'Where is your mother?'

He looked shifty. 'What do you mean? My mother died when I was younger. She had mental health problems. She killed herself. I think it's pretty frightful of you to bring that up.'

'Oh my god they locked her in an asylum,' I said when he hurried away quickly.

'You have a dark mind,' Cameron said, looking impressed. 'I think we might have this, you know.'

Beth was telling Izzy what to write down as Miss M appeared. 'Have you heard any rumours about the former Lady Devilton?' Beth asked Miss M eagerly.

'Ah, that poor woman,' she said, shaking her head. 'She apparently had a lot of mental health problems. She took her own life, so the family said, but there were rumours that things weren't all as they seemed to be. I did warn my god-daughter but she said it was just gossip. Although I've always found that gossip has a lot of truth in it, haven't you?'

Beth was grinning like a Cheshire cat. 'We've solved it guys. We make a really good team,' she said, jumping up to find the Inspector.

'We really do,' I said, lifting my wine glass up towards Cameron. He clinked it and we watched as Beth told the Inspector our theory that Lord Devilton was the murderer – silencing the Reverend from telling his new wife that their marriage was a fraud as his wife was still alive, and being kept in an asylum. The butler witnessed the murder and had been threatening to tell the Inspector so he had to kill him too.

'Is this true, Lord Devilton?' the Inspector cried out. The room fell silent, all eyes turning to Lord Devilton, who tried to make a run for it. 'Grab him!' the Inspector cried out.

Cameron, who was the closest to the door, jumped up and grabbed the escaping murderer, who surrendered easily, probably to make sure no one actually got hurt, and the Inspector dashed over to handcuff him. The room erupted into cheers and Beth came back over and high-fived us all. I saw Heather shake her head when she real-ised Beth had won yet another game, and I found myself unable to stop smiling.

–

'There you are.' I stepped out onto the terrace to see Cameron leaning on the rail looking out at the grounds, a clear indigo sky above him. We'd been in the lounge drinking merrily when I realised he had disappeared. Izzy and Luke had been sent to bed despite their protests, and the rest of us had found a corner table to toast our crime-solving triumph and enjoy the rest of the night. It was still strange to see us all in our 1930s costumes. I felt like we were in another time, another world, and it led me to slip out beside him and not worry that I shouldn't.

'Just needed a moment outside,' he said, smiling as I leant next to him.

'That's how I'll always think of you. Not in a crowded bar drinking but outside with nature, quiet and calm,' I said, feeling rather tipsy by this point and, as a consequence, being more honest than usual. You would have thought I would have learned my lesson about that by this point but the cocktails just tasted too good frankly.

Cameron turned to me, eyebrow raised. 'Basically, an antisocial loner?'

'If the shoe fits.' I nudged him with my elbow and he chuckled, which made me smile. It was always good to hear him laugh. 'And don't forget crime-solver extraordinaire.'

'I wouldn't have got there without you. We made a good team back there,' he said.

'You're right.' I looked up at the twinkling stars. 'Why does that scare me so much?'

Cameron gently put his hand over mine on the rail. 'It scares me too. Anna, I can't stop thinking about you. But I can't give you my heart. It's not whole anymore.'

I looked at him. 'Mine isn't either. I've never even been in love. At least you know you can love. What if I just can't?' I whispered the last words. Cameron made me say things out loud that I didn't even want to think. But deep down, that was what worried me the most. That even if I found someone special, even if I found everything I wanted, I still wouldn't be able to let go of the past and make a life with them? What if I'd never have what Brodie had with Emily? Worries flowed into my mind as Cameron looked at me but they were suddenly erased when he leaned in and kissed me. Gently, tentatively at first, but then deeper. The kiss was full of longing and yearning and I kissed him back exactly the same. I wrapped my arms around him and his slid to my waist, pulling me closer, kissing me like no man had ever kissed me before.

I pulled back to look at him. 'Maybe we are broken, Cameron.'

'Maybe we can fix each other.'

'I don't think it works like that.'

'I don't want to let you go,' he said urgently. He leaned in again and I kissed him back because I was unable not to, even though I knew it wasn't a good idea.

'One of us is going to get hurt,' I said when I could let go of him again.

'Right now, I don't care. Come to my room with me. Please,' he said, reaching out to touch my hair.

'It's a bad idea,' I whispered but every part of me wanted to go with him.

'Is it? Maybe there's a reason we met this summer. I had a good time tonight. Probably the first time I've let myself enjoy something for so long. And when I kiss you, I feel... happy.'

'Me too,' I admitted. I put my hand in his. 'But you said it yourself, our hearts aren't whole.' I wanted to go with him though, so much. 'And we only have the summer.'

He picked up our entwined hands and kissed mine gently. 'Then we should be together tonight.' And even though I was sure one of us was going to get hurt, even though there were a million reasons why we shouldn't, I nodded.

We walked around the side of the hotel and upstairs together, avoiding the others in the lounge, disappearing into our world of two inside Cameron's room.

We closed the door behind us as we walked through, and I knew that we both wished that we never had to come back out again.

Chapter Thirty-Two

'Tell me how you fell in love with Kirsty,' I said to Cameron in a low voice. We were under the covers in his bed, facing one another, naked but with the sheets pulled up. The night was fast fading into the early hours of morning but neither of us seemed to want to fall asleep. It was like we were under the spell of the night and if we fell asleep, we knew the spell would be broken when we woke up. I wasn't sure I had ever wanted a night not to end before but tonight that was how I felt. I wanted to get to know every inch of him – body and mind – and I'd never felt like that with someone before.

Cameron traced his fingertips across my shoulder. 'Kirsty was my first… everything.'

I lifted my head. 'Your first?' I raised an eyebrow.

He nodded. 'I grew up in the middle of nowhere remember. There was no one at school that I really liked. I wanted to wait until I found someone that I loved. And Kirsty was the woman. Is that crazy?'

I shook my head, still reeling from what he had said. 'I think it's really sweet. I've never met anyone that I wanted to be with for long. I was hurt by my first. He didn't want me after we slept together. Maybe that made me wary to trust again, I don't know. But then I'm always moving around so I've never wanted a tie, never wanted someone that would keep me in a place. So, I suppose I don't let anyone get close to me.'

'Do you want to let someone in?'

'Sometimes,' I admitted. 'Especially here, surrounded by all these happy couples. But it scares me so much.'

He nodded. 'Love is scary. I was scared when I fell for Kirsty. You feel so happy but also vulnerable because you don't know if they really feel the same way about you or how long it will last. I was destroyed when I saw her with someone else, and then to lose her completely. I don't know… It's made me scared too. Scared to love anyone else again.'

'So, you don't let anyone close either,' I said. I pushed back a strand of his hair. 'Has there been anyone else since Kirsty?'

Cameron's eyes met mine. 'Only you.'

The two words I wanted desperately to hear but the two words that completely freaked me out too. When I had said one of us was going to get hurt, I had really been unsure who I meant and now I wondered if it would be both of us. 'What are we going to do?' I asked him then, hoping he had an answer for me.

'What do you want to do?' he asked.

'Stay here with you,' I answered truthfully. My stomach fluttered with nerves and excitement. I had never felt so content and so uncertain all at once.

'I want you to stay too.'

I was both relieved and nervous as Cameron leaned in to kiss me again. When we pulled apart, I moved closer to him. 'What do you see yourself doing in five years?' I asked.

'Is this a job interview?' He grinned.

'I want to know. If I came back to find you in five years, what would you be doing?'

Cameron thought for a moment. 'I'd like my own farm. I love the farming life. I thought I wanted to do something completely different but honestly working at Hilltop has saved me, I think.'

'And a family?' I asked, not meeting his eyes, tracing a finger across his bare chest.

'That's what I always thought. I wanted to get married and have children. But what if I don't deserve to have that now? What if I lost my chance at that?'

I shook my head. 'I don't think you did at all. What happened was an accident. You aren't to blame and one day you'll be able to see that, and you'll meet someone and fall in love and have that family. You're a good man, Cameron. You're still grieving, you're still shocked by what happened and that's so understandable. But you will let it go one day. I know you will.'

'What about you? What about your five-year plan? Will you realise that you also deserve to be happy?' he asked, stroking my hair, speaking gently.

'I hope so. Realising the truth about the accident has helped. And knowing my family do want me around. But I'm not sure yet what will make me happy. All I know is that how I've been living isn't making me happy. It's hard though to see a way out, to change the habits of a lifetime.'

'You will though,' he said firmly. 'Because you know you need to. There's no rush anyway. You like Glendale, don't you?'

I nodded. 'I do but this job is only for the summer. I have a flight booked to Ibiza in September.' I bit my lip. The thought of it wasn't as appealing as it had been.

'September is ages away,' he said, leaning in to kiss me.

I wish I had his faith that I could change my life. I wish I had as much faith in myself. It was funny how we believed that the other person would find a way to make their dreams come true but we didn't yet believe it for ourselves. Cameron wrapped his arms around me and I rested my head on his chest, listening to the sound of his heart beating steadily, grounding me in the moment. I closed my eyes. I was always thinking of the next place I was going to go to, but in that moment I couldn't think of anywhere else I wanted to be.

–

Sun streamed into the breakfast room of the hotel the following morning. I had woken up and slipped out of Cameron's room before he opened his eyes, heading to mine for a much-needed long, hot shower. Once dressed in jeans and a t-shirt, I walked downstairs to find the others already at two tables next to one another, tucking in to a hearty breakfast. Cameron was next to Rory, who was chatting away to him while Cameron sipped black coffee. He looked up when I walked over to the buffet and smiled. Relieved, I smiled back. I'd been worried that things would be awkward between us in the cold light of the day.

'Did you sleep well?' Beth asked, coming over with an empty plate to join me. Like me, all traces of her glamorous 1930s self had gone. 'I still can't believe we solved the murder last night.'

'It was really fun,' I replied with a smile, trying to ignore the flashback I was having of Cameron's arms around me. 'Did you enjoy it?' I was starving, I realised, so loaded up my plate with toast, scrambled eggs, mushrooms and grilled tomatoes.

'Loved it. And I think everyone did thank goodness. It's not easy trying to find something we all will enjoy. And you didn't mind sitting with Cameron, did you?' Beth asked me. She was filling her plate up with bacon and sausages and fried eggs. I glanced behind me and saw Cameron watching me. I felt my cheeks heat up.

'I knew you'd planned that,' I said, shooting her a hard stare. I added two hash browns to my plate and started to make my way back to the table but she made me pause, taking me by the elbow.

'I'm sorry. Heather just said she thought there might be a mutual attraction going on and I'm a wedding planner. It's really not my fault, I can't help it,' she said, holding one hand up in defence. 'I would never want to make anyone uncomfortable. I hope you know that.'

She looked worried that I might be annoyed with her so I shook my head. 'It's fine. We're just friends though,' I said firmly, hoping she couldn't see the way Cameron smiled at me as I sat down next to him with my food.

'Of course you are,' she said as she sat down opposite me, next to Izzy and Drew, dropping me a wink when no one else could see.

I rolled my eyes but I just couldn't help smiling. She was shameless but I had to concede that her heart was in the right place. Under the table, Cameron brushed his foot against my leg and warmth travelled up my body. I felt like an infatuated teenager. When I glanced across at him, I could see he too looked like he was finding it hard not to grin at everyone. I wasn't sure how we could stick to our 'just friends' pact now. Then again, if I was really honest with myself, I really didn't want to.

Chapter Thirty-Three

'Anna!'

I walked downstairs to hear Izzy calling me loudly a few days after we came back from the stag and hen do. 'What's up?'

She rounded the corner and her face lit up. 'Hurry!' she cried, grabbing my arm and pulling me along with her. 'Come on, Anna.'

'I'm coming,' I said with a laugh. I'd never seen her so impatient before. She led me to the closed door of her reading room then let go of me, cleared her throat and turned to look at me so seriously I almost laughed again.

'The reading room is finished and as you helped me so much I wanted you to be the first to see it before I let anyone else in,' Izzy said, grabbing the door handle.

'I'm honoured,' I said, touched that she wanted to show it to me first. Once all the decorating had been finished, and the shelves had been put up while we were at the murder-mystery weekend, Izzy had closed the door and forbidden us all from entering on pain of death so she could finish it off on her own. Well, with Luke. Obviously, he had been allowed in – the room felt as much his as it was hers anyway.

'Okay.' She took a deep breath. 'Let's go in.' She opened the door with a flourish and stepped inside to let me through. The room felt bigger now it was no longer piled with stuff. There were two walls of bookshelves and Izzy had colour-coded them all so it looked like there were two rainbows in the room. There were two armchairs on each side of the room, with cushions and cosy throws draped across them. On one of them Ginny, Izzy's cat, was curled up fast asleep, giving the room her seal of approval. There was a reading lamp by each armchair. And there was a picture hanging on the book-free wall with the quote – 'She is too fond of books, and it has turned her brain'.

I smiled when I saw that. 'It's perfect, Iz. Really,' I said. And it was. A comfy snug of a reading room that had clearly been put together with a whole lot of love. I wrapped an arm around Izzy's shoulders to give her a quick squeeze.

'I love it so much,' she agreed, beaming around the room. 'I've wanted a reading room since we moved in here. I love this house so much and now it really is perfect. I hope I never have to leave. I mean, there are places I want to go but I'll always come back here, you know? To this. My home.'

I wasn't sure why, but a lump rose up in my throat at her words.

'And Luke is so jealous,' Izzy continued, oblivious to my sudden silence. 'But I got this second armchair for him so we can read together. Especially when it gets colder. Can you imagine curling up in here with a hot chocolate?' She clapped her hands together. 'It's going to be so cosy. You okay, Anna?' she asked, looking at me then.

I snapped myself out of my reverie. 'Of course. It's a great room, Iz. Why don't you show your mum?'

'Good idea.' She hurried out to find Beth and I folded my arms across my chest and leaned against the wall. Although I wasn't a big reader, I did feel envious of Izzy.

Mainly because she was so sure that this house was where she wanted to be. I wanted to feel like that about some-where.

Beth came in then and gasped. 'Oh wow, guys, this room is so cute and cosy. And you colour coded the books too. Great job, Iz. And you too, Anna, I know you helped a lot. I feel like I need to spruce up my office now. Maybe I'll pay you to do it, Izzy. You could be an interior designer.'

'Mum, you know I'm going to be a writer.'

Beth smiled. 'Never hurts to keep your options open. I've made us some lunch, come on.' She led Izzy out and I followed them slowly. I glanced back at the room before I left it. I liked the idea of having helped make something that would stay at the Hall long after I left it, maybe even for generations. I mean, if Izzy ended up having kids then they could be reading in here one day. She had left her mark on this house at the age of fourteen. What had I left my mark on? Nothing. But I wanted to.

After I had eaten toasted cheese sandwiches with Beth and Izzy, I left them in the kitchen and finished off making the beds and then I did the pile of ironing that had accumulated in the laundry room. The house now looked so much better than when I had arrived – surfaces sparkled and everything was crisp and fresh and when the sun streamed in through the windows, there was no dust floating in the air. When I had finished my jobs for the day, I peered out of my bedroom window to see Beth and John in the garden heading to the greenhouse to pick produce for the shop. Luke arrived, having walked from the village to see the finished reading room. Caroline was out having lunch with a friend and Drew was out at work.

Heading downstairs to the kitchen, I prepared a stew for dinner and put it into the Aga to cook slowly while I headed out to Hilltop Farm. I hadn't seen or heard from Cameron since we came back from Edinburgh but I didn't want to wait for him to get in touch. What was the point? If we only had this summer together, why pretend that I didn't want to see him? Although as I drove there I did feel some nerves about whether he would want to see me or not but at least I would find out either way.

Hilltop crept into view in a gap through the trees after I had driven down the winding country roads. The sky was cloudy today and there was a chill in the air, the Scottish summer deciding not to play ball. I parked outside the farmhouse and spotted Cameron carrying logs through the woods towards the house. He was wearing jeans, a flannel shirt and boots. This was how I would always picture him, I felt. He just seemed so much more comfortable out here than in a fancy hotel wearing a suit. I wondered where I seemed more comfortable to him, as I left the car and met him at the door to the farmhouse, which was flung open. 'Hey, stranger.'

Cameron looked up and smiled. 'Hey yourself. Just getting the house ready for our new guests arriving tomorrow.' He nodded. 'Come in with me.'

I followed him inside and watched as he piled the logs up by the fire and then led me into the kitchen. 'I've missed this place,' I said, hopping up on one of the stools and running my hand along the marble counter. 'It's a dream kitchen.'

'You seem very at home here. It feels empty without you cooking up a storm in it,' Cameron said, heading to the coffee machine to make us a drink. I smiled at his back, pleased that he missed seeing me in here. 'I wanted to phone you,' he said as he made us both a coffee. 'But, honestly, I wasn't sure what to say.'

'Me too. I had some free time so thought I'd come and see you. I'm not a very patient person.' I smiled as he carried our cups over and sat down on the stool next to me.

'I'm glad you're here,' he replied simply, sipping his coffee.

'A man of few words but I like them. So, what have you been doing since we got back? Obviously not pining for me…' I grinned as I took a long gulp of the coffee and let out a contented sigh. I had missed that machine. It was so much better than the coffee at the Hall.

'I've been giving everything a clean ready for the new guests and I had to go with Rory to an auction. We've bought some sheep for the hill and so I've been putting up a new fence ready for them. There's always loads to do. But I have thought about you,' he added, glancing at me. 'My mum came for dinner last night. I told her about you.'

'God, what did you say?'

'That you've made me feel like there is a way to move on, I guess.'

'It's the same for me. Are you close with your mum?'

'I'd say so. As my dad wasn't around, we relied on each other. I felt like I needed to be the man of the house at a young age. I mean, we had Angus, of course, but he lived out on Fraser Farm and, let's face it, he's better with cows than with people.'

'I bet she's pleased you're still in Glendale. They both must be. And you're farming like your uncle too. My parents are so happy that Brodie lives nearby and that he's a minister, they are so proud. I always felt a little jealous of that if I'm honest.'

'My mother has no one to compare me to, that's why I'm okay. Seriously, though, I bet they don't think like that – they are happy you're here this summer. They love you and are just as proud of you, I'm sure.'

'I don't know about that.' I smiled. 'I think I need some fresh air, I've been stuck inside all day, that's never good for over-thinking. Fancy a walk with me?'

'You never need to ask me twice to go outside.'

We put our coffee cups in the dishwasher and headed out of the back door towards the woods, walking side-by-side along the path. I heard the birds in the trees above us and in the distance could see the Fraser Farm cattle grazing on top of the hill that joined the two properties. Some of my tension eased immediately as we strolled together in silence. Cameron was good for that. He never felt the need to talk. I usually did, but with him I found that I was okay just thinking for a minute. After a while, he reached out and took my hand in his. It was nice to feel his skin against mine. I'd never been a hand-holding type of woman before. But maybe I could be. If it was with Cameron.

'What did you like doing when you were younger?' I asked as we disappeared into the trees. With the clouds above us and the trees blocking the light, it felt as if we'd suddenly moved into the early evening. I was glad I had long sleeves on now.

'I liked visiting Angus on the farm, seeing the animals, playing in the field, and I liked to watch my mum cooking in the kitchen. We'd sing along to the radio together.' He smiled, remembering. 'What about you?'

'Watching my dad play guitar, walking in the park with my family, listening to music in my room, going shopping with my friends to town, buying a nail varnish and spying on boys, and, to be honest, going to church. We'd all go and then have a roast on a Sunday. The four of us. I miss that sometimes.' I sighed. 'But that was all before my accident.'

'What changed then?'

'I took a long time to recover, Brodie went off to study to be a minister, and my parents were just so worried about me all the time. And I felt like I couldn't be honest with them. They never wanted to talk about the accident. I misunderstood the reason why. It became a wedge between us, I think. I was trapped in all kinds of ways. I felt so guilty and I couldn't tell them. So, I escaped, and have kept on moving. I do miss who I was before though.'

Cameron thought for a moment. 'I think you're still the same person. You went through something traumatic and obviously you had to grow up so much but I reckon you'd still enjoy doing all those things you did before. Maybe you just felt like you had to change after something so huge happening to you but maybe it was okay not to, to keep your life how it was. You put so much pressure on yourself to live this amazing life but really how many people do that? Most of us just live day to day in our corners of the world. Life is about the small things that bring you joy when it comes down to it, don't you think?'

I stared at Cameron. It was the longest speech I'd ever heard him make.

'Maybe people think my life here is small. Maybe it is. But look around you. It's peaceful and beautiful and I wake up every day grateful for that. I'm starting to think that is enough.'

'I worry that I'll never be able to just appreciate this though,' I said, gesturing with the hand that wasn't holding his. 'That I'll always keep running.'

'It's up to you though, isn't it? You were right when you said that I spent too much time thinking that I could have helped Kirsty. I kept thinking what if I had done something different that night but I hadn't thought that even if *I* had, she might not have done. She broke up with me. I couldn't have done anything to stop her.' He stopped then and turned to face me. 'And you couldn't have stopped the drunk-driver who drove into your dad's car. We can only be responsible for our actions; do you know what I mean?'

'I do and you're right. I like it when you talk. You should do it more often.'

He chuckled and leaned down to kiss me.

'And you should definitely do that more often too,' I said, wrapping my arms around his neck. He pulled me closer for a long and lingering kiss in the quiet of the woods.

Chapter Thirty-Four

A breeze ruffled my hair as we walked back to my car. I asked Cameron if he wanted to come back to the Hall for dinner. 'I've made loads. Brodie and Emily are joining us too... it could be fun,' I said. It was unlike me but I realised I was quite happy with the idea of spending the evening with Cameron. His company was soothing and I liked the idea of having someone there with me when I would be surrounded by couples if we left the children out of it.

'Why not. I was just going to have beans on toast. You know though that they will talk about this,' he said, raising an eyebrow to check that I really did want him to come. We all knew that the Glendale Hall gang, however much we liked them, were gossips.

I shrugged. 'They're talking already. Besides, I never worry what people say about me.'

'I think we really are opposites.'

'No pressure,' I said opening the car door. And I meant it. I would never push him. It just wasn't my style. I wanted him to come but I knew you couldn't make people do things they just didn't want to.

'You know I want to spend more time with you,' he replied, jumping into the car. I hid my smile as I climbed in beside him.

'So, are we still sticking to just being friends?' I joked as I drove us away from Hilltop.

'I thought you didn't like labels.'

'You're right, I don't. But I have a feeling you do.' I glanced at him. It was so strange this connection I felt with someone so different from me. But I suppose two lost people could find each other, and it felt like that was what was happening with us. I just wished I wasn't equally excited and scared by that idea. How did people fall in love? How did they just take that leap? I couldn't fathom it yet.

'I think I've learned they don't mean anything.'

Even though he had only loved one woman, he had loved before, he had been in a long-term relationship whereas I never had. Relationships were alien to me whereas my love life was probably equally as alien to him.

We drove the rest of the way in companionable silence, and when we arrived smiled at one another as we got out of the car and went inside.

In the kitchen, Beth, Drew, Izzy, Caroline, John and Sally were there and Brodie and Emily had arrived with Iona. The smell of my stews (I'd made a meat and a veggie one) cooking filled the room, and everyone was chatting happily as they gathered drinks and sat down at the table. I didn't think I'd been in a kitchen with so much warmth in it before coming here. And it was down to the people. I wondered if Beth knew how lucky she was to come home to this every night. 'Sit down everyone and I'll get it all dished up,' I said, aware of eyes turning to me and Cameron. I slipped into the kitchen, leaving him to deal with their curious looks. I felt bad but he had known what he was getting into.

'So, you and Cameron...' Brodie appeared beside me to pour two glasses of red wine, handing me one, as I tipped each stew into a serving pot and spooned the roast potatoes that had been crisping up while I was over at Hilltop into another dish.

I looked at his twinkling eyes and despite myself, I smiled. 'We're just hanging out,' I said, nudging him with my hip. 'Make yourself useful and carry something over.'

'Fine but it's nice to see you smile. Oh, and I have something to tell you... I'll wait till we're sitting down.' He carried off one of the stews and Drew came to help me bring everything else over. We also had runner beans grown at the Hall cooked in butter and everything looked delicious. It was a bit more of a winter meal but it was a cool evening and no one minded a hearty meal here, I had found.

'This is as tasty as ever, Anna,' Beth said after everyone had piled up their plates.

'I have to admit you're giving me a run for my money,' Sally said to me after she had tasted it.

'That is high praise,' Beth told me.

'I'm honoured,' I said, pleased. I had a taste of my veggie stew, it was spicy tomato flavour, and I was happy to see some of them eating that either instead of or with the meat version.

'So, one of my parishioners came to see me earlier,' Brodie said. He was opposite me with Emily on one side, Cameron on the other. I was relieved we weren't next to one another, this was strange enough already for me. 'And he mentioned that his son works at a cookery school in Inverness. He gave me his number, said he'd be more than happy to talk to you about doing one of their courses...' Brodie slid the business card across the table to me. Everyone was listening by this time. 'I think you should make this your career. You could open your own restaurant one day.' He said it so simply, like it would all be that easy.

'How could I ever afford to open my own restaurant?' I asked, looking at the card.

'We would think of something,' Brodie said. 'If it's what you want. You're such a good cook, Anna.'

'You definitely should do it,' Beth said. 'And I'd love to help you, Anna. Your talent shouldn't go to waste. Maybe you could even open the restaurant nearby, I mean we only have the pub in Glendale, don't we?'

I looked around the table, everyone was nodding and smiling like they had all of my future planned out. I looked at Cameron, the only one looking down at his plate unsure. If I stayed in Glendale, what would that mean for us? Would he even want me to? 'This is all a bit much. I'm only here for the summer.'

'There's no reason why you can't stay though,' Beth said.

I knew she meant well but she was so bossy. Anger flared up inside my chest at their assumptions. 'You think you have it all planned out, don't you? Like I don't get a say in my own life?'

Beth's mouth fell open. 'That's not what I meant…'

'No,' Brodie said at the same time as her. 'Of course not. Just trying to give you some options. We want to help.'

I put my cutlery down with a clatter. 'But I didn't ask any of you for help, did I?' I wasn't sure why I was so annoyed. I think it was because they all seemed to know what was best for me without taking into account that I might want to make my own life choices. 'I know you're all used to being in each other's business all the time but I'm not you, okay? And I didn't ask for any of you to butt in like this.' Even after all we had talked about, my brother still thought he knew what was best for my life. And Beth seemed to want to control everyone. I stood up. 'I'm quite capable of deciding what I want to do, okay?' And even though it was maybe childish of me, I couldn't face the rest of the meal with them so I stalked out of the room.

Chapter Thirty-Five

It was Emily who had evidently drawn the short straw as she was the one who came to find me sitting on the stairs, fuming. She walked over, hands up in a peace offering stance. 'I know it's annoying when people say they know how you feel but I really do this time. I have been on the receiving end of people trying to fix my life,' she said, coming to sit beside me. 'When I left my boyfriend in London, everyone told me that I should move here to open my own bakery. But they don't mean to be bossy, they just like to help people. I totally get that you didn't ask for any help, and that's fine. But, honestly, they really didn't mean to upset you.'

'And you just went along with their plans for you?'

Emily smiled. 'I had always wanted my own bakery and my old boss offered to give me the money to set one up. I grew up here and coming back did feel right. But I didn't make the decision until I was one hundred percent sure. And it wasn't because Beth told me to or that I knew it would make my aunt happy, or even because it would mean I would be living near your brother. I did it because I knew deep down in my heart it was the right move. I knew that it was going to make me happy. I also knew that it would be bloody hard work, and it was, and my life felt such a mess at the time but it was like a life raft. And I knew I would be crazy not to grab hold of it and use it to pull myself up. And look at me now.' She touched my arm. 'But that doesn't mean it's the same for you. You're right about one thing – it's your life, your choice to make. Just go easy on them in there, okay? They honestly just mean to be kind, I promise.'

I nodded slowly, my anger deflating. 'I know that really. It came out of nowhere though. I felt like they were trying to take over my life. I'm not used to asking or needing or wanting help from anyone else.'

'I get that. But it's also okay if you do, you know?'

'I only meant to stay for the summer. I'm supposed to be going to Ibiza next.'

'Plans can change, Anna. Look at all of us in there. Did any of us plan to be where we are right now? Definitely not. But hopefully you can see we are all pretty happy. I'll tell them all to back off but don't hold this against them, will you? They're good people.' She stood up. 'As are you. Remember that.'

I watched her go and felt really bad for my outburst. I had always been hot-headed but it was more than that. I had been alone for so long that it wasn't in my nature to let people into my life. But it seemed that at Glendale Hall they pushed their way in regardless. Should I still be annoyed or should I admire them for trying? I wasn't sure, truth be told.

Cameron came out into the hallway then. 'Fancy a drink?'

'Hell yes.'

–

Cameron and I walked into the village together and headed straight for the Glendale Arms. It had been a quiet walk. Cameron seemed as thoughtful as I was and I longed to ask him what he had made of that meal but I was nervous to as well. We got our drinks and found a corner table. It was too chilly to sit outside. The pub was quiet as it was still early and none of his friends were in there thankfully.

'Was I wrong to get upset?' I worked up the courage to ask Cameron after taking a long gulp of my wine.

'Maybe you were a tad harsh on Brodie and Beth but no, not wrong if that's how you feel,' he replied. It was a diplomatic answer. 'You know, my mum and uncle did a similar thing to me. When I came back from uni, I was pretty broken. I had no idea what to do next. I was grieving. I'd lost Kirsty, and our future. I was down. Maybe even depressed, you know?' He paused to take a sip of his beer while I waited. 'Then my uncle came over and told me that Rory and Heather were buying the next-door farm, and that he was helping them under the proviso that I got first refusal for the manager job. I told him there was no way I was up to it and he actually swore at me. He told me to get up, have a shower, get dressed and come and see the place. He told me that his heart had been broken once and although he had never fully healed, he'd found a life that gave him purpose and peace, and that was what I needed. So, I went to see Hilltop and I saw it clearly. It was a place that would give me purpose and peace. And it did, and still does.'

'So, you're saying I should do what they're telling me to do?'

'No. I'm just saying we can't always see things clearly, maybe sometimes we do need people who care about us to step in and just show us the way a little bit. But even if you don't agree with what they said, I don't think they said it to upset you. Your brother really cares about you. And Beth does too.'

'I feel even worse now.'

'I don't want you to feel bad, just trying to say I understand the feeling of wanting to tell people to get out of your business, I really do. It's just sometimes maybe we need them to get in it. I don't know. I'm not good with words.'

'You're better than you think you are.' I finished my drink. 'I've never really thought far ahead, you know? Made a big plan for my life or anything. I don't even know where to start. Or if I want to. Staying here was definitely not what I pictured. I still can't.'

Cameron nodded. 'I get it. You need to think about it, decide for yourself. But it's good to know you have people who want to help, if you ask them to.'

'I know. God, was I such a brat back there?'

He laughed. 'You're spirited, not a brat. But maybe you might need to apologise to your brother and Beth when we get back.'

I sighed. 'Okay. God, could I really be a chef one day? That just sounds so crazy to me.'

'It's not crazy to follow your dream. I mean, it won't be easy but I thought you didn't want an easy life, anyway?'

I picked up my beer mat and threw it across the table at him as he chuckled, making me smile.

'You did say that you were fearless, I'm pretty sure you did,' he said, taking hold of my hand.

I swallowed hard. 'I think I was lying to myself and you. Because right now I'm terrified.'

'So am I but maybe it's a little less scary doing it together?'

'Maybe,' I said, squeezing his hands. 'Just a little bit.'

Chapter Thirty-Six

Cameron walked me back to the Hall after our drink and then I drove him to Hilltop. When I returned, everyone was still at the table talking over coffees despite it being near to ten o'clock. I gestured for Beth and Brodie to come into the kitchen with me, which they did willingly. They were better people than me but then I already knew that.

'Sorry for storming out earlier,' I said. 'You took me by surprise with all these plans you were coming up with, and I really don't know what I want to do next.'

'Look we all know that I can be bossy,' Beth replied, good-naturedly. 'I can't help it. I like to try to make everyone's lives better but you're right, I need to stop and check that they actually want my help in the first place. I'll let you two talk and I'll butt out, okay? Unless you actually ask me to do something.' She rubbed my arm and headed back to the others, as cheerful as ever. I wondered what it would take to break her good nature. But then I remembered her telling me she'd been forced to run away. Maybe something that big happening when she was so young had made her resilient now and she was able to shrug off small problems. I needed to learn how to do that.

'I'm sorry if you think I was trying to control your life,' Brodie said once we were alone. 'I certainly didn't mean to do that. It was just Graham telling me about his son, this little light bulb went off but you're right that I didn't even ask if cooking was something you wanted to do in the first place. I think I just got excited about the idea of you sticking around.'

I felt really bad now. 'I was just taken by surprise. I felt blind-sided by this plan you guys had laid out for me. I'm used to doing things by myself, on my own terms. I need to find my own way, you know?'

He nodded. 'I know. I just want you to be able to reach out if I can help. I want you to be happy. I just saw how much you enjoyed cooking and, yes, I took a hundred steps ahead of you. I see that now, but it doesn't mean that you have to completely dismiss what we said. Think it all through. I'll support you no matter what. You're my little sister and even though you might hate it sometimes, I want to protect you.'

'I'm old enough to look after myself.'

'Maybe, but we all need a helping hand sometimes.' He leaned in and gave me a quick squeeze. Emily called him over then as it was time to take Iona home. I watched him go and felt something in my pocket. I reached in and pulled out the business card that he'd slipped in there when he hugged me. I shook my head but I wasn't as angry as before. I just had no idea what I wanted to do.

I slipped the card back in my pocket and joined the others.

–

The second Glendale wedding was not as lucky with the Scottish weather as the first one had been. Rain poured down the windows of Glendale Hall from the moment we woke up on Saturday, and didn't stop.

'I don't think the gazebo ceremony will be going ahead,' Beth said as she drank a huge cup of black coffee and stared mournfully out of the kitchen into the garden. It was early and there was no sign yet of any of the wedding party or the people coming to help run the day. It was just us in the kitchen and it very much felt like the calm before the storm. 'It'll all have to take place in the marquee. What a shame.'

'You can't make the weather play ball,' I said, passing her a plate of pancakes as I joined her at the table. 'It will still be beautiful in the marquee.'

'I hope so. Grant and Paul really deserve it.' She took a sip of her coffee and looked across at me. 'Are you still heading to Hilltop today?'

I tried not to smile but it wasn't easy. 'The retreat guests are leaving late morning so I'll go then and have lunch with Cameron. If you're sure you won't need me.'

'It was never part of your job description to help with the weddings and, besides, there will be plenty of people here soon to do the work. I'm just glad that you're spending time with Cameron. You two deserve to have fun. I'm kind of jealous, I'm an old boring married woman now.'

I scoffed. 'No one would describe you as that. You and Drew are still so in love, anyone can see that.'

'You and Cameron will be like us soon,' she said with a grin.

'Honestly, I could never see myself settling down. Getting married, having a family, I don't think it's me.'

'That's fine, life would be boring if we all wanted the same things. But it doesn't mean you can't build a life with someone. If you find the right person.' She ate some of her pancakes. 'I'd marry you for your cooking alone,' she added with a laugh.

'It's funny. Until I came here, I'd never cooked for anyone but myself. I just helped out in kitchens. You guys are the first people I've actually made meals for. And I do love how much you all enjoy it.'

'Honestly, we love our food here, so if you can keep us happy, you have a good future ahead of you.' She smiled. 'Right, I'd better get dressed before the chaos begins. Enjoy today. I know that you might not be here for very long but life's too short to worry about what happens after the summer. If you and Cameron are happy now then that's enough, right?'

'I think so,' I said. I was tired of worrying about what to do next. I just wanted to enjoy these summer days despite the current rain for a bit longer. 'Good luck today.'

'Thanks. You know me, it'll all be okay. I just want to make it perfect. I remember my wedding to Drew and it was everything I wanted it to be. That's what I want to do for my weddings. Especially for Heather and Rory. I'm so nervous to get their day right.'

'Honestly, when it all comes down to it, they will be happy because they are going to spend their lives together.'

She grinned. 'I told you if you stayed here Glendale would start to work its magic. That sounded almost romantic.' She left the room chuckling to herself. I shook my head. Romantic was something I would never be but I supposed I was starting to see benefits to this falling in love lark. Maybe my time would come one day.

Until then, I was going to just enjoy myself.

After I finished tidying the kitchen and did the last of the week's ironing, I did some yoga. The rain was relentless now and I didn't fancy running through it so

I did stretches to some calming music and felt ready for the rest of the day.

When I was finished, I peered out of my window down at the garden. The place was a hive of activity. The marquee had already gone up but now people were filing in and out of it, carrying things covered up with hoods and umbrellas; the florist was running with flowers from the main house. I could see Beth down there directing everyone. She really was born for organising events like this.

Slipping out of my room, I went downstairs and paused by the reading room. Izzy was curled up in the armchair reading with her cat asleep on her lap. She looked so happy. I thought back to lying on my childhood bed listening to my dad's vinyl record collection, thinking that nothing bad could ever touch me while playing The Beatles or Queen or any of the other bands we loved. I wish sometimes I could go back to those moments and relive them. Maybe that was the problem with growing up: you forgot to have moments like that. There seemed to always be something to do or think about that you didn't often just let yourself… be.

I left the Hall to drive to Hilltop Farm and walked from the farmhouse down to Cameron's cabin as quickly as I could, my hood pulled up against the rain, my arms wrapped around my chest as I shivered in the cool wind, the grey clouds swirling above me.

Chapter Thirty-Seven

'You're here,' he said, opening the door with a pleased smile. 'And you're soaked, come in.' Cameron helped me out of my hoodie and told me to sit by the log fire, which was crackling with much-needed warmth. He grabbed a throw from the sofa and I wrapped it around my shoulders as he disappeared into the kitchen.

'Here,' he said, returning with two mugs of tea. I had sat down by the fire and he joined me down on the floor. 'Summer seems to have come to an abrupt halt. Are you warm and dry now?'

'This is so cosy,' I said, leaning forward to give him a kiss. I'd never had a man do anything for me so this was something new. In fact, everything with Cameron had been new so far. Sitting in his small living room, wrapped in a blanket, holding my tea next to the fire, I looked across at this handsome, quiet man and I felt more at home than I ever had before. 'I can see why you love it here.'

'It's better with you here,' he said. 'More than I thought it could be. Shall I go get us some food?' he asked, smiling as he got up to go back into the kitchen.

I smiled back, closing my eyes while he was gone, letting the peace settle over me. I had always been nervous of quiet like this but now I wasn't. It felt restorative rather than something to fear. Cameron came back in with a tray for us and sat back down on the floor, where we seemed to have settled in for the afternoon. He'd made butternut squash soup, and there was fresh crusty bread, cheese and grapes.

'A girl could get used to this,' I said, tucking in eagerly.

'I don't think I'd mind if you did. Although you could do a much better job with the food.'

'I know that I kind of went off on one when Brodie and Beth started talking about me being a chef one day but it would be fun, wouldn't it?' I said taking a bite of the bread. It was from Emily's Bakery, I could tell by how tasty it was. 'I loved working in the farmhouse kitchen, more than I thought I would.'

'Do you think you might look into that course your brother suggested?'

'I don't know. I'd planned to go abroad, not do a course in Inverness.' I avoided his gaze, uncertain.

'I should have said the other night... If you wanted to stick around Glendale, you don't need to worry about us. I would love you to stay here. Even if we weren't... well, you know, doing this.'

I smiled. 'Thank you.' I put the bread down. 'Does that mean you want to stop "doing this"?' I put the words into air quotes.

Cameron shook his head. 'Not right now, thank you.' He leaned in to kiss me. He tasted of soup and held me close. 'I thought you were hungry?'

'I can wait,' I replied, pulling him down onto the blanket with me.

–

When I opened my eyes, I smiled to see Cameron asleep beside me, his arm draped over me. We'd had an accidental nap after we'd eaten, warm and satisfied by the fire and still naked under the blanket. I moved and Cameron shifted his arm so I could sit up. He murmured sleepily. 'It's okay, I just need the loo,' I half-whispered as I reached for my clothes.

'Okay, Kirsty,' he murmured back, his eyes closing again.

I froze as I pulled my hoodie on. Did he seriously just call me by his ex-girlfriend's name?

I walked outside quickly, needing to get out of there. The room which had until a few moments ago felt warm and cosy now felt claustrophobic. This was why I had always resisted getting close to someone. Other people just always let you down. Outside, the rain had eased off and was now just lightly falling in the breeze. I breathed in the cool air.

My phone vibrated in my pocket then. I picked it up absent-mindedly. 'Hello?' I snapped as I paced outside Cameron's cabin, agitated and to be honest pretty hurt by what had just happened. I had hoped that he was moving on from the past but it was clear he was still haunted by his ex-girlfriend. That he still missed her. That maybe he also still loved her.

'Anna! How are you?' a bubbly voice cried down the phone line. 'It's Chloe,' she added when I didn't answer straight away.

'Oh hi, Chloe,' I replied, surprised that she was calling me. I walked a little further away from the cabin and shivered a little. It was cool beneath the trees and now I was away from the fire, and Cameron's arms, I felt the sudden drop in temperature. 'What's up?'

'I have a proposition for you and I hope you'll be as excited as I am about it…'

I listened to Chloe telling me all about this project that she was involved with and wanted me to be a part of too. I think if she had phoned just an hour ago I would have said I wasn't interested. I had actually been starting to feel content here in Glendale, and had been wondering if I would really want to leave as planned in September. Curled up with Cameron, I had let myself imagine sticking around Glendale past the summer. And then there was Brodie's idea of going to cookery school…

But then Cameron had called me by Kirsty's name, and suddenly Chloe was offering me a very different next move. And I was extremely tempted by it.

Chloe hung up, with me promising to let her know by the end of the day if I was up for it. After I put my phone away, I turned around to see Cameron in the doorway. He was shirtless, just wearing his low-slung jeans, looking sleepy and confused to find me gone. My stomach dropped like I was in a car rolling over a hill.

'Where did you go?' he called over to me.

'I didn't exactly want to stick around after you called me Kirsty,' I flung back.

'Huh?'

'You called me Kirsty. I knew that this was a mistake.' I turned to go and he darted out from the cabin after me, taking my arm to pull me to a stop.

'Don't go, Anna, please!'

Frustrated, I turned to look at him. 'You're clearly not over her. Do you wish I was her?'

'No, god.' He ran a hand through his hair, agitated. 'I didn't mean to do that. I was half asleep. I guess I was thinking about her. I mean, I told you, you are the first woman I've been with since her.'

'I thought we were both moving on from the past but I was so deluded. Of course we're not! We are no good for one another. We're too messed up.'

'No, that's not true!' He took my hand but I pulled it away. 'I'm sorry. I didn't mean to do that. I would never… Anna, you have changed everything.'

I met his gaze. 'Not everything,' I said, bitterly. 'You don't need to worry. I'm going to do what I do best. Chloe just phoned me and offered me a job in London. I'll be on the next train.'

He stared at me. 'Don't do this, Anna. It was a mistake.'

'You're right about that.'

'No, not us. Don't tell me that being in my arms just now didn't feel right. I know that you feel the same way. We have a connection. There's something between us, don't walk away from it.'

'I thought there was. But I'm not Kirsty. I never will be. So I'm not what you want. And you're not what I want.' I was fighting back tears now, which annoyed me. I didn't want to cry in front of him. 'This is what I do. I run. You knew that. I told you that one of us was going to get hurt. Looks like both of us have.'

'If you're hurting doesn't that tell you that you have feelings for me too?'

I hated that he was right. I hated that I had feelings for him. The first man to make me feel something was still in love with his ex. Talk about the universe having a twisted sense of humour. 'It doesn't matter. We're both broken. And we can't fix each other. I need to go, Cameron. I was never going to stay. And this is a great opportunity.'

'What about working here and studying cookery? What about being a chef one day?'

'This is a cooking job. And a fresh start.'

Cameron shook his head. 'You told me you didn't want to run anymore.'

'And you told me that we should just be friends. I should have listened.' I turned around again. 'I've made my decision. Don't follow me, okay?' As I walked away, the tears came. I made myself not look back but I could feel him watching me until I disappeared through the trees. I let out a breath then and broke into a run, wondering how anyone could bear falling in love when it hurt like this.

Chapter Thirty-Eight

I couldn't bear to look at them. A sea of disappointed faces. It was Sunday morning and everyone knew by now that I was catching a train to London soon, and no one was happy about it.

'But what about Heather and Rory's wedding?' Izzy asked me as she trailed behind as I descended the stairs, coming face-to-face with Beth and Drew, Emily and Brodie with Iona, who was asleep in her pushchair, and the only one not judging me with her eyes.

'Chloe's boyfriend is opening up this pop-up restaurant now, I have to go,' I repeated. Ever since I'd returned to the Hall and told Beth about Chloe's phone call, I had to tell everyone in turn why I was suddenly leaving. Chloe's boyfriend, Ashley, had wanted to open a restaurant with his best friend and a French chef called Pierre for ages. A premises had come up for a short lease so they had decided to try a pop-up restaurant to see how it went. They had hired a team to help but realised that they needed one more person so Chloe had asked me. I would be doing prep work in the kitchen, nothing more, but it was a chance to learn from a talented chef and get a feel for restaurant life. I'd never lived in London either so that was appealing. But mostly, it provided me with a reason to leave Glendale sooner than I'd planned, and I really needed to get some distance between me and Cameron.

I had told Chloe about my flight to Ibiza in the middle of September, two months away now, but she was fine with it – the pop-up was due to open next weekend and close around that time so it worked out perfectly. She was even giving me her spare room until I got settled too.

However, the people in front of me now really didn't understand why I wanted to go. I put my bags down with a thump in the hallway. 'It won't be forever,' I said, trying to console Izzy.

'I can't believe it's taken so long to get you to come to Glendale and you're leaving before the summer is even up,' Brodie said. I hated to see the disapproval on his face. But it was something I was used to, at least. It had been nice to connect with him again. To even become friends with him. And it had felt nice to ask his advice. But his advice had led me to Cameron. I was better off on my own.

'We'll miss you,' Emily added kindly.

'How am I going to manage?' Beth said, shaking her head. 'Drew, will you take her bags out to the car? Anna, come here for a sec.' She took my hand, brooking no protest, and pulled me into the living room, shutting the door behind us. 'Are you really sure about this? I know it seems like a good offer but you'll be just washing dishes probably, not studying cooking, or building up to getting your own place.' She bit her lip. 'I know that I'm interfering again but I thought you liked it here in Glendale?'

I sighed. I could see she was genuinely worried about me. 'I did... I do but I only planned to stay until September, and this is too good an opportunity to miss.'

'What about Cameron, then?'

'That didn't work out. But that's not the only reason I'm going. I need to make my own way in life. I always have. If I stay here, I'll end up relying on you guys.'

'But we want you to,' she protested.

'That's not me. I know you mean well but I'm independent and...'

'Believe me, I know exactly how you feel wanting to make your own way in the world. It's admirable. But running away is a different thing. You have family here and friends. You have a chance to build a career here, and we all want you to stay.'

'Thank you. It's nice to hear. But I need to do this.' I gestured around us. 'I'm not made to settle down in a small town seeing the same people every day.'

'I thought you weren't happy with always moving,' she reminded me. 'I thought you were happy here.'

I hesitated. I was. But it had all been a fantasy, hadn't it? I had let my guard down and now I was paying the price. 'I can't stay, Beth.'

'Please know that you can come home whenever you want. Don't think because you're leaving now that you can't come back. Will you?'

I shook my head. I'd run out of words. Drew called out then that we needed to go if I was going to make my train. I hurried out before Beth could stop me. I gave everyone a hug, swallowing the lump in my throat down hard.

'Ring me when you get to London, please,' Brodie insisted. 'I want to make sure you're okay. And if you need anything. Anything at all...'

'I'll be fine,' I said. I forced on a smile. 'Wish me luck.'

They all mumbled 'good luck' and I followed Drew out, who was going to take me to the station, glancing back to see them all huddled in the doorway. I waved but my heart wasn't in it and nor was it in theirs to wave back.

I looked up at the Hall. It had seemed so grand when I arrived, intimidating even, but then it had felt more like home than any place I'd lived in apart from the house I grew up in. Because it was filled with love. But I didn't belong there. I knew that. I had been pretending but it wasn't real. I would always end up running. That was clear. I just needed to accept that I would never be like my brother or his friends here. It was better I left them now before it got too hard.

Even so, it was more difficult than I expected to climb into the car and watch Glendale Hall fade into the distance as we drove away.

It was even worse getting on the train, waving goodbye to Drew, who watched from outside his car, lifting his hand as the train pulled out from the platform. I sank back in my chair and watched Glendale roll past the window. It felt like I had been there for such a long time, even though it had only really been five weeks. I had known I wouldn't be there long but I had thought I'd last the summer.

But this was the right thing to do. I was going to work in a London restaurant. I tried not to think about the fact that I wouldn't have this offer without being at Hilltop, without Beth and Heather encouraging me to cook, without my brother telling me I could do it, because that hurt too much. I couldn't let myself think about Cameron at all. I would just do what I always did. I'd walk away and start again. Start somewhere new with new people, people who didn't know me, and I wouldn't let myself care again. I had learned my lesson on that front.

My phone rang but I sent the call to voicemail. It vibrated with a message.

Heather has told me you've left Glendale. Please don't leave like this. Can we at least talk? Don't walk away from us, Anna. Please.

I read Cameron's text with a heavy heart. How could I talk to him? What was the point? He couldn't move on and nor could I. People didn't change. We both were too haunted by our past. It was better that we had no more contact. Better we carried on living alone like we had before.

I put my phone away and focused on watching the landscape change out of the window. I'd always wanted to go to London. I needed to be excited about this next step, and not be upset. I wasn't used to regretting anything. It was unsettling. I didn't like feeling like I'd left part of me behind. That was crazy. I'd always moved on without a backward glance before. I was sure this feeling would pass. It had to.

I needed to forget Glendale and everyone in it.

Picking up my phone again, I scrolled to Cameron's name and I deleted his contact from my phone.

Chapter Thirty-Nine

When I arrived in London, I got a taxi to Chloe's flat, not wanting to brave the tube on my first day in the city. It all felt like a blur. I was tired from the long train journey and the past couple of days. Emotional tiredness was proving to be a real thing. I didn't feel much as I watched London roll past the window of the taxi as we drove to Islington. I had always thought my first time in London would be such a thrill. But I was numb. I told myself I would feel a whole lot better in the morning.

Chloe's flat was in a pretty square in a converted townhouse. She opened the door when I buzzed. 'You're here! Come in, you must be shattered.' Her blonde hair and make-up were flawless and she wore a bright blue velour tracksuit. I felt crumpled and knackered in comparison but her enthusiastic smile when she saw me did cheer me up a little bit.

'I am,' I admitted, carrying my two bags over the threshold. She pulled me in for a hug, which was slightly awkward with my bag in the way. Chloe lived on the ground floor with her boyfriend and she showed me into the spare bedroom so I could dump my bags. It was tiny but I was used to that and it looked out onto the square. The walls were white and the floor was polished wood but Chloe had decorated it beautifully in soft grey and the bed looked so comfortable after sitting on the train for so long.

It was completely different to Glendale Hall but that was what I was looking for.

'Let's have some food and drink and then I'll let you rest.' She led me into the open-plan kitchen and living room. It was all tastefully decorated in neutral colours and she had scented candles lit and lots of green plants so it did feel homely, if small. 'Ashley is at the restaurant so we're on our own. I'll take you there tomorrow. I'm so excited to show you. Sit, sit!'

I climbed onto one of the bar stools as she pottered around the kitchen. 'Can't wait,' I said but my voice lacked half of her eagerness.

'Okay. I'm not a cook as you know but even I can't get this wrong.' Chloe came to sit next to me handing me a glass of red wine and taking one for herself. She placed a tray of crusty bread and a melted pot of cheese down between us.

'Just what I need,' I said, smiling. We tucked into it as Chloe told me all about the pop-up restaurant.

'It's going to be so brill. I'm helping decorate the space. We've gone for a really cool vibe, I can't wait to show you, and Pierre is doing a small but gorgeous French menu and Ashley is doing all the promo and will be front of house. With you helping, and the sous chef – Eddie – and the wait staff we've hired it should be a great team. Opening night is Saturday, which feels crazy soon, but we already have the first two weeks booked up thanks to the power of social media.' She gestured to her phone. 'I'm so glad you're here,' she said, taking a sip of her wine. 'It felt like a long shot as I could see how much you loved Glendale. I mean, I loved it too! I said to Ashley that we need to go back in the winter together. Can you even imagine how cosy it must be there at Christmas time?'

I swallowed my mouthful of bread. 'Really cosy. I just felt like this was too good an opportunity, you know? They all understood,' I mumbled, not even sure if I was lying or not. I gulped down more wine and Chloe topped us both up again.

'Even Cameron?' she asked, giving me a sideways glance. 'I couldn't help but wonder if there was anything going on between you two? When you looked at one another... And with Ashley not here I can admit that Cameron is hot.'

I couldn't even force on a smile at that. 'I thought maybe but no.' I shook my head firmly. 'I've always wanted to come to London. I'm excited.' That was true but I wasn't sure why I couldn't feel that excited in my heart. Hopefully, I just needed a good night's sleep.

'Well, I want you to enjoy it. And you know how much I want you to show off your culinary skills. Pierre will be so good to learn from and I've told him and Ashley how much I loved your cooking. Obviously, the restaurant will be different to that homely style of yours but I think you'll grasp it quickly.'

I knew that this was going to be a gourmet restaurant, different, as she said, from my style of cooking but I enjoyed the food I made and that was the main thing. I also knew that people enjoyed eating it. I knew in my heart it was the type of food I would want to make if I ever did make this a career but I kept quiet. I didn't think she would understand. To her, French cooking was the pinnacle. I tried not to think about what the Glendale gang would have said if I'd given them food like that at dinner time. I smiled into my wine glass. Even though they lived in a mansion, they were neither pretentious nor stuffy. I would always admire that.

Chloe's phone rang then and she walked over to the sofa to chat to her friend, telling me that we'd head off at eight a.m. tomorrow. I took that as my dismissal for the night so I jumped down off the stool and took a glass of water into my room. Closing the door, I let out a breath and went over to the bed, lying down on it still clothed. It was as soft as I had imagined it would be. Outside, a lamppost created a pool of yellow light through the gap in the blinds. I could hear traffic and a group of men talking outside. The sounds of a city again. I hadn't thought I would ever enjoy peace and quiet but the noise tonight was startling after my time in Glendale.

I couldn't even be bothered to get undressed. I turned off the bedside light and closed my eyes, willing sleep to come, but it turned out my insomnia was still very much there. It had just been taking a holiday while I'd been at the Hall. I heard Chloe go to bed an hour later and then another hour later Ashley slipped in through the front door. I heard their low voices before the flat went dark and silent. Still I stayed awake, finally pulling myself out of bed to change into my PJs and climb under the covers.

I was exhausted but still I couldn't sleep. I tried to stop myself but I replayed the final conversation I'd had with Cameron over and over on a loop. Those would be the last words we ever spoke to one another. I told myself I needed to forget all about it but my mind wouldn't let me. Finally, at three a.m. I was so tired that I drifted off to sleep but I dreamt of that cabin in the woods and the feel of Cameron's strong and solid arms around me.

When I opened my eyes, it was six a.m. and light slipped through the blinds into the bright white room, waking me up. I could hear traffic outside, and not birds, and it took me a minute to remember where I was. I yawned. My body ached and my eyes stung. The poor night's sleep hit me harder after sleeping so much better recently and I sat up slowly, heavily, and ran my fingers through my tangled hair from all my tossing and turning.

I slipped into the bathroom and had a hot shower and tried to shake off the remnants of my restless night. After I had got dressed and tried to make myself look as human as I could, I went into the kitchen. Ashley was buttering toast and Chloe was in the middle of the living room doing yoga.

'Hi, Anna, you need coffee?' her boyfriend asked. He wasn't how I'd pictured him at all. Short and stocky, he wore a grey suit and had slightly copper coloured hair. He looked out of place in the stylish kitchen but his warm smile endeared me to him.

'As strong as possible please,' I said, sitting on a stool.

'Want to do some yoga with me, Anna?' Chloe called over.

'I'm too tired this morning. I need caffeine and carbs,' I called back.

Ashely poured a cup of coffee for the two of us and clinked my cup with his. I took a long gulp and felt slightly better. 'You better get ready, Chlo, we need to leave soon,' he said to her as he pushed over a rack of toast towards me.

'Okay, I'm going to have a shower,' Chloe said, getting up and gathering up her mat. 'I can't wait to show you the restaurant,' she told me with a smile.

'I'm looking forward to it,' I said, and it wasn't a lie, I was curious to see it. I drank my coffee and thought that maybe this wouldn't be a complete disaster. I needed to focus on why I was here – the job. And once I had my first wages, I could rent a flat. Go out and meet people. Build a life for myself in London. And then I would forget all

Chapter Forty

The premises that Ashley and Chloe had secured for the pop-up restaurant was an unused warehouse. An empty shell a couple of roads back from Angel tube station. A prime location, but the warehouse looked rough from the outside so I understood why it hadn't cost too much to hire for the summer. Inside, though, Chloe had put her magic interior touch on it. Instead of hiding the warehouse, they had embraced it, with exposed bulbs hanging from the ceiling beams. The floor had been sanded and polished, and the bricks left exposed. The tables were reclaimed wooden park benches with black chairs, and there was a giant chalkboard at one end with the menu written on it. It was very... hip.

'Wow, this place is perfect for London,' I said, looking around. It certainly wasn't the type of place I would picture wanting myself but I knew it would be popular with the trendy city crowd. 'What about the kitchen?' I asked.

'There's a restaurant across the alley,' Ashley said, pointing to the open fire door at the side of the room. 'They're closed for refurbishment but the kitchen is finished so we're renting that out. Pierre knows the owner so we're not paying a fortune but it does mean we need to be fully booked to make a profit from this. It's not the end of the world if we don't – we want really to build a buzz around our name so when we open our real restaurant, people will be excited, you know? I guess we just want to make sure we work well together and it's a viable plan.'

'Of course it is,' Chloe said, threading her arm through his. 'You're brilliant.'

I looked away. The sight of her adoring smile made my stomach tighten. Everyone was sitting in a circle close to the open fire door, which let in much-needed air. The morning already felt far too humid. Summer in a city, I supposed.

'Ah, there you are,' the man in the middle said when he saw us three. He spoke with a thick French accent so was clearly Pierre, the chef. I stopped short and Ashley almost walked into me. He and Chloe gave me funny looks as they sat down. But I was so stunned. Pierre looked at me and slowly one of his eyebrows rose as he recognised me.

'Joining us, Anna?' he asked after a moment, his accent even more pronounced as he said my name. I nodded once and sat down slowly, ignoring Chloe's stare. I couldn't believe it. I knew Pierre. As in, we'd had a fling once. I mean, what were the chances? I hadn't even thought to ask Chloe anything about the chef. But then he hadn't been Pierre when we had met. I crossed my arms over my chest as he talked about the restaurant, avoiding my gaze. I certainly had only been looking for casual relationships when I had met him but I hadn't lied about my name like he had.

After Pierre had gone through what still needed to be done before opening night, Chloe said she'd introduce us but I told her there was no need and I hurried after him when he left through the fire door, clearly keen to get away from me. Which wasn't going to work as we were meant to be working side by side for the next few weeks.

'Luc,' I called.

He stopped, his shoulders sinking as he turned around. He put two hands up in a defensive stance. 'Hey, Anna, look…'

'That's funny. My name *is* Anna. Yours on the other hand…'

'I'm sorry,' he said although he didn't really look it. I remembered his arrogance then. 'But, you know, it was four weeks of fun, wasn't it? You didn't want anything more than casual. Nor did I.'

'Why lie about your name, then?'

He sighed. 'Because women say they want casual and then they change their minds. It always happens.' He tilted his head. 'Not with you, in the end. I was surprised to wake up one morning to find you gone.'

I had done that to annoy him. I had known he was used to using women, not the other way around. We'd met when I was in Paris for a weekend – he was good-looking and charming, and I'd admired his food, so when he'd invited me to come and stay at his family's home in the south, I'd gone, happy to have a holiday from real life. We'd spent four weeks together and I'd enjoyed long lazy days by the pool, eating and drinking well, and steamy nights in his bed. But I'd become bored and decided I should go back to Scotland and find a job. I'd done a midnight flit while he slept, thinking I'd never see him again.

Pierre shrugged. 'Look we both had fun, that's all we wanted. I'm happy to work together if you are?'

'Sure,' I said. 'Why not?' I couldn't be that angry. He'd been just like me. I watched as he walked back to the kitchen and wondered why relationships like that had made me think I was happy. I turned and went back into the warehouse to find Ashley and Chloe waiting for me, both curious as to what was going on. I explained I'd met Pierre in Paris, leaving out the gory details. As Ashley showed me the menu, I couldn't help but compare my month with Pierre to my month in Glendale. With Cameron. They were worlds apart. Why hadn't I realised how unfulfilled I had been living like that? Pierre had meant nothing to me. I'd walked away without a second glance. This time around, I wasn't sure I was going to be able to.

'What do you think?' Ashley asked me, shaking me out of my thoughts.

The menu was exactly what I would have imagined Luc, aka Pierre, creating for his first restaurant. I knew the food would all be full of flavour and presented beautifully. He could have won *MasterChef* if he didn't think it was a travesty of a show. 'I think people will love it.' And I genuinely did. Foodies would flock to this pop-up. But was it food that you would remember for years to come? Food that brought back memories and made you want to create it for the people you loved? I still thought of Christmas dinners cooked by my mother. I still longed to make one myself. That was the kind of food that I wanted to make.

'But not you?'

I was startled by Ashley's knowing look. I shrugged. 'I can't help but prefer less fussy food, more home-style. That's what I would love to do if I was a chef. I know it's not trendy though.'

'Chloe raved about your food. Sometimes people want comfort food. Sometimes they want food like this. That's the beauty of it – enough room for everyone. I love what Pierre cooks but…' Ashley leaned in closer and dropped his voice. 'Sometimes I need a Big Mac afterwards.'

I snorted with laughter. I remembered sneaking to the fridge while Pierre slept one night to eat chocolate after one of his meals, so I knew exactly what Ashley meant.

'Okay, I need to head off,' Chloe said, reappearing after a phone call. 'I have a photo shoot. Let's all eat together later, yeah?' She kissed Ashley and gave me a wave. 'Enjoy your first day, Anna.'

'Thank you,' I called after her retreating back. 'Right, what do you need me to do?' I asked, ready to get stuck in and forget about Glendale for the day.

Chapter Forty-One

Ashley and I went back to the flat after a day at the restaurant. I had been calling suppliers most of the day so my throat was dry but it had worked – my mind had been kept off all I had just left, focused on what I was doing now. Pierre had kept his distance but soon we'd be in a kitchen together. I still couldn't believe he was the chef I was supposed to be learning from. It would look good on my CV though. He was well-known and this restaurant would be a success, I could feel it.

'Chloe just messaged,' Ashley said when I walked into the kitchen after changing. 'She won't make dinner. She'll be back late.' He sighed. 'I do wish sometimes her job wasn't so busy. How about we order a takeaway?'

'Sure,' I said, pouring us both a glass of wine. It seemed we both needed it. 'So, how long have you and Chloe been together?'

'Five years. We met at university. Opposites attract and all that. Her career took off so much after we left and I can't help but miss her sometimes. That's why this pop-up has been so good, something we've worked on together.'

'You seem to make a good team.' They certainly did appear to be opposites but they both seemed happy. I wondered what it was like to live and work with someone. To be with someone for five years and share a life. I still couldn't picture me doing that. Although seeing Pierre again had shown me that what I used to think about relationships wasn't really how I felt now. What did I want instead though?

As we waited for the Chinese, my phone rang. I slipped into my room to answer Brodie's call, realising I hadn't contacted him. 'Hey, big brother.'

'You were supposed to let me know you got there okay!'

Oops. 'I'm sorry, I'm fine though.' I wasn't used to checking in with my brother. I perched on the bed. 'I've been to the restaurant, it's really cool. I think it will do well. And Chloe has a nice flat. Her boyfriend is really friendly so it's all fine.'

'Well, I'm glad. You hurried off so quickly, I was worried. We all were.'

'I do feel bad about letting Beth down.'

'She would never think that, you know her. She just wants you to do what will make you happy. I do hope you can come back for Heather and Rory's wedding at least.'

'I don't know, Brodie. The restaurant is fully booked already and it's not like you're just down the road.'

'Don't decide now. See how it goes. Everyone would love you to come, I just wanted to make sure you knew that.'

It was on the tip of my tongue to ask if Cameron felt the same way but I didn't. 'Okay,' I whispered.

'Mum phoned. She was surprised to hear you'd left Glendale. Did you think about talking to her? About everything you told me?'

Something I really didn't want to do. 'I will. Let me get settled here. Look, I really do have to go now.'

'Okay, Anna. Well, I'm pleased you got there safely. Take care of yourself, okay? Emily sends a big kiss too. And Iona. And the bump, too.'

I tried not to think about how much the bump would grow without me being around to see it. 'Thank you. Send a kiss back to them. My food is here.' I needed to hang up before I let myself think I'd made the wrong decision in leaving Glendale.

'I'll let you go but please keep in touch. I don't want to go for weeks without speaking to you like we did before.'

I nodded even though he couldn't see me. 'Bye, Brodie.' I hung up and took a deep breath. Why did speaking to him make me feel so emotional?

'Anna, food's up!'

'Coming!' I called back to Ashley, standing up and exhaling. I knew I was kidding myself that I could forget about everyone in Scotland so easily. Just hearing Brodie's voice had sent me straight back there.

—

The rest of the week was hectic. It was a mad rush to get the restaurant fully ready for opening night on Saturday. Chloe was publicising it like crazy, Pierre was trying recipes out over and over again, Ashley was making sure it looked perfect, and I was doing whatever any of them asked me to, becoming an assistant to the three of them. We worked long days and then in the evenings we either went out for drinks or ate at Chloe's flat, and Pierre spent most evenings with us. I remembered how he was good company, with his stories of France and how liberally he poured the wine. Ashley was quieter than his friend and girlfriend, the sensible one of the three, and Chloe worked harder than anyone I knew. But she liked to let her hair down hard too, so we drank a lot and had fun, but as soon as my bedroom door closed and I was alone again, my heart ached for things that I couldn't put into words.

And then it was the night of the grand opening. Chloe had invited influencers, journalists, food critics and her foodie friends so the place was packed. I was in the kitchen with Pierre and the sous chef, handing dishes to the wait staff who ferried back and forth from the warehouse. The kitchen was hot and loud and Pierre barked orders at us all evening. I didn't have a chance to think about anything other than the task in hand and the adrenaline was in full flow. I loved it. I might not have been creating the dishes but I was part of it and I thrived on the energy.

'That's it,' Pierre said as the clock struck ten. 'The final dish has gone out.'

I slumped against the counter. 'Blimey.'

He looked at me. 'Blimey? I should remove you from my kitchen for describing the night like that.'

I grinned. 'Fine. That was amazing. I loved it.'

He came over to me and lifted me up on the counter. 'It's like taking a drug, isn't it? Pumping through your veins.' He brushed back my hair. 'I hate the pink by the way. You should go back to being blonde.'

'And you should learn not to be such a twat,' I replied.

Pierre leaned in and kissed me on the lips. For a second, I kissed him back but then I came to my senses and pulled sharply back. He raised an eyebrow. 'No?'

'It's a hard no.' I jumped down and hurried outside. Guilt flooded through me, which was crazy. It felt like I had been about to cheat on Cameron. I stood in the alley, letting the evening air cool down my flushed cheeks. Why couldn't I forget about him? Why couldn't I go back to easy flings with men like Pierre? Go back to roaming the country, the world even, without caring about anyone?

Because I did care.

I answered the question for myself.

'You okay?' Ashley came out of the fire door to see me lost in thought. 'It was a great night. The last tables are just finishing up. Everyone loved the food. You should be smiling.'

'The night was great. I'm really pleased. It's just…'

'What?' he asked gently.

'I miss Glendale.' I shrugged. 'It's so stupid.'

'Why is it stupid? I've lived away from my hometown for five years but I still think of it as home. Come on, Chloe wants us to toast the night.' He gestured for me to come in so I followed, one of his words turning over and over in my mind.

That word was 'home'.

Chapter Forty-Two

I couldn't believe that I had been in London for four weeks. It was mid-August and summer was reaching its peak. The heat in the city grew unbearable. The restaurant was going really well. It was completely booked for the duration of the pop-up now and the reviews had been as good as I had predicted. Ashley, Pierre and Chloe were already thinking about the future, finding investors and looking for a full-time premises, and they'd made it clear they wanted me to come along with them. The problem was, I still felt lost.

It had been enjoyable. I liked working hard and the thrill of the busy kitchen excited me, and I felt so satisfied by the end of the night. I enjoyed cooking, I knew that, but now I knew that I loved working in a kitchen. I started to fantasise about what it might be like one day having Pierre's job. But it just didn't seem like it was possible for me. I didn't know how to make it happen.

And then there was the constant feeling that I was in the wrong place being in London. I was still staying in Chloe and Ashley's spare room. It just made sense with all the time I was at the restaurant and we got on so well. But what would I do once the pop-up closed? Carrying on working with them and find my own flat in London? Or should I still go to Ibiza as I'd planned next month? The thought of working in a beach bar didn't excite me as it had before. I kept willing the universe to give me a sign but I was worried that it already had, and I'd ignored it.

It was Saturday and I got up early for a run. Running in London was an experience I was still getting used to. Pounding busy pavements with traffic beside me wasn't my favourite but there was a park near to Chloe's flat that I could run in with more peace and enjoy the morning warmth. I hated that I was comparing everything to my stay in Glendale but it was hard not to think back on my runs there fondly.

I ran for a long time. It had been a late night at the restaurant, which had been packed with the Friday night crowd, and we'd gone to a bar afterwards so I was feeling a little worse for wear and I wanted to shake the night off.

When I returned to the flat, I opened the door to the sound of voices, which was surprising as both Ashley and Chloe had still been in bed when I had left for the park. And then I froze as I shut the door because I definitely recognised one of those voices. My heart sped up even more than it had on my run as I walked slowly towards the open-plan living room and kitchen.

There were five people in the kitchen. And they all turned around as I walked in.

I hadn't quite believed it from the voices but now I had to believe my eyes.

Chloe and Ashley were in the kitchen and so were Beth, Heather and Emily too. I stared at them, wondering what the hell they were doing here.

'Hi, Anna.' Beth broke the silence, smiling warmly at me. Emily gave me a cheerful wave and Heather a hello nod. The three of them were all sitting on the bar stools while Ashley and Chloe were making teas and coffees.

Emily looked like she was about to fall off her stool – in the weeks I'd been gone, her bump had grown even more and I wondered how she'd even got up onto the stool in the first place.

'What are you doing here?' I asked, still in the doorway, dumbstruck.

'We just fancied a little trip to London,' Beth said with a shrug. 'And thought we'd come and say hi.'

I raised an eyebrow. 'You expect me to believe that?'

Emily laughed. She was glowing even more now that she had a tan and with her bigger bump. 'I told you she'd never buy that,' she said to Beth.

'Fine. We came to talk to you,' Beth admitted. 'Do you want to get dressed? Let's go out for brunch. Please?' she added.

Why was Beth so hard to say no to? 'Fine, fine,' I mumbled and shuffled off to the bathroom, my mind whirring as to why they were here. Were they trying to get me to come back to Glendale? My gut instinct was to say no, obviously, and yet just seeing them had put a smile on my face. I jumped in the shower and tried to use the hot water to calm myself down but it was impossible. I wondered if I could ask them about Cameron but I shouldn't, should I? I had to leave him well alone. Did he know they'd come to see me today? I wanted to shout at myself to stop thinking about him but it had already proved impossible for me to do that.

I got dressed quickly in a t-shirt and jeans, pulling my hair into a ponytail and not bothering with make-up. I was too curious to see what the three of them had to say, too eager to find out what I'd missed the past month. I pulled on a pair of Converse and grabbed my bag, hurrying back into the kitchen where they were all chatting over hot drinks. 'I'm ready,' I found myself saying a little shyly. It had been four weeks since I'd seen them and they were so close. We'd never gone out as a foursome and I had no idea why they'd come all this way to see me. I realised, though, I was pleased that they had.

'Let's go. Chloe has given us a recommendation around the corner,' Beth said, hopping down from her stool. She helped Emily climb off hers.

I smiled. 'Chloe knows all the best places.'

'Have fun,' Chloe said with a cheerful wave. She wrapped herself around Ashley, who kissed the top of her head. As always when they were affectionate, I looked away because it was still painful to see them so happy when I felt so lonely. I led Beth, Heather and Emily out of the flat and into the summer sunshine outside. We walked in silence around the corner to the café Chloe loved for brunch, and we found a table in the corner. The waitress came over and we ordered drinks and food. And then there was no putting off the conversation.

'How are you?' Beth asked me. 'We haven't heard from you since you came down.' She gave me one of her not-impressed looks. It was so strange to see the three of them in a London café. To me they seemed completely out of place down here. But then again, I had been feeling that so was I.

'I'm good,' I said, which was a half-lie. 'I really enjoy working at the restaurant,' I added, which was true.

'That's great,' Emily said. 'I knew you'd love the atmosphere, there's nothing like creating things for people to enjoy.'

I turned to her. 'More importantly, how are you? Should you have even travelled down here?' I gave her bump a significant look.

'I wasn't going to miss out when these two said they were coming,' Emily said with a wave of her hand. 'I'm not due until the end of September, and I'm feeling full of energy actually. Although I love Glendale, I do miss living in London sometimes, so I thought I'd better grab my chance to come as I doubt I'll be back again anytime soon.'

'But why did you guys come?' I asked, still unsure if they had just come to see me or not. And if so, why?

'It was my idea.' Heather spoke then. She pushed back her curly hair. 'We had our final dress fitting a couple of days ago and it just felt like someone was missing. And I said to these guys that it just won't feel right me and Rory getting married without you there. So, we thought we should come down and persuade you.'

'Really?' I asked in surprise. I mean, I really liked Heather but I hadn't known her for long. To think she'd come all this way for me…

'I really want you there. So does Rory. So does everyone. But Brodie thought you probably wouldn't want to come back to Glendale so we thought if we came down, you'd have to say yes. Plus, I deserve a pre-wedding break so we're staying the night. We have twenty-four hours to persuade you to come to my wedding. And you know us, we will do it.' Beth and Emily both nodded in agreement.

I was saved from having to answer as our food and drinks arrived. I was both taken aback and touched that they'd come all this way to get me to come to the wedding. I hadn't contacted any of them because I'd been too scared I'd hear their voices and want to rush back to Glendale. I wanted to go to the wedding, but I was scared. 'I just don't know,' I admitted finally when we were alone again

Chapter Forty-Three

'He did?' I said, my surprised voice rising in pitch to almost only-dogs-could-hear-me levels.

'He was really upset when he found out you'd left.' Emily took over the story. 'He said he'd tried to contact you but you didn't reply. He didn't know what to do. He knew he'd hurt you but he told us that it was all a massive misunderstanding. He is desperate to tell you how he feels.'

'I know how he feels,' I replied, picking at my scrambled eggs. 'He can't get over what happened with his ex.'

'But that's just it, Anna,' Emily said gently. 'He says that meeting you has changed everything. He wants to explain what happened. Honestly, he's gutted that you've gone. He's so miserable, isn't he, Heather?'

'It's kind of annoying,' Heather agreed. 'But listen, it's up to you if you want to talk to him or not but please don't let him stop you coming to the wedding. You're part of the family now, you have to be there.'

'And if you make up with Cameron so much the better,' Beth added. She never gave up, did she? 'Show her the letter,' she told Emily.

'When we told everyone we were coming down for the weekend, Cameron gave us a letter for you. He really hopes you'll read it.' She pulled an envelope out of her handbag and slid it across the table to me.

I stared at it. 'What does it say?'

'He wouldn't tell me,' Emily said. 'But he looked broken, Anna. Really.'

Could he have missed me these past few weeks? Did I want him to have missed me? I mean, of course I did. But the thought that he might miss me, might feel the same way... it was also terrifying.

'Think about reading it, it's up to you. But please don't let Cameron keep you away,' Heather said. 'I'm getting married in two weeks and I'm so excited but I'm also nervous. I need all of you there with me. It's going to be so emotional without my mother, getting married in the place she loved and always wanted to—' She broke off, her voice cracking. Beth squeezed her hand and Heather gave her a grateful smile.

I felt like such a cow for letting her down. How could I say no? 'I'll have to see if Chloe can spare me though,' I said.

'She already said yes,' Beth replied.

Of course Beth would have already asked her. I rolled my eyes. 'One day someone isn't going to do what you want them to.'

She grinned. 'But then I'd have a lot of fun persuading them, wouldn't I? I'm sorry, I know I'm too much, but we have missed you. We just really wanted to see you.'

I was moved by that. To be honest I'd never had anyone follow me when I had left a place before. A couple of times I'd heard from people on social media or had a couple of messages before they gave up when I didn't respond, but no one had ever come after me like this. 'I'm glad you're here,' I admitted. They all smiled happily at that. I tucked into my breakfast, feeling for the first time that I actually had proper friends. Despite all my protesting that I didn't want to be tied down by caring about people or having people care about me, it felt really good to have them here. I eyed Cameron's envelope and when I'd finished eating, I put it in my bag to be dealt with later, when I was alone and could decide if I wanted to read it or not.

'I think we need a shopping trip,' Beth said when we'd finished. 'We never come to the city. We need to make the most of it. And we all deserve a treat.'

'I've got a couple of hours before I said I'd pop in and see Mum and Dad,' Emily agreed. Her parents still lived in London but I knew they were planning to retire to Glendale next year to be closer to their family.

We wandered around Islington and found some great independent clothes and homeware shops plus we had a mooch around the bookshop, where Beth bought Izzy a few books. I couldn't remember the last time I'd gone shopping with other women. Maybe not since I was a teenager with my mum. I was surprised by how much fun the four of us had.

'How's my brother doing?' I asked Emily in a shop as we waited for Beth and Heather to pay for what they wanted. I had picked up a vintage leather jacket and a print of one of my favourite album covers. I had hesitated as I had never hung things on walls, or bought much home décor, thanks to moving so much, but Emily had encouraged me as it had made me smile to see it. I felt good for having bought it, and hoped I'd get to hang it up one day soon in a place I wanted to stay long enough to put it up.

'Brodie talked about you a lot once you left,' Emily said, moving towards the door. I followed. She clearly wanted to speak to me without the other two. 'He really loved getting to know you better once you came to Glendale.' We stepped outside. The sun was out in full force. I wondered if it was as hot up in Scotland at the moment. 'It felt to him like when you were younger.'

I smiled. It was lovely to hear that he thought that. 'We were close when we were younger. Obviously, he was older and I was his annoying little sister but we were a close family. And then he kind of went off with his friends and my parents were worried, and I didn't really understand, you know? And then the accident happened, and it changed everything for all of us. We couldn't talk like we used to and there was a lot of misunderstanding, which I only realise now.'

'It's amazing how just talking can help so much. I'm glad the two of you got to reconnect. I hope you'll come back to Glendale. I know Brodie would love it. Family means so much to us. I think he just hopes he can be part of whatever you do next.'

'I would like that too,' I admitted. I thought about how I used to get really annoyed that Brodie had everything figured out. I compared myself to him. I thought our parents compared me to him. I thought I'd never be good enough for my family. But I didn't feel that way now. I had to find my own way in the world. And they would love me regardless. I felt bad for not speaking to my parents like my brother had suggested. We did need to put the past to rest. I could do that if I returned to Glendale.

'So, do you think you have finally found what you want to do?' Emily asked.

I smiled. 'I do love working in a restaurant. I love cooking and I want to learn more. It's just deciding how I do that. I'm used to doing things my own way and being independent. I need to feel like I've earnt things for myself, you know?'

'I do understand, but even if you get a helping hand along the way, it doesn't mean you don't earn your success. Beth rented me my bakery space. But it's mine. I have built it up to be successful, she just gave me that first footing on the ladder. It doesn't take away my own hard work.' She turned to see Beth and Heather coming out of the shop. 'I like that you're a free spirt. Even if you do come back to Glendale, even if you do accept help, you'll always live your own way. Because that's who you are.' She smiled at the others. 'I need to go to my parents' now.'

'Shall we drop Anna home and then head to the hotel?' Beth said to Heather. She turned to me. 'Chloe's booked us in to eat at your restaurant tonight.'

We all headed off. My mind was whirring. I thought about Emily believing that, whatever happened, I could do things my own way and I liked that idea. I wanted to stop running from people and places but I would always want to be free. It was who I was now. Was there a way to do both?

–

I worked my shift and then I joined Beth, Emily and Heather in the restaurant after their meal. They seemed to be having a great time on their girls' night away. They were so at ease with each other. I had always felt like I didn't fit in but they made me feel like I had been part of their group forever.

'I have had far too much wine,' Beth said with a giggle. 'I'll need a taxi back to the hotel, I can't walk straight.'

'I'm so annoyed that I have to be the responsible one,' Emily said, touching her stomach but she smiled. I knew she really didn't mind one bit.

'What's he like?' Heather asked, nodding towards Pierre, who had come in with me to say hello to his friends and hang out with Ashley. He kept his chef's hat on, of course. He loved being the centre of attention.

'He's a brilliant chef and has an ego to match,' I replied with a laugh. I wasn't going to tell them about our fling. I would never be ashamed of my past, of having fun like I had, but it wasn't something that I still wanted to pursue. I was moving on so there was no point in dwelling on it. 'I've learned things from him, from working here though, and that's been really useful.'

'Like how you might run your own restaurant one day?' Beth asked slyly.

'Or how you would run the kitchen at Hilltop,' Heather added, giving me a really exaggerated wink and giggle. How much had they been drinking?

'I suppose it has got me thinking about what I want to do,' I admitted, taking a sip of my wine. 'I have loved working in a kitchen.' I had also, sometimes, late at night after work when I hadn't been able to sleep, made some notes about it on my phone. Ideas of recipes, themes, plans – not that I would admit it or show it to anyone yet.

Emily leaned in and lowered her voice. 'Honestly, I would much rather eat your food, Anna. I mean, this tasted good but it's so rich and the portions were tiny. I might need a burger when we get out of here.'

Beth nodded vigorously. 'Too high-brow for my tastes, I'm afraid. We are unrefined, maybe, but there it is.'

'Well, don't tell Pierre, but I agree with you,' I whispered back. I was pleased that they thought the same way about the food as I did. It was top quality, but it wasn't food that filled you with joy. That's the kind of food I wanted to make.

'I'd want people to leave my restaurant happy,' I declared. Everyone needed a place like that to enjoy. To look forward to eating at. A place where you'd go for birthdays or anniversaries or special occasions.

Beth stared at me. 'Did you just admit that you want to open your own restaurant one day?'

They all looked at me expectantly. I drained my wine glass dry, enjoying making them wait for my answer. I was maybe high on the night and from the sudden injection of alcohol and the fact they had come to see me, but I didn't want to hide from it anymore. To pretend that it wasn't my dream. I nodded. 'Yes, yes I did!'

'Yay!' Emily cried as Beth cheered and Heather clinked her glass against mine. I smiled at their happiness for me. They wanted me to succeed. I'd never experienced that before. It felt good. I wanted to do something for them in return.

I turned to Heather. 'And I'm coming to your wedding,' I told her. I didn't want to think about Cameron's letter for the evening. I just wanted to have fun with my friends. And they really did feel like my friends. For maybe the first time in my life. And I didn't want to let them down. They wanted me at the wedding, so much they had come all the way down to London. And I realised as Beth topped us all up with more wine, I wanted to be there too.

'Okay,' Beth said, gesturing for us to quieten down. 'I need to make a toast. Firstly, to excellent company this evening. I love you gorgeous women, and honestly you all inspire me. I'm so excited that Anna has decided to follow her dreams. We will help as much or as little as she wants us to.' She grinned at me. 'And I can't wait to celebrate Heather's wedding to Rory. There is no one who deserves happiness more, and you two will be together forever. It won't be an easy day, I know.' She paused to look at her friend. 'But we will all be there with you and it will be so special, I promise. I suppose what I'm trying to say is here's to a wonderful future for all of us!'

Even I felt a lump in my throat as I clinked Beth's glass with mine. Emily's eyes were brimming with tears and Heather couldn't meet anyone's eyes. I understood what bonded these women and I realised that it wasn't a weakness to want their support sometimes. They were there for each other whenever they were needed and somehow I knew they would be there for me too if I wanted them to be. I promised myself that I would do the same in return for them.

And then I drained my second glass of wine and the evening grew hazier but I would never forget it, I knew that. Beth, Heather and Emily had given me something that I had never had or thought I wanted or needed. And I didn't need it – I was just fine on my own, I knew that, but it was okay to want it and to enjoy it. I hadn't let myself think like that before but now I could.

I smiled. I was excited for the future that night. And that was definitely a feeling that I wanted to keep.

Chapter Forty-Four

I let myself into Chloe and Ashley's flat just after two a.m. I had gone to Beth, Heather and Emily's hotel bar for drinks and finally staggered into a taxi as they went to bed after giving me two rounds of hugs. I was feeling more than a little bit tipsy and keen to collapse in bed but when I closed the front door both Chloe and Ashley called out for me to come into the kitchen.

Walking in, I was greeted with them wrapped around each other, an open bottle of champagne, and two glasses in their hands.

'Anna! We've been waiting for you. Guess what?' Chloe cried out, waving her hand in front of me.

After all the booze I had consumed, it took me a minute to focus on her hand but when the light from the Jo Malone candle lit on the breakfast bar caught it, I could see the sparkling rock that now sat on her finger. 'Is that…?' I asked, stepping closer to see better.

Chloe broke into the biggest smile. 'It is! We're engaged!'

'Oh, wow. Congrats guys.' I went over to hug them both. 'I'm so happy for you.'

'Thanks, Anna,' Chloe said. 'I just can't get over how perfect this ring is!' She looked at her hand again. It was pretty dazzling. 'And you picked the exact style that I've always wanted.' It was a stunning ring. As if I would expect anything less from this couple though. It was platinum with a massive square diamond and I caught sight of the Tiffany's box on the side. The thing was, though, I couldn't begrudge them anything. They liked the flashy lifestyle, sure, but they were sweet and kind and were head over heels in love. It was hard not to feel a pinch of envy. Not that I'd changed my mind about marriage but it would have been nice to have someone to share my life with like they had.

'I can take hints you know!' Ashley laughed and they leaned in for a kiss.

'I'll leave you two to celebrate,' I said, backing away. I was pleased but I felt like I was intruding on a moment that was just for them.

'Ooh yes, I need to post on Instagram,' Chloe said, grabbing her phone.

Maybe not that private, but then it wouldn't be Chloe if she didn't instantly share their news. I left them posing for selfies and headed into my room. I had sobered up somewhat. My wine buzz had definitely gone. I was left with a strange empty feeling in the pit of my stomach. I went through the motions of getting ready for bed – taking off my make-up and brushing my teeth, pulling my hair into a ponytail, and changing into my pyjamas. I climbed into bed but I knew it would be a long time until sleep found me.

I could hear Chloe talking loudly on the phone. Clearly, she and Ashley were ringing around friends and family despite the late hour, too excited to wait to share their news, which I understood. I thought about their engagement and how a wedding would be on the cards, and the wedding I'd agreed to travel back to Scotland for. All these happy ever afters around me. It was hard not to be affected by them. I lay there alone and then my eyes found the bedside table. Inside it was Cameron's letter. Just waiting for me to decide whether to open it or not.

Pulling it out, I sat up in bed with it on my lap. I prided myself on not being scared of anything. I wanted to be fearless. But this scared me. I wasn't sure what I wanted his letter to say. What I wanted to hear from him right now. Or even if I wanted to hear from him at all.

Then I thought of Chloe and Ashley. They had a connection. It didn't make much sense on paper. I would never have picked them out to be a couple. I didn't think anyone would think they went well together, and yet they did. It worked. And I knew that curled up with Cameron in his cabin I had felt that same way about the two of us. Of course, it had then been snatched away from me but, for that one moment, I had felt happier and more contented than I had in years. I longed to feel that way again. Now I'd had it, I didn't feel quite whole without it.

Even if this letter said that he never wanted to see me again, it would be better to know rather than torturing myself as to what was in it. And if there was even a small chance that our connection had been real, I knew that I couldn't allow myself not to find out. I had done what I always did and run away. But Glendale wasn't letting me get off that easily. Beth, Heather and Emily had already proved that. And now I had this letter.

I knew I couldn't hide away any longer. I had to face whatever was in it, and only then could I decide what I should do next.

I had to rip that plaster off.

Curling up into a ball facing the bedside light, I opened Cameron's letter.

Anna,

I haven't been able to stop thinking about what happened before you left. You might not want to hear from me. I understand that. Which is why I asked Emily to give this letter to you. Then you can decide whether to read it or not. I really hope you do. But I'll understand if not.

I have no idea how it must have felt for you to hear me say my ex-girlfriend's name like that. But I'm jumping to the end. I need to explain it all from the start. Words, as you know, aren't my strong suit but I hope this will all make sense...

The first time I saw you I almost hit you with my tractor. I was so panicked. You know why now but you didn't then. You just thought I was overreacting. I didn't see you clearly that day but I remembered your pink hair, the way you looked in your jogging gear, that eyebrow you raised when you were being sarcastic. Then I saw you again at Glendale Hall. And I was pleased. It was this strange surge inside me. I hadn't felt it in so long. I had closed myself off. You know that. And you understand why. But suddenly, I didn't want to do that anymore. Because of you.

Then I saw you about to get into Adam's car after he'd been drinking. I don't think I've ever moved so fast. I wanted to – no, I needed to – protect you. And it wasn't just because of the past. I couldn't even think about something happening to you.

That scared the hell out of me so I tried to push you away. But we were constantly being drawn together. I know sometimes I was rude. I'm so sorry for that. I was trying to make myself not care by making sure you wouldn't care about me. But it got harder and harder. You were so alive. So full of fire. You don't realise how much you shine, I don't think. So honest, so fearless, so beautiful. You just rocked my world. You turned it upside down.

I kept telling myself I needed to stay away. I honestly felt so much guilt about Kirsty. I thought there was no way I could deserve you in a million years. But every time I saw you, I felt this pull towards you. There was this spark between us. This connection. This force. You were like a magnet.

Somehow, I think you felt it too. When we kissed, it felt so right. But I was haunted by the past. You were so honest with me about how you were too. For the first time, I felt like I could open up to someone. And I wanted to.

Being with you felt like the part of me that had been missing had been returned.

I felt so many different things. I don't know how to explain it. I was so happy but so scared and so guilty. You made me feel like I could move on. That I should move on. That it was okay to. I don't know if you'll ever realise how much you've changed my life in such a short space of time.

Then that day in my cabin...

When I had my arms around you and you fell asleep, I knew it. I loved you. I think maybe I had loved you from the first moment I saw you, if

I'm being honest. I wanted to tell you but I was nervous. You always seemed like such a free spirit. You made it clear we were casual. That you were moving on at the end of the summer. That you didn't want to be tied down by anyone. So, I fell asleep and I didn't tell you how I felt.

God, I regret that.

Every day.

I must have been dreaming about Kirsty. Maybe it was my way of saying goodbye finally. Of letting her go. Of letting my guilt go. Of being happy with you. Of feeling like the future was mine again. That's why I said her name. I had been thinking about falling in love with you. Not her. I'll always regret what happened with her. And it was so tragic. I miss what we had. I miss her. I wish she'd had her chance at life, of course I do. But I don't love her anymore.

I thought I was to blame for what happened to her. But I know now that I wasn't. You made me see that. I closed myself off the night she died. But you opened my heart again.

I hope you believe that I love you. But I know that might not be what you want to hear. You left and I hope you're happy. I want you to be happy. But I had to tell you how I feel. In case you might feel the same way. If you do, just know that I'm terrified. But that's okay. We can be scared together. We don't need to make any promises. We don't need to plan anything. We can just love each other for as long as it feels like the right thing for both of us.

And it does feel right to me. You feel right. And if I feel right to you then please come back to me, Anna.

Cameron

Chapter Forty-Five

The sun rose outside my bedroom window but I hadn't slept a wink. I had pretty much memorised Cameron's letter, having read it so many times during the night.

I didn't know how to feel about it. On one hand, I was relieved that he felt the same way as I did. I hadn't imagined our connection.

But I was also terrified. I hadn't even let myself admit that what I felt for him might be love. I'd never been in love before. Cameron had declared himself but what the hell should I do next? If I admitted that I loved him too, that would mean starting a relationship, me going back to Glendale and sticking around, settling, building a life there, with him... and these were all things that I had actively been avoiding since I was eighteen and first left home.

How did people do this?

I could hear activity in the flat so I was thankful I could get up and stop my over-thinking. I padded through to the kitchen in my PJs and found Ashley making coffee. 'Please tell me that is really strong,' I said, shuffling over to a stool and climbing up. I knew I must look awful. I felt it.

Ashley gave me a sympathetic look. 'Couldn't sleep? Neither could I. Chloe is fast asleep. If I'm nervous or excited, I have no chance of a good night's rest,' he said, coming over with two big mugs of black coffee.

'Same. Or if I do manage to fall asleep, I have nightmares.' I took a gulp even though it burned my throat. 'Can I ask you something?' He gestured for me to go ahead. 'How did you know you were ready to propose to Chloe?'

'We went to a wedding. It was a close friend from university so we all met at the same time. I looked at them getting married and I thought "that should be us". We are just a great team. I can't imagine going through anything in life without her by my side.'

I felt so envious of his certainty. 'You do make a great team,' I agreed. 'I've never really seen myself settling – in a relationship or a place or at a job – but I've loved working with you guys this month. I would love to have my own restaurant one day. I just don't know how to get there.'

'I would say take it one step at a time so don't think "oh god I have to own my own restaurant". Think about the first step to get there.'

'I'd love to work as a chef. I mean, it's such a long way to opening my own place. I want to study some more. I saw this...' I showed him the chef diploma course at the college in Inverness that Brodie had told me about.

Ashley nodded. 'That looks like a great course for you. Definitely the first step. So just focus on that. That's it. Don't think about what's next. Think about where you'd want to do the course and apply and if you're accepted, find somewhere to live nearby. And that's it. Don't think further than that. Otherwise it will get scary.'

'Even that feels scary. But exciting too.' I smiled. Then I pulled out my plane ticket to Ibiza. 'It would mean not doing what I had planned next though. A course would start around this time. It is a refundable ticket though,' I mused as I looked at it.

'Perhaps you weren't as sure as you thought you were about going there if you paid for a refundable ticket?' Ashley suggested.

I looked at him. 'Huh. I hadn't thought of it like that.'

'So have you decided not to come with us to our new restaurant? I'm guessing by thinking of doing a course that you have. And you're heading back to Glendale.'

'All I've agreed to is going back for Heather's wedding but my brother knows the guy who runs this cookery school. It would make sense to go there. I don't know though. My brother is always offering to help me but I'm so not good at letting people do that. I've always thought I have to be independent, I suppose.'

'That's what family is for, though. The silent investor in our pop-up was my dad. I don't see it as a hand-out, just a leg-up when I needed it the most. And I'll pay him back. So it was more like an interest-free loan. Think of your brother's help that way – a way to get started. I think you can do it, if that means anything. You just need to really want it.'

'I do,' I said. It was a relief to say it out loud. I had been so annoyed at Beth and Brodie for making all these plans for me when I hadn't even decided what I wanted but I think it was because I knew instantly deep down that they were right about what I should do. I just needed to make the choice for myself. And working here in London had decided it for me. I wanted to be in my own kitchen one day for real. I knew that it would be a long road to get there but, finally, I had a direction for my life. And it felt good. I didn't feel as lost anymore.

Chloe came in then. 'Why are you both up so early? And why are you smiling like that, Anna? It's freaking me out.'

'It's freaking me out too,' I replied with a laugh. I felt a hundred times lighter.

'You're looking at a future chef over here,' Ashley said, leaning to give her a kiss. The diamond on Chloe's finger sparkled even more in the morning light.

'Of course I am,' Chloe agreed. 'I told her that the night I tasted her food for the first time. And I'm always right.'

I rolled my eyes as Ashley shook his head. She grinned at us. 'I bet I'm right about something else too,' she said, pouring herself a coffee.

'What's that?' I asked, feeling a little bit nervous to hear what she had to say.

'That you left a piece of your heart back in Glendale.'

'On that note, I'm going for a shower.' I slipped off the stool as she protested it wasn't fair for me not to answer and Ashley laughed heartily at us. I skipped into the bathroom. I had no idea what to do about Cameron's letter but I knew one thing, Chloe was right. I had left a piece of my heart behind me in Glendale. I just needed to decide whether to go back to get it or not.

—

Chloe came into my room late on the Thursday night before I was due back in Glendale. It was Heather's wedding on Saturday so I was getting the train in the morning and I was packing a bag ready. Beth said I could have my old room at the Hall for the weekend and it was strange to feel like I was packing to go home. But the Hall was the closest I'd had to a home since childhood. I was excited to go back but nervous too. I still hadn't decided what to say to Cameron but I was hoping that when I saw him, I would know.

'Thank you for coming down here to help,' Chloe said, perching on the bed as I packed. 'Even Pierre said you were a life-saver,' she added with a smile. 'He won't admit it but that red wine sauce worked so much better once you worked your magic on it.'

'He definitely will never admit that,' I agreed. 'This has been such a great opportunity and it's really made me want to do it for myself one day. I knew I loved cooking but honestly until we met, I had never thought about it seriously as a career. So, I'm the one who should be thanking you.'

Chloe waved her hand. 'It was selfish – I wanted the best team for Ashley and Pierre and that included you. I'm glad that you've seen sense though, that you should be doing this as your job.'

'It's been a long road. I haven't known what I really wanted for a long time.' I shrugged. 'I can't complain about all the places I've seen but maybe it's time to focus on what I want to do.'

'I'm proud of you. And, listen, I know there are a couple of weeks left until the pop-up closes, but we'll be absolutely fine without you. I get the feeling that once you're back in Glendale, you might not want to leave it again.' She stood up. 'No need to decide either way now. I just didn't want you to feel like you had to come back. Sometimes when a fresh start is beckoning, it's better to start straight away. What's the point in waiting?' Then she winked.

'What are you planning, Chloe?' I asked. I knew her well enough by now to recognise the mischievous look on her face.

'I couldn't possibly say but, remember, follow your heart, okay? Promise me.' She hovered in the doorway for my response.

I sighed. 'I will promise to try,' I said. That was all I was willing to agree to for now.

'You've got this, Anna. I'll be eating at your restaurant one day, I know it.'

With that, she skipped out, always a bundle of enthusiastic energy. I hoped she was right. I carried on packing and found myself humming as I did so.

Chapter Forty-Six

I had been in London for longer than I had lived in Glendale but the sight of it was more welcome than I could have imagined. Brodie was waiting at Inverness train station to collect me and drive me to the village and as we passed by the sign I felt my body relax in a way it just hadn't done while I was down in London.

'It's been much quieter without you, you know,' Brodie said as we drove through the village. I had sat up in my seat to look out of the car window at the shops rolling past. I turned to give him a glare, and he broke into a grin. 'We missed you.'

'Well, good. Can we pull over a sec? I want to talk to you before we get to the Hall.' I knew that everyone would be there and I needed to speak to my brother alone first. Brodie looked curious but did as I asked and stopped just on the road to the Hall. It felt so familiar to me and it was good to see it again. I already couldn't wait to run out here again. I had missed my solitary mornings outside in the countryside. Even the air felt different to London.

'Is everything okay?' Brodie asked once we'd stopped and he'd turned off the engine. He had on what I liked to call his 'serious vicar' face, even though today he was just in jeans and a t-shirt. I wondered if he'd always be nervous when I asked to talk to him. And if I'd always feel nervous to do so. Hopefully one day we'd get there, I wanted us to talk more.

'I hope so,' I said with a nod. 'I've been doing a lot of thinking down in London. I thought I'd be able to just move on like I always do. Start over and forget all of this.' I gestured outside the car. 'But I couldn't. I enjoyed being here more than I thought I would. Much more. I love living at the Hall, I've made friends there, being close to you and Emily has been great too, and cooking for you all has been so much fun. I've never had people to cook for like that before.'

'I was so surprised at how talented you were, and the smile on your face when you're cooking and serving it all, I can tell how much you love it.' Brodie smiled with genuine pleasure. I could tell he really did want to see me happy.

'And then getting to work for the past few weeks in a proper restaurant just sealed it for me. I've spent so long being kind of aimless, I suppose, thinking that I needed to try everything and see everywhere, but I didn't ever stop to think about whether doing that was making me happy. I think I needed to go off and experience it, though. I needed to come to terms with everything that happened. I didn't know who I was and I needed time to discover the person I am and want to be. Now I know what I want. And a lot of that is down to you and everyone here.'

'Well, I'm pleased. So, what do you want to do next? Are you going back to London? Or are you still heading abroad?'

I shook my head. 'Chloe said she was fine with me not finishing my last couple of weeks at the pop-up. It's all running well, they will be absolutely fine without me. I was planning on going back but when she said that, I thought why not just get started on what I want to do, you know? I had a refundable ticket to Ibiza so I've got my money back. It's not where I want to be right now.' I took a deep breath. 'I called your contact at the Inverness cookery school,' I said, knowing that I was rushing to get my words out. I still felt kind of awkward baring my soul to my brother but it was getting easier. And I needed to get all of this out. 'I've got a place if I want it on their diploma course in September. But I need to go and look around the college and meet with him. I wondered if you'd come with me?'

'Definitely,' he said quickly. 'I'm so proud of you. I think you will be amazing. Do you need help with the course fees?'

'Actually, I think I have enough. I can put the Ibiza ticket towards it and everything I've saved this summer. Plus, it's a part-time course so I can work at the same time.' I took a breath. 'I'm going to ask Beth if I can continue working at the Hall while I do it. I think I can manage most of what needs to be done at the Hall and the course is in the evenings anyway. I know that Heather said she might hire a chef for Hilltop next year but I think I would rather do things this way.' I felt like I'd be more independent this way, and Cameron was in the back of my mind. I wasn't sure working at Hilltop, or even living there – which I supposed I would need to do if I took the chef job – was a good idea, no matter what happened between us. I needed my own life whatever relationship I had, I was sure of that. I would always want to live on my own terms.

'I think it's a great idea,' Brodie agreed with a nod. My chest sagged with relief. I hadn't realised how important his opinion was to me until I heard it. 'I'm thrilled you'll be staying in Glendale while you do this. Even if you're not here forever, I'm really looking forward to spending time with you and the fact you'll be around when the baby comes makes me really happy.'

'Me too,' I said with a smile. I was going to be an auntie and I'd actually get to know my niece or nephew. It was pretty cool. 'One more thing I'd like your help with... I need to go and see Mum and Dad. I've put it off ever since we talked about the accident. But I can't chicken out anymore, especially now I'm moving here. I want to see them more. I want to put the past behind us as much as we can. I wish I had talked to you all more but I can't change the fact I didn't, I can just do better from now on.'

'It works both ways. We should have talked about the accident too. We should have seen that you weren't okay. That you blamed yourself. We'll go and see them and we'll talk it all through. It will be okay, Anna, I know it will. I have faith.'

I smiled. 'Good, one of us needs to.'

I was taken aback then when Brodie suddenly leaned over to give me a quick squeeze. 'You are stronger than you'll ever know,' he said into my ear.

'Right, we should get going,' I said, clearing my throat. I hid my pleased smile from him. I felt like I finally had the chance to have my family back in my life and that made me happier than I could have guessed.

'Right,' he agreed, starting up the car. I always thought my brother had a holier-than-thou attitude but I think that was just because I thought he disapproved of my life; I now knew it wasn't that, he had been trying to look out for me. But I had needed to make my own decisions. And that was okay, I thought. He was here for me if I needed him, but I also knew I would always try to do things for myself. That was part of who I was. And I liked who I was.

Now I was free of the guilt that had haunted me, I didn't have to worry that I didn't deserve to have what I wanted in life, I could instead focus on achieving it.

I watched as the gates of Glendale Hall came into view, open ready for us, and I smiled to see the house rising up in front of me. Its grand exterior was different to the warmth within I knew. I had been intimidated when I had first arrived here but coming back to it now was just like coming home. I understood why Beth and Izzy felt so rooted here; why they never wanted to leave. Beth had been right about its ability to work magic – it had for me. I thought you'd have to have a heart made of stone not to fall in love with this house.

It was a grey day but nothing could dampen my spirits as I climbed out of the car and walked up to the door with Brodie, carrying my bags as I had done when he had first brought me here, but feeling like I was at a completely different point in my life two months later.

The door opened before we knocked. 'You're home!' Beth exclaimed when she saw us, bouncing on her bare feet. She wrapped her arms around me. 'So happy to have you back.'

God, was I going to cry? 'I'm happy to be back,' I managed to say through the lump in my throat. I walked into the hallway, and I took in the grandfather clock, the vase of fresh lavender on the side table, and the chandelier hanging from the ceiling, and I broke into a wide smile.

'Take your things up to your room, I'm just getting lunch ready, everyone is in the kitchen,' Beth said as she ushered Brodie in and closed the front door. I walked up the stairs as they went off into the kitchen. The house was quiet as I made my way to my room, peeping in to the other rooms as I went. The house was nowhere near as clean and tidy as it had been before I left, which actually made me feel needed – the house felt as if it had missed me like I had missed it. Which was probably crazy to think, but still.

Pushing open the door to my room, I carried in my bags, putting them down on to the floor and walking over to the window to look down at the grounds below. I had missed this view so much. All the open air and green outside of my window. I would never take that for granted. Turning, I saw there was something on the four-poster bed. It was a notecard that said 'Welcome Home!' and, on the back, everyone at the Hall had signed it – Beth, Drew, Izzy, Caroline, John and even Sally. Then I couldn't help it. A little tear poked out of my eye. I brushed it away, embarrassed at myself, glad no one else was here to witness it.

But I'd never had a place to call my own. It was still temporary, I was certain of that. I wanted to be a chef and have my own restaurant and my own place to live one day but for now, this was where I both wanted and needed to be. For now, it was home.

I opened my bag and pulled out the print I had bought in Islington. I was going to hang it up in here. For the first time, I was going to make the room I slept in feel like it was actually mine.

I smiled as I thought about Beth calling Glendale Hall my home.

It really did feel that way.

Chapter Forty-Seven

Lunch at Glendale Hall. I had missed the chaos, the laughter, everyone talking over one another, and the food. Sally had been in charge today as Beth wanted everything to taste amazing and there were lots of treats from Emily's Bakery too, of course. As well as the Hall gang, Heather, Rory, her dad Don and little Harry were joining us and of course Brodie, Emily and Iona too. Izzy's cat Ginny even made an appearance crying for food. Izzy snuck her some ham when her mum wasn't looking.

It was difficult not to feel the absence of Cameron, and even Angus, but they were working on their farms and I also knew that Cameron wouldn't come until I let him know if I wanted to see him or not. He'd bared his soul in that letter and now it was my turn. But I couldn't help but want to put that off. It certainly wasn't easy to change the habits of a lifetime.

For now, though, I focused on how good it felt to be back. I piled my plate up with crusty bread, potato salad, cheese, veggie sausage rolls, cold pasta, salad, and boiled eggs and joined everyone crowded around the table with extra chairs for those who couldn't fit. The French doors were flung open out to the garden and a fresh breeze blew in. There was wine for the adults and homemade lemonade and juice for the kids, and Emily of course, and

I'm not sure there was a more enjoyable lunch to be found anywhere else in the world.

'Okay, you have to tell us all about London,' Izzy begged me from across the table. 'Did you go to the British Library? Or King's Cross Station?'

'I not sure Anna did the Harry Potter tour,' Beth told her daughter fondly.

I smiled. 'I didn't. I was working mostly. The restaurant was so busy and we had such late nights that in the day I mostly chilled. I did do some shopping, though, and I ran in the park most days.' Izzy grimaced at that. Like her mother, she was averse to most exercise. 'I loved being in the kitchen. It was a real adrenaline rush every night.'

'I get that in the bakery on busy mornings,' Emily said. 'So I can only imagine what a restaurant is like. What was your favourite thing to do?'

'Making the sauces. Pierre let me help after a while. You have to ease him in to change. He's a real control freak but he is a talented chef. He'd turn his nose up at this kind of spread though. He's way too fancy. I loved helping him to get the flavours just right... It's really an art.'

'I liked his food,' Beth said. 'But honestly, the portions... It was ridiculous!'

'I was still hungry afterwards,' Heather agreed. 'I hope your restaurant will do proper portions,' she said to me, gesturing to her full plate.

'It will,' I promised, thinking how strange it was to be talking about having one of my own one day. It still felt so far off into the future but I was determined to get there. It wouldn't be easy but I loved a challenge and I knew now it was what I wanted to do. I looked at Beth, Heather and Emily. All businesswomen running successful

317

companies during a time when having a small business was so difficult, and in a small town too. They were all an inspiration. And I knew I could count on their help and support too. Which made it all feel a little less scary.

After lunch, Beth asked me to help her pack up some greenhouse produce to take to the Glendale shop. I knew though it was an excuse for us to be alone so we left the others and walked across the lawn towards the large greenhouse. They grew all sorts of things at the Hall and some we ate and some were sold in the shop. 'You looked like you had things on your mind,' Beth said as we walked side-by-side. She had on her garden boots, even though it was summer, and a long cardigan as the breeze was chilly.

I had to walk quickly to keep up with her long strides. I explained what I had told Brodie earlier. 'But that's only if you would still need me here, of course. I completely understand…'

'Of course we need you!' she interrupted. 'I didn't want to say because I didn't want to pressure you or make you feel guilty, but honestly this place is already starting to fall apart. I feel like the chore list gets longer and longer so we definitely need you and we will work around your studies.' She opened the greenhouse and we went inside, the warmth a welcome from the breeze outside. 'I'm so pleased. I thought maybe you'd stay for the wedding then go back to London. But you're coming home! We honestly think of you as one of the family already.'

'That means a lot to me,' I said. She handed me a box, which I started filling with strawberries. 'In fact, Chloe said I didn't need to come back at all if I didn't want to. And until I arrived in Glendale, I was still in two minds. But being back here just sealed it for me. Right now, this is where I want to be. It feels like where I'm meant to be, even.'

She nodded as she packed up tomatoes. 'I know exactly how you feel. When I came back at Christmas after being away, I couldn't wait to escape back to London again but I really think this place gets under your skin. It worked its magic and I couldn't leave. I had to stay. Dare I ask about Cameron?' She gave me a sly look.

'I'm still thinking about that. I might wait to see how I feel when I see him at the wedding. Then maybe I'll know.'

'God, Anna, we are so alike,' she cried, shaking her head in wonder. 'I thought the same about Drew when I saw him again after ten years. It was like no time had passed and I knew in that moment we were meant to be. It wasn't quite that easy to make it all work but my heart knew what it wanted. You will definitely know when you see him. And at a wedding too, so romantic! I know you're not a wedding fan but I promise you when you see Broomfield Castle, you will feel the magic in the air.'

'I don't know if I'll ever feel the same about weddings as you do but I promise I'll go with an open mind towards magic,' I replied with a laugh. 'I can't believe Heather is getting married tomorrow. She, and Rory too, and you for that matter… you all seem so chilled about it.' I couldn't imagine being so comfortable with the idea of being with one person for the rest of my life as they all appeared to be.

'To be fair you haven't seen us the past few weeks, it has been pretty fraught because the photographer pulled out due to bereavement and then Heather changed her mind about which flowers she wanted but getting away to London to see you really helped us all just to have a break. Everything is on track now. We'll be at the venue tomorrow morning and then hopefully we can just enjoy the day. The woman at the castle who organises the weddings there is such a pro. And even if things don't quite run like clockwork it's such a gorgeous place, I don't think anyone will mind.' She sealed up her box, and I did the same. 'I think Heather and Rory have been through so much together already, this is a walk in the park. Great, let's carry these to the house and Drew is going to drop them off for us. It's so nice he's got the weekend off from the hospital so we can all enjoy this wedding.' The smile on her face was pure joy. I tried to think when someone had made me feel that happy as we went back to the house. I could only think of being in Cameron's cabin, in his arms.

My stomach danced a little. Tomorrow I would see him again. How would I feel? How would he feel? Did he still feel the same way as he did when he wrote me that letter? Did I?

Chapter Forty-Eight

If I was honest, I had put more thought and effort into my outfit than I usually would. I couldn't help it. It would be the first time Cameron had seen me in four weeks and I wanted to look good. I also wanted to feel good for myself. It would give me confidence. And I couldn't let the side down – the Hall gang had gone all out for this wedding.

We met by the front door to wait for the car to pick us up and take us to the venue. Beth had left much earlier with Izzy as they were bridesmaids, and to make sure everything was okay. Drew had stayed with his brother last night – the rest of us followed on at lunchtime, ready in good time for the ceremony. I was wearing a dusky pink dress that reached just below my knees and had a silky top and pleated bottom. Over the top was my leather jacket as it was a cool day. Peep-toe black ankle boots completed the look. I carried a clutch bag and had curled my candy floss hair over my shoulders. I liked to think that Chloe would label my outfit as rock chic. John wore a kilt and Caroline was elegant in her camel-coloured suit. Sally had on a pretty floral blouse and skirt. We were picked up by a sleek black car and driven out to Broomfield Castle.

The grey tower of the seventeenth-century castle rose up above sloping hills after we had wound around country lanes. The grounds we passed were perfectly manicured and then we drew up towards the iron door. The castle was open for the public to walk around but the chapel and the function room were sectioned off for weddings and there was a separate entrance that we could use too. Watery sunshine peeped through the clouds as we walked through to the chapel but I was glad I had a jacket on as it was cool in there.

The chapel had been draped in wild flowers, providing gorgeous colour and scent, and there was a gold runner down the aisle. At the altar were two huge displays of flowers and standing there was Brodie, dressed for the occasion as he was conducting the ceremony, and Rory and Drew both in their family kilts. They were all chatting quietly and looked in good spirits. I wondered if Rory was nervous at all. I recognised most of the guests as I followed Caroline nearer to the front to take our seats. I told myself I was looking to see everyone who was here but I knew that really I was looking for one guest in particular.

My eyes found him in one of the front pews next to his Uncle Angus, with Hattie, the lady who worked in Heather and Rory's farm shop. Caroline led us to the front pew on the other side of the aisle. Cameron looked up as we filed in and our eyes met. His dark hair was slightly messy from the breeze outside. It was a jolt to see him again. And I was right. When his lips twitched into a smile, mine did the same. I knew exactly what I felt. My stomach danced and my pulse sped up. I couldn't stand there staring though – Sally was behind me. So I sat down next to Caroline and John and moved my eyes to the front but I could feel him there. I waited a beat before I looked at him again. He was still watching me. I couldn't stop my smile then and neither could he. Angus nodded in greeting at everyone and Sally gave them both a cheerful wave.

Music started up then. A harpist, who was off to one side of the chapel, began to play soft, romantic music. The wedding so far was tasteful and elegant, which I had come to expect from Beth's hand, with a nod to the Scottish countryside too with the flowers. I knew that Heather had chosen this venue because her mother had always wanted to get married here, and I could see why. It really was a beautiful place.

The music changed then and Brodie ushered Rory and Drew to the front, gesturing for us to all rise. We stood up and turned to the door in anticipation. I definitely would never be a 'wedding' person but even I was stirred by seeing the people who I now felt so fond of walking down the aisle. First came Beth, Emily and Izzy – the three bridesmaids. I knew Beth and Emily felt slightly too old for the title but they had each been bridesmaids at their other weddings and Heather had wanted to continue the tradition. Beth and Emily wore long floral dresses, which matched the theme perfectly. Emily looked glowing with her bump and Beth looked like a model. I saw Drew beam with pride when he locked eyes on her. They both held bouquets of flowers matching the ones in the chapel, in shades of pink, purple and white. They were followed by Izzy in a shorter prom-style floral dress, her hair in a pretty bun. She held the hand of Harry, Heather and Rory's toddler, who wore a little kilt and looked so adorable that everyone in the chapel murmured when they saw him.

And then it was Heather's turn. On the arm of her father, Don, resplendent in his kilt, she looked stunning. Her hair was in its natural curls, pinned up with a veil and a gold tiara. She wore a beautiful ivory lace dress that spread out across the ground with a small train, off the shoulders. I was used to seeing Heather on the farm in her outdoor-friendly clothes and not in such an elegant dress. I caught a glimpse of a pair of ivory heels as she walked up the aisle. She was smiling so widely, it was sweet to see. She looked radiant and happy.

Heather and Don walked up to the altar as the bridesmaids and page boy stood off to the side and Rory grinned as he took his almost-wife's hand in his. The look they gave one another could have melted the coldest heart. Even I felt a little chocked up to see the pure joy on their faces. As we were all told to be seated by Brodie, I looked again at Cameron. I couldn't help it. I realised then that he, like most of the men here, was wearing a kilt. He was looking right back at me I was pleased to see. I was suddenly anxious for the ceremony to be over so I could talk to him. I still wasn't sure what I was going to say but I didn't really care, I just wanted to hear his voice again.

My knee bounced with an eagerness I tried to hide as Brodie conducted the ceremony. My brother's voice rang out deep and strong in the chapel as he talked through the importance of marriage, glancing occasionally to smile at Emily. He talked about how strong Heather and Rory were as a couple and the fact that they had both been through difficult times but had come out of them stronger together. Heather losing her mum and Rory losing his parents and how they had built both a strong family together and two thriving farms too. Rory and Heather kept their eyes on one another as they made their vows, both of them shaky and emotional when it came to that part. I looked at Heather's dad and he was sobbing into his hanky bless him.

And when Brodie pronounced them to be husband and wife, the whole chapel erupted into claps and cheers, which I had never experienced before. I saw Harry jumping up and down with excitement too.

'That was so lovely,' Sally said beside me, her eyes glistening. 'I just love a good happy ending, don't you?'

'They're a lovely couple,' I replied diplomatically. I still wasn't sure I believed in happy endings. I glanced at Cameron, who was enthusiastically shaking Rory's hand as the couple made their way down the aisle hand-in-hand as husband and wife. Harry bounded over to them and Heather scooped him up in her arms. Her eyes were full of tears too as she smiled at everyone, holding her son close, Rory looking at them both with so much love I admit my eyes did well up. There was so much joy around me. Maybe Beth was right about the magic of Glendale because I could feel it in the air in this chapel, there was no denying it.

'Look at my make-up,' Emily said to Beth as they trailed behind the couple. 'Ruined! Why didn't I use waterproof mascara?'

'That really was a schoolgirl error,' Beth deadpanned in response.

'Hey, I'm a schoolgirl and I'm wearing waterproof mascara,' Izzy told them.

'Come on, dear,' Sally said to me, walking into the aisle after the wedding party. I followed her, my eyes on Cameron as I passed his pew. He smiled at me and I nodded with my head towards the side door. I slipped out through it and found myself at the side of the castle, the cool breeze whipping through my hair as I breathed in the air, hoping it would clear the pinkness in my cheeks.

Seconds later, Cameron was out there with me.

Chapter Forty-Nine

'You came,' he said simply. I tried not to look down at his muscly legs on show under his kilt but it was hard not to. I wasn't sure what was worse – the legs or looking up to meet his piercing gaze and seeing the small smile on his lips. The way he was looking at me made it hard to speak.

'I came,' I agreed, rather stupidly. He stepped closer to me. 'Thank you for your letter.'

'When I didn't hear anything...'

'I know, I'm sorry. I had to think about it. I had to think about a lot of things, I suppose. And then I thought maybe I'd know what to say when I saw you again here.'

He took another step closer and I hitched a breath. I could smell his musky aftershave around me. 'And do you?' he asked, gruffly.

I saw his gaze flick to my lips. And then it was really hard to think coherently. 'I think... I think...' I started, stepping closer so now there were just inches between us.

'Anna?'

I really didn't want to think at all once he said my name. I wrapped my arms around him and just caught his smile before our lips met. His hands found my waist, drawing me to him, and I really didn't want him to let go.

Our kiss deepened and my fingers threaded into his hair. His hands slid up to the small of my back and, for a second, I wished we weren't outside a castle at a wedding.

Pulling back before I wouldn't be able to, we both looked at each other sheepishly. 'Well, that's what I thought,' I said, and I started laughing. Cameron took my hand in his as he chuckled.

'I enjoyed that thought,' he replied, drawing my hand up and kissing the back of it.

I smiled. 'I have other thoughts, I promise, but the wedding fever just got to me.'

'Anna! Come on, we need you for photos!' Izzy suddenly appeared around the corner calling for me. She stopped when she saw us. 'Oh, errr…' She stepped back, embarrassed.

'We're coming!' I called, giving her a wave. I looked at Cameron as she fled as quickly as she had arrived. 'Busted, wouldn't you say?'

'Anna,' he said as I started to pull away. 'I meant every word in that letter, I just want you to know that.'

'I know,' I said, forcing myself to push through my fear. 'Can I stay with you tonight? At the cabin? There's so much to say. You know I don't find it easy though.'

He grinned. 'You want to stay with me. That's more than enough for me right now. Yesterday I wasn't sure I'd even see you again. Come on, we'd better do our wedding guest duty or we'll never hear the end of it,' he said.

We walked around the castle hand-in-hand and joined in with the photos, the castle providing a stunning back-drop to the shots. Heather looked happier than I'd ever seen anyone. But I felt like I was almost as happy. I kept glancing at Cameron and he would be looking at me, both of us smiling when our eyes met. It was so hard to stop smiling. I felt kind of giddy. If this was what it felt like to really like someone then it wasn't so bad really, was it?

'I knew I'd make a wedding fan out of you in the end,' Beth said into my ear as she came over to me.

'I might be enjoying this wedding but let's not get carried away.' I ruined it though by grinning rather stupidly.

She squeezed my arm. 'It's so good to see you smiling, seriously.'

'Right,' her mother said, joining us. 'Time to get everyone inside, I think.'

'Who's the wedding planner, Mum?' Beth tutted but she checked the time and agreed, hurrying off to nudge the castle wedding planner.

'Are you doing okay?' Brodie asked from behind me then.

'It was a lovely service,' I said. 'You really do weddings well.'

Brodie smiled. 'It helps when you know the couple as well as I know Heather and Rory. Now I just need to find *my* wife...' I watched him go off in search of Emily and I turned to follow everyone as we made our way through into the reception, which was to take place in the large function room next to the chapel. I glanced back to see Heather and Rory having a last couple of pictures together. Rory leaned down to whisper something to her and she gazed back at him adoringly.

The reception room was as stunning as I had imagined it would be. Flowers stood everywhere again and in dramatic centrepieces on each table with large candles, and there was a board featuring pictures of Heather and Rory through the years as we walked in.

I glanced at the table plan and I looked around for Beth. She was by the top table talking to a waiter. I shook my head even though she couldn't see. I had never met such a meddler in all my life and what was more annoying was that I was pleased by her meddling. I would never tell her that though. She certainly didn't need any encouragement.

I walked over to my table, where Cameron was already hovering, waiting for me. We had been placed next to one another on the round table with Caroline and John, Sally, Hattie, her husband Hamish, and Angus. My brother was on the top table, of course, with the bridesmaids and their partners, and Heather's dad. Waiters came over to pour wine and water and give out crusty, freshly baked bread. Off to the side, a pianist provided an elegant accompaniment to the meal.

'What a beautiful service. I do love a wedding,' Hattie said to us. 'And they are so dear to me.'

'It was lovely,' Sally agreed. 'And not a dry eye in the house. They did so well the both of them, it can't have been easy with so many loved ones missing. As we know...' she trailed off and glanced at Angus.

Seeing me confused, Cameron spoke low in my ear. 'Sally lost her husband and my uncle lost the love of his life so they know what it's like to miss people today,' he explained. I knew, of course, that Rory's parents had died when he was younger and Heather had lost her mother. I thought about how much I felt I had lost after my accident but I knew I needed to count my blessings more. I still had all my family. Under the table, Cameron gave my knee a gentle squeeze, which made me smile.

The food was delicious. As if I had expected anything else. We started with bruschetta with caramelised onions and a rocket salad followed by chicken in a wine sauce with mash for the meat eaters, and for me a goat cheese tart with roasted vegetables, and then there were chocolate brownies for dessert. I loved listening to the others talking through the dinner, telling stories about Glendale over the years. All of them had lived in Glendale all their lives and for Sally, Angus, Hattie and Hamish that was over seventy years.

I laughed a lot when I heard about how the village was scandalised at the thought of such a young minister coming after their previous one had died and the idea that because Brodie was good-looking he wouldn't be a good minister. The women who threw themselves at him at first, and how there was some bitterness when he chose Emily, although her kind and sunny personality mixed with her delicious cakes had won everyone around in the end. How Beth had saved the shops in the village from being sold off by the council and turned into flats, which I already knew something of. How Heather and Rory's farm had featured on *Countryside Watch* to the thrill of the village, although they were annoyed that the High Street hadn't been filmed for it.

And before anyone I knew had come to Glendale, the story of Caroline's relatives building Glendale Hall with their whisky fortune and how the family had basically founded the village. It was so interesting that the meal flew by. I kept asking them all questions. I was eager to learn more about the place I would now be living in for a while and they were all so animated when they spoke about the past, their love for the place clearly deep rooted.

I was surprised when the sound of clinking glass, signalling the start of the speeches, cut Caroline off as she was telling me how her grandmother once met the queen.

Don, Heather's father, stood up as the room fell silent and all eyes turned towards the top table. Beside me,

Cameron topped our glasses up with wine and I leaned back to listen.

'Please forgive me if I get emotional,' Don began. 'I don't think I've made it through this speech without crying and that was just me reading it to the pigs on the farm,' he said, to titters from around the room. 'But it's hard not to be emotional today. My only daughter's wedding day. And what a daughter. Heather is such a wonderful woman that sometimes it's hard to remember that she was once a girl who I could hardly get to come out of her room to eat as she was so absorbed in one of her favourite books. But, Heather, you've grown up to be such a capable businesswoman and a wonderful mother. I couldn't be prouder to see how your two farms and the shop are thriving, to see how well you look after your son, Harry, and how you get up every day come rain or shine at the crack of dawn and put on wellies, which we all know how much you hate.'

More laughter at that.

'What I've been most happy to see is how you've created such a lovely family for yourself. You and Rory are such a strong partnership. I think everyone in the room sees that. You've both suffered such big losses in your lives but they have made you so determined and such caring people too. You love your family so fiercely and I know you'd do anything for them. And for me too. Inviting me to be part of your family was such an honour and I love living at Fraser Farm with you.

'Seeing you two get married today makes me so proud and happy for you both. I know this has been a long time coming, that it wasn't easy to stand up there today without some of the people who we miss very much, but I know that they are right here with us. Your mother, Heather, was watching today and she was incredibly proud of you, and your parents too, Rory.'

He paused then to clear his throat. Everyone was starting to get emotional now. Rory was holding Heather tightly beside Don as they listened.

'You have been through so much together that there is no doubt you'll be together forever and will continue to weather any storm, anything that life throws at you, with all your strength and good humour too. This is really a lifelong partnership. I want to thank everyone here today for supporting Heather and Rory, and for cheering them on always. This community is so special, I know we all know that, and we will always be rooting for you both. We will always be here for you.'

'Hear hear!' Angus said from next to me. Everyone murmured their agreement too.

Don nodded his thanks to the room. 'This is Heather and Rory's special day but I know that we all share in it. I wish I had some wisdom to give you both but I learn as much from you two as you learn from me. You will live happily ever after because you have chosen the very best person to navigate life with. So, here's to finding your partner in life and to never taking that for granted.'

As he raised his glass to the couple, Don completely choked up and had to sit down and bury his face in a hanky. Everyone cheered and raised their glasses as Heather hugged her dad and Rory clasped his shoulder tightly. God, even I felt a tear roll down my cheek.

I turned to Cameron and leaned in so only he could hear me. 'I love you too.'

'Really?' he checked, which made me chuckle.

'Yes, really, you fool.' I leaned in to kiss him and, in the background, I heard someone wolf whistle and I didn't mind one little bit.

Chapter Fifty

Once I had told Cameron how I felt, I felt a hundred times lighter. I had been so scared to just say the words but once I had, I felt fearless. And I didn't want to waste a moment with him.

After dinner, we all headed outside to wait for the floor to be cleared for dancing. Cameron took my hand and we slipped away from everyone, walking around the castle as the sun started to dip in the sky. It was chilly now but I felt perfectly warm as Cameron wrapped an arm around my shoulders, pulling me close as we walked. I felt giddy from the wine, the emotion of the day and being by his side again. And the thought of being alone with him later too.

'Well, this is definitely one wedding I won't forget,' I said as we looked out at the countryside, the castle standing tall behind us.

'What brought you back to me?' he asked. I leaned in closer, enjoying the warmth and strength of him next to me. I wondered how it was that I could feel like I fit beside him so perfectly when I hadn't even known him that long. As if we were two puzzle pieces that had been slotted together.

'I had been thinking about it all the time I was in London, even though I tried not to. I missed Glendale. All of it. The place, the people, the Hall, my brother, and you too. But I told myself to forget it, that I needed to move on, and I was annoyed that I couldn't do it. And then there was the work. I loved it, Cameron. I knew that this was what I really wanted to do. But you know me, the fear soon kicked in.' I smiled wryly. 'It was the same with you. That day in your cabin. I felt it then... but when you said... well, you know, I freaked out that you didn't feel the same way about me and I did what I've always done best, and I ran.' I shrugged.

'I'm so sorry that you thought that. It's haunted me why you left that day, why you wouldn't speak to me. I couldn't stop thinking about you. I knew I had to try to tell you how I felt.'

'I'm so glad you did.' I looked up at him and he gave me a soft kiss. I smiled. 'Then suddenly Beth, Heather and Emily showed up. It was like I was trying so hard to move on from you all, but they decided not to let me.' I chuckled. 'And then reading your letter... It just cemented what I'd been thinking and feeling but trying not to. Basically, I knew I needed to come back here.'

'You did?' he asked in surprise.

I remembered then that I hadn't told him any of my plans. I turned to face him then, even though it was hard to leave his side. 'So I have come up with this idea but I just realised, I mean maybe you might not...' I stopped myself. God, what was wrong with me? I didn't want to be scared anymore. We had both told each other that we loved the other person. 'I want to move back to Glendale. I want to live and work at the Hall and study for a cookery diploma. One day I want to own my own restaurant. I've never stayed put anywhere, you know that, but this feels right. I want to follow my heart for once and maybe I'll suck at it, maybe I'll want to run. But right now, this just feels right.'

Cameron broke into a wide smile. 'You're staying?' he checked.

'I mean maybe not forever, I don't know—'

He stepped forward and put his hands on my waist. 'But right now, you're staying?' he interrupted my babbling.

I nodded. 'Right now, I'm staying.'

He picked me up by the waist, spinning me around in the air. I cried out in protest and he put me down, both of us laughing. Maybe if I'd have known how good this love lark felt, I would have opened my heart up sooner. But as Cameron kissed me, I realised that, no, I wouldn't ever wish that. Because it was meant to be Cameron who opened my heart. The same way I had opened his. If I was sure of anything in this life, I was sure of that.

—

We went back inside for the dancing, and twirling in Cameron's arms on the dancefloor was something I felt like I'd always enjoy. I received many nods and winks and nudges and smiles from our family and friends throughout the night but I didn't care. I knew that I was smiling like a loon and I wasn't bothered in the least. For once, I just enjoyed being with Cameron. I wasn't worried about what came next. I was perfectly happy just enjoying this moment.

We had the wedding cake, baked to perfection by Emily of course, and we danced until midnight, when the reception ended and we piled into cars to take us all back to Glendale, apart from Rory and Heather, who were staying the night at a nearby hotel. They had decided not to have a traditional honeymoon as they didn't want to leave either Harry or their farms. I went with Cameron back to Hilltop, which I knew had been noticed by everyone and would have probably been high on people's talking points of the night but I was too happy to mind that. It was annoying that Beth had been right all along, and my brother too, but nothing is perfect, right?

Cameron's cabin was dark and silent as he let us inside. He went over to the fireplace to light it and then made us both tea in the kitchen. It was chilly but we curled up on the floor with a blanket draped over us as we sipped our tea in front of the fire. We were both quiet after such an eventful day and night until he turned to me, the flames from the fire flickering in his eyes. 'Are you really sure, Anna? About us, I mean?' I caught the vulnerability in his gaze as he asked me the question. I wondered if he was thinking about his ex, not because he still had feelings for her, but their relationship ended so tragically. I kept thinking about how scared I was considering an actual relationship for the first time but I needed to remember all the hurt and pain he had been through too. This wouldn't be easy for us. We had been closed off to other people for a long time but our connection had opened up our hearts. We were fragile, though. What we had was still fragile.

I nodded. 'I'm scared. I think I will be for a long time. But being away from you made me miserable. I feel like this is where I'm supposed to be.'

'Me too.' He reached out and stroked my hair back from my face. 'Everything has changed since you turned up in Glendale with your pink hair and honesty and passion, and I feel like I've changed. I don't want to hide away here. Well, unless you're with me, and I feel excited

337

Chapter Fifty-One

Light streamed in through a gap in the blinds, pooling on the bottom of the bed as I opened my eyes and felt Cameron's arms still around me. I smiled at how cosy I felt, and how well I'd slept too. As if finally having everything settled had put my mind and body to rest in a way it had struggled to do for years. Glancing at the beside clock, I raised an eyebrow. It was late morning. I'd slept for nine hours. Which was completely unheard of for me.

Cameron was facing me and he opened his eyes as he felt me move a little under his arm. His lips curved into a super sexy smile. 'Morning, gorgeous. Did you sleep well? I slept like the dead.'

'The best in a long time,' I agreed. Cameron leaned in to kiss me gently. I had been half wondering if things would be the same between us this morning. We'd had so many false starts since we met. But his kiss sent a warm wave through my body and I knew that it hadn't all been a dream. This was real.

'I'm going to make us breakfast in bed,' he said, sitting up and stretching. I eyed the muscles in his stomach. 'Don't move,' he half-warned. Perhaps he was worried it had all been a dream too.

'I wouldn't dare,' I replied with a smile. I watched him leave the room and then I sat up, pulling a knot out of my hair. I looked around. Like me, Cameron kept his bedroom décor plain and functional. I thought maybe we both needed to change that. Now that we might be finally planting some roots. Together. I smiled again. God, I was starting to annoy myself with this happiness. But I had to admit it had been a very long time coming.

Cameron returned with a tray of coffee and toast with pots of homemade jam from Heather and Rory's farm shop. 'I might get used to this,' I warned him as he came back into bed and put the tray down between us.

'I don't mind. I'm just so happy you're here with me. You know, you don't have to go back to the Hall.' He shrugged. 'If you didn't want to.' He busied himself by buttering his toast, avoiding my eyes.

I laid my hand on his arm and he looked up at me. 'It's not that I don't want to stay with you, but I still think we should take things slowly. This is really new to me. I don't want to freak out and run again. I need to be independent. I can't help it.'

He smiled. 'I know, and it's one of the things I love about you. I just wanted to make sure you knew that if you wanted to I'd be more than fine with it. But you're right. We should take things slowly. It's not like you're far away. It just felt so good to wake up with you.'

'We will do a lot of that, I promise,' I said, giving him a kiss then snatching his toast out of his hands and taking a bite of it. He shook his head and got himself another one. 'I know that everyone will be looking for our happy ever after. It's what Glendale seems to be all about,' I said. 'I've only been here for one summer and I've already seen three weddings, for goodness' sake, but for me this is a happy ending, you know? I like us just like this.'

'Just like this,' he agreed, brushing back my hair and looking into my eyes in that way of his that both thrilled and unnerved me. It was like I was being seen for the first time properly in my life. 'Always and forever,' he added in a whisper.

Goosebumps pricked my arms as I pulled him to me and we kissed, our mouths full of love, hope, trust, contentment and toast.

—

There were two things I needed to do next. I had told almost everyone I wanted to that I was coming back to Glendale but I still had four people on my list. The first were Adam and Lorna. I felt like I... not 'owed them an explanation', exactly, but I wanted to be open and honest because I genuinely liked them and hoped that we could be friends. I knew they both meant a lot to Cameron too – he'd been friends with them since school, after all. I wanted to speak to them without him first, though, just in case. I messaged them and asked them to meet me at the pub for an afternoon drink.

Cameron drove me in his truck to the village before heading off to Fraser Farm to help his uncle with the chores there in Rory and Heather's absence, and I wandered into the pub alone. Adam and Lorna were already seated at a table in the back. It was another cloudy day so the beer garden had clearly not appealed to then. The pub was busy as usual for a Sunday afternoon, people eating roast dinners with a drink, settling in for a relaxing time. I ordered a glass of wine and took it over to them, feeling a little bit nervous as I sat down.

'This is a nice surprise to see you back,' Lorna said with a warm smile. It was a relief that she seemed pleased to see me. Adam nodded in agreement.

'Thank you, it's so nice to be back.'

'Are you here just for Heather and Rory's wedding?' Adam asked as he sipped his beer. Although they hadn't been invited, of course they knew about it from Cameron and, to be honest, most of Glendale knew each other's news anyway.

'I did come back for that but actually I wanted to talk to you both about my plans next…' I explained that I was going to move back to Glendale to study cooking and continue to work on at the Hall.

'That's great news,' Lorna said enthusiastically. 'It was a shame getting to know you and then you leaving for London.' She glanced at her brother. 'It'll be great to have you around again.'

I was nervous for Adam's thoughts but he smiled genuinely at me. 'You will definitely have to cook for us now.'

'I promise I will. In fact, Cameron had an idea to throw a kind of dinner party at his cabin,' I began hesitantly. This was potentially the awkward part but I had always been honest and I knew it was better to just tell them and hope that they would be okay with it. 'Because at the wedding, well, we actually got together. Uh, became a couple, I mean.'

They exchanged another look. I held my breath. 'I knew it,' Lorna said but she smiled. 'I said to Adam there was something between the two of you. I sensed it the first time we met.'

'She did,' he agreed with a nod. 'Told me I was wasting my time,' he added wryly. He didn't seem too angry though.

'I'm sorry, Adam. Honestly, I really didn't realise that there was something until there already was, if that makes sense? We had this connection and I didn't understand it. I'd never really had that before.'

'It's okay,' he said. 'Cameron told me after you left that he had feelings for you. He thought you'd gone for good, so I'm pleased for him, for both of you, that you're back. Honestly,' he added. 'All's fair in love and war, right?'

'I never meant to hurt you, I hope you know that,' I said, feeling a little bit less nervous now. Still, I took a gulp of wine just in case. I was glad Cameron had been honest with his friend. I knew how important it was to have friends you could be honest with now. Glendale had shown me that this summer.

'I'm a big guy, Anna, I can handle it. You were always honest with me.'

I looked at Lorna then. 'And, Lorna, I know that you liked…'

She put up a hand to stop me. 'Seriously, my heart is completely untouched. Honestly, it's always been more the people around us trying to get me and Cam together.' She gave her brother a hard look and he smiled sheepishly at her. 'We were never more than friends, even growing up, well before you came long. And then he went off to uni and fell in love and I knew when he came back that he wasn't ready for anything else. But when you arrived, that changed, and I wasn't mad about it. Obviously, ego-wise it smarted a bit,' she said with a laugh. 'But we are just friends. He's good-looking, and a good lad. I'll always think that but that's it. He's just a mate and I hope you are too. And I'm always happy for my friends. I'm still looking for my person.' She shrugged. 'I'm pretty happy on my own anyway, and so are you really,' she said to her brother. 'It'd be nice to meet someone but I'm living my best single life until then.'

'Amen to that,' I said raising my glass. They both clinked it. I was so relieved. 'I hope we can all hang out, I missed you guys when I was in London.'

'Definitely,' Lorna said firmly. 'We've had a lot of fun this summer, long may that continue.'

'And if I get some free meals out of it too...' Adam winked, and we both laughed.

'I will need to test out all my dishes on you guys,' I said. 'You won't be able to get out of it.'

'Speaking of food, shall we order some?' Adam said, grabbing a menu.

'Always hungry, this boy,' Lorna said, rolling her eyes.

I grinned. I loved their sibling relationship. They made me think of Brodie. I'd missed his church service today as I was with Cameron but next Sunday I'd be there. I wanted to be as close to him as Lorna and Adam were. And that made me think of the next people on my list. It was time to repair my relationship with my family. It had been a long time coming after all.

Chapter Fifty-Two

Brodie drove us to Inverness on Monday evening. It was still daylight as we left Glendale to go back to our childhood home together. I hadn't been there since Christmas but now I lived so close I was determined to improve on my usual annual visit.

'I can't believe it's almost September – the baby will be here so soon now,' Brodie said as we drove. I had changed his radio station to one that didn't send me to sleep and the sun was warm on my elbow hanging out of the open car window. 'Emily wondered if you'd like to come and see the nursery when we get back? We redecorated while you were in London... Well, I did, while Emily supervised.'

'I'd love that,' I said. I would never be maternal myself but I was excited to be an auntie, and I wanted to feel part of their family. No, actually – *my* family.

He smiled, pleased. 'I'm glad. It's really nice having you here. Right, here we are.' He parked outside our childhood home. It was always strange walking back in as a grown-up. Sometimes I felt like I went back in time after I walked through the door, becoming younger in an instant, as if I'd stepped through a time portal. It was the memories that hit, I supposed. It was hard not to look at the sofa I used to lie on after the accident, a blanket draped over me, bored and restless but the pain preventing me from doing much to occupy myself, looking out of the window longingly.

'Hello, darling,' Mum said when she opened the front door with a warm smile. She leaned in to kiss Brodie and then she saw me and did a double-take. Brodie had told them he was coming around but hadn't mentioned me.

'Surprise,' I said, hoping she'd be pleased to see me.

'You're back,' she said haltingly before leaning in to kiss my cheek too. 'Well, well, come in you two, your father is in the living room.' We passed her and she closed the door. I felt her eyes on my back as I followed Brodie into the living room, the one that been my convalescence room. I knew it was one of the reasons that I avoided returning home for long visits, I really didn't enjoy the reminder of that time, but I needed to try to move past that. It was just a room. My parents were here – that was a reason to come back. I needed to focus on them and not thoughts of the past. This summer had made me realise how much I needed to try to move on.

'Anna!' my dad cried when he saw me. He jumped up to hug us both. 'We didn't think we'd see you again so soon.' It was sad how shocked my parents were to see me so soon after they had come to Brodie's house.

'I'll get the teas,' Mum said, hurrying into the kitchen.

'How's the guitar playing going?' Dad asked me as we all sat down. I sat in the armchair – I still avoided that sofa.

'I'm enjoying it. I'm going to sign up for some classes, I think.' I glanced at my brother. 'The college offers music lessons.'

'The college?' Dad asked.

I waited until Mum returned with cups of tea and a plate of homemade biscuits, and then I explained. 'I've decided to do a chef diploma at a college in Inverness. It will be a part-time course so I can carry on working at Glendale Hall while I study. Beth is happy for me to do that. So, I'm back in Glendale for the foreseeable.'

'You've decided to live there?' Mum said, her voice going a little high-pitched. My dad put down his tea in surprise. 'Past the summer?'

I nodded. 'The course starts at the end of September. I really love cooking, I'd love to work in a restaurant, even open my own one day, if that's at all possible. And it just makes sense to do it here so I can earn money at the Hall and have a place to stay as well. I don't know what will happen after the course but, for right now, I'm staying.'

'Oh, Anna, I'm so pleased!' My mum jumped up and hurried over to hug me. Now I was the surprised one in the room.

'I'm really proud of you,' Dad agreed, his voice catching at the end. Oh god, was he going to cry?

'So, we will be seeing a lot more of Anna,' Brodie said with a smile. 'Which is great news, isn't it?'

'I'll say,' Mum replied, sitting back down, looking a little overcome. 'And you're going to be a chef too! Oh my goodness, are these biscuits okay?'

I laughed. 'Delicious.' I was so happy that they were happy. I had spent so long feeling like a disappointment to them but now I didn't feel that way at all.

'Maybe I'll get a guitar and take some classes with you,' Dad said then, his eyes lighting up. 'I've been wanting to for ages.'

'That would be brilliant,' I agreed. I felt bad that he had stopped playing after my accident. 'I also wanted to talk to you both about…' I tried to steady my voice. 'The accident.' They looked surprised again. 'I know it's something that we don't talk about, and I know that's been

347

my fault. I made you think I didn't want to talk about it, but the truth was I was scared to bring it up because of how guilty I felt over it.' I explained, falteringly at first, but soon my courage rose and I told them everything – how I'd believed it had been my fault, the guilt I had carried, and how I felt like I didn't deserve my second chance at life. 'I think that's why I've kept my distance from you all. I thought you blamed me as well and it was better if I stayed away.'

'Oh Anna, how could you have ever thought that? We missed you so much!' my mum cried. She came to sit beside me and took my hand. 'Of course it wasn't your fault.'

'I blamed myself,' my dad said then, his voice breaking with emotion. 'I couldn't bear seeing you in so much pain. I wanted to protect you, shield you from it all. I didn't realise you didn't know the truth. I've let you down.'

I shook my head. 'No. I don't want us to argue about blame or guilt anymore. We need a fresh start. I need to move on from what happened and I want us to rebuild our relationship, to be close like we were before. I mean, if you do too.'

'Of course we do,' Mum said, pulling me in for another hug. A minute later, my dad was there too. I looked up to see Brodie grinning at us, and I knew this was the first step for us and that we would get there. We would be the family we were once again.

A bit later, I followed my mum into the kitchen to catch her alone. 'Mum, do you remember after my accident that I had some therapy? Do you still have Dr William's contact details? I just thought that maybe I should pick it back up again for a bit...' It was hard to get the words out but I knew I needed to. I didn't want to walk into this house and be haunted by the past again nor did I want to keep running, I wanted to settle and find a life that I loved, and I thought maybe I needed a little help to get there.

'I definitely do,' Mum said. She reached out and touched my shoulder. 'I am so proud of you, Anna. I hope you know you can always talk to me too. I know things were so hard for you after what happened… after the accident,' she amended, as if remembering we were no longer ignoring it. 'Maybe I didn't help you in the right way, I don't know, but I want to help you. I always have, I just didn't know how to reach you, I suppose.'

I shook my head. 'I didn't want you to reach me. I needed to go off and try to find my own way. But I took it too far, I went too far. I would really like to find my way back now.'

She smiled. 'I think you already have.' She reached out and hugged me again. I leaned against my mother and smiled as she held me tightly. It was weird. I hadn't had a good hug with her for so long but sometimes you still just needed a hug from your mum, didn't you? 'Everything is going to be all right,' she promised me and, for once, I really did believe that it would be.

Chapter Fifty-Three

I was cleaning Izzy's reading room when my phone rang. Izzy was back at school and wasn't there to hover, making sure I didn't move anything around, so I could get on with the dusting and hoovering undisturbed. The whole Hall was quiet at this time of day as everyone was busy doing something so I could get on with my chores before I went into the kitchen to start dinner and they all returned home hungry and chatting about what they had all been doing. We had settled into a routine already and I was enjoying it.

I turned off the hoover to grab my phone, smiling when I saw who it was. 'Hey, Chloe,' I said as I put her on speaker so I could carry on with the dusting. 'How are things?' The pop-up restaurant had closed. They had FaceTimed me on the last night so I could raise a glass with them to the successful summer stint. Chloe and Ashley and even Pierre had all wished me well when I said I was staying in Glendale – everything was running fine without me and they knew I didn't want to leave Cameron again. Chloe had sent on everything I left in the flat and the guys were almost ready to sign their investment deal and find a location for their proper restaurant. I was already eager to go and eat there when it opened.

'Very good, very good,' she said, the smile clear in her voice. 'I'm at the airport ready to get on a plane.'

'Oh, where are you off to?'

'Las Vegas!' she half-screamed down the phone and I heard Ashley shout the words too. 'We're eloping.'

I almost dropped my duster. 'What?' I cried. 'I need to see this!'

Chloe rung me back on FaceTime and she and Ashley stood arm-in-arm at the airport, waving at me, grinning like a pair of teenagers.

'You're seriously eloping?' I checked again. I honestly thought Chloe was planning a spectacular wedding somewhere.

'I know no one believes me but I never wanted the big wedding. I just want me and Ash together celebrating us, you know? But don't worry, we're going to throw a huge party at Christmas for all our family and friends. We've been phoning everyone and they're all very shocked but I knew you'd understand!' Chloe explained, her face just glowing. Ashley looked equally full of joy.

I smiled. 'I'm so happy for you guys. You should definitely do what works for you two, doesn't matter what anyone else thinks,' I told them firmly. 'I can't wait for the party though! Congratulations guys. Honestly, you both deserve a lifetime of happiness.' They would always be one of my favourite couples.

'We love you, Anna!' Chloe called as Ashley told her they were being called to their gate.

'Send me a photo from the chapel!' I called, waving as they hung up. I laughed aloud to myself. I loved that Chloe had done something so unexpected. She and Ashley were so different but they just worked. I thought about Cameron then. Things were going really well between us. It was as if once we were honest with one another about our feelings, we were able to enjoy being together. We made each other happy and that was everything.

I finished up cleaning and headed into the kitchen. Everyone was coming around to the Hall tonight – it was Friday night and I had told them I'd make pizzas. It was twelve weeks since I first arrived in Glendale and so much had changed in my life it was crazy. I wanted to say thank you to everyone who had made me feel so at home here this summer.

I turned on the radio and tied my hair up, pulling on an apron, and making the dough. Izzy's cat came in and rubbed my ankles hopefully. I filled up her food bowl and carried on cooking.

People started to arrive home and join me in the kitchen then. Izzy and Beth arrived from school in high spirits. Beth had had a call from a couple who wanted to get married at the Hall this Christmas at the end of the Christmas trail and Izzy had got an A on a short story she had written in English. They told me their news excitedly as they got themselves drinks and I started to make the tomato sauce for the pizza. Caroline returned from the Hall shop and John came in from the garden – she sent him straight to wash before letting him sit with them. Then Sally walked in from her cottage, and Drew got back from work looking exhausted but cheerful as usual. Brodie, Emily and Iona arrived next from the village and then I turned with a smile to see the door opening with Heather, Rory, Don, Angus and – finally – Cameron walking in from the farms.

'Gang's all here,' Beth said, handing me a glass of wine. She nudged me. 'I'd be happy to put on more than one wedding this Christmas, just saying!'

I threw a tea towel at her. 'Wedding's aren't my thing but you can plan my next birthday if that helps.'

She sighed. 'Fine. But I won't stop dreaming.' She grinned at Cameron, who came over to kiss me. 'You're just too cute. I can't cope.'

'I'd rather not be thought of as cute,' Cameron said to me when we were alone. 'I would prefer ruggedly handsome.'

I looked up at him and laughed. 'I bet you would. I'll make sure Beth knows for the future. Now help me carry over these bowls, if it's not too much hard work for someone so handsome?'

He grinned and gave me another kiss. 'You know me, always at your beck and call.' He went through into the kitchen and I watched him, still amazed that the two of us were where we were. Somehow the universe had pulled us together and I would be forever grateful. Maybe all along we were meant to find each other in this quiet corner of the Scottish countryside. Either that or we just got lucky. I shrugged and followed him with the bowl of salad.

I had made five pizzas with different toppings, salad and garlic bread and everyone tucked in with gusto, as usual. Italian was my favourite to make and eat, I was realising, and in the back of my mind I dreamt about the Italian restaurant I might open in the future. But I would just take it all one step at a time. Like I had told Cameron.

Sometimes life was more fun when you just let it take you where you were meant to go. I had run for so long but Glendale had made me want to stay and I was going to enjoy it for as long as it felt right to be here. And, as Cameron said, if that turned out to be forever then I was happy to go with it. I knew, though, that wherever I did go next, he would be right by my side. We were like Chloe and Ashley – unconventional but perfect for one another.

'Okay, everyone,' I said, calling for order. As usual, it took a minute to get everyone to be quiet. 'I wanted to say a massive thank you to you all for welcoming me as part of the family and for letting me stay on past the summer, and not even reminding me about how often I told you all I would be long gone by now.' I smiled as they all laughed. 'I haven't had a place that I wanted to call home for a long time, seriously, but you guys made it feel like my home straight away and I know that even if I move on in the future, there will always be a place for me to come back to and that is something I never thought I would have. So, here's to Glendale – our forever home!'

Everyone echoed my toast as we raised our glasses and Cameron met my eyes and smiled as we clinked and I knew that he felt exactly the same way as I did.

Epilogue

Autumn was in the air as I walked through Inverness city centre in the final week of September.

There was a cool breeze blowing some of the leaves from the trees gently down in front of me. Some of them were just beginning to turn from green to gold above me and I passed by a group of kids in school uniforms walking home from school, the summer already behind them. I still couldn't believe that I was going to be a student again. I was nervous but excited as I reached the college induction talk. I hadn't studied since I was eighteen and, let's face it, I didn't stick that out for long. This time felt different. I had a spring in my step. I was going to improve at something I was passionate about, so I was eager to get started.

I walked in, following the signs for the induction session in the main hall. Everyone doing a cookery class this term was invited to this talk. I felt a little thrill of excitement as I went in to take my seat with the other students. At the front were all the tutors at the school and, as I sat down, I did a double-take because up there was a familiar face that I hadn't expected to see here at all.

'Every term we invite an actual chef to come and talk to us at this session to give us all some inspiration before we start,' the head of the school, the son of Brodie's friend, said after he had welcomed us to the school. So that's why he was here.

I shook my head as Pierre was introduced to everyone.

—

After the talk, I lingered outside the school and waited. Soon, Pierre came out, lighting a cigarette and coming over when he spotted me. 'Small world,' I said with a smile.

'Anna.' He kissed me on each cheek. 'Actually, I knew this was where you were going. Chloe told me. So, when they asked me, I thought I had to come and wish you well for your study,' he said as we fell into step together, walking away from the building.

'Well, it was nice to see a friendly face. I spoke to Chloe last week. She said you've found a location for your restaurant? It's all on track?'

He nodded. 'We're hoping for a spring opening; full steam ahead, isn't that what you say? They talk about you often. Chloe and Ash. They definitely think they had a hand in you wanting to be a chef. I like to think that I did too.'

'Of course you do.' I rolled my eyes. He would always think things were about him. 'I enjoyed working in your kitchen though,' I added. Which was true. We paused at the gates.

'Even when I kissed you?' He raised an eyebrow.

'Actually, yes. You made me realise what I did and didn't want.'

'I knew when we met that I'd never forget you, Anna. And I certainly won't. If you ever want to work in my kitchen again, just call.'

'I will keep that in mind,' I said, knowing that he really did mean that. 'Take care, Pierre.' I gave him a kiss and a wave before I walked off to my car.

I got in and checked my phone but there were no missed calls or messages. Emily was almost at her due date and it felt like we were all on tenterhooks waiting for her to go into labour. Relieved I hadn't missed anything while I was in the talk, I set off for Hilltop Farm. I felt really positive about my course, and it had been nice to see Pierre again and know that the past didn't always have to carry with it bad memories. We hadn't meant much to one another when we were in France but he was right: I would never forget him and it felt good to part on better terms now, both hopefully better people than we were then. I was excited for my course to start properly on Monday but, for now, I was going to spend the weekend with my boyfriend. I smiled as I turned up Queen on the radio and sang along. Calling Cameron that still hadn't become old.

Hilltop took a while to come into view but I enjoyed the country drive listening to my favourite music, and the sun began to set as I turned into the gravel drive and parked outside the farmhouse. Guests had left the last retreat earlier in the day so we would have the place to ourselves and it was my favourite thing to spend quiet alone time with him out here. We were usually surrounded by family and friends so we enjoyed our nights alone on the farm.

Well, not completely alone as sheep now grazed on the hill.

I walked towards the woodland, smiling over at them as they looked up to watch me pass. The sun had dipped behind the trees and the sky had turned pastel pink, the same colour as my hair, as I walked under the cover of the trees. The noise of Glendale was blocked out now. All I could hear was birdsong. I weaved along the path until Cameron's cabin appeared through a gap between the trees. The cabin was always peaceful and it made me feel calmer just to see it again.

Practically skipping up to the door, I didn't need to knock because it swung open in front of me. 'Well, hi there.'

'Hey, babe.' Cameron leaned down to kiss me. 'How did it go? Coffee?'

'Great. And yes please,' I said, going inside. Cameron wrapped an arm around my waist to stop me, kissing the side of my neck. I gasped. 'Miss me or something?'

'Always. Right, I'll put the kettle on, you tell me all about your day.' He slipped past me into the kitchen. I watched him go, aware that I was smiling rather stupidly. I'd never had anyone to just share my day with. I liked it.

I sat down on the sofa, curling my legs up as Cameron listened to me talk while he made us both a coffee. Behind me, the sun set slowly on the day and on the summer. A summer that had changed everything. A summer that I would always remember.

Forever.

A letter from Victoria

Dear readers,

I can't believe I'm writing the letter for book four! I really didn't think there would be four Glendale Hall books so thank you so much for how you've taken this series into your hearts – this book is here because of you, and that's why I've dedicated it to you.

This time, we are following Anna's journey. I was always intrigued by Brodie's little sister – the reason that he became a minister. I wanted to explore how the accident that led him to his vocation changed her life. And Anna's life after the car accident has definitely not been as smooth sailing as her brother's and she's been on a journey to find what she wants in life ever since. Saddled with guilt, Anna has struggled. But this summer, she finally makes her way to Glendale and we all know that Glendale has a magic to it – a magic that can heal a heart and soul…

I hope you will take Anna into your hearts. She's so different from our other main characters and brings a breath of fresh air into the village. She is very complex and is haunted by the past but she's also fun and passionate, and I just love her pink hair and feisty spirit. I hope you will too!

I also hope you'll enjoy being reunited with everyone we know and love in Glendale, seeing how Hilltop Farm is working, watching Beth become a wedding planner and meeting another farmer – Cameron – a man who is haunted by his past just like Anna. But who also, just like Anna, has a heart of gold.

My favourite scene to write in this book was the murder mystery weekend that our Glendale family go on and I hope you will all love reading it too. It was particularly special to me as it gives a little hint to my next writing venture – a brand new crime series! I am so excited for you all to read *Murder at the House on the Hill* so please do look out for it coming in September 2021!

Thank you for all your lovely messages about Glendale – they really do make my day! I hope you will love book four just as much as the first three. If you do, please do pop up a review on Amazon or any other retailer and let me know on social media.

I hope you're all staying safe and well!

Lots of love,

Victoria

Instagram: @vickywalters
Twitter: @vicky_walters
Facebook: VictoriaWaltersAuthor
YouTube: Victoria Walters
Blog: www.victoria-writes.com

Acknowledgments

Wow, Glendale Hall 4! Thank you so much Keshini, Lindsey, and the Hera and Canelo teams for making this possible. Big thanks also to Hannah and everyone at Hardman and Swainson for all your hard work and support. Thanks also to my copy-editor, Eleanor Leese, and Vicki McKay, and Cherie Chapman for another lovely cover.

A huge thank you to all the bloggers, reviewers and readers who are so enthusiastic about this series – book four was only possible because of how much you love the Glendale books! I'm so grateful to all of you. Special thanks to my Facebook Book Squad too for being such great cheerleaders.

Special thanks to Kiley Dunbar, Lisa Swift, Anna Bell and George Lester for being so supportive and for all our chats this past year. It's helped more than you know!

As always, a huge thank you to my mum for your love and support and for listening to all my plot problems too. And, of course, Harry for always being by my side.